With the care he would give an infant, he removed his coat from her body and slid his hands beneath her. Taking care to keep her head from bouncing too greatly, he eased her onto her back. A faint moan tumbled free, a noise so soft and anguished, Farran's heart twisted.

"Noelle, can you hear me?"

When she did not do so much as twitch, he moved to her feet. Sliding his hands along her legs, he checked the alignment of her bones. Pressure on her left hip provoked another throaty protest. The sound gained strength as he examined her ribs.

Frowning, he moved to her exposed shoulder where the blood ran in a thin stream. She lay still as he pressed her collarbone. He pushed aside her sweater's shredded sleeve, following the trail of blood, and froze.

In the moonlight, the torc glinted with subtle color. A decoration he could not hope to ignore, no matter how he might wish to.

"Jesu," he swore softly.

A rush of fiery rage surged through his blood. A seraph!

TOR BOOKS BY CLAIRE ASHGROVE

Immmortal Hope
Immortal Surrender
Immortal Trust (forthcoming)

Immortal Surrender

The Curse of the Templars

Claire Ashgrove

A TOM DOHERTY ASSOCIATES BOOK • NEW YORK

This is a work of fiction. All of the characters, organizations, and events portrayed in this novel are either products of the author's imagination or are used fictitiously.

IMMORTAL SURRENDER: THE CURSE OF THE TEMPLARS

Copyright © 2012 by Valerie M. Hatfield

All rights reserved.

A Tor Book
Published by Tom Doherty Associates, LLC
175 Fifth Avenue
New York, NY 10010

www.tor-forge.com

Tor® is a registered trademark of Tom Doherty Associates, LLC.

ISBN 978-0-7653-6759-4

First Edition: October 2012

Printed in the United States of America

0 9 8 7 6 5 4 3 2 1

For my mother,
who never stopped believing.

All my love.

Acknowledgments

To my wonderful agent, Jewelann Cone, and my equally wonderful editor, Whitney Ross, for your constant support and enthusiasm, most particularly when the writing becomes "work" and the details become painstaking. Cassandra Ammerman, you make the other aspects of authorial life all fun! Thanks for your dedication.

To my mother and my boys, your patience is amazing, even when the days run together and seem never-ending. Without you, there would be no *Curse of the Templars*. Your faith, belief, and support keep me focused and directed.

To Jason, my rock when the world around me turns into a landslide. Your support is amazing. Your patience even more so. Thank you for being a bright light and a beacon of hope.

As always, to my invaluable critique partner, Dyann Love Barr, there simply aren't words to convey how much I appreciate and treasure both your knowledge and your friendship. And, Dennis, thank you for always keeping the coffee warm.

Jackie Bannon, it's been a long road, one I'm proud to walk beside you on. Thank you for countless hours on the phone, for wisdom, and for the ability to cut through the muck and get to the point of the matter.

Diana Coyle, Alicia Dean, Cathy Morrison, Goldie Edwards, Sunny Cole, Elisabeth Burke, Judy Ridgely, and Linda Kage, your insight as beta readers and trusted co-workers makes my visions come to life. Alfie Thompson, you are a mentor above all others, and you gave me the courage to pursue this project from the get-go. You kept the faith when times got rough. Thank you from the bottom of my heart.

To the members of Heartland Romance Authors, Midwest Romance Writers, and Mid-America Romance Authors, you teach, you guide, you laugh with and dry tears with. Thanks for being family away from home.

To my readers, you're the reason I do this, and I thank you for not just your constant support, but for everything you bring to my in-box, my blog, and my day-to-day work. I greatly appreciate your dedication.

The Curse

In 1119, nine knights rode with Hugues de Payens to the Holy Land, becoming the Knights Templar. All were bound by marriage or by blood. Eight were recorded over time. The ninth vanished into history.

Beneath the legendary Temple Mount, the knights uncovered holy relics, including the Copper Scroll—a document written by Azazel's unholy hand. For their forbidden digging, the archangels exacted a sacrifice. The knights would spend eternity battling the demons of Azazel's creation, but with each vile death they claimed, a portion of darkness would enter their soul. In time, they would transform into knights of Azazel, warriors veined with evil, destined to fight against the Almighty.

Yet an ancient prophecy remained to give them hope. When darkness raped the land, the seraphs would return. Female descendants of the Nephilim would carry the light to heal their dying souls.

Centuries have passed. Azazel's might grows to intolerable limits. With the acquisition of eight holy relics, he will gain the power to overthrow the Almighty.

Six Templars stand above the rest in duty, honor, and loyalty. But each is haunted by a tragic past, and their darkened souls rapidly near the end. As they battle both the overwhelming power of evil and the nightmares of lives they left behind, the seraphs are more than tools to victory.

They are salvation.

Prologue

Whence comes the teacher, she who is blind will follow.

The one who digs in dust precedes the finding of the jewel.

And she who understands the sword precludes the greatest loyalty.

When darkness rapes the land, the seraphs shall purify the Templar and lead the sacred swords to victory.

—ANCIENT PROPHECY OF THE
KNIGHTS TEMPLAR

You must save your seraph. Azazel knows of her existence. I cannot come.

Gabriel's adamant warning pounded through Iain's head as he jogged down the darkened alley the archangel bade him to follow. At the end of the street, Bianca Moreau's weatherworn apartment building sat in the shadow of a hulking modern high-rise. Forgotten and neglected. Like the woman within.

Iain knew she had suffered much in her young life, but he knew not what he would find. Whether she would be lovely or plain, refined or crude. However, his heart took wings at the prospect of binding himself to the seraph who would heal the darkness in his soul. He would take her from this cold, unfeeling city of Paris and care for her. Devote himself to her. And like the American Templar commander, Merrick, Iain would know coveted peace.

A greater gift, the Almighty could not grant.

He set his hand on the doorknob, and a slight smile tugged at his mouth. Convincing her to accept her role might prove a more difficult chore than battling Azazel's minions, but 'twould be worth the effort.

Hurry. We haven't much time.

Gabriel's words rose to his memory, and Iain dismissed the quandary of how to explain all to his immortal mate. He turned the knob, finding it unlocked as Gabriel foretold. As he eased open the door and stepped into a musty hall, a rat scurried across his boot. He kicked the vermin aside, briefly reminded of a different season, a different century, when he had walked the streets of France and witnessed the horrific destruction by the plague. How he despised the city. A seraph should not be bound to these degrading conditions.

He took the dingy staircase to the fourth floor, aware of the strange quiet that clung to the hall. No muted televisions echoed beyond closed doors. The insects stayed within the walls. Even the air stilled. He breathed deeply, searching for the putrid scent of rot that would identify one of Azazel's foul creations.

Only dust, the aroma of human bodies, and stale sex filtered to his nose. Dimly, a soft feminine moan rose to his ears. A sound of pleasure, he realized with a wry smile.

Hurry.

He strode down the short hall to number eight and reached for the lion-head knocker. As his fingers grazed the tarnished brass, the door moved beneath his light touch. It swung open a good six inches. Unlocked. Her door should not be unlocked. Not here. Not in this indecent building.

The hair at the nape of his neck lifted. He dropped his hand to the hilt of his sword. His fingers closed around air, and he silently cursed. He had left the weapon in the SUV, afraid 'twould frighten her and make his task more difficult. Saints' blood, he had been foolish!

He set his hand on the painted wood and pushed the door open. Darkness flooded her front room. Her kitchenette. The hall. The oppressive silence clung more thickly here, and Iain's pulse tripped.

Faint light at the end of a short hall caught his eye. He breathed easier as a rustling drifted to his awareness. The sound of a mattress creaking. Covers unfolding as she put herself to bed.

Yet the nagging suspicion something was amiss prevented him from calling out and making his presence known. Quietly, he approached the light.

"Please . . ." she begged softly. "Please."

His throat tightening, Iain stepped into the doorway. The sight before him stilled his heart. Nude, two figures lay atop her bed, oblivious to his presence. Her long blond hair spilled across the pillow. Her lips sought the masculine mouth that hovered over hers. She arched her back, a mewl bubbling in her throat, as the man eased his hand between her parted legs.

'Twas not, however, the sight of her sexual pleasure that constricted his chest. 'Twas the man. For as Iain's gaze traversed his broad spine, he glimpsed what only centuries of living amongst angels could reveal. From powerful shoulder blades two cloaked wings spanned toward the ceiling. And there could only be one angel who would indulge in carnal delight.

Azazel.

"You will serve me," he cooed against her engorged nipple. "Please me. Do my bidding."

She answered with a moan.

Rage, unlike any Iain had ever experienced, surged through his body. It overpowered the fear that came with Azazel's unholy presence and possessed him like a mad man. He threw himself at Azazel, knowing 'twas futile, hoping he could pull her from her trance enough to bid her to run.

"Bianca!"

With a malicious snarl, Azazel reared off her body. With one effortless swing of his arm, he flung Iain across the room, sending him crashing into the wall. Something inside his chest cracked. Pain erupted, white hot and engulfing.

With the distraction, Azazel's magic collapsed. But in the half second where he clung to his human form before his fathomless black wings could emerge, Bianca regained her senses. She lifted her legs and kicked Azazel in the chest. It sent him staggering.

"You have doomed her," Azazel hissed.

Iain struggled to rise. Agony dropped him to his knees, scarcely able to breathe. Helpless to aid his seraph, the only woman in this world who could save his soul and aid the Templar purpose, he watched as Bianca scrambled across her bed in a vain race for the door.

Azazel snatched at her shoulder. Claws dug into flawless flesh, whipping her around to face him. Before she could do so much as whimper, he thrust his hand into her chest. She screamed. Her body convulsed in his deadly embrace. Azazel released the hand that supported her back, and she fell to the floor. Her heart remained in his vile hand. Blood poured down the length of his arm.

A smirk drifted to Azazel's lips as he carelessly tossed her heart atop her broken body. "A pity. She was most entertaining. I could have enjoyed her company a good while before that became necessary."

Unable to form words through his blinding pain, Iain spit at Azazel's feet, daring the Lord of Darkness to take him next. To put an end not only to his physical suffering, but also to the eternal damnation of his soul.

Yet Azazel would not grant him such respite. He chuckled at Iain. "You will serve me soon enough. I await the power of your sword."

A fetid breeze stirred, and Azazel vanished.

Iain's gaze fell to Bianca's bloodied form. He closed his eyes to the hot rush of tears. Fighting against the searing heat that taunted him with the bliss of unconsciousness, he dragged himself across the carpeted floor to her lifeless side. With a shaking hand, he pushed her thick hair away from her face. Long lashes graced high cheekbones. She had been beautiful.

His heart broke as he touched her still-warm cheek. He had failed his seraph. Failed his brethren. There would be no salvation for his tainted soul. Not now. Not ever. He would suffer until the darkness overcame him. When it did, he would know escape. But he would raise his sword against his brethren and join Azazel's ranks to conquer the Almighty.

Condemned.

Eternally.

CHAPTER I

✦

"How's it feel to prove the existence of Christ?"

The wavering masculine voice invaded Noelle Keane's laboratory as a door clicked shut. She looked over her shoulder to greet aging archaeologist Gabriel San Lucee with a smile.

"Morning, Gabriel." She turned back to the cloth.

Thirty-three inches of fragile cloth swathed the laboratory table. Laid out with less care than anyone had given the delicate weave in centuries, it bore dark stains in the wrinkled center, telltale marks of its original insignificance. But though it had once been little more than a scrap meant for the trash, millions revered it. Now the flimsy piece of material would gain more respect and attract thousands of devotees. All in the name of a mythical being who no one could prove existed.

Noelle ran her gloved hand across the rough surface, smoothing out wrinkles that would never see an iron. In her other hand, she held a typed printout of her carbon-dated findings. The evidence was there, and yet all it proved was that the Sudarium of Oviedo covered a body in the approximate year 33.

Not what body. Not which month. Not even where it had been used. Supposition laid claim to all those things. Scientific fact, however, verified only its age. That and the blood type AB. All the rest of the findings—such as pollen type and traces of myrrh that had been verified in the midnineties—could relate to any number of ancient funerary practices in Palestine.

She folded it into a loose square, small enough to fit into the airtight canister that protected it.

"You didn't answer my question." Pulling on gloves, Gabriel joined her at the table and leaned a hip on the edge. He extended a wrinkled hand toward the metal container. "May I hold it?"

She passed him the canister. "I haven't proved Christ existed. Until they dig up his bones, that won't happen. And even if they *do* dig up his bones, barring your God suddenly appearing to tell us otherwise, we can't *prove* the bones are Jesus Christ's."

He clucked his tongue as he pulled the veil-thin cloth out and draped it between his palms. "You still haven't come to see the truth?"

"The truth is here." Noelle wagged her paper beneath his nose. "Black and white."

A lazy grin crinkled the corners of his gray-blue eyes. He put the Sudarium back into the canister and reverently set it in the middle of the table. "Tell that to all the people lined up outside and the throngs of Christians waiting to follow that little can to the airport."

"I suppose that's why you're here?" She picked up her travel log, signed the necessary forms to verify she'd performed the accelerator mass spectrometry herself, and stuffed them all into her briefcase. She couldn't remember a time Gabriel hadn't dropped into her sanitized laboratory unannounced. Since she'd accepted the lead scientist position in D.C. six years ago, he popped in almost monthly.

Truthfully, she already knew what brought him here today. Gabriel had been part of the team of scientists that dated the Shroud of Turin in the eighties. He'd want to see this supposed counterpart.

"Well, yes and no." He slung a leather satchel that had seen better days over his shoulder and set it on the table. "Yes, I wanted to see the Sudarium. But I needed to talk to you as well."

"Make it quick. I've got a flight to catch. That little baby has to be back in the Cámara Santa tonight. If it's not, Father Phanuel will have a coronary." She shrugged out of her lab coat, hung it on the wall, and went to the mirror to tighten her ponytail. "He's convinced someone's going to steal it."

"With good reason, Noelle." Gabriel pulled out a rolling stool and sat down. "The same reason I wanted to talk to you. People coveted that cloth before it came here. Now, people would kill just to touch it. Let alone possess it."

She shot him a glance through the mirror and adjusted her glasses. "I think I can handle escorting the thing back to Spain. I got it here, didn't I? Seth's going to meet me at the airport and keep me company across the ocean."

"Ah yes, your faithful shadow, Seth." Humor lightened Gabriel's eyes. He pushed a hand through short, thick, white hair, and a frown tugged at bushy eyebrows. "I don't think you should trust anyone with this, Noelle. It's too significant."

Slowly turning, Noelle dropped her gaze to the gnarled cane resting against Gabriel's left leg. He'd devoted his life to proving the Shroud of Turin was legitimate. Now he was almost eighty, and all he had to show for his research was a shroud that dated from the thirteenth century and a crippled leg. His shooting upon that shroud's return was the reason for her cadre of governmental guards.

She met his concerned gaze with a warm smile. "I'll be fine. There's four cars ahead and behind me. The Church owns the plane. My assistant will be with me— I'll be just fine."

His eyes narrowed as he studied her expression.

She'd seen that look enough times to know Gabriel was about to dump some revelation on her she wouldn't like. The hairs on the back of her neck lifted, and unease rolled in her belly.

"I've arranged for a personal guard."

"You what?" She blinked. Her glasses slipped down her nose, and she hastily shoved them back into place.

"I spoke with the director. We both feel it would be a good idea to have someone with you. Driving you. The caravan is nice, yes. But the men inside are strangers easily bought. It's not like Pope Benedict arranged for the Secret Service to escort you."

Noelle folded her arms over her chest and scowled. "I thought you retired. Doesn't that mean you can't piddle around in my lab and interfere at will?"

A hearty chuckle rumbled in the back of his throat. "Come now, don't be cross. It's one day out of your life. Besides, I brought you something to make up for it." He flopped open his satchel and stuffed a hand inside.

"More like something to bribe me with." Unable to

keep her grin under wraps, Noelle sidled into a chair next to him. Gabriel's trinkets were always fascinating. But whatever he brought for her always included a personal request. Date some little object he'd picked up from someplace he wouldn't say, in some corner of the world he'd forgotten. She suspected half of them ended up on eBay.

True to form, he pulled out two felt-wrapped parcels tied with a white string. He selected the smaller and gently tugged at the ties. The ribbon fell away. Gabriel plucked the folded fabric apart. He held his open hand beneath her chin.

Noelle looked down on a gold ring set with a vibrant red stone. She gingerly took it between thumb and forefinger and held it to the light. Intricate etching along the band formed a crude basket weave pattern that lacked even a hint of patina. Yet the artistry was old. Imprecise and rough—a product of an era where everything came from the hands of men. She brought it closer and traced a short nail over the prominent cabochon. Etched into the polished surface, a clubbed chevron had been spared the scars of centuries.

Though beautiful, she'd seen many of similar type. "Roman."

Gabriel nodded. "I know that much. But I want to know if it's empire or republic." He nudged her elbow. "Try it on."

Smirking, Noelle gave in to the tradition. If she had a jewelry box for all the ancient decorations Gabriel had made her try on over the years, she'd never want for accessories again. She slid the ring onto her finger and cocked her hand, allowing him to inspect the trinket.

"Lovely. Can't you see who might have worn it? She

would have dark hair like yours. Elegant hands." He caught her fingertips and turned her wrist under the light. "It would glint at banquets, a symbol of her husband's wealth. Perhaps she was an empress. That's gold, you know."

She retracted her hand and slipped the ring off. "I figured as much. There's no tarnish on it at all. This doesn't look polished—but we won't know until I get it tested. We might find chemical residue."

He winked in the affectionate way that always reminded her of her long-gone father. "You'll tell me if you do." Freckled hands pressed the protective cloth into hers.

She wrapped it up, twisted on her stool, and stuffed it into the bag that would hold her precious cargo. When she swiveled around to face him again, Gabriel had the next package unwrapped. Sitting on the tabletop, a heavily patinaed arm torc waited. The patches of green and red iron oxide shimmered in iridescent color, marking it as bronze.

Noelle picked it up to examine it more closely. Triple wound, it coiled in a near-perfect circle. On each end, a tiny serpent's head came to rest in the center. Each bore fragments of some jewel, or perhaps glass, which served as onyx eyes. Cross-hatching behind the miniature heads created masterful scale work.

"This is gorgeous," she murmured. She turned the torc beneath the light, and her eyebrows furrowed. Out of place with the other artwork, a Templar cross had been etched into each serpent's head. "That's odd."

"I thought so too. Can you see if there's any difference in the age between the crosses and the rest of it?"

She brought the torc closer and squinted at the miniscule carvings. "I'll do my best. When do you need these back?" Before he could instruct her, she eased the torc up over her elbow, fitting it snugly onto her arm. She pushed her shirtsleeve to her shoulder, then twisted to admire the piece. For the first time since Gabriel had started bringing her objects on the side, she could see what he saw—a visual of the long-ago person who might have cherished the forgotten object.

"It's really pretty, Gabriel."

His heavy hand clapped her shoulder. "I'm glad you like it. That one's yours."

"Mine?" Noelle's eyes widened. "I can't accept this. It's got to be worth a fortune."

Features that still held a hint of color from all his years in the field lifted with a smirk. "Where'd my skeptic go? You don't know how old that is."

A flush crept into her cheeks. "I know it's authentic. You've never brought me a fake. No matter how old this is, it's still got to have significant value." She pushed at the trinket to slip it off her arm. "I can't accept it."

Gabriel grabbed his satchel, snapped it shut, and stood. "You can. Consider it your reward for successfully dating the Sudarium." He slung his bag over his shoulder, then braced himself on his cane. "Come on. I'll introduce you to the men I hired."

Noelle pushed at the torc again, but it refused to budge. Under her breath, she muttered an oath. She should have known better than to shove it onto her arm thoughtlessly. The last time she'd tried on something that was a little too tight, she and Gabriel nearly had to cut it off. If not for his brilliant idea to soak her hand in ice water until her fingers almost froze, she'd have destroyed a ring worth thousands.

"Try soap later," he commented.

Noelle watched Gabriel limp toward the door. A frown pulled at her forehead as his long-ago accident sifted into her mind. He hadn't expected someone would try to shoot him, especially not after disproving the theory on the shroud. Maybe his guard wouldn't be such a bad idea after all. She glanced at the canister. "I need a few minutes, Gabriel. I don't have this packed right."

Knowing glinted in his eyes. "I'll hobble over to the candy machine. Want anything?"

Noelle shook her head.

When the door to her laboratory thumped shut, Noelle picked up the canister and shoved it inside her oversized purse. She lugged the larger satchel Father Phanuel had packed it in to her locker, and stuffed in the change of clothes she kept on hand in case of a chemical spill. Satisfied it didn't look too bulky, she snapped the tiny padlock on the fastener shut and pocketed the key. Stopping at her cluttered desk, she scribbled a note to Seth instructing him to pick up the relic at the boarding gate. While she'd like to convince herself Gabriel was being overprotective, she knew in her heart he was a practical man. He wouldn't caution her unless he felt she had reason to worry. Better to take precautions, even if they were unnecessary.

Still, the idea he'd hired private security niggled at her pride. She did a reasonable job living on her own in D.C., even with her apartment being in a shadier side of town. She hadn't been mugged, hadn't been threatened, and hadn't once felt as if she needed a protector. Accepting Gabriel's suggestion that now might be a wise time to become dependent on someone else just didn't sit well.

A knock signaled Gabriel's return. She tossed the bag

and her purse over her shoulder, grabbed her coat, and pulled on her winter hat. Winding her heavy scarf around her neck, she headed for the door.

In the hall, she handed Gabriel the canister's satchel. "Take this to the airport for me, would you? Gate 23— I'll meet you there with Seth."

Gabriel reached down, and in a gesture that could only be marked as fatherly, he clasped her hand in an affectionate squeeze. "I'll have Lucan do the honors."

"Who's he?"

"One of the men I hired."

Even better. Gabriel might observe the weight difference. Someone unfamiliar with transporting artifacts probably wouldn't catch on. When she arrived at the airport, she'd reclaim the bag, and no one would ever be the wiser.

Gabriel urged her toward the back stairs. "We'll go this way. There's a slew of reporters on the front steps."

Noelle rolled her eyes. The things people would do over a myth. She'd never understand religion or the power it held over mankind. It was so much easier to comprehend the properties of science, the genetic links between the different species, as opposed to trying to sell the creative fiction of a greater power. Science could be proved. Theology only existed as long as people believed.

She followed Gabriel up the musty metal stairs reserved for employees onto the rooftop parking lot. The sun glared off high banks of snow, a false illusion of warmth against the frigid blast that whipped through her hair. As they stepped around the first row of multicolored vehicles, the front doors on a silver SUV opened. Two men climbed out. Two giant men who looked like they could turn that SUV on its side with little effort.

Noelle bristled. Gabriel hadn't hired security, he'd hired damn bodyguards. "I won't forget this, Gabriel," she mumbled under her breath.

His chuckle only annoyed her further. Gritting her teeth, she sank into her coat and accepted she didn't have a choice. Maybe she could have gotten out of this back in her laboratory. But not now. Not after she'd agreed. And certainly not when she couldn't pry his bribe off her arm.

As they approached the waiting vehicle, Gabriel gave her a sideways glance. "I'll send Lucan ahead with the Sudarium. I would trust him with my life, so you don't need to worry about its safety. Farran will escort you to your apartment, then take you to the airport when it's time to leave." He came to an abrupt stop and pulled on her elbow to turn her around. Bracing his hands on her shoulders, he dropped his head to meet her gaze. All traces of good humor drained from his expression. His eyes glinted with warning.

"When you get to Spain, Gareth will meet you at the baggage claim. He'll have a red armband over his jacket. Allow no one but him to escort you to your hotel."

A chill worked its way down Noelle's spine, and she shivered. In all the time she'd known Gabriel, she'd never seen such deadly seriousness.

She opened her mouth to ask for an explanation, but Gabriel silenced her question with a gesture at the waiting men. "Dr. Keane, please meet Lucan."

To her utter surprise, the dark-haired man took her hand and kissed the back of it. "A pleasure." Silver eyes shone with sincerity, a striking contrast to the tousled locks that brushed against his shoulders.

Before she could recover from the surprising greeting,

Gabriel cut in. "Lucan, you will take the second car with me, and we will go to the airport ahead of Dr. Keane."

With a respectful, subordinate nod, Lucan accepted the directive.

Curiosity pulled Noelle's gaze to the larger giant at the same time Gabriel addressed him. "Farran, this is Dr. Keane. You will escort Noelle to her apartment so she can gather what she needs. Do not leave her side."

Noelle's gaze traveled over the imposing figure leaning against the driver's door. Blond hair tumbled in the crisp winter breeze. A slight wave to his long lengths gave them a softer appearance. He dwarfed her easily, his broad shoulders a good five inches taller than the top of her head. Dressed in faded blue jeans that hugged thick thighs, and a well-worn leather jacket that accented a trim waist, he cut a breathtaking picture. As her gaze drifted up, taking in his well-defined chin, high cheekbones, and nose that sat slightly off center, it skidded to a stop and locked with an intoxicating pair of ale-brown eyes.

Her heart kicked into her ribs. Wow. Maybe Gabriel's bodyguard wouldn't be half bad. She could spend a few hours with this guy and live off the resulting high for months to come.

With a tentative smile, she extended her hand.

Farran glanced at it. Then, on an indistinguishable mutter, he scowled. Not even bothering to accept her handshake, he pushed off the door, yanked it open, and climbed behind the steering wheel.

To her shame, Noelle wilted inside. Although his gruff rebuke stung, his reaction didn't surprise her. Men like Farran had never found her remotely attractive. Then again, glasses, ponytails, and lab coats didn't appeal to many men, period. If Farran hadn't brushed her off now, he would have when she tried to talk to him and all that came out was drivel about elements, reactive compounds, and carbon footprints.

Anger rose on the heels of her hurt, and she shot Gabriel a look meant to kill. Except Gabriel had already crossed the parking lot, leaving her the only option of getting in Farran's vehicle. She grumbled to herself, crossed to the passenger's side, and opened the door. So much for that euphoric high. In this man's company, time would crawl at a turtle's pace and with each agonizing tick, remind her of all her shortcomings.

CHAPTER 2

Farran curled his fingers around the steering wheel as Noelle's perfume assaulted his nose. The faint sweet scent of jasmine soaked into the air, making it impossible to pretend she did not sit beside him.

A woman. A cursed woman. He had been sent to guard the Sudarium, not to act as maid to a woman. God's teeth, did Gabriel seek to punish him? For what, Farran could not fathom. Yet he could think of no other reason the archangel would assign him to such a menial task.

Aware he could not sit in the parking lot forever, he slid his gaze sideways to the wench occupying his passenger's seat. "Where is your apartment?"

"Go right at the end of the block, left at the next, and left on the third block. It's the townhouse without Christmas lights." She did not look at him, rather kept her gaze fastened out the side window. Still, he could not help but notice the way she slunk down further into her seat.

Good. So she sensed he cared not for this distraction from his purpose. If he had known Gabriel intended to have him serve as chauffer, he would have insisted on staying in the stronghold with the other Templar knights. Whilst their commander, Merrick, healed, there was much Farran needed to do.

Tamping down a rush of annoyance, he shifted the SUV into drive and eased onto the gas. Would that this chore ended quickly, for he could not stomach hours of idleness. Not when so much lay at stake. Not when they had all been warned Azazel would attempt to take the Sudarium. The master of darkness coveted the cloth's power. 'Twould give him another victory in his quest to overthrow the Almighty. Whilst Lucan could fend off a great many of Azazel's demons, if Azazel sent a fallen Templar knight, 'twould take both their swords to protect the holy cloth.

He glanced through the rearview mirror into the backseat, ensuring Lucan had not forgotten his blade. Only one silver scabbard sat in sight, and Farran allowed the tension in his shoulders to dissipate. He would speak with Gabriel on his return and make his displeasure known. Until that time arrived, however, there was naught he could do except cart the woman where she instructed.

They drove in silence, a welcome sound to Farran's ears. The less she engaged him in conversation, the better. If not for the subtle aroma of her perfume when she shifted, he could dismiss her presence. At least Gabriel had not sent a comely wench to torment him. This one's brown ponytail did not taunt. Her oversized coat did not cling to shapely curves. And her complete lack of conversation did not plague him with the need to find words he did not wish to speak.

As he wound down the twisting residential street, she pointed at an aged, brown brick building. "It's there."

Farran pulled to the curb and shut the engine off. She gathered her purse to her chest with one hand, opened the door with the other. "I need to shower. I'll be a little while. You want something to eat? Or drink?"

Nay, he wanted neither. But Gabriel had ordered him to not stray from her side. He dared not linger outside. He let out an exasperated sigh and opened his door. "I will have water."

Noelle rounded the front of the car, leading the way up the building's front steps. As she bounced up the snow-covered stairs, her ponytail bobbed against the middle of her back, catching the rays of afternoon sunlight. Farran's gaze fixed on the unexpected, reddish brown sheen. 'Twas not the color of a mouse's coat after all. A most startling discovery, for naught about the tiny little woman had caught his attention upon first meeting. Naught beyond her wire-rimmed glasses and the passing thought that he knew no woman who preferred the bits of glass to contacts.

She punched her pass code into the security system, and the bolt on the doors clicked open. He followed wordlessly down the hall, up another flight of stairs. She unlocked her apartment and entered, leaving him to shut the door.

Inside, Farran halted. The apartments he frequented were small, unlike the vast expanse of her front room. Polished planks of wood adorned the floor, and where he had anticipated crisp modern furniture and appliances, he found simplicity. A couch, a coffee table, a plush rug. He glanced around, noting the same lack of frivolity applied to her dining area, the sparse but tasteful hangings on her walls. Even the open kitchen, he noted, held naught that could be considered luxurious.

Not what he expected to find in Washington, D.C.

Nor had he expected to find a gray cat lounging in the nearby chair.

He blinked as Noelle scooped up the feline and buried her nose in its fur. "Hey, fella." The way she nuzzled her cheek against the cat's head and closed her eyes struck a chord of dissonance deep inside his soul. 'Twas so tender, so natural, he felt at once out of place. Oversized. Too harsh.

When she opened her eyes and her gaze met his, Farran realized he was staring. He gave her a curt nod, then distanced himself by sitting on the couch. A colorful magazine atop her coffee table caught his eye, and he picked it up to thumb through it whilst she attended to her affairs.

From the kitchen, he recognized the sound of a can opener. The anxious meows that accompanied the noise told him her pet expected dinner. A plate clattered onto the countertop. Silverware pinged against the dish.

"Here you go, Scat Cat."

Scat—what manner of person named her pet the very word meant to drive a cat away? For some unexplainable reason, the oddity of her chosen name amused him. Long dead humor stirred, and he felt the corners of his mouth twitch. Listening with more interest, he tracked her movements through the house. Behind him, she shrugged out of her coat. After she entered the kitchen once again, ice cubes plinked against glass. The sound of running water blended with the melodic sound of her voice as she hummed a tune he did not recognize.

Her footsteps approached the couch. Her perfume tickled his nose.

She leaned over his knee and set the glass of water on

the polished tabletop. "Are you sure I can't get you anything else?"

Farran's heart skidded to a stop as her gaze locked with his. Her glasses removed, eyes the color of a doe's hide and every bit as soft drew him in. They shone with warmth, a natural friendliness that her silence obscured. Where he had thought her plain less than thirty minutes previous, he looked upon features as delicate as porcelain. Creamy skin bore no mark of time, no suggestion of a hardened life—unlike the whores he entertained himself with. Neat white teeth peeked behind full lips as she offered him a hesitant smile. And her nose possessed just enough uplift at the tip to belie a spriteful spirit.

Jesu, Gabriel tortured more severely than the days spent in the strappado at the Inquisition's mercy.

"Nay," he grit out through clenched teeth.

Even his traitorous wife did not compare to the picture of loveliness that stood at his side. Especially when he considered the twinkle in Noelle's eyes. Nay, that foul creature he married centuries ago had never held such sunlight in her stare.

He jerked his gaze away at the tightening of his gut.

"You don't talk much, do you?" she asked as she vanished behind him.

The same could be said for her. Yet, at her subtle rebuke, the discomfort in his gut intensified. He had no cause for rudeness. 'Twas no more her fault he sat here than Lucan's. He set the magazine aside and pulled in a deep breath. "I have little to say."

"I see that."

As the silence lapsed between them, Farran's mind wandered to the temple and his fellow knights. Were he with them, he would no doubt be aiding Merrick in teaching Lady Anne the use of a sword. In comparison to spending an afternoon with *that* particular woman, this one seemed much more benign. The last time he had cause to spar with Anne, he could not walk right for three days, such was the damage her knee did to his groin.

Aye, mayhap he could suffer worse assignments than guarding Noelle. 'Twould be a short reprieve from the duties of his immortal cause. Here he would not confront Azazel's creatures and would not wonder if the next battle would be his last.

He listened to the sound of running water and laid his head on the back of the couch. Closing his eyes, he sought a moment's rest. But behind his lowered eyelids, those fawnlike brown eyes gleamed bright. He snapped upright with a mutter and snatched the magazine back into his lap. Damnation, he did not need this distraction. Nor did he desire it. He belonged with Lucan, protecting the Almighty's sacred treasure. The sooner he delivered Noelle to the airport, the sooner he could return to usefulness.

Noelle squeezed a liberal amount of shower gel onto the torc around her arm. Gnawing on her lower lip, she worked the slippery liquid around the three coils, slid her finger under, and saturated her skin. Then she shoved her wrist between her knees and pushed on the bangle with all her might.

The torc refused to budge.

"Damn it," she mumbled. Straightening, she twisted her arm to inspect for swelling. Strangely, the only evidence that she'd managed to get an ancient antiquity lodged onto her arm came from the red marks where her nails had scraped into her skin. The thing *looked* loose.

For that matter, she couldn't even really feel a squeeze around her bicep. Yet two attempts with the shower gel and it still hadn't shifted a bit.

She edged her body away from the spray of tepid water and eyed the conditioner. She'd never get a brush through her hair without it. But the idea of stuffing her head back under the last dregs of cool water from her hot water heater made her shudder. Hot showers she could do. Cold—*ugh*.

On the other hand, she'd rather die than look like Broom Hilda with Farran around.

She grabbed the bottle and quickly conditioned. With a deep breath, she braved the even colder water. A gasp wrenched free as what amounted to buckets of ice dumped on her head. She rinsed as fast as her fingers would go, then whipped the faucet off. Shivering, she wrapped her arms around her body. Towel. Where'd she put the towel?

Through the glass door, a flash of pink near the sink answered the quandary. She lunged out of the stall and quickly toweled off. She'd wasted precious time trying to get that stupid torc off, and now she'd be lucky if she had an hour to make it to her flight. Rushing into her bedroom, she glanced at the clock and confirmed her suspicions. They'd have to hurry, not a good thing given the conditions of the roads after last night's snowfall.

She yanked on a pair of clean jeans, stuffed her feet into comfortable heeled boots, and rummaged through her closet for a top. Planes always made her hot, no matter the time of year. Still, she needed to look presentable. Her first task involved delivering the Sudarium, which would likely lead to dinner with Father Phanuel. Much as she'd prefer to wear a T-shirt, she couldn't.

She eased into a short-sleeved sweater, lightweight

enough to keep her cool on the flight. As she passed her
mirror, she combed her fingers through her hair. The torc
glinted in the late afternoon sunlight, and she lowered her
arm, admiring the piece. It really was pretty. And even if
it looked a little out of place, the subtle sheen of color
complemented her fair skin.

Grabbing her glasses, she pushed them back onto the
bridge of her nose and hurried out of her bedroom. "Okay.
Sorry about that. I'm ready, if you are."

Farran eased to his feet, all six foot something of him.
He'd loosened his coat, giving her a remarkable view of a
dark green jersey pulled tight across his broad chest. Her
stomach did a flip-flop. Man he was yummy. Some days
she'd give anything to be blond and perfect. Men didn't
scowl at Barbies.

Only, as she lifted her eyes to his face, this time Farran
wasn't scowling at all.

All the air in Farran's lungs lodged in his throat as he
turned around to acknowledge his tardy little ward. Hair,
more rich and thick than he had imagined, draped around
her shoulders. The damp waves tumbled to her waist,
long and free, reminding him of the thick vines that covered the grotto where he played as a boy. Her glasses were
not cumbersome. If anything, they enhanced the saucy
upturn to her nose.

They tempted too. Called to his fingers and begged
them to pull those wire frames away from those fawnlike
eyes. And the mouth he had believed was plain, smiled
with such innocent hesitation, he could not help but wonder if it had ever known a man's lustful touch. Full and
lush, her lips would be soft. Mayhap as silky as her hair.

He curled his fingers into a fist and turned away. Saints'

blood, he would have to pay a visit to Leah upon his return. Clearly, he had spent too long away from her willing arms if this scrap of a woman could warm his blood.

"Are you ready?" Noelle asked.

"Aye."

She picked up her purse and coat, crossed to the door, and pulled it open. "It's rush hour. Seth said we should probably go south out of town and then head west on the outskirts."

"You will guide me. I have not been to D.C. in quite some time."

Again, her smile graced her face, and his stomach balled into a hard knot. He ground his teeth against the uncomfortable twist. A few hours more, and he would be free of her. She would fade into memory, no more significant than any other woman he had encountered throughout time.

Farran entered the hall, waited for her to lock up her house, then followed to the stairs. He furrowed his brow as he recalled the cat. "Someone will tend your pet?"

"Scat?" she let out a soft chuckle. "Yes. Seth said he would stop by over the weekend."

The fist around his innards clamped harder. This Seth, did he enjoy the softness of Noelle's mouth? He could not silence his curiosity. "Seth is?"

"My assistant at the lab."

Invisible fingers released their hold, and Farran breathed deeply. He had no cause to feel relieved, yet 'twas no mistaking he did. More reason for him to satisfy his oath to Gabriel and return to the temple.

Outside, the sun sank into the horizon, and long shadows emerged atop the piled banks of snow. He opened Noelle's door, then jogged around to his. But as the doors thumped shut, the silence he had treasured became

oppressive. Enveloped by the sweet fragrance of her jasmine perfume, Farran became aware of the woman beside him. The rustle of her coat when she moved scraped
against his nerves. Her bright smile rose within his mind
to torment, and his thoughts steered down a treacherous
course. A path that led to visions of those long lengths of
hair secluding them away whilst he explored the softness
of those damning lips.

He gripped the wheel in both hands, silently cursing
his fate.

"So this is what you do? Security?" Noelle's voice vibrated with a touch of nervousness.

Security—'twas an interesting way to describe his
duty. Somehow he doubted she would care to hear the
truth, or that she would believe if he explained. He settled
for the easier response. "Aye."

She twisted in her seat to look at him more fully. "Are
you from here? From America, I mean? Your speech—you
have an accent and distinct dialect, but I can't place it."

"Aye." He glanced at her, gauging how much to reveal.
"I was born outside of Clare, in England." The only son
of a long-dead lord and one who left his family in shame.
Lost to time like the rest of the world Farran understood.

"That's in Sussex, isn't it? I went there once in college.
We were doing research at Sutton Hoo."

"Aye."

"Turn here." She tapped on the window, indicating the
approaching narrow road.

Dutifully, Farran slowed for the turn. As he rounded
the corner, he chanced a glance at her. Posture relaxed,
expression full of animation, she looked at ease. Naught
like the uncomfortable woman who tried to hide in the
seat on their first journey together. Her gaze slid to his,

surprising him with the same hesitant smile. A touch of pink rose in her cheeks, and she hastily cast her eyes to her lap.

Beneath the rising lavender of twilight, they left the hustle-bustle of D.C. proper and emerged into a remote stretch of fields. The houses spaced farther apart. Fields rose between them. Trees even peppered the landscape. Great hulking trees with twisting branches that rose like skeleton arms to embrace a winter's sky.

"Do you miss it?" Noelle asked. "England. Home."

A more conflicting answer he could not imagine. Aye, he missed England, but not the one she knew. He missed the fields of green, the days spent on horseback, the harder, yet simpler life he had known so long ago. At the same time, the thought of home filled him with such loathing he could not stand to think upon it. Farran settled for, "Sometimes."

"It's so pretty over there. Everything has character. And oh . . ." She let out a wistful sigh. "There are so many old things there. I get glimpses when artifacts come into the lab. But seeing everything under the microscope just doesn't compare. I can't imagine leaving, if I'd been born there."

He had once felt the same. Now, with Azazel's darkness running in his blood, England only spurned fury. Anxious for a change in subject, he asked, "You were born where?"

"A little farm in Iowa. My folks raised pigs." She pulled down the visor to fiddle with her hair. "Hey, that looks like Seth's car behind us. I guess I won't have to worry about finding him at the airport."

Farran glanced in the rearview mirror. Several yards away, a yellow Chevy Camaro rapidly approached. Despite the rolled-up windows, he caught the stench. The revolting scent of rot. A smell so foul, it still made his stomach roll even after hundreds of years of combating it.

Evil.

Mayhap her Seth followed, but somewhere near, Azazel's minions lurked.

He gripped the wheel tight and stepped on the gas. Jaw clenched, his gaze riveted on the mirror. The Camaro's grille bore down on them, its headlights mere feet away from their bumper.

Not somewhere near, he rationalized. Right behind them.

"Hold on," he barked. Stomping on the accelerator, Farran gave the wheel a fierce jerk and skidded through a sharp right-hand curve.

From the corner of his eye, he caught Noelle's furrowed brow. She opened her mouth to speak, then quickly snapped it shut. She grabbed for the overhead handhold and shrank into the seat.

Farran's pulse bounded to life. His chest tightened, and his heart hammered into his ribs as he tried to outmaneuver the creature behind the wheel. But already exceeding eighty, he dared not attempt more speed. Not with a mortal sitting at his side. Too great was the risk he would lose control on this slick highway.

In his side mirror, the sports car gained. It surged around his rear fender, barreled down the oncoming lane. Farran glanced out his window, catching a brief glimpse of a man behind the wheel before it sped past. The foul odor filled the car and tightened his throat. Beside him, Noelle gagged.

When the taillights evened with their front bumper, Farran expelled the breath he had been holding. Azazel's minion wanted the Sudarium, not the woman at his side.

Best to alert Lucan. He reached between the seats for his cell phone.

As he flipped it open, Noelle let out a shriek.

Metal ground against metal in a sickening scream. Somewhere glass shattered. His hands slipped from the wheel as his body lurched to the left. Where pavement had stretched out before them, brown grass and clods of dirt flew by.

In the next heartbeat, everything went black.

CHAPTER 3

The throbbing in Farran's head became angry drums
that pounded against his skull. Faint lights flashed
behind his eyes with each pulse of his blood. Groaning,
he squeezed his temple. Pain arced down his arm, and he
struggled to make sense of the cold.

It seeped into his bones, intensifying the ache in his
body. Wetness blanketed his back, plastered his jeans to
his thighs. He cracked one eye open and stared up at a
cloud-covered moon. Outside. What was he doing out . . .

Memories slammed into him. The Camaro, the impact, the rolling vehicle. They had been run off the road.
How long had they been here?

Noelle.

He sat up, ignoring his body's protests. Whatever injuries he had received were insignificant. They did not
come from a Templar blade, nor had Azazel's demon in-
flicted them directly. He was immortal—he would heal.
Not so Noelle.

Rising to his feet, he searched their surroundings. The

SUV lay on its roof in the ditch, four black tires barely discernible in the dark. No lights marked nearby houses, and the closest streetlamp failed to shine.

A shiver rolled through him. He pulled his twisted coat down to cover his dampened clothes. Where was she? Had the demon taken her?

Stumbling, he approached the wrecked vehicle. Thoughts sifted into firm place, despite the blaring noise inside his head. Other than aches, he felt no significant pain. Nothing broken. Nothing damaged. He felt the truck, the cold frame telling him they'd been here quite some time. An hour, maybe two, gauging from the moon's height.

"Noelle!" His voice rasped through the night.

Silence answered.

His legs gained strength with each step, and he quickened his pace. Trudging through banks of plowed snow, he rounded the vehicle. Bits of glass speckled the ground, glinting against the intermittent light of the moon. Twisted at a grotesque angle, the passenger's door stood open. His heart skipped a panicked beat when he stuck his head inside and found the seat empty. Only her purse remained. Dangling by one handle, it hung motionless on the jagged corner of the door. The other strap stirred in the faint breeze, tap-tapping against a dull brown stain.

Farran whipped around, his gaze scanning over the expansive field. Wherever she was, she bled. If she was here at all.

His breath caught as a swathe of reddish brown caught his eye just beyond the SUV's rear end. "Noelle!"

He choked back bitter unease and rushed to her side. For a handful of heartbeats, he could do no more than look down on her. She lay on her stomach, her lower body

in a wide indentation in the snow where the SUV had hit.
Arms stretched above her head, her hair covered her face.
The tattered remnants of her coat clung to her right arm.
Beneath her left, the snow soaked up her blood. Fresh
blood.

She was alive.

Farran dropped to his knees and gently pushed the hair
away from her face. Through lips the color of violets, she
breathed shallowly. "Can you hear me, damsel?" he said.

Shucking his coat, he covered her with haste. Then he
stumbled back to the vehicle. Amidst a barrage of vile
oaths, he searched for his cell phone to no avail. He found
his sword, the map Gabriel left behind, a tube of lipstick
that escaped Noelle's purse, her glasses. A glance over
his shoulder told him Noelle had not moved, and he resumed his search once more.

Faint but persistent ringing stilled his hands. He cocked
his head, listening. The notes came not from the SUV.
Instead, they drifted from where he had lain.

He raced around the vehicle and the tune stopped. Farran lifted his eyes to the heavens, and in a moment of rare
faith, begged the Almighty to make it ring again.

For the first time in more years than he could remember,
his prayers did not go ignored. The chiming began anew.
Snow flew as he dug for the sound. His fingers touched the
cold plastic, and relief surged through Farran's veins.

He snapped the phone open. "I need help."

"Where are you?" Lucan's voice filled with urgency.

"On the south side of town." He turned a circle, looking for a street sign, a marker of any type that would
identify their position. Damnation, why had he not paid
attention to where Noelle instructed him to turn?

"You come here oft," he snapped at Lucan. "Tell me where I am."

"Are houses nearby?"

"Nay." And no passing cars, much to his frustration. "We turned off about two miles from her apartment. Ask Gabriel."

"Gabriel left once we were out of sight."

Farran ground his teeth together. 'Twould figure that the archangel would vanish. God's messenger did naught but create headaches.

Rustling on the other end of the line indicated Lucan used his map. Farran returned to Noelle. He pressed his fingers to her delicate throat. When he found her pulse intact, he breathed deep.

"I am not certain, Farran. There are so many places . . ."

"For the love of the saints, phone Merrick," Farran barked. "Have him locate the vehicle. My ward is injured. Get here." He snapped the phone shut and jammed it into his pocket.

He must get Noelle warm. And yet he feared moving her. If she had injured her neck, he could damage her further. Still, he could not risk the chance she bled someplace he could not see.

With the gentleness he would give an infant, he removed his coat from her body and slid his hands beneath her. Taking care to keep her head from bouncing too greatly, he eased her onto her back. A faint moan tumbled free, a noise so soft and anguished, Farran's heart twisted.

"Noelle, can you hear me?"

When she did not do so much as twitch, he moved to her feet. Sliding his hands along her legs, he checked the alignment of her bones. Pressure on her left hip provoked another throaty protest. The sound gained strength as he examined her ribs.

Frowning, he moved to her exposed shoulder where the blood ran in a thin stream. She lay still as he pressed her collarbone. He pushed aside her sweater's shredded sleeve, following the trail of blood, and froze.

In the moonlight, the torc glinted with subtle color. A decoration he could not hope to ignore, no matter how he might wish to.

"Jesu," he swore softly.

A rush of fiery rage surged through his blood. A seraph! Gabriel sent him to guard a seraph and failed to include that important bit of information.

God's teeth, 'twas a wonder the demon had not killed her.

He slammed a fist into the snow and ground his teeth together until his jaw hurt. He did not want this responsibility. 'Twas bad enough she was a woman. A seraph, the promised salvation for the weakened Templar knights, would mean trouble tenfold. Anne's arrival had proved that. And yet he could not escape this duty. Not as long as they remained away from the temple. Once he returned her there, however, he would gladly pass her safekeeping to Lucan.

Scowling, he tossed his coat over her body. As his gaze fell to her face, something deep inside him rolled around like a ball of lead. He had failed her. As well as his brothers. The most sacred gift to the Templar, and he had neglected to even consider Gabriel might have cause to keep her safe.

He tucked a strand of her wet hair behind her ear and brushed his thumb over her cheek. "I will get you someplace safe," he murmured.

Headlights flashed across the snow, accompanied by the squeal of tires. Farran snapped his head up, instincts on alert. Too late, he remembered he had left his sword in the upside-down vehicle.

Looking to the road, his gaze settled on a silver SUV. He expelled a long breath, and fitted his hands beneath Noelle's shoulders as Lucan jumped out.

"I was not far away," Lucan supplied. "How does she fare?"

"I do not know." Farran glanced down at her delicate face, his frown deepening. "Help me get her into the back. I shall take her to Louise's adytum. 'Tis nearby, is it not?"

"Aye, brother. Within a half hour from here."

Lucan reached for Noelle's feet, but before he could touch her ankle, Farran scooped her into his arms. "I will attend her. Fetch the things from the truck."

Though he tried to be careful, he stumbled as he rose. The jostle brought another faint groan from her lips. Farran grimaced. Saints' blood, he should have allowed Lucan to carry her. Lucan possessed more grace, a gentler nature. He would not have aggravated her wounds.

As Farran made his way through the snow to the running vehicle, he glanced down at Noelle's pretty face. Without her glasses to cover her eyes, he noticed tiny freckles adorned her high cheekbones. Faint sun marks placed there to make her appear more youthful. A smile tugged at his mouth, but he squelched it before it could transform. 'Twas naught to smile about. He had contributed to her injuries, and lest he managed to keep the archangels uninformed, 'twould be hell to pay.

Under his perusal, her lashes fluttered. Farran paused, less than a yard away from the SUV's rear door. He drew in a sharp breath, held it whilst he waited. They stirred again, dusting the tops of her cheeks like butterflies wings. She opened her eyes. Closed them. Then with an airy exhale, she tried a third time. Those fawn-brown eyes lifted to his, and for a moment, his heart stopped.

"Farran," she whispered.

The hand she kept in her lap lifted. Her fingers curled into his shirt as if she clung to a safety rope. Ever so slightly, she shifted, bringing her cheek closer to his chest. Somewhere deep inside him, buried in some forgotten portion of his soul, something did a long, slow roll.

"Aye," he murmured as he cradled her closer.

"I'm so cold."

Protective instincts he had thought long dead rose like a fierce tide. He fought them back with clenched teeth. Yet 'twas futile. They stormed through him, awakening every particle of his body to the woman in his arms. He swallowed with effort and trained his gaze to the open hatch door. Too many years had passed since he had held a woman this way. Too many centuries. Once he had believed 'twas his purpose to protect the fairer sex. Once he would have died to uphold that fabled notion. Brighid changed all that. Changed everything. He could not allow himself to forget, no matter how helpless a woman might appear, beneath the surface they were as deadly as any man.

Choosing silence, Farran eased Noelle into the truck. He leaned against the wheel well, his legs stretched before him. Still she clung to him, her shivers now strong tremors. They vibrated into him, making it impossible to hold on to his resolve. With a defeated sigh, he wound his arms around her more tightly and pressed her body flush with his.

Lucan shut the door, extinguishing the light. In the

darkness, the fall of Noelle's breath against Farran's neck taunted his senses. Heat rushed through his blood. Against his thigh, he felt the stirring of his shaft. On a silent mutter, he shifted.

"When I was little," she said on a soft chuckle, "I used to dream of being rescued."

Wincing, Farran tried to ignore the sensations her words stirred. He had not rescued her, he reminded himself. He had, in fact, injured her. Whatever misplaced thoughts she entertained, they were naught more than a product of the injury to her head. "You should rest, damsel."

To Farran's relief, Lucan climbed inside. He flipped on the overhead light and looked back at Farran. "Do you not think we should take her to the hospital?"

"Nay, 'tis unnecessary."

"Farran, she is but a woman. She may bleed inside. Uriel is far from here."

Farran answered with a shake of his head. "To Louise's, Lucan."

Noelle's hold on his shirt lessened, and he glanced down to find her once again at rest. He lifted his gaze to Lucan once more and lowered his voice. "She is a seraph. She will heal when her mate is found."

Lucan's eyes widened like saucers. In the rearview mirror, his gaze dropped to Noelle, and then he turned around. "Does she know?"

"I do not think so. Let us go to Louise's. Lady Anne has catalogued the marks of our men. I shall contact her and ask for the list."

With a slow dip of his chin, Lucan faced forward and dropped the SUV into gear. "How did you learn of this?"

"She wears the serpents."

Farran leaned his head against the window and allowed

the discovery to settle in. A second seraph. Gabriel foretold of their coming, as much as the prophecy did. It made sense now—*Whence comes the teacher, she who is blind will follow.*

Anne had been the teacher. Noelle's sight marked her as the next.

Would she belong to Lucan? Mayhap Caradoc? Mayhap someone else all together. Whilst Lady Anne's journal documented all the Templar in America, it only catalogued the few knights who had visited from Europe. Noelle could belong to one of them. Or another much farther away.

The Sudarium leapt to life within his mind, and he jerked his head up. "What trouble did you encounter at the airport?"

Lucan's low chuckle preempted the amused shake of his head. "'Twas one demon. A young one at that. He took no care to conceal himself and 'twas over before it began."

"And the cloth?"

Extending his arm above the seats, Lucan held up the small bag Noelle had given him earlier. "'Tis here."

"My sword?"

"Open your eyes, brother. You nearly sat on your belongings."

Farran frowned at Lucan's good humor. Looking down at the collection of things from the wrecked vehicle, he inventoried what he remembered—her purse, her glasses, his sword, the tube of lipstick.

"She is pretty," Lucan remarked.

"Aye." *As lovely as an English field.*

"Mayhap she is mine."

"Mayhap," Farran murmured. Though the thought tightened his gut so fiercely, he could scarcely breathe.

She was too pretty to belong to Lucan. Too delicate for Caradoc. Too quiet for Declan.

Damnation, what was the matter with him? He did not want a seraph. He much preferred the inevitable death that loomed ahead. For feeling naught would be a greater freedom than learning to feel again.

CHAPTER 4

With Lucan on his heels and Louise leading the way, Farran carried Noelle up the adytum's old mahogany staircase to a small room on the second floor.

"Set her here, Farran." Louise patted the tall four-poster bed. "I'll fetch my robe. Get her out of those wet clothes. Lucan, you go down and fix some tea."

Farran laid Noelle in the bed and backed up a step. Undress her? He could not. Though he was more than familiar with the hidden treasures of a woman's body, she belonged to a knight. What lay beneath those soaked clothes he had no right to see.

"Come now, sir knight." Louise's smoky voice carried a note of laughter. "Do you expect me to believe you've never seen a woman naked? More than once, I've heard the whispered murmurings of your brethren and their maids beneath these rafters." She gave Lucan's shoulder a push and nudged him out the door.

With a frown, Farran stared at the tiny woman in the bed. He could excuse witnessing her nakedness to duty.

He fished his cell phone out of his pocket and punched in Merrick's number.

Lady Anne answered on the second ring. "Farran, are you all right?"

Uncomfortable with the concern in her voice, Farran bristled. "I am well. Allow me to speak to Merrick."

"He's right here. One minute."

It took less than three seconds for Merrick's voice to ring in Farran's ear. "What happened?"

"A demon ran us off the road." He glanced back at Noelle, remembering the shrill cry she had let out moments before the impact. Approaching footsteps in the hall announced Louise's return, and he tucked the phone against his shoulder to ease Noelle's boots off her feet.

"Is the Sudarium safe?"

"Aye. 'Tis still with us. Mikhail shall need to send word to Phanuel."

"Phanuel has been informed. Will you be returning?"

Farran set Noelle's boot on the floor near the bed and reached for the other. "Aye, soon."

Drawing in a deep breath, Farran dropped her other boot to the floor and let his gaze settle on the torc around Noelle's arm. He picked up her right hand and plucked off one soaked glove. He held her fingertips against his palm, admiring the slender lengths. Short nails bore no trace of polish. Soft skin disguised her line of work. Reluctantly, he laid the hand across her belly and announced, "Dr. Keane is a seraph."

A heartbeat of silence passed through the line. Wariness fringed Merrick's voice as he asked, "Are you certain?"

Farran pursed his lips against an exasperated retort. Was he certain? 'Twas not a claim he would loosely make. "She bears the serpents. I am not blind, Merrick. Send me the document of our brethren's marks." He picked up Noelle's left hand and tugged on her glove. "I shall have her paired before—"

A scar on the back of Noelle's hand choked off his words. He stared, dumbstruck, at the meaty flesh between her thumb and forefinger. There, spanning up to her wrist, the whitish mark formed a perfect replica of a dagger, complete with a ringed pommel.

"Jesu," he whispered.

The phone clattered to the floor, closing as it fell. Farran backed away, scalded by the sudden heat in Noelle's palm. Reflex brought his hand to his belly in a vain attempt to cover the identical scar beneath his shirt. Surely his eyes deceived him. He did not want a seraph. Not now. Not ever.

"Damnation," he hissed through clenched teeth.

He stalked back to the bed. No longer concerned for her injuries, he snatched up her fingers and inspected the scar once more. Nay, his eyes did not play tricks. She bore a dagger on her hand. It matched his as if someone had miniaturized the eighteen-inch-long weapon and scalded it into her flesh.

She belonged to him.

The door opened, and Farran's head snapped up. He returned Louise's pleasant smile with a glare. "You may undress the wench." He shouldered past the aging caretaker, ignoring the way she spluttered.

So Gabriel sought to pair him with a maid, did he? 'Twas no wonder the archangel did not forewarn him of her nature. Gabriel well knew Farran would rather swallow his own sword.

He took the stairs two at a time, in desperate need of

fresh air. His fingers twitched with the need to pummel something. A seraph! *His* seraph! God's teeth, would he be allowed no mercy? Could he not just leave this world and be done with life?

In the wide front room, Farran braced his hands on the table and squeezed his eyes shut. Duty bound him to accept the pairing. With the oaths they were fated to take, the Templar would gain much needed strength. Much as he would like nothing more, he could not walk away from the woman in the bed upstairs.

And yet . . . he did not have to stay either.

"Brother? Is something amiss?" Lucan's voice drifted down the stairs.

Farran turned around and raised his glower to Lucan's face. "You will go to her apartment. Fetch her cat. Fetch her things. Deliver them all to Mikhail."

Lucan's gaze narrowed with suspicion. "I trust you do not seek to have the maid to yourself?"

"Nay!" God's teeth, nay. He would no more touch her now than he would touch a snake. He would say his oath, deliver her to the temple, and leave with the first light.

Cocking his head, Lucan studied him. Slow dawning filtered into his expression, and he answered with a thoughtful nod. "You recognize her mark. I shall have her mate sent here."

Farran exhaled through his teeth. At his thigh, he clenched a hand into a tight fist. "There is no need for such."

"Farran, you cannot be serious. She must be paired at once. 'Tis written—"

"She is mine, Lucan." With the vile truth exposed, Farran stormed out the door.

* * *

Noelle stirred inside her warm cocoon. Snuggling deeper into what felt like a pile of down, she savored the last fragments of the dream where Farran had held her. Such wonderfully strong arms. Hard and gentle all at once. And he smelled good too. Like wet woods and oranges. All man.

Eyes still closed, she smiled and rolled over to cuddle with her pillow. As she moved, the dull throb of pain cut through her early morning bliss. She winced and opened her eyes. Instead of the muted blue of her room, warm yellow covered the walls. Frowning, she searched for the explanation as to how she got here.

"Good eve, damsel." Low and rough, Farran's voice washed over her.

In a flurry, reality crashed into her. Not a dream—he'd saved her after the SUV flipped. He'd carried her to another vehicle, and he'd rescued her from the cold.

The heavy blanket covering her slipped as she sat up. It caught on her breasts, exposing bare skin to chilly air. She clutched at the brushed cotton, desperate to cover herself, and felt the heat of embarrassment crawl up her throat. Naked. How absolutely mortifying.

"There is no need for modesty, Noelle. I have seen it all before. 'Twas I who undressed you when you proved too difficult for Louise to shift."

The heat in her cheeks intensified, and she dropped her head to hide her humiliation. He'd seen her naked. No one had ever seen her naked. God, he'd know how small her boobs were, discover her bra was padded. Covering her burning face with her hands, she groaned. "You were supposed to be my hero, not my humiliator."

Heavy footsteps approached the bed. "I am no one's

hero, damsel. How do you fare? Your head, does it pain you?"

Fingertips moved through her hair, pushing it out of her face. A strong hand cupped her chin, tipped her head toward the light. He brushed his thumb over her temple, and she winced. "Ouch."

"'Tis no wonder. You have a baseball of a knot."

She stared at his abdomen as he inspected her wound. This close, the scent she'd remembered so vividly engulfed her. Memories of how comfortable his arms had been swamped through her, and she resisted the overwhelming temptation to lock her hands around his waist and rest her cheek against his massive chest. How this giant of a man could possess such a gentle touch mystified her. Yet his fingers were nothing less than tender.

With a satisfied nod, he stepped away. His gaze lingered, probing her with unsettling ale-brown warmth. "Your ribs. Can you breathe without pain?"

She nodded. "They hurt, but I'm okay."

He reached for the blanket, as if he meant to inspect them as well, and Noelle scrambled backward into the pillows. Consternation creased his brow. The light in his eyes sharpened. "God's teeth, woman, you cannot be that innocent. Let me see your injuries."

Noelle blinked. For half a second she debated blurting out the truth. But for some unexplainable reason, she didn't want Farran to know she'd only been kissed a handful of times. At twenty-nine years old, she *should* be more experienced with men. And this man clearly had no hesitancies around naked women. Besides, the last man she'd told had laughed so hard it had taken her weeks to confront her reflection in the mirror. She couldn't stand the thought of Farran laughing at her.

Twisting sideways, she lowered the blanket to her hip, careful to keep her breasts covered. He set a knee on the bed and supported her opposite side with a large palm. Roughened fingertips grazed over the purplish marks on her ribs, firm enough she could feel his caress, yet gentle enough he didn't disturb the lingering ache.

His touch sent a shiver down her spine. Warmth flowed through her veins, heating her from the inside out. It fanned into her belly, fluttered wildly, then spread lower. She averted her gaze and gnawed on her lower lip, trying to pretend this was normal. That men like Farran touched her intimately all the time. That this was no different than going to the doctor.

As she did when she had to face the degrading necessity of a yearly gynecological exam, she sought conversation. "Where am I?"

"In the adytum Louise tends."

His breath washed over her shoulder, stirring the fine hairs on her skin. She squeezed her eyes shut and swallowed down a whimper. "The what?"

"'Tis a friend of mine's home. Does that pain you?" He pressed his thumb into the spot he had before.

"No." She snapped her eyes open. *Stay normal, Noelle.* She took a deep breath to temper the sudden erratic beat of her pulse. "How long have I been here?"

"You have slept for thirty-six hours."

As he pivoted her to look at her back, his long hair tickled her arm. Unable to suppress a nervous giggle, she squirmed. The hand at her opposite side tightened. "Hold still."

"Sorry." Thirty-six hours. That meant . . . She twisted out of his hold to face him. "Oh, crap! Father Phanuel."

Farran moved away from the bed. "The Sudarium is with Lucan. Phanuel has been informed. He is most understanding, I assure you."

She scanned the room, in search of her purse. Had it survived the crash? "My purse, Farran. Did you find it?"

He pointed behind her, and she turned to look. Hanging from one of the mahogany posts, she found the oversized black bag. Relaxing, she sank into the wealth of pillows propped against the headboard and closed her eyes. "Thank you for taking care of me. I suppose I should be getting home now. I'll have to call my boss and make arrangements for another flight."

"Are you hungry?"

In answer to his question, her stomach rumbled. "I could eat."

"Very well then." He crossed to an overstuffed wingback chair and picked up what she assumed was her clothes. Setting them on the bed beside her, he added, "I shall bring you dinner. You may dress. Your sweater was ruined. Louise has given you a sweatshirt."

With another disturbingly cold nod, he strode through the door.

Noelle looked after him for several long minutes, a wistful smile playing at her mouth. He was out of her league. One hundred percent the kind of man who pointedly ignored her on the few occasions she went clubbing. But damn, he was handsome. And the eccentric way he spoke stirred something so deep inside her she couldn't explain it. He made her feel alive in a wholly feminine way she hadn't ever experienced before.

For the first time in her life, she really wanted to be something other than the science geek with glasses. Especially something other than the terribly inexperienced twenty-nine-year-old she was.

Sighing, she leaned forward to pick up her bra. A pillow snagged on her arm, and she glanced down to find that damnable torc still wound around her bicep. Damn it. She'd lost her clothes, but she hadn't managed to get rid of that thing.

Maybe not eating for thirty-six hours would help. She pushed at the trinket. Not surprisingly, it didn't slip.

With a mutter, she slipped into her bra and eased her legs over the side of her bed. At least Farran had left her in her panties. He hadn't seen *everything*. If he had, she didn't know how she'd ever look him in the eyes again. She tugged on her jeans and stood on unsteady legs. Now, to find some lotion and try to get this ridiculous gift of Gabriel's off.

Before Farran came back and found her half dressed.

CHAPTER 5

✝

Farran hefted the wicker tray Louise had given him to one hand and twisted Noelle's doorknob with the other. As he pushed the door open, he stilled, his head cocked to the side. Standing at the edge of the bed, engaged in a fit of temper, Noelle held her boot in one hand and smacked it into the heavy comforter. A throaty growl of frustration accompanied the harmless strike before she repeated the action again.

If he were not quite certain her mind was intact, he would have questioned her sanity in that moment. For such a tiny little woman, her temper seemed wholly out of place. She looked much like a hornet attempting to break through a glass prison. All fury, yet no bite. God help him—he chuckled.

The noise so surprised him, he nearly dropped her supper. He could not remember when last he laughed.

Yet he was not the only one surprised by his humor. At his short bark of amusement, she dropped the shoe and turned wide eyes his way. Her features changed to ash. Her jaw dropped with a squeak of surprise.

He could not still his tongue. "Tell me, damsel, what offense did the bed commit?"

She puffed out a breath that stirred the stray tendrils of hair around her face, and her shoulders slumped. 'Twas then she recalled her state of dress. Crimson flooded her cheeks as she wrapped her arms around her to cover her bra. Her modesty intrigued him. If he allowed himself, he could almost liken her to the maids he had once known. Those who would have rather died than be caught un-clothed with a man in their chambers when they were unwed.

"I can't get this thing off." Her back half turned, she presented her left arm and the serpentine torc.

The subtle reminder of their circumstance squelched his misplaced humor. His smile died before it could take life. They would have to speak of this soon, for he could not keep her from the temple. Nor could he self-ishly ignore his duty and pretend he knew not what she was. Still, he could not bring himself to confront the truth. Once he informed her, there would be no turning back.

He set the tray on the nearby dresser. "I brought you a bit of everything. I did not know what you would like." He indicated a bowl of fruit, several slices of roast beef, a fried chicken leg, mashed potatoes, green beans, and a hunk of sourdough bread.

Her gaze followed his upturned hand, her eyes widen-ing at the feast. "Thank you." Still holding her arms over her chest, she bent awkwardly to retrieve her sweatshirt. As she slipped her unadorned arm in, she paused. A deep frown creased her brow, and she glanced over her shoulder. "I don't suppose . . . Would you see if you can get this thing off?" She extended her arm.

Farran bit back a mutter. He eyed the twin serpents, debating. When he touched the torc, he could no longer delay explaining her circumstance. What happened then, only God knew. He held no hope she would embrace the knowledge. At best, she would do as Anne did and deny. At worst, she might well turn that temper on him.

Noelle wagged her arm in the air. "Yoo-hoo? It's stuck. Can you give it a try? I put lotion on it."

With a heavy sigh, he went to her and took her hand. Like a willing lover yielding to a mate, the torc slid easily to her wrist. Noelle's gasp of surprise cut through the room. "How'd you do that?"

"'Twas not difficult." He slid the torc back up her arm, fitting it neatly into place.

She gave him a look of disbelief. "Why'd you go and do that? I've been trying to get it off since we were at my apartment. I'll never get it free now."

Farran sat down on the edge of her bed, feeling much as if leaden weights hung off his legs. "I am quite certain 'twill give you no trouble."

Her features scrunched together as if he had spoken in his native tongue. Testing his claim, she pushed at the torc with one finger. It dropped to her elbow. 'Twas the last bit of proof Farran needed to know, without a doubt, they were fated. As long as he was present, the torc would feel no need to lock itself in place.

"Did you stretch it?" She peered at him quizzically, then tried the armband once more. Again, it glided over her skin with no resistance.

"Nay. It recognizes me." He let out a heavy sigh and pushed a hand through his hair.

"Huh?"

"Sit down, Noelle. We must talk." 'Twould not be easy either, judging from the cockeyed eyebrow she arched his way.

She tugged the sweatshirt over her head, pushed her left arm through, and flounced onto the bed at his side. With a teasing smile, she tipped her head to the side and asked, "You aren't going to tell me it's magical, are you?"

He hesitated for a heavy heartbeat. Then, he locked his gaze with hers and answered, "Aye, I am."

The giggle started before Farran finished his brief response. It bubbled up Noelle's throat and skipped free, the first bit of humor she'd felt since she'd rolled out of bed the morning of the accident. Magical torcs. Of all the absurd things. His sense of humor crept out at the most unexpected times. "Uh-huh. Nice try. You stretched it, didn't you?"

"Nay, Noelle, I did naught."

His deadpan expression made her giggle even harder, and she covered her mouth with her hand. If she could count all the artifacts she'd dated that came with some legend about curses or magical properties, she'd end up near a thousand before she slowed down enough to think. Not a one of them had brought her bad luck. Nothing helped her win the lottery, and no single object had healed the chemical burn on her hand.

Gabriel had tried to pull a couple of good ones on her too. Like the spear she'd dated for him three years ago. He claimed it tied back to the days of Christ. He'd sworn its authenticity so vehemently he'd almost convinced her. Until her research, however, disproved his theory when the data indicated it couldn't be older than the late dark ages.

But Farran wasn't laughing. Which meant—if he was anything like Gabriel—he wasn't ready to confess his joke. She'd play along, humor him until he became satisfied he convinced her enough to grin and tell the truth. She swallowed down her smile and assumed a sober expression. "Okay. Tell me more."

He pulled a leg up onto the bed and twisted to face her more fully. "'Twas created before the angels fell from grace and succumbed to Azazel's influence. The serpents symbolize Nehushtan, the sacred snake of healing and salvation. It identifies those born from divine power, the descendants of the Nephilim."

Oh, now this was definitely interesting. He'd even twisted theology to exclude Satan. Noelle choked down another renegade laugh. The man was good.

"When the floods came, they were given a choice—keep their powers and die, or surrender their divinity and become as man. Those who chose to live returned their torcs and were stripped of their longevity. The Almighty promised when the need arose, they would return to his grace and serve. They lived, they labored, they died."

Interesting indeed. *New* theology even. If there was a modicum of truth in this, it would turn the zealots upside down. Everyone would be screaming for the angels to return. Especially in this politically charged world.

Noelle dipped her head, encouraging Farran to continue.

"You are a descendent of that power, damsel. The living breath of the Nephilim. The torc recognizes you. 'Twill use whatever means necessary to ensure you assume your place."

Aha! He had slipped. Time to turn his words back on him and watch him squirm. Her mouth curved with a smirk. "But you said it recognizes you."

Without missing a beat, Farran agreed, "Aye. It does. I am . . ." He paused, looking to the ceiling. Noelle resisted the urge to call his bluff right there, and leaned back on her hands as he furrowed his brow in search of what to say next.

The deep frown returned to his handsome features, and he cast his gaze to his lap. "Nine centuries ago, I joined a small gathering of men in the Holy Land. You would know them as the Knights Templar. I have spent centuries fighting Azazel's evil creations and protecting man from his unholy desires. Our power weakens with each evil life we take. The seraphs . . ." His eyes gleamed with soft light as he lifted them to hers. "You . . . are the strength we need. I am your mate. We shall take vows. You shall gain my immortality, and I shall gain the light that lives in your soul."

Noelle couldn't help herself—she burst out laughing until tears gathered in her eyes. Wiping them away, she expired into chuckles. "Oh God, Farran, that's a good one. I've heard some doozies, but that's great. I'm sorry. I shouldn't laugh. I don't mean to spoil your joke. But that's just amazing."

In the blink of an eye, his serene expression morphed into a dark scowl. "You do not believe me."

"No," she answered on a chortle. "Did you really expect me to? I'm sure someone else would—you've put so much feeling into the tale. But I'm a scientist. I don't even believe in God." To soften his disappointment, she reached between them and patted his hand. "You did good though. Better than some of the things Gabriel has told me."

He abruptly pulled his hand away. "Everything Gabriel has ever told you is true, damsel. He is an archangel. Whilst he may behave most strange, he is God's messenger and cannot lie."

Gabriel an archangel. Oh man, the two of them were in this together. When she saw him next, she'd buy him a drink for this. She grinned at Farran and shook her head. "You two are something else. I swear, I should have known. He tries to do this to me all the time."

"Woman," Farran barked. "'Tis no jest! You are branded as mine." He grabbed the hem of his shirt and yanked it over his head. "Look for yourself."

Noelle gaped at the vision that sat before her. Smooth bronzed muscle lacked any trace of hair and bulged even as he sat still. The chest she remembered so vividly was nothing less than a wall of corrugated stone. Thick forearms led to even thicker biceps, arms so strong she felt three times smaller than normal. He could crush a man—or so her imagination said.

Her appreciative stare dropped to his belly and stopped on her gasp. Scored into his taut abdomen, a white scar ran from his ribs down beneath the waistband of his jeans. A good three inches wide, and easily three times as long, the scarred flesh assumed the distinct shape of a ring-hilted dagger. Someone had heated metal and pressed it to his skin.

"My word," she whispered.

Drawn to the horror of the mark, she leaned in and traced a fingertip down the length of the hilt. The pain he must have felt—her heart twisted hard. "What happened to you?" She glanced up at his face.

Eyes closed, he sat utterly still. "'Twas meant to gain my confession."

Noelle winced. Looking back at the ugly scar she couldn't take her hand off of, her chest tightened. What sort of person could do that to a man? His stomach bunched beneath her fingertips, mystifying her even more. As deep as the wound had been, he was lucky he could feel anything at all. Whoever had done this was sick. Sick, sick. "Were you in the war?" she asked quietly.

"Aye," he exhaled.

"Oh, Farran, I'm so sorry." And she was—sorrier than she'd ever been for anyone. All the stories she'd heard about beheaded captives, tortured soldiers, and political screw-ups amounted to nothing when faced with the stark truth of what he'd been through. He'd suffered. Through some miracle, he'd survived a wound that would have killed a lesser man.

On sheer impulse, she leaned in and pressed a kiss to the ringed pommel.

As she leaned back, Farran's palm cupped her chin. He lifted her face, locked his eyes with hers. The light that always burned so bright within those ale-brown depths now glowed a rich golden color that reached down into her and touched some unnamable part of her soul. Her heart skipped a beat, then launched into erratic rhythm. She drew in a short breath, and Farran's lips touched hers.

She'd been kissed a handful of times before, but nothing like this. Compared to the sloppy, inexperienced searchings she knew, no hesitation came with the caress of Farran's mouth. He slid his hand from her chin to her hair and settled in, knowing what he wanted and exactly how to take it. Velvety warmth nudged her lips apart, and Noelle yielded with a surprised gasp. The tip of his tongue coaxed hers to join its seductive dance. As the quivering in her belly turned into liquid heat, she all too willingly complied.

Sensation burst through her veins as his woodsy-orange scent soaked into her. So clean, so tempting, so completely masculine. The softness of his mouth, so unlike the hardness of his body, had the effect of wine on her thoughts. It made her dizzy, yet she couldn't get enough. She braced a hand on his shoulder to steady the rapid swirl of her head and eagerly tangled her tongue with his.

A husky murmur rumbled in the back of Farran's throat. His fingers tightened against her scalp, and he tipped her head back. Where he wanted it, where he could explore more thoroughly. As his mouth took on more pressure, demanding something she didn't fully comprehend, the heat pooled in her belly fanned into her blood. Her skin felt tight. Restlessness possessed her body.

The feel of Farran's palm against her breast soothed the need to move. Those strong fingers lifted and squeezed. Firm, but like every other time he'd touched her, filled with an underlying tenderness. So unlike the fumbling attempts of her one, almost lover right after college, he knew how to touch a woman. Knew it well. And the unrelenting caress stirred that aching need to move to intolerable limits. When his thumb grazed across her swollen nipple, Noelle shuddered. Her womb contracted. The heat in her blood spread uncomfortably between her legs.

Then everything changed. Farran abruptly drew away, his kiss terminating with his raspy gasp. He stood. Ramrod straight, his back faced her. He stared at the wall as he spoke. "We are fated. You will come with me."

It took a minute for his words to reach her brain. When

they did, she laughed. That again. If he wanted to date her, this was a bit ridiculous. All he needed to do was ask. "I have to get home, Farran."

As if he hadn't heard her, he pulled on his shirt. "I apologize for my trespass, damsel. 'Twill not occur again whilst you reside in the temple. Though we are fated, you shall have freedom to the pleasures you wish, and I shall take mine elsewhere."

Her features scrunched together as she tried to process his meaning. The temple, reside . . . "What?"

He gave her an incredulous look. "Do not be daft. You may have the men you wish. I prefer whores. You shall have no demands from me in that respect. But damsel, you *will* come with me. We both must answer duty."

Shock rocketed through her. She stared, speechless. He was still clinging to that ridiculous tale? Was he nuts? He had to be. Whatever had happened to him as a captive had affected his brain. Made him think he was stuck in a different time. "Don't be absurd, Farran. I'm not going anywhere but home."

His glower silenced her protests. He took four purposeful strides and opened her door. "Ready yourself to travel. Whether you wish it or not, you are mine. Lord knows I do not want you, but the choice is not mine."

The door clanged shut with an angry shudder. Stunned, Noelle sat in the middle of the bed. As the understanding she'd just been kidnapped slowly filtered into her consciousness, she made a mad lunge for her purse. She hauled it onto the bed and dumped out the meager contents. Lipstick, tampons, car keys, canister . . . but no cell phone. She'd left it on her nightstand, plugged in. Despair crashed into her.

She hurled the empty bag across the room with a frustrated scream. This wasn't happening. She hadn't been run off the road and taken to some house she didn't know. Gabriel's guard hadn't turned out to be some psychotic veteran who'd decided to take her prisoner. And she hadn't just been kissed senseless, only to have the stark reminder of her innocence thrown into her face. He preferred whores. Then what the hell did he want her for when she evidently couldn't get a single kiss right?

She dismissed the displaced thought and gnawed on a short fingernail. She'd been kidnapped. Now wasn't the time to lament her inadequacies with men. She had to find a way out of here. And if Farran's twisted convictions started with this damn torc, she'd begin by getting rid of it.

She tugged her arm out of sweatshirt and pushed on the brass adornment.

To her complete horror, it refused to move.

Swallowing another frustrated howl, Noelle grabbed her glasses off the nightstand and raced to the window.

CHAPTER 6

Farran braced his hands on the kitchen countertop and dragged in deep lungfuls of air. Squeezing his eyes shut, he willed the trembling in his body to subside. God's teeth, that wench provoked something deep inside him. A feeling so buried in his darkened soul he thought he had snuffed the life out of it centuries ago. 'Twas not just desire the brush of her lips stirred, but a sensation far more damning. The gentle sweep of her mouth against his scar carried compassion. Tenderness he had once believed in. Tenderness he learned 'twas naught more than deception.

Noelle knew men. And like the black-hearted Brighid he had sworn his life to, Noelle knew well how to manipulate him. 'Twas evident in the readiness of her mouth, the willingness of her body. If he had not come to his senses, he would now have her splayed beneath him, and she would have wrenched his vow of loyalty free.

He would give her the oath to bind them, but he would never pledge himself to her. No matter how comely she was, no matter how she might attempt to coerce him, he would resist. Once had nearly destroyed him. The loss of his wife, his son, his kinsmen's respect . . . He would never make that mistake again.

"Sir Farran?"

Louise's voice intruded on his thoughts. He pulled in another haggard breath and lifted his head. "Aye?"

She crossed to the large window that overlooked the backside of her expansive lawn. Leaning a hip against the counter, she cocked her head and looked up toward the overhanging gables. "How are your climbing skills?"

His brows furrowed into a tight line. He did not have time to retrieve her cat. With two days between Louise's adytum and the temple in Missouri, he must get to the halfway point whilst he still possessed the energy to travel. Still, after all she had done for Noelle, he owed Louise the courtesy of his aid. "Why do you ask?"

"I'm afraid you have a little problem."

The hairs on the back of his neck lifted in alarm. Noelle. He knew it before Louise ever answered. Grinding his teeth together, he strode to the window. "Where is she?"

Louise pointed a bony finger toward the white eave. "There. On the trellis outside her window. I noticed her when I was in my room and the bottom half of the trellis broke free. It dropped past my window. She can only go up."

A low growl rumbled in his throat. He detested heights. Few things could make his stomach churn, but to look down from anything more than a horse had a worse effect than any severed limb or foul demon's breath. His stomach knotted at the very thought.

"There is no other way down?"

"Oh, there is." Louise nodded. "An iron ladder on the south side of the house. But if she's sneaking out windows, good luck convincing her to come to you."

"Then I shall wait. Unannounced." He grabbed his coat off the chair. Another look outside told him Noelle would have to come down sometime soon. She wore only her sweatshirt. "Lock her window, Louise."

A knowing smile tugged at the caretaker's mouth, and she left the room humming a soft tune.

Farran did not share her good humor. Muttering, he stalked out the front door and made his way through the snow to the south side of the house. He eyed the rusty iron ladder to ensure he did not doom Noelle to a fall. Strong bolts, void of any trace of rust, held it firmly in place against a newly mortared brick wall. It climbed the two stories, fit neatly against the white eave, and rounded onto the roof between a pair of tarnished copper gargoyle heads. Satisfied the ladder would hold, Farran folded his arms over his chest and prepared to wait.

Noelle kicked off the brick exterior and grabbed the next thin trellis slat above her head. Silently, she cursed her luck. If she hadn't tried to climb down at full speed, she'd have noticed the weak board. Now, with her window too far below to drop onto the sill, she squinted through the sunlight and willed her body to cooperate. Her left side burned. Her shoulder screamed against the effort of holding on. And the wind whipped through her, making stronger muscles weak.

She grabbed at her courage and climbed higher. Another foot, at most two, and she could rest. Then, she'd find another way down. The lack of shouts within the house told her Farran hadn't realized she'd escaped. She still had time. Not much, but enough to get to the ground and down the road to the house at the bottom of the hill.

With a grunt, she climbed up the last of the trellis. She swung her leg, hooked her heel on the eave. Finding finger holds in the sturdy boards, she tuned out the protests in her left side and hauled herself onto the roof. For several minutes, she did nothing but lie on the shingles and pant. Two years of regularly attending the gym was nothing compared to that kind of workout. Scaling the side of a building made forty minutes with weights seem like child's play. Never mind that in the gym she didn't have to worry about falling and breaking her neck.

When her breathing evened out, she pushed to a cross-legged position and took stock of her body. Her right arm trembled as she swiped her hair out of her face. Her ribs felt like someone had kicked her with a steel-toed boot. Everything else ached, but she could ignore the dull pain. She'd feel it tomorrow. Right now, it was insignificant.

Scanning the roofline, she searched for a means down. Old houses like this almost always had a ladder somewhere. With the decorative gargoyles, the intricate gables, and the narrow attic cupolas to her left, this one wouldn't disappoint. They were too clean, too cared for, to not have easy access. Unless, of course, the owner removed the old access route in favor of a metal portable.

Her gaze flicked across two protruding handles, and Noelle exhaled with relief. Down. Away.

Finally.

Careful to keep clear of the edge, she crawled along the steep pitch on all fours. Slow and steady. One hand, one knee, in front of the other. When she reached the distant house, for Gabriel's sake she'd make no mention of her near kidnapping. She'd come up with a plausible excuse and beg for a ride back to her apartment. Maybe the owners would believe she'd had a fight with her boyfriend and he'd left her on the side of the road.

She glanced at the still street. *Right.* No car had passed in the twenty or thirty minutes since she'd made her grand escape. She dismissed the voice of her conscience with a shake of her head. What the owners believed didn't matter. She'd get a ride to her apartment, grab her cat, and take refuge with Seth. There she'd stay until she reached Gabriel. When he called off his security guard, she'd go back home.

The ladder loomed before her, and Noelle resisted the urge to shout in triumph. Easing to her belly, she poked her head over the eave to inspect the ladder. This time, she wasn't going to be hasty. If that length of steel pulled out of the bricks, she'd have a whole lot more to worry about than getting away from Farran. Broken legs, arms . . .

Her thoughts screeched to a halt as her gaze dropped to the ground below. There, standing not more than two feet from the bottom rung, Farran stared back. And he didn't look at all happy to see her.

Damn. Damn, damn, *damn.*

"Come down, Noelle." He didn't raise his voice, but the low, even tone held strict warning. *Come down, or I'm coming up.*

She dropped her forehead to the shingles with a mutter. She'd give anything for a nice spring day so she could outstubborn that man. As it was though, her teeth chattered in the December breeze, and the patches of snow left on the rooftop had soaked into her clothes. Still, she couldn't accept defeat so easily. Maybe there was another way down.

She inched backward, away from the ledge.

"Noelle!" Crisp, clear, his voice cut through the stillness. "There is one ladder. The very one I am standing beneath."

Cringing, Noelle bit back a string of obscenities. How the hell could he possibly know what she'd intended? This was insane. Ludicrous. All she wanted to do was go home. At this point, if she'd had her cell phone she'd call the cops. To hell with Gabriel and his reputation.

For now, the greater concern remained being in the cold. Before she could get *home,* she had to get *down.* She pulled in a deep, fortifying breath. Down it was.

Stretched out on her belly, she inched around until her feet touched the top rung. She pushed backward, easing her knees over the ledge, then her thighs. As she grabbed for the handles, her right foot slipped on a patch of unseen ice. For a terrifying moment, everything moved in slow motion. Her legs went out from under her. The ground flashed before her eyes. Farran let out a shout. She twisted sideways.

Noelle clamped her fingers around the handles and hung on. Half on the ladder, half dangling against the brick, a fierce burst of white-hot heat lanced up her arm. She cried out, and tears stung her eyes. Blinking them back, she edged herself back onto the ladder and wrapped the handholds through her elbows. She leaned against the cold metal, her heart drumming against her ribs.

Trembles broke through her body. Paralyzed by fear, she bowed her head to the slick rung. She couldn't go up, she couldn't go down. "I can't do this," she whispered. Louder, she repeated, "I can't do this."

"You can. Climb. Go slowly."

At the mere thought of letting go at all, her tears burst free. She bit down on her lower lip, trying to stop them.

But it was useless. She was stuck and scared. More frightened by the prospect of moving than by the man at the bottom of the ladder. He might be crazy, but he hadn't hurt her. As her tears coursed freely down her cheeks, she shook her head and choked out, "I can't move."

Farran stared up at Noelle, cursing her bad luck, the Almighty, and his fate. He well knew how terror could trap a person, had seen it countless times with unseasoned knights. In her unmoving position, he recognized the signs too clearly. This was no act meant to gain his sympathy. 'Twas no ploy to soften his anger over her attempt at escape. She was truly terrified.

"Damnation," he muttered beneath his breath.

He closed his eyes with an inward prayer his stomach would not revolt and made the mark of the cross over his chest. Eyeing her, he strode to the ladder. She would pay for this later. He would find a way to make certain she came to regret her attempt at escape.

Do not look down. He chanted the mantra as he climbed the icy rungs. In less time than he had imagined, he arrived at her feet. Holding on with one hand, he placed the other on her calf. "I am here. Climb down."

'Twas then he noticed the shaking of her shoulders, heard her muffled tears. When she did not move, he gave her leg a squeeze. "Noelle, come down. I will not let you fall."

"I'm scared," she murmured.

Saints' blood, she did not intend to make this easy. Aye, indeed, he would lock her in her rooms at the temple for a week.

He assessed her position, made note of the little space her tiny body occupied. Carefully, he tucked his feet between hers and the side rails and eased his body up her legs. When he had pinned her between the ladder and his chest, he stopped. "Grab on to me."

She let go with one hand, then clutched at the rail with a fierce shake of her head. "I can't. I can't, Farran."

At the sound of her broken voice, all his defenses shuddered like a door under the barrage of a battering ram. The anger her defiance provoked dissolved with her sniffle. Deep in his gut, a heavy knot unwound. He pressed his body into hers, molded his thighs around her legs. Holding on with one hand, he pried her fingers off the metal and guided her hand to his shoulder. "Turn around, damsel," he encouraged quietly. "Wind your arms around my neck, and we shall descend together. I swear to you, I will not let you fall."

Dropping his hand to her narrow waist, he steadied her as she pivoted. When her chest brushed against his, she threw her arms around his neck in a stranglehold. Farran grabbed the ladder with both hands and began the slow climb down. With each step, he supported her with his body. Their closeness was enough to torment his senses. The sweet scent of jasmine combined with the way she meshed all around him, set his blood to simmering. He kept his stare fastened on the brick house, knowing if he chanced a glance at her, 'twould be his undoing. He would forget his purpose, use their forced position to take advantage of that sweet mouth once more.

As his boot crunched into the snow, he expelled a long breath of relief. 'Twas over. He could escape her damning nearness and tuck her safely in the SUV where she could not run. He gave her shoulder a firm push. "Let go, Noelle."

Her face tucked into his shoulder, she answered with an adamant shake of her head.

God's teeth, she could not still be scared. What in the heavens was the matter with her? His frown firmly intact, he increased the pressure of his hand. "We are on the ground. Let go."

Against his chest, her ribs expanded as she took her first normal breath. She lifted her head and looked over his shoulder. Instead of letting go, she tightened her arms, and her body relaxed against his. The embrace reached in and turned his innards upside down. He clenched his teeth against the rush of pleasant sensation. Reminded himself he had not come to her aid for her sake, but for the Templars' purpose. If she had fallen to her death, the holy Order would lose much needed might.

"That's the second time you've rescued me," she murmured. "Thank you."

Farran backed up like demons chased him. He set his fingers on her waist, pushing her down and away. In his hurry to free himself, his feet tangled with hers. He grabbed at the rail to steady his fall, but the momentum he put into his shove made her stumble. She toppled into him, upsetting his already unsteady balance. They fell to the ground in a heap.

For a long silent moment, Farran stared up at the sky. Unbelievable. She weighed no more than two sacks of grain, yet she toppled him as easily as if she wielded a club. His mouth quirked at the irony. And then he chuckled. For the second time in one day, a short burst of air constricted his lungs in a way they had not stretched in more years than he could count.

Before he could fully savor the lightheartedness she provoked, she scrambled to her feet. "I'm sorry. I'm so sorry." Crimson colored her dainty cheeks, and her eyes widened to twice their normal size. "I'm a klutz. I fall over everything. My cat—" She clamped a hand over her mouth to silence her rush of words and swallowed hard. Behind her fingertips, she muttered, "I'm sorry."

His brimming laughter died in his throat, but he could not stifle the smirk that pulled at the corner of his mouth. With a disbelieving shake of his head, he stood. He clamped her wrist in his right hand and started for the SUV. "'Twas a grand attempt at escape. Now we must attend to duty."

Noelle dug her heels in and pulled against his hold. "I'm not going to be your prisoner, Farran."

Her protest erased all traces of his good humor. He whirled on her, pinning her in place with a furious scowl. "Have I hurt you?"

She backed up a step. "No."

Tightening his hold on her wrist, he pulled her back in front of him. "Have you been placed in chains? Are you secured to a wall? Have you been denied food, damsel?"

With an ashen expression, she answered, "N-no."

"Then do not speak to me of being prisoner. You know naught of the meaning!" He spun around, and with a fierce tug, dragged her to the vehicle. He opened the door and roughly pushed her inside. Stepping back, he fixed her with a warning glare. "Do not attempt to disappear whilst I retrieve your things. Or I promise you, damsel, you shall come to understand the life of a prisoner."

CHAPTER 7

✝

Noelle itched to run. Every nerve ending in her system demanded she kick open the door and bolt down the street. But the idea of what might happen if Farran caught her rooted her in place. She stared at the house, watched his shadow ascend the stairs behind the front windows. A prisoner. While his definition and hers might vary, nevertheless, she'd lost her freedom. He'd stripped it away just as if he'd tied her up.

She wanted nothing to do with wherever he intended to take her. Visions of a solitary room without a window played with her imagination. Trays of meager food. Days without showers. All in some vain quest to prove his ludicrous claims. At best, he'd only prove his mental instability.

The compassion he'd shown her was the only thing that kept her from being truly terrified. He'd saved her twice, a blunt truth she couldn't overlook. Not only that, but from what she assumed, he'd looked after her while she recovered. True, behavior like that could go hand in hand with psychopathic madness, but she didn't think so. He'd had ample opportunity to bend her to his wishes. For that matter, he could have taken her to this *temple* while she slept, skipping the explanation all together.

Besides, he worked for Gabriel—Farran's one, ultimate saving grace. Gabriel was meticulous enough that he'd surely conduct background checks on people he hired to protect a holy relic. If Farran were truly psychopathic, something would have shown up. Gabriel wouldn't trust the Sudarium to someone he didn't implicitly trust.

Which must mean he knew Farran well. Which must also mean Gabriel thought Farran's post-traumatic stress disorder wasn't terribly threatening.

Noelle took a deep breath and reclined in the seat. Post-traumatic stress disorder—Farran exemplified that in triplicate. Their accident threw him into memories, and he reacted with the only defense he knew—a fictional story that masked over the horrible reality. If she needed any proof he'd served with the military, his physical strength and his no-nonsense demeanor provided plenty. Not to mention the nerves of steel he'd exhibited when they had a yellow Camaro running up their ass.

Opening her eyes again, she caught his silhouette bounding down the old staircase behind the glass. Her heartbeat kicked up a notch. She needed to think of something quick. Any minute now, he'd be out here. Behind the wheel, ready to take her to some place she'd never heard of. A place she had no intentions of ever seeing.

Too late.

Farran hurried out of the house. He jogged down the porch and to the driver's side, her meager things in hand. As he slid behind the wheel, he tossed her purse into her lap. "Indeed, you do have wits."

Anger sparked at the insult, and Noelle gripped her purse between her hands, resisting the urge to swing it into the side of his head. She hadn't become a recognized expert on radiocarbon dating by being an idiot. "You could benefit from the lesson my mother used to preach—if you can't find anything nice to say, don't say anything at all."

Hands on the wheel, he sat still, his gaze trained on the house they'd just left. Slowly, he nodded. "Aye. Then silence 'tis. Nice is not a part of me." With a press of his boot to the accelerator, they reversed out of the drive.

A traitorous portion of her subconscious rose up screaming in protest. He could be nice. She'd seen that more than once. He didn't have to come up the ladder after her. True, he might still be waiting for her to come down, but he came up and coaxed her down not just with niceness, but with that same damnable gentleness he gave her injuries. What was with this guy? He had to be an anomaly of science. All hard and calloused on the outside, but down there where he didn't want anyone to see, he was as sweet as a kitten.

Something she doubted he'd care to hear.

"Where are we going?"

Farran turned the corner, still not bothering to look at her. "The temple is in Missouri. 'Tis the middle of the nation, suitable for a central stronghold for our defenses."

Missouri. Noelle's pulse jumped. Just south of Iowa, and what remained of her family. This might not turn out so bad after all. She'd be within hours of help.

She slid her gaze sideways, hoping her excitement didn't show in her words. "What part of Missouri?"

"'Tis just north of Kansas City."

Not just hours away from help—*four* hours away. Noelle bit back a smile. She couldn't ask for better luck.

"When we arrive at the temple, you and I will take our oaths. Then we shall part ways. Mikhail shall see to the Sudarium's return. 'Tis safer. I am quite certain Phanuel will support this change in arrangements."

Noelle blinked, the obvious staring her in the face. The Sudarium. Regardless of what Farran thought of her, he and Gabriel believed in the cloth. Farran also believed the cloth was with his friend. She didn't need to run. She'd leverage the Sudarium for her freedom. When they made arrangements to return the cloth to Father Phanuel, they'd discover her bag held nothing but clothes. All she had to do was tell them she knew where the Sudarium was and refuse to help return it until Farran agreed to let her go.

She might be his prisoner, but that damned cloth was about to become her hostage. All she needed was a suitable hiding place. Someplace a bit more secure than the bottom of her purse.

Careful to keep her excitement out of her voice, she asked, "Are we driving through the night? It's twenty-three hours or so, isn't it?"

Steely ale-colored eyes held hers for a heavy heartbeat. He glanced back to the road, tightened his hands on the wheel. "Nay. We shall overnight at the adytum in Ohio. Should you try to run again, Noelle, I warn you I will not hesitate to deliver you to Mikhail in ropes."

Farran kept his stare fastened on the road. He refused to witness the certain anger his warning had aroused in his seraph. He mused over how Gabriel liked to provoke. It came as no surprise that Gabriel chose a woman more difficult than the willful Anne as Farran's mate. 'Twas not the first time God's messenger saw fit to destroy his life. Nay, the first came when he granted the gift of immortality.

Yet Gabriel showed no mercy this time. Where the promised hell of immortality came with the salvation of a possible death by a Templar blade, this pairing doomed Farran to eternal existence. The darkness that seeped into his soul with each demon he killed would no longer guarantee an execution. Nay, instead, he would walk the lands timelessly, tied to a woman he did not desire and consumed by memories of one he once had. Branded forever as a traitor.

He had come so close. A few more fights and the darkness would claim him. With that transformation, his Templar brethren would still his foul-beating heart. And he would at last know peace.

Now, peace was as distant as the homeland he once loved.

He tightened his grip on the wheel until his knuckles turned white.

Noelle held power over him already. Tremendous power. The way her soft curves provoked unexpected hunger was dangerous enough. The way her fawn-colored eyes struck the deep need to protect her increased her danger tenfold. Yet all those things he could exorcise with one phone call to Leah. Nay, Noelle's charms lay in something deadly.

She possessed the ability to make him laugh.

One moment he wanted naught more than to wring her dainty neck. In the next, he found himself disturbed by the most ridiculous of things—the tirade with the shoe, her unique name for her cat, and most of all her clumsiness. Graceful deer she was not. On her, however, the fumbling awkwardness that garnered her the most precarious of positions gained her uniqueness. A special kind of elegance that enhanced the pert upturn of her nose and those damnable eyes.

Why could she not have proved to be as he first assumed—plain as a mouse? Were she, 'twould be an easy task to accept this preordained fate and the coinciding oaths he must swear.

He sighed inwardly. Much as he might not care for his predicament, he must do what the archangels expected. With their fated joining, he would be one more knight capable of fighting off Azazel's fallen Templar. The power the dark lord amassed warranted nothing less than Farran's full cooperation. If he turned his back on his brethren, he would become exactly what his black-hearted wife branded him. A traitor. To the Templar, to the archangels, and to the Almighty himself.

From the corner of his eye, he caught Noelle's movement. She leaned forward and flipped the dial on the radio. The quiet twang of a male country voice seeped through the speakers.

Farran cringed again. She did not even know how to appreciate music.

Unable to tolerate the steel guitar and the nasaly voice, he nudged her hand aside and retuned the station to his preferred. Boosting the volume, he kept time against the wheel with his fingers. Angry guitars screeched. The low sultry tone of bass accompanied by insistent drums sank into his simmering blood. A scratchy voice screamed the cold notes of solitude.

"Metallica?" Noelle asked incredulously.

"'Tis far better than the whining song of a broken heart."

Noelle let out a soft snort. "Spoken like a true guy."

With an eyebrow lifted in reproach, Farran asked, "I beg your pardon?"

"Nothing." She winced as the guitar hit a drawn-out soprano chord. Leaning forward once more, she turned the volume down. "That's a guaranteed prescription for a headache." She pressed her fingers to the side of her head. "Not that I'd gotten rid of mine anyway."

Farran's brows drew together, and one corner of his mouth pinched. 'Twould be just like a woman to play to a man's sympathies with claims of ailments. He pushed aside the twinge of sympathy that tugged at the edge of his thoughts. Soon enough they would reach their destination and she could rest.

The silence between them carried the weight of leaden mallets. Twelve hours stretched before him, a time more agonizing than the days he had spent under the Inquisition's brutish hand. He would gladly suffer a day of coals beneath his feet in exchange for this intolerably small space. At least there, in the pits of the Inquisition's foul prison, his nose would take comfort in the smell of death, as opposed to suffering the heady lightness of Noelle's subtle perfume. It clung to her like a veil, despite her clothes having been washed. As if it came from within, as opposed to a mere scent lathered upon her skin.

He shifted against his growing awareness of Noelle's presence. As much as he despised the thought of conversation, he could not tolerate another moment of this infernal silence. He glanced her way once more and found her staring out the side window.

He cleared his throat. "The adytum we shall stay at this eve is smaller than the one we left. Bethany, the keeper, feels her years more than Louise. We shall be responsible for our meal."

She cocked her head with a quizzical crinkle of her eyebrows. "These women, these houses—are they family? I mean, you come and go at liberty?"

"Nay and aye. They are women who Gabriel has offered to care for in exchange for their accommodations. We come as we are needed. When we work within range of the adytum. We are given rest and reprieve. In turn, they are protected, their lives are extended, and their needs are met."

"Gabriel? I never knew he did shelter work. You said you protect them—are they from abusive situations?"

"They possess gifts that make them targets for Azazel's vengeance. All this you shall come to understand in time. For now, you need only know if you should travel, you have safe passage in these many halls."

Her delicate eyebrows arched. "I can travel?"

"When our vows are sealed, you have complete freedom. The only time you need put aside your outside duties is when we are called to battle. We shall be required to fight together."

"I see."

He caught the rolling of her eyes before she turned her face to the window. With a heavy sigh, he stared at the road. Convincing her to believe the truth would be far more difficult than he had ever imagined. The Templar prophecy marked the second seraph as one who was blind. He had taken that expression literally. Whilst Noelle's glasses told of her vision's suffering, her eyes held not the problem. 'Twas her complete lack of faith. Never would he have believed he would have to teach someone to believe in the Almighty. Especially not a woman who descended from angels.

And he did not desire the chore.

Nor did he believe he could emerge the victor without help. 'Twould require the temple's entirety to bring her misguided thoughts around.

Noelle bolted forward in her seat as if someone had shoved her to the edge. "Farran, what happened to Seth? I'm positive that was his car—it had his vanity plates on it. Yet you said Lucan had the Sudarium still. Seth should have flown over with it."

Farran's throat seized at the question. So far, he had avoided the subject of her friend in hopes her injury would keep the memory locked away. She did not believe in the holy hand. She would never believe in demons, nor that her associate was the same.

Choosing his words carefully, he answered, "Seth was not present when the plane boarded." 'Twas truth. The juvenile demon had never made it to the airport's front doors. Mayhap he misled her, but in his heart, he understood that should he tell her Lucan had killed the creature, what little cooperation she exhibited would vanish. She did not appear to fear her circumstances, and he would do naught to give her cause to bolt again.

She chewed on her cheek, picked at her thumbnail. Her expression carried the weight of worry when she lifted her head and turned her gaze on him. "That wasn't an accident was it? He ran us off the road on purpose."

The tightness in Farran's throat spread to his chest. On a shallow breath, he answered, "Aye."

"Why? I mean, I've worked with him for two years. I gave him equal credit on the report, and this would have cemented his future in our field. Why would he do something so stupid?"

The answer came easily. "He wanted the Sudarium."

Dismayed, she shook her head. "That's just silly. There's

no gain in that. What did he think he'd do—sell it? Like that wouldn't land him in jail."

"Mayhap he intended to give it to a greater power."

Noelle chuckled quietly. "Yeah. Like Israel. For that matter, the Palestinians. Hamas would pay a pretty penny for it."

He refrained from comment, sensing any remark about Azazel would restore her sarcasm. She would learn in time.

In a sudden change in the course of their discussion, Noelle exclaimed, "Oh, crap! My cat! Farran, no one's watching Scat!"

A satisfied smirk broke free. He could not help himself, the opportunity to gain his hand over her taunted too much. Flashing her a quick grin, he answered, "Your cat is with Lucan."

She blinked once. Twice. "Scat Cat? Really?"

"Aye. Whilst you slept, I instructed Lucan to retrieve your cat."

Her hands caught his arm, her grip firm and uncomfortably pleasant. Joy filled her words, her exclamation breathless. "Oh, Farran, I could kiss you!"

His blood ran cold at the thought. Another kiss he would not survive. The first still haunted him. Something wholly unique hid within that tantalizing mouth of hers, a sweetness he had never before experienced. On the heels of the icy shudder that rolled down his spine a distasteful warmth filtered into his veins. Visions of her thick lashes dusting her cheeks as she closed her eyes in surrender leapt within his mind. He pushed them aside, determined to keep the memory of that damnable lapse in judgment locked in a far corner.

He shrugged free of her grip and fished in his pocket

for his cell phone. He needed a distraction. Anything to avoid this gratitude of hers.

Flipping it open, he punched in Merrick's number. On the second ring, he reached Anne.

"Hey, Farran." Her bright voice rang through the line, making him cringe.

He grunted in answer. "Where is Merrick?"

"In the training yard with Declan. Do I need to get him?"

"Nay. I need to know if Lucan has arrived, and if he bears Noelle's cat."

Light laughter filtered through the receiver. "Only just. He's waiting on Merrick too. I'll tell them you called."

"There is no need. We arrive tomorrow."

"Wonderful! I can't wait to meet her. It'll be nice to have another woman around here."

Muttering, Farran hung up. Aye, 'twould be nice for her—another cohort to plague him. If Anne had her way with Noelle, no doubt she would teach Noelle how to wield a knee so sharply a man felt the reminder at the mere sound of her voice.

God's teeth, why could Noelle not belong to Lucan? He was far more suited to the needs of women.

"Was that a woman?" Noelle asked.

"Aye. Merrick's troublesome wife."

"There's women where we're going?" Her voice lifted with disbelief.

Farran nodded. "Two. You and she." Unwilling to admit it, he mumbled, "You will like her."

"And Lucan has Scat Cat?"

Saints' blood, every time he heard the feline's name he felt amusement bubble. Tamping it down by gritting his teeth, Farran answered, "Aye. He has only just arrived."

CHAPTER 8

Lucan set his elbows on his knees and bowed his head with a heavy sigh. Merrick's expectant stare bore into the top of his skull. At his left, Anne waited, hands folded in her lap, a barely contained smile tugging at her lips. At his right, Caradoc hunched into the overstuffed chair, his rigid posture conveying that the ache in his bones plagued him more than usual.

Lucan should have been elated to bear the news of a new seraph. With the second discovered, the prophecy proved undeniably true. More would come. One for every tainted knight who managed to survive long enough. Mayhap more.

Yet the discovery of Noelle stirred questions he did not wish to consider. Her assistant, Seth, had known her well. What manner of things had she inadvertently revealed to Azazel? Gabriel had briefed him and Farran on both Noelle's responsibilities and her team. Only the archangel left out the important fact Noelle's direct second spawned from Azazel's unholy power. Why? Had Gabriel sought to challenge them? Mayhap force one into an untimely death?

He squeezed his hands against his temple to block out the unwarranted suspicion. These days, he could do naught to stop it from crawling into his thoughts. God's messenger had always behaved most strangely. The fact he omitted the danger that Noelle trusted a demon should not surprise him. Gabriel had his reasons. He and the Almighty were the only ones to share the purpose.

"Lucan? The cat—what is it doing here?" Caradoc asked for the second time.

Lucan expelled a long breath and lifted his head. He glanced at the gray feline curled up on Anne and Merrick's sofa, contentedly grooming itself. It had yowled the entire drive. Now it seemed oblivious to the change in environment. "Farran ordered me to retrieve it."

Merrick's hearty laughter filled the sitting room. He sat forward and dropped his hand onto the cat's back. His amused gaze met his wife's smiling eyes. "Well, little demon, that confirms it."

"Confirms what?" Lucan looked between the pair, searching for the knowledge they shared.

"She belongs to Farran."

At Merrick's proclamation, Caradoc sat upright. Jaw slack, he stared at their commander. "You cannot be serious."

"Aye, I am. He dropped the phone and has not seen fit to make a return call. His swearing made me suspicious. The cat—Farran would not order its presence lest he had cause to concern himself with the maid's comfort."

Lucan rubbed his hands together between his knees. "Farran does not share your amusement."

Anne's laughter joined Merrick's. "Of course he doesn't. Does that surprise any one of you?"

As Lucan let his humor escape on a low chuckle, Caradoc joined in. Lucan shook his head. "Nay, it does not."

Anne leaned back against Merrick's side and stretched her feet out, propping them on the table. "She must be beautiful. Something has to crack through that shell of his."

"On the contrary, milady. She is pretty, aye. But Farran's whore is far more lovely." A fact that only stirred the suspicion lurking in Lucan's darkened soul further. To any who knew Merrick, his attraction for his seraph had been visible from the start. That Farran did not share the same left Lucan wondering if mayhap Noelle could not be some great deception of Azazel's. None but Farran verified the mark. No one witnessed whether the serpents responded to Farran as well. It could all be a fiction within Farran's head, planted by the demon when it ran the pair of them off the road. Even now, Noelle could be learning secrets Azazel craved.

On the heels of the thought, another occurred. Mayhap Farran did as Tane had with Anne. Mayhap he craved salvation so much he saw things that did not exist. Mayhap Noelle belonged to another.

He frowned at the straying thought. Nay. Farran had no cause to covet. Of all of them, Farran embraced their fate. He looked forward to the day darkness claimed his soul and the inevitable death Mikhail, or whichever knight stood at Farran's side, carried out. Farran did not wish to exist forever.

"You are troubled, Lucan," Caradoc observed.

Lucan leaned back in his chair and folded an ankle

over one knee. "'Tis naught more than what plagues you, brother. I find myself doubting even the things I would swear upon."

A reassuring hand clamped onto his ankle, gave a squeeze, then pulled back. Caradoc nodded. "The darkness grows within us all."

All except Merrick. He alone knew healing.

As if he sensed Lucan's thoughts, Merrick rose to his feet and went to the window, his back to the small gathering. "'Tis not as quick as you may think. The darkness lurks inside me as well, but I am beginning to believe again. My concerns lay with neither of you, however. Nor with Farran." He pushed aside the curtain and braced a hand on the glass pane. "If Farran resists the vows, we must insure what happened with Tane does not occur again."

Lucan's gaze pulled to Anne. Her kidnapping had forced their brother from the temple. Yet in the weeks since, Lucan had yet to witness any form of hostility from her when Tane came into discussion. Even now, she watched Merrick with tender eyes. Naught like the gaze of agreement Lucan had anticipated.

"'Twill not happen," Caradoc affirmed. "Noelle's rooms are already prepared. They lay just beyond yours, Merrick. Mikhail has assigned the four of us to guarding her door."

Merrick's voice dropped, and he bent his head toward the window. "'Tis precisely my fear. Have you not noticed Declan withdraws from us? He is not present now. I could not begin to tell you his whereabouts."

A heavy silence descended on the room. For several long moments, they all avoided eye contact. Though none would speak the obvious, all had observed Declan's subtle changes. What could not be explained was the reason for such. The injury Caradoc dealt him had not yet healed enough to allow Declan to fight. His soul had taken no further damage. Still, the change was marked. Declan's once frequent smile came with less abundance. His constant laughter diminished. He spent long hours brooding in silence, never offering to share what plagued his mind.

Anne broke the stillness. "Have hope, Merrick. I see the same changes in all of you. Caradoc's pain increases. Lucan, you just admitted your suspicion deepens. Farran gets angrier and angrier."

"Aye, but we fight. Declan does not," Lucan argued.

"True. Still, if you were confined, you'd get hostile too. All of you would. Declan's been bound to the temple for weeks. I'm sure it's nothing more than cabin fever."

"If we all possessed your hope, Anne, we would conquer Azazel overnight," Caradoc replied on a chortle. "'Tis as she says, my brothers. She is the only one of us who can see clearly. Let us not concern ourselves with possibility. I shall pick up Declan's guard should he fail to attend to Noelle as Mikhail ordered."

"I shall also," Lucan added. In so doing, he would assure himself the seraph was not false.

Merrick gave a sharp nod. "Then we are agreed. Should Farran refuse the vows, Noelle shall come to no harm."

"Aye," Lucan and Caradoc answered in chorus.

"Then off with you both." Merrick turned from the window with a wide grin. "'Tis late. I desire time with my wife."

Lucan rose to his feet with furrowed brows. Did Merrick truly wish time alone with Anne? Or did he have concerns he did not wish to voice in front of Caradoc and himself? Annoyed with the wayward path of his thoughts,

Lucan grasped for the conviction of faith. He would not doubt Merrick.

However, he would report his concerns to Mikhail. He picked up the satchel Noelle gave to him. "Aye. I must turn this over to Mikhail. He will wish to know of Farran's pairing."

Merrick answered with a supporting nod. "Farran relayed they shall arrive tomorrow. Be at hand so you may give your oath of loyalty."

"Aye," Lucan agreed as he followed Caradoc into the hall.

Anne turned to Merrick, concerned. She watched him pace in front of the television, followed the path of his hand as he raked it through his dark hair. "What is it, honey?"

Merrick stopped and expelled a heavy sigh. He turned around, his expression fraught with conflict. At once, she knew. The only time his emotions warred so fiercely nowadays was when Tane concerned him.

"Armand informed me Tane came by the temple today."

She extended her hand, seeking Merrick's. He crossed to her, clasped her palm in his much larger one, and sank into the cushions.

"I do not want him here, Anne."

Leaning closer, she pressed a soft kiss to his cheek. "He's part of what brought us together. You don't need to carry my burdens for me. I'm not fond of him, but I don't hate him, Merrick." She trailed her fingers through his long black waves. "What did he want?"

"He wants funds from the Order to open a shelter for homeless teenagers."

Anne's lifted an eyebrow, perplexed. "Aren't there some already established?"

"Aye. But Tane does not wish to open something large scale. He intends to create a family environment. Long-term residents like the young woman Marie he knows. No more than six or eight at a time. Teenagers who must meet criteria and follow regulation to stay within the program. He intends to fund college educations for them."

Anne let out a low whistle at the prospect. She'd have never guessed that buried inside Tane's jealous soul he carried that much compassion. Definitely a noble venture. If it worked, he'd really make a difference. No transitionary beds. A real place to call *home*. "He told this to Armand?"

"Aye. He requested Armand relay the request to me."

Picking her words carefully, Anne asked, "What did you tell him?"

Merrick shook his head. "I have not answered."

The tension that had accumulated in Anne's spine relaxed. In truth, Tane had scared her, but he hadn't harmed her. She felt little fear when it came to him, for that matter. The animosity existed solely between her mate and his former brother. Still, she didn't want to contribute to Merrick's hostility. Didn't want to encourage him to keep Tane at a distance. If the man wanted to do good with his excommunication, then he should be allowed to do so. For that matter, after he'd fought for the Order in Louisiana, he shouldn't have been evicted. But nothing would have convinced Merrick out of that idea.

She slid her hand down Merrick's broad shoulders to the small of his back and snuggled in close to his side. Inhaling the heady scent of spice she loved so dearly, she rubbed her cheek on his shoulder. "If you're resisting because of me, don't. Just like the knights who remain, Tane can't help himself." She bit her teeth into her lower lip debating how far to go. Did she tell him the obvious?

That if Tane's seraph appeared, he would have to return to the Order?

As Merrick bristled, she decided the argument would fall on deaf ears. Merrick wasn't ready to let go of his anger. Wasn't ready to forgive what he viewed as a risk to her life. Truth be told, Tane wouldn't have harmed her. The darkness that ate at his soul just created illusions Tane couldn't resist. But she'd tried to explain that so many times she already knew the outcome. Merrick would storm off, unable to understand how she could see what he couldn't.

"Tane acted without honor. He broke the oaths of brotherhood. He betrayed us all by acting on his own selfishness. If something had happened to you . . ." He trailed off, his jaw so tight the faint scar there pulled white.

Anne slipped her fingers beneath the hem of his shirt and caressed his warm skin. In a low voice she murmured, "I know. That's how I feel about you too."

Merrick's arms came around her fast and tight. He dragged her sideways onto his lap and cradled her in his strong embrace. In moments like this, they needed no words. As it had always been between them, they spoke from their hearts, words that came out through their bodies. As she understood Merrick's deep love for her, he knew hers intimately. Just as he understood what she couldn't bring herself to say—Tane might be gone, but his absence would only be temporary. As second only to the archangel Mikhail, Merrick held the decision for Tane's fate. And he would inevitably have to allow Tane to return home.

When the time came for him to confront the reality, she would make sure Merrick knew she supported the decision.

CHAPTER 9

✟

Noelle fought the call of sleep as the SUV wound down a sweeping drive just outside the heart of Columbus, Ohio. Overhead, stars twinkled on glistening snow, blending with the rays of a silver moon. In the luster of winter, a two-story brick house stood out against a tree-covered backdrop. More a box on stilts than any sort of grandiose manor, the architecture was every bit as old as the house they'd left behind in D.C. The early 1800s home came complete with tall white shutters framing narrow windows and two columns supporting a white-trimmed front porch. It offered warm welcome. Not only did every light burn a soft yellow, but a lighted Christmas wreath dangled from the double chimney.

A vision of her childhood home took root in her mind, and Noelle let out a wistful sigh. If she'd been able to keep the property after her parents' death, it would look much the same this time of year. Even with the wreath. While Noelle didn't believe in Christ, she loved the festive tradition she always associated with home. She just couldn't bring herself to participate alone.

"She keeps it up well," Noelle remarked.

"'Tis all handled by the Order. Each summer, we spend time traveling to the adytums to repair, replace, and landscape." Farran gestured at a stone-encased pond where a fountain sat dormant beneath a pale blue light. "Four summers ago, I aided with the construction of that."

She cocked her head with a lifted eyebrow. "Construction? You mean you put it together?"

"Nay." He slowed their speed as they passed the granite replica of a fantasy piece. Mounted on an armored horse, a knight bowed his head before a castle's gate. Atop the tall tower, a dragon perched on the ramparts, its fearsome jaws opened in a timeless assault.

"What do you mean then? My aunt and uncle installed a fountain. They ordered the center piece, but had to connect the lines and electricity."

"Five of us cut the stone. It took us all summer and well into autumn. I carved the knight and his mount. Declan crafted the castle. Caradoc the dragon. Gottfried and Ranulf cut and laid the stones for the basin."

Noelle blinked. She looked to the fountain, almost lifelike in its precision. Then she looked to Farran, dumbfounded. The giant beside her didn't seem capable of carving something so meticulous and delicate. Those large hands looked like they'd break that stone. But then, she'd experienced the gentleness in his hands, hadn't she? That surprised her too.

"Where'd you learn how to do that?"

He shrugged. "It has been so long I have forgotten. 'Tis part of me now. Nearly all of us have the ability to carve."

That put the missing link in place. Freemasons. His friends must all be part of an order of Masons. Which explained how his post-traumatic stress disorder fabricated the Knights Templar part. A wave of pity washed through her veins. He could really do something with that talent if he didn't have his head all mixed up. And if he managed to straighten out those mental issues, he'd be one hell of a catch for some lucky woman.

After that kiss, if she'd thought she had a chance at all, she'd have thrown her hat into that race too. But she *didn't* stand a chance. He'd made that perfectly clear—he'd rather have a whore.

She shook off the misplaced envy and forced her attention on the house. Whom Farran preferred didn't matter. She'd be gone in a few days anyway.

He parked in front of the porch and let himself out. Making no attempt to get her door for her, he bounded up the steps. With a mutter, Noelle climbed out and slung her purse over her shoulder. She huddled into her sweatshirt, joining him beneath a hanging iron porch light.

Farran let them in without ever producing a key. The hall light burned bright, as if the caretaker expected his arrival, despite the fact he hadn't phoned during their drive. This had to be family. An aunt, a great aunt—no one just walked into a house without so much as a knock unless he visited family.

"Bethany? 'Tis I, Farran."

A door opened at the end of the hall. A woman stepped out, her white hair in a long thick braid. She wore nothing more than an ankle-length gown with long sleeves, attire that made her look every bit as old as the house itself. "Sir Farran?" Her frail voice carried a note of delight.

"Would you like some tea? Are you hungry?" She approached at a slow shuffle, then stopped as her gaze fell on Noelle. "Oh, I'm terribly sorry. You have company."

To Noelle's surprise, Farran smiled. Not an all-encompassing smile that lit his eyes, but one of genuine affection. Almost like a son might give a mother. Definitely like a nephew would give an aunt.

"Nay, madam. Do not trouble yourself. The hour is late. I did not wish to alarm you, however."

"Are you certain?" Bethany's gaze flicked between Farran and Noelle, her curiosity unmistakable. "It's really no trouble."

Farran dipped his head with respect. "Aye. Rest, good lady. We shall help ourselves to the kitchen, and I recall where the rooms are."

Noelle shifted her weight as Bethany's curious stare penetrated through her clothing. Farran couldn't be ignorant of the woman's subtle hint at an introduction. Even she, who'd never faced the awkward situation of meeting a boyfriend's family, recognized the unspoken question, Who is she?

Noelle glanced around in search of a hole to crawl into. Spying an inviting velvet-covered chair in the front room, she sidestepped away from Farran.

He grabbed her wrist before she could escape. Firm fingers pulled her back into the hall as Bethany's door closed. "The kitchen is this way." He skated his hand up her arm to her elbow and steered her in the opposite direction.

The kitchen was the only room in the lower level of the house without a light on. He fumbled at the wall, in search of the switch. "I apologize for not introducing you. She would make the association with who you are and feel obligated to wait on us. I cannot allow her to jeopardize her health."

Though the explanation carried a significant degree of compassion, Noelle heard what he didn't say—he didn't want his family thinking she was his girlfriend and asking questions later. The truth shouldn't bother her. But her pride refused to accept the slight. She might not be beautiful, she might not be a man's ideal catch. Still, she wasn't a scrap of yesterday's trash.

She bit the inside of her cheek to temper the sting and pulled her arm out of his grasp.

The lights came on, a row of recessed luminaries along the far wall above the sink. Another flip of a switch, and the lights over the island glowed steadily. Noelle shrank back against the wall as Farran wandered to the refrigerator to rummage through the contents.

"What do you wish to sup on?" he asked over his shoulder.

"Sup?" His odd speech caught her off guard.

He continued to rummage through the shelves. "Eat."

"Oh." She wound her arms around herself, wanting nothing more than to fade into the woodwork and disappear. Man, it just didn't get worse than this. She'd screwed up one kiss so badly not only did he feel it necessary to tell her how displeased he was, but he evidently didn't find her worth the time to give her the courtesy of a name. "I don't think I'm really hungry."

"You must eat. You are naught but skin and bones."

Behind her, the refrigerator thumped shut. Something heavy rattled against the island's counter. The clatter of silverware and plates followed.

Noelle meandered alongside the wall, taking in the rows of hanging photographs. Old photos. Men dressed in military uniforms and women dressed in bustles and long, draping skirts. An occasional black-and-white of a country farm interrupted the portrait gallery. "Who are these people?"

"Bethany's family."

Wow. It must be nice to have heirlooms as old as this. Most of Noelle's family relics had disappeared over time. She owned a quilt her great-grandmother made as a young girl, but nothing like the pictorial timeline hanging in Bethany's kitchen.

"Will you have soup, or a pastrami sandwich?"

As she traced a finger over the brittle glass that covered the face of a little girl with springy curls, Noelle forgot about the slight Farran dealt her. "Pastrami." She moved further down the wall and stared at a black-and-white wedding scene with the very house she stood inside rising in the background.

"So this must have been her family's home then?"

"Aye. Bethany was born here."

Another stab of longing lanced through Noelle. Family . . . Some days she missed her parents so much she wanted to pack up her things and leave D.C. forever. The family she had now amounted to little more than cousins she'd met at a handful of small reunions. People who would come to her aid, but folks she really only knew by name. Her parents had been the only people to ever understand her, to really accept her for all her social flaws. But running away wouldn't bring them back. Nothing could reverse that fatal tornado.

"Come. We shall eat in our rooms."

Noelle snapped her head up, Farran's voice jerking her out of memories. A quick glance around showed he'd already cleaned up after himself and now stood waiting at the door with two plates in hand. Embarrassed to be caught so deeply in thought, she hurried to join him. Halfway across the room, however, she failed to notice the island stool that sat cockeyed from the bar. Her toe caught on one leg, and Noelle tripped.

Half lying on the stool, she scrambled to right herself before it scooted all the way out from under her and she went flying to the ground. Her glasses slipped down to the tip of her nose. Her hair flipped forward into her face. Time suspended as she waited for the wobbling to stop, each agonizing second adding to the increasing heat that burned into her cheeks. What a fool she must look like. Talk about a bull in a china shop. She was the only person she knew who could fall over a toothpick lying on the ground.

When the stool steadied, she took a deep breath. Expelling it, she puffed her hair out of her face, slid her glasses back into place, and glanced at Farran, hoping against all hope he hadn't noticed.

He had.

Leaning on the doorframe, he stared at her. His mouth quirked with amusement. Those mesmerizing ale-colored eyes sparkled. "'Tis a wonder your cat survived kittenhood."

Noelle pushed herself upright. Shooting him a scowl, she grumbled, "Oh, shut up." Before he could comment further, she adjusted her lopsided purse and scurried through the door.

As she passed, however, she caught the muffled rasp of a chuckle.

He stepped around her, effectively leading her up the stairs. A narrow hall spanned left and right at the landing, and Farran gestured to the left with a plate. "Where

I will sleep." He inclined his head to the door directly in front of them. "Your room is here."

Noelle took the plate out of his hand and opened the door. One foot over the threshold, Farran caught her elbow. She swiveled to look up into his narrowed eyes.

"There is no trellis outside your window. My door shall remain open. Need I remind you what will happen should you attempt to run?"

Only the dull ache of her empty stomach curbed the urge to throw her sandwich in his face. She jerked her arm free, stalked inside, and shut the door. For good measure, she pushed the lock in place.

For several long minutes, she waited for him to pound on the door with a demand to unlock it. When the only sound that met her ears was the retreat of his feet, she gave in to the brimming string of curses. Run? Here, where she didn't have a clue about where to go? Did he really think she had no sense? D.C. was different—she could find her way back to her apartment from any main road. If he thought she'd try to flee when she was as lost as a sailor without a compass, he had to be stupid.

She set her plate down on a round, claw-foot table and shrugged her purse off her shoulder. The rumbling in her belly demanded she eat. But before she could take so much as one bite, she needed to do something with the Sudarium. Once she had it appropriately hidden, she could consider her stomach.

With a quick glance around the room, she surveyed the antique furniture—sleigh bed, tall ornately carved wardrobe, wood and metal traveling trunk, vanity with an oval mirror. All done in deep cherry. On the bed, a thick off-white quilt bore a flowered circular pattern in the middle, it's off-centeredness a hint it had been made by hand.

Here too, the portraits on the walls carried age, only where the ones in the kitchen had been small photographs, these were vibrant oils.

Much to her disappointment, she found no closet. But then, that shouldn't have surprised her—houses built in this one's day didn't often contain them. They were considered rooms and taxed accordingly.

Hands on her hips, she gnawed on her lower lip. Under the bed was out—too obvious, and the lack of a bed skirt made the empty underneath visible. She went to the wardrobe, pulled the doors open. The pungent aroma of mothballs flooded her nose. Holding her breath, she flipped through empty hangers to the concealed corner and rapped on the wood in search of a fabled false side.

When no deeper echo resonated, she tapped lightly along the rest of the walls and the bottom. No difference. Dismayed, she eased the doors shut and went to the vanity. Six drawers all produced the same results—empty, save for the fine liner of tissue paper, and no false bottom.

"Damn," she whispered.

This was supposed to be easy. Not an exercise in frustration.

She crossed to the foot of the bed and the old trunk adorned with various customs stamps. Inside, she discovered bedding and more old quilts, these with the telltale must clinging to the worn fabric. She rubbed at her nose to stifle a sneeze and shoved her hands along the neatly folded stacks until she reached the bottom.

Nothing.

Straightening, Noelle scanned the portraits. A sizeable depiction of a woman in pink silk hung cockeyed, drawing her attention. She squinted. Had dusting knocked it sideways? Or was something behind it?

She took a step forward, onto a threadbare Oriental rug. The thin fabric muffled the heels of her boots, but she slowed her step anyway as the overwhelming feeling she was snooping filtered into her consciousness. If something *was* behind that portrait, it had been hidden for a reason. And her eyes were most likely not welcome.

Halfway across the room, a board creaked beneath her step. As she moved off the plank, her heel connected with a hollow *thump*. Noelle froze. No way. She had to be imagining things.

She looked to her boots, lifted her right heel, and tapped it against the floor. The same dull sound answered. Checking to ensure she hadn't misjudged the obvious sound of a normal floor, she tested the surrounding area. With each drop of her heel, the boards answered in sturdy fashion. She tried the off-sounding board once more and bit back a squeal of delight.

No doubt about it, that particular board was different.

Rejuvenated by a burst of excitement, Noelle hurried off the rug and picked up a corner to ease it out of the way. When she had the place where she'd been standing revealed, she tested the floor a final time. The distinctly hollow echo confirmed her suspicions.

She dropped to her knees and ran her hands over the plank. Fingertips met a raised corner, found tiny nail heads standing above the smooth surface. Pulled loose on purpose, or just a product of time, she couldn't say. It didn't matter either.

Prying her nails beneath the lifted edge, she pulled.

The board offered no protest as it bent in the middle and lifted away from the floor a good four inches.

Noelle peered into the opening, noting bits and pieces of lint, thick dust bunnies, and a handful of mouse droppings. Nothing indicated Bethany knew this board was loose, or that anyone other than the mice cared about this little gap between the ceiling below and the guest room's floor.

Delighted, she let the board fall into place and went to the trunk for a pillowcase. She shook it out, straightened the pile of linens, and shut the arched top. From her purse, she retrieved the Sudarium's canister and twisted off the top. The hole wouldn't hold the unbendable metal, but out of its container, the thirty-three-inch cloth was a perfect fit.

She eased the Sudarium inside the pillowcase, folded it into a narrow strip, and returned to the board. It took a little maneuvering, but the protected cloth wedged in tight. A perfect place to hide it, until she needed to retrieve it.

The board in place, she rolled the rug out straight and gave in to a self-satisfied smirk. Now, when Farran and his friends discovered the satchel Lucan had held nothing but her clothes, she would be home free.

CHAPTER 10

With morning's light, the shadows in the hallway dimmed. Farran turned his gaze from the doorway and rolled onto his back. The ceiling proved no more interesting than it had throughout the night. Nor did the light of dawn chase the images of Noelle from his head. As the grandfather clock at the top of the stairs droned the passing of each hour, she rooted into his mind. Each time he closed his eyes in search of sleep, she lay waiting, those fawn-colored eyes beckoning. Her silky mouth inviting.

He relived their kiss a hundred times or more. Bathed in the memory of her sweet jasmine perfume. Suffered the tantalizing weight of her breast beneath his palm.

God's teeth, she tormented long after the stirrings behind her door ceased. 'Twas a miracle he had slept at all. Were it not for the rest the previous day denied him, he would still be chasing the elusive arms of slumber.

A rustle through the walls snapped his eyes wide. He

lay still, listening as Noelle moved through her room. Did she dress? Don that scrap of silk and satin he had once removed from her? The vision tugged at his mind once more. Against his thigh, his cock stirred. With an annoyed hiss, Farran sat up and swept the covers aside. He jerked on his jeans.

Ten hours more, and he would be free of her. They would speak their oaths, and he would not waste one moment longer to find comfort in Leah's embrace. Once he expelled this rush of lust, Noelle would cease to plague him.

Her door opened, bringing his gaze to the hall. Soft footsteps padded closer. Through the gray light, her silhouette took shape. She poked her head through his doorway and greeted him with a hesitant smile. "Where's the bathroom?"

As if a cool breeze caressed him, his body tightened at her whisper. His gaze swept over her. Tousled long hair revealed her night had not been as restless as his. Sleep still clung to her features, softening her full lips and the brightness of her eyes. She wore the sweatshirt the larger, more robust Louise provided. And 'twas all she wore.

His gaze locked on the thick fabric that dusted the tops of her trim thighs. Barely long enough to qualify as decent covering, it gaped near the juncture of her legs. When she shifted her weight, he caught the briefest glimpse of ivory that covered her feminine flesh.

Jesu.

Farran swallowed hard and coiled his hands into the bedding at his sides. He dragged his eyes away, but made the mistake of following the short length of her slender legs. She rubbed a toe against the inside of her dainty ankle. Fire lit in his gut. A slow burn that threatened to spread and consume him. The tightening in his groin intensified, and he struggled to breathe.

"Farran? I need to use the restroom."

He jerked his gaze back to her face. Before he could collect himself enough to direct her to the opposite end of the hall, she lifted a hand to cover a yawn. The sweatshirt pulled. Lifted to expose one hip. A strap so insignificant he could gnaw it in half wound around her waist, securing her damnable undergarment. Though he had glimpsed her underclothes whilst he attended to her injuries, they had not vexed him whilst she slept. She had not moved, had not animated limbs. Had not yet poisoned him with the taste of her silken mouth.

Self-conscious in his silence, she dropped her hands and smoothed her shirt. Her dark eyebrows pulled with worry. She reached around behind her and tugged the hem over her buttocks. "Um." Glancing at her legs as if she inspected herself for spots, she fidgeted side to side. "Farran?"

He shook his head to clear away the fantastic images that leapt to life within his mind, and glared. 'Twas women's trickery. The innocent guise. The widening of her eyes. The act as if she knew naught of what her near-nakedness would cause. She wanted something—likely her freedom. As Brighid had done countless times, she sought to soften him. 'Twould not work. He had been the fool once. He would never make the same mistake again.

He pushed to his feet, strode across the room, and grabbed her by the shoulders. With gritted teeth, he turned her so she faced the door at the end of hall and ground out, "There."

She took a step forward and he tightened his grip.

Bending near to her ear, he warned, "Do not attempt to bend me to your wishes by parading your wares beneath my nose. I assure you, damsel, you will fail." He loosened his fingers. "We leave in fifteen minutes."

With a none too gentle shove, he pushed her toward her destination and barred her from his sight with the slamming of his door.

Noelle spluttered as she gaped at the barred doorway. Her wares? Bend him to her wishes? Had the man lost *all* his marbles? It wasn't as if she had a dresser full of nightgowns to wear. Judging from his half-dressed state, and the way his fly hung partly open, he hadn't slept fully dressed either.

She glanced down at the hem of her borrowed sweatshirt and rolled her eyes. Midthigh, it exposed nothing. Summertime would find her in far less, even if she couldn't bring herself to wear a bikini to the beach. He really believed she'd chosen this as provocative?

The pressure on her bladder increased, and she mumbled beneath her breath. She stalked to the bathroom, shoved open the door, and flipped on the light. A sweatshirt seductive—of all the ludicrous things. If she'd known heavy cotton that bagged around her torso could do the trick, maybe she'd have had a lover or two by now.

The cold porcelain stool made her shiver, and she huddled down into the thick material. Catching her reflection in the wide mirror, she stared at the fuzzy lines of her face. Even without her glasses, she could see the dark circles under her eyes, the wild mass of knots her hair had become. How Farran could think she'd try to seduce him when she looked like the Wicked Witch of the West defied all rationality. On her best day, she wouldn't get far enough to elicit a response. She wasn't stupid enough to believe Farran would find her attractive after a restless night of sleep.

Her business finished, she flushed and turned on the sink. A few splashes of cold water eliminated the drowsiness that clung to her eyes. She gasped at the icy sensation and blindly fumbled for the towel that hung near the light switch. Drying off, she peered at her reflection again.

Nope. No better. Sleep removed, there was simply nothing there to add credence to Farran's ridiculous insinuation. Her glasses at least made her look intelligent. And her hair . . . it would take hours to try and tame that mess.

Opting for the easiest solution, she turned to the bathtub and spun the tap. When the water ran a comfortable lukewarm, she stuffed her head beneath the faucet. A tiny bottle of hotel-room conditioner sat on the overhead ledge next to its twin shampoo. She quickly applied a liberal dose and combed her fingers through the tangles. When her hands slid freely, she rinsed and wrung out the ends.

Rising, she returned to the mirror. Wet hair wasn't much better than tangles. But at least in an hour or so, she'd have somewhat manageable locks. If she were lucky, she wouldn't catch a cold as well.

As she exited the bathroom, she observed Farran's door stood open once more. A glimpse of wide bronzed shoulders had her scurrying into her room and shutting the door before he could turn around. She took a deep breath, determined to ignore the way her heart tripped into her ribs at the sight of powerful muscles and a tapering waist. Damn . . . Why did the nuttiest man she'd ever met also have to be the most gorgeous one?

She refused to give the splendid vision further thought

and dressed with haste. Judging by his sour demeanor, it wouldn't be the wisest move to keep him waiting. Jeans, boots, and coat donned, she yanked her hair into a ponytail then picked up her purse. With a backward glance at the hidden board, she stepped into the hall, ready to confront whatever Farran concocted.

As she stepped onto the top stair, her gaze slid to Farran's open door. Dark and empty, the room held no sign he'd been there moments before. He'd even made the bed—more than she could say for herself.

Shaking her head at the man's idiosyncrasies, she descended the stairs. One minute, he created the perfect ideal of what a man should be. The next, he turned into a psychiatrist's dream project.

She found him in the kitchen, wolfing down a bowl of cold cereal. He paused long enough to lift his spoon and gesture at an identical bowl near the countertop's edge. "Break your fast."

It took a moment for his meaning to register. When it did, she declined with a shake of her head. "No, thanks. I'm not really a breakfast person."

He arched an eyebrow, but said nothing. Three more spoonfuls, and he set his bowl into the sink. "You are ready then?"

"Yeah." In truth, ready had nothing to do with anything. She didn't have a choice. All her agreement accomplished was a little peace and quiet. At the very least, a pretense of cooperation could only work to her advantage when she needed to leverage the Sudarium. The less Farran had to complain about, the more he'd be apt to set her free.

With a curt nod, Farran indicated the door. He slung a heavy bag she hadn't observed the night before over his shoulder and eased into the narrow hall. As she followed, she noticed something else she hadn't seen when they first entered the house—a silver scabbard. It poked out one corner of his black duffel bag and glinted as they passed beneath the overhead light. Where had he come up with a sword? More important . . . What did he intend to do with it?

She eyed the back of his head warily. Maybe this was where his virtual kidnapping turned into danger. If he knew how to use that thing, she couldn't exactly claim this journey to Missouri was harmless. Weapons put her circumstances in a whole new light.

Then again, given his attachment to his illusions of the Knights Templar, the sword could be just a prop. If he were taking her to a gathering of fellow Freemasons, it could be ceremonial as well.

Nevertheless, she kept a wide berth as she let herself into the SUV and surreptitiously watched to ensure the sword didn't land within arm's reach of the driver's seat. He tucked it neatly into the back, along with his bag, then slid behind the wheel.

As they backed out of the driveway, Noelle chanced a cautious glance his way. His jaw still held the tight lines of annoyance, but the overall harshness his earlier anger created had eased. His eyes held concentration, not the sharp glint of fury. Encouraged, she braved conversation.

"So. What exactly will happen when we get to this . . . temple?"

Farran rolled his fingers closed around the steering wheel. With measured words, he answered, "You shall meet Mikhail. You shall meet our commander, Merrick, and his seraph, Anne. We shall exchange our oath, and then you shall be released to your chambers."

A frown tugged at her brow. "My chambers?"

"Aye." He repositioned his hands and relaxed into the seat. "Gabriel left orders after Merrick's pairing. For weeks, men have worked to prepare the rooms that belong to you. You will enjoy them."

Determined to catch him in a conflict with his stories, she challenged, "I thought you said I would be free to leave when I took this oath?"

Slowly he dipped his chin in a nod. "Aye, you shall be. But the rooms are yours for eternity. Whenever you choose to return, when you lend aid to our battles, you shall have a bed to call your own."

Noelle let out a heavy sigh. The man was unshakable. Either he'd practiced this game before, or he really believed this stuff. Or . . .

A shiver crept down her spine. Maybe she wasn't the first girl he'd dragged off to an abandoned corner of the Midwest. Maybe this was some sick cultish practice.

She glanced at him from the corner of her eye. "Farran? Will any portion of this . . . oath . . . hurt?"

His frown scolded as he glanced at her. Returning his gaze to the road ahead of them, he answered, "'Tis words, damsel, not a blood pact."

The touch of sarcasm lacing his response sent heat rushing to her cheeks. She hung her head, sank deeper into her seat. But on the heels of her embarrassment, annoyance sparked. He had no right to shame her. Any rational person would be worried about harm. If anything, Farran ought to be glad she hadn't screamed her head off or done something drastic to get attention.

She stiffened her spine and returned his scowl. "Why are you doing this? It's absurd. It's against the law, for that matter. I don't know what you intend to do with me, but I swear to you, if this turns into some sick sexual deviancy, I'll find a way to bring every authority in and gloat when they take your ass to jail."

Though he didn't look at her, his eyebrows lifted almost to his forehead. A soft snort rang out over the low radio. "Must I remind you, I do not wish to bed you?"

She folded her arms across her chest, ignoring the sting to her pride. "No, I think you've made that perfectly clear."

"Then we are agreed. I shall not touch you. You shall not expect me to touch you. In return, you may take the lovers you desire." He paused, then slid a meaningful stare her way. "You will not choose another knight."

Unable to resist the taunt, Noelle retorted, "No? Why not? I'm not good enough for them?"

His eyes narrowed. His jaw worked. He opened and closed his fingers, repositioning his hands. "Only a fool would make the mistake of touching you."

Though she longed to be immune to the age-old pain, his brutal honesty cut like a knife. Hadn't she learned the truth long ago? When Brett Thornbow laughed at her for asking him to the sophomore Valentine's Day dance, he'd said pretty much the same thing. Her prom date, whom she'd truly believed wanted to attend with her, disclosed she was nothing more than a pity date. The frat boy she'd thought was interested in college echoed similar remarks. Over and over again, she'd confronted the depressing reality that she was an embarrassment. Even Seth, as close as they were, couldn't help but chuckle when he caught her staring a bit too long at attractive men who entered her lab.

Biting the inside of her cheek to stop a rush of sudden tears, she looked out the window. When her eyes welled anyway, she tugged her ponytail free to cloak her face. She wouldn't cry in front of Farran. Just as she'd learned she embarrassed men, she'd also learned tears only made it worse. They laughed a little harder. Goaded a little more.

She should be used to this by now. Only, for some reason she couldn't fully explain, hearing the nutcase beside her shared the same thoughts hurt far more.

Damn it all, she had to get out of here. Back to her lab. Back to the inanimate objects that had stories to tell, but no voices that could speak.

CHAPTER II

Stars peppered the night sky with pinpoints of light. Farran blinked into the darkness, his eyes dry as bone and his muscles as tight as a belt. Before him, the stretch of Missouri highway wove through wide fields, a ribbon of rolling hills determined to plague him with the need for sleep.

He rolled his shoulders and pulled in a deep breath. The twang of country music filled his ears, turning the knotted muscles in his neck into even tighter belts. Yet he made no move to change the dial. 'Twas his peace offering. A silent apology for the remark he knew Noelle took with offense. Even now, it dominated his thoughts. Screamed inside his skull.

Only a fool would touch you.

Only a fool would say such to a woman and believe she would take it as he intended. 'Twas not a slight on her— though he wished, in truth, it were. That she was not quite so comely nor quite so tempting. A knight who touched her would be the fool, for in so doing, he would lose his life. Whilst Farran had no intention of pledging himself to her, he suffered no compulsion to stay his hand should betrayal lurk within his brethren's minds. He would slice the man's throat before he could so much as stutter a worthless apology.

As he should have done centuries ago.

He let out a soul-deep sigh and forced the memory from his mind. Seeking to rouse his drowsy eyes, he scanned the landscape as he eased off the two-lane asphalt onto the exit ramp. To his right, a twisting outer road wound through tall trees, and he took the turn. Greenish streetlamps faded to black, the neon glow hampered by the thick growth of hackberries and maples.

His gaze skimmed sideways to rest briefly on Noelle's sleeping face. A pang of guilt stabbed through him as his stomach rumbled. He had denied her dinner. In his rush to reach the temple as early as possible, he made no attempt to even inquire if she wished to sup. And as twilight faded into night, she drifted off to sleep without a single protest.

Then again, she had remained silent most of the day. Thanks to his idiot's tongue.

A shadow skittered across the road.

Farran jammed on the brake. Dread rolled around in his gut as he looked to the scrub. Through the heating vents, the scent of rot infiltrated the vehicle. Demons.

He shifted in his seat and eased onto the accelerator. Azazel's fiends had no place on this narrow stretch of road that led to the temple. Barred from entering the temple grounds by the might of the holy hand, there could be only one purpose for their presence—the seraphs. Noelle and Anne.

God's teeth, Azazel grew bold. To walk here, within

reach of the knights' swords, would mean certain death. What was his purpose? Surely he must know his minions would fail.

Lest . . .

A shiver rolled down Farran's spine and twisted his gut into a mass of knots. He swallowed hard.

Lest they planned to ambush a seraph before she could find safety behind the iron gates.

Between the sparse boughs, a glint of yellow-green caught his eye. Another, just below the first, turned the uncomfortable heat in his veins to a rush of fiery anger. Row after row of beady eyes lay within the trees, waiting. Lurking.

From between the trunks, a figure emerged. Tall and lithe, it took the form of a human sentry. In a gnarled fist it carried a thick wooden club. It took two steps toward the driver's door, and Farran caught the shifting light behind its haunted eyes. A flash of darkness that cloaked the yellow-green glow.

He stepped on the gas and roared toward the gates. At the SUV's rear fender, the figure lunged in pursuit. A dull thump echoed over the country-and-western song, telling Farran the beast behind him made contact with the vehicle.

Reaching above his head, he hit the button on his visor that opened the gates and reached across the center console to give Noelle's shoulder a violent shake. "Wake up."

Gravel spun beneath his tires as he sped across the threshold. He punched the button again, stared in the rearview mirror, and watched as the gates eased shut. When the clang of iron meeting iron rang out, he allowed himself to release the breath he held. Ignoring the ghostly howl of rage that cut through the night, he swiveled in his seat to shake Noelle a second time. In a softer voice he coaxed, "Noelle, we have arrived."

He glanced into the mirror again, noticing two figures now stood beyond the protective barrier. Turning to face the wheel once more, he eased closer to the temple's columned front porch and a parking space near the steps. They could not harm her, but he would not put it past them to coerce her beyond the Almighty's ring of power. Until she understood the danger, he dared not let her observe the creatures beyond. Her curiosity would place her directly in Azazel's hands.

She stirred with a stretch. Balled fists scrubbed at her eyes. Blinking, she dropped her hands to her lap, picked up her glasses, slid them onto her nose, and stared at the building's abandoned facade. "This is a *temple*? Surely you could come up with something better?"

His gaze traversed the weathered brick, the askance shutters, the peeling paint. Aye, disguise served its purpose, if she thought this an abandoned building. He had long ago adjusted to the decrepit appearance of the exterior, and though she could not see it, the backside fared better. They worked steadily to improve the building, to limit the curious who sought to investigate a rumored haunt. Yet winter came before they could address the street-facing walls.

"'Tis not as it appears."

Noelle let out a soft snort of disbelief. "What, you dusted? The sheets on the furniture are clean?"

Farran stifled his tongue. 'Twould be wasted breath to argue. She would understand within moments.

He opened his door and motioned for her to do the same. Her heavy sigh made her displeasure clear, yet she did as he requested. Outside, she stretched with catlike grace, then turned questioning eyes on him, and Farran beckoned her ahead.

Home. He had returned alive . . . though unscathed remained to be seen. 'Twas time to take the oaths. When they were spoken, he would attend to the creatures lurking in the street. Then, with his sword reinforced as fate demanded, he would take his leave.

Noelle trudged up the steps beneath the curious glow of a hanging lamp. She took in the pitted brick, the peeling columns. More evidence this was some fantastic fiction Farran wanted her to believe. Everyone knew the Freemasons meant money. Hoards of it. If he were part of some branch that descended from the once-noble Templar, she felt certain they wouldn't hole up in a building that looked like a strong wind would topple it in on itself.

Farran reached around her to open the door, giving her a good whiff of the woodsy-citrus scent that clung to him. Her heart stutter-stepped, and she stiffened against her natural response. She had no business getting lightheaded over this man. Beyond the fact he had issues that would take a team of psychologists years to cure, he'd made his opinion of her more than clear. No, the only choice she had was to go along with this until the Sudarium offered her a way out.

He pushed open the door, gave her a little nudge forward. Shoulders high, Noelle stepped through the neglected entryway. One foot still lingering in the cold, she came to an abrupt halt and blinked at her surroundings.

Contrary to the dilapidated exterior, the rooms that opened before her were spotless. A wide central entertainment room sported several plush couches that gathered before a wall-mounted flat-screen television. To her right, a smaller alcove contained four billiards tables, all presently in use by men who matched Farran in size. The hall she lingered in reached toward a second story, its artfully painted ceiling easily twelve feet high.

Farran's hand settled into the small of her back. With gentle pressure, he guided her inside and pulled the door shut. "'Tis not what you expected?"

Noelle gathered her senses with a shake of her head. Before she could find words, the men playing pool jockeyed through the archway into the hall. The scrape of steel rang out as they withdrew swords from scabbards that mirrored Farran's. As she furrowed her brows, all ten or so dropped neatly to one knee. In the same fluid motion, they laid their swords down in front of their braced feet and bowed their heads.

She blinked. What in the world? For several long moments, she could do no more than stare. Yet Farran's none-too-gentle elbow in her side snapped her out of her stupor, and she turned her frown on him. "This really is a bit overboard, don't you think?"

His ever-present scowl deepened. With a jerk of his head, he indicated the gathered men. "You must accept their service. Wish them well." He gave her a hard look before adding, "In the name of the Almighty."

Just how exactly was she supposed to do that? If they believed so heavily in God, then surely they'd think her attempt bordered on blasphemy.

Farran's low whisper near her ear stirred her hair and sent tingles rippling down her spine. "Do not shame them, and do not test me, damsel. Do as is expected."

Instinct dared her to ask, *or what*. Instead, she swallowed the gut response and searched through the forgotten prayers of her childhood. Bits and pieces gathered, none of which made any coherent sense. At a complete loss, she settled for the parting words her family's preacher had used to dismiss the congregation every Sunday. "Go and be with God. We will meet again with light in our hearts."

The man closest to her extended a hand. His fingers closed around the sword's pommel, and he slowly lifted his head. Bright green eyes locked with hers, then crinkled with the faintest hint of a smile. He rose to his feet, slid the sword into the silver scabbard that hung at his hip. As he moved, the others shifted in unison. Each offered her a brief nod before they simultaneously stood.

In a blink, they'd returned to their billiards game, taking up their places as if nothing had transpired.

Dumbfounded, Noelle looked to Farran for an explanation. The only one she found was the hard light behind his ale eyes and the firm set of his jaw. He looked beyond her, down the hall.

She turned to follow the path of his stare and cringed inwardly. She recognized Lucan immediately. Flanked by two men, he greeted her with a wide smile. But what set Noelle's nerves on edge had nothing to do with the trio of giants who shook hands with Farran. No, it was the shockingly beautiful redhead who looped her arms around Farran's neck and greeted him with a fierce hug that made Noelle wish she could crawl into a black hole and never come out. No wonder he didn't want her. With women like this around, she could never hope to be more than the plain, unexciting little mouse.

The woman let go of Farran and turned her smile on Noelle. "You must be Dr. Keane. I'm so very glad to meet

you." She extended her hand. "I'm Anne. Lady du Loire—
Merrick's wife."

Anne's gaze drifted over her shoulder, her smile no-
ticeably brightening as she locked eyes with a dark-haired
man whose very presence intimidated Noelle further.
Unlike Farran, he smiled. But also unlike the grouchy
man she'd grown accustomed to over the last two days,
Merrick's handshake lacked the gentleness that lay behind Farran's fingers. He squeezed too hard. His calluses
scraped the back of her hand. This man made it impossible to deny her petite size—or the fact that he could cause
her serious harm.

Instinctively, she edged closer to Farran. She searched
for courage, pulled it from a dark corner of her soul.
"Yes, I'm Dr. Keane."

Farran's hand wrapped around her wrist. He took one
large stride forward and tugged her toward a descending
stone stairwell. "Come. You shall make your acquain-
tances before Mikhail. I wish to have our oath completed."

Noelle dug her heels in, but to her consternation, no one
attempted to dissuade Farran from dragging her down the
dimly lit stairwell. At least none of the men. Anne's gaze
touched hers, sympathy reflected in her apologetic smile.
She hurried around Noelle to set her hand on Farran's
forearm. "Farran, maybe you should let Dr. Keane—"

"Nay." He shook off her hold and gave Noelle another
tug.

Unable to resist his strength, Noelle fell into step behind him. Their footsteps echoed through the winding
corridor of stone. Each step took them deeper into cool
air that carried the faint scent of must. As if water had
once run through these cut stones.

Maybe it had. Missouri was known for its caves. She'd

explored several wild caves on weekend college trips. Maybe whoever built this house chose it because of the natural cubbies where they could store food. It certainly was old enough to support the idea.

The absence of stalagmites or broken stalactites reinforced her theory. If water ran through here once, it eroded the cavern until what was now a footpath stretched smooth.

As they rounded a corner, a series of thick wooden doors emerged in the hall. In the silence, her imagination leaped into action. Had the Mob been here? Had some gangster from the forties used this place during Prohibition? With cubby after cubby hidden behind those metal-studded doors, someone could hide a whole trainful of liquor and never worry about someone breaking in. For that matter, it would take a powerful gun to cut through those slabs of wood. Simple bullets wouldn't make a dent.

Farran led the small group through a series of twists and turns. On occasion, a head popped out from behind one of the doors to inspect the procession, but no one made an attempt to speak. They wove through the maze of identical closed-off rooms until Noelle couldn't decipher whether they walked north or south. Or any other direction in between. Everything was identical—soft sand-colored stone, mounted iron torches, metal-studded doors. Even the footing remained constant, with its complete lack of divots or lumps that would answer the nagging suspicion they were walking in circles.

He halted abruptly before a door engraved with the Templar cross. With a light rap of his knuckles to announce them, Farran opened the door, but pulled Noelle aside. The others filed in quietly.

She turned to him with lifted brows.

Farran dropped his voice and held her gaze, his look full of quiet meaning. "I care not how you look upon me. But, damsel, you will give the archangel the respect deserving of his station. Are we clear?"

It took all of her willpower to hold an amused snort inside. The deepening of the crease between his eyebrows, however, told her the humor reached her eyes. She didn't know what Farran expected to happen once they entered, but she was pretty damn sure his expectations didn't begin to match what she had in mind. Smothering a smile, she answered, "Of course."

CHAPTER 12

Farran escorted Noelle inside Mikhail's spacious chambers to stand before his desk, all too aware of the eyes that followed their path. Noelle had done everything possible to demean his claims, and on the chance she might denounce Mikhail, he would rather broach this alone. Where Anne had expressed disbelief, even Merrick's headstrong lady had not dared insult the Almighty's chosen warrior. Anne possessed faith. Noelle, as Farran well knew, did not.

His fingers still firmly wrapped around her delicate wrist, he guided her to a halt. Behind the massive wooden desk that bore the scars of centuries of work, Mikhail rose. His features warmed with an inviting smile, and he gave Farran a respectful dip of his chin. "Sir Farran, I understand you have discovered your seraph."

From the corner of his vision, Farran caught the rolling of Noelle's eyes. He squeezed her wrist tighter, silently instructing her to behave. "Aye. I wish to swear the oath as soon as possible. I have other matters to attend."

Mikhail arched a reddish-brown eyebrow. "Do you, now? Perhaps 'twould be courteous for you to introduce your lady before you rush away."

The low, flat tone of Mikhail's voice scolded Farran for his impatience. He gritted his teeth, flexed the fingers on his free hand, and exhaled long and slow. With the demons lining the nearby lane, he dared not waste precious time with friendly overtures. Nay, better to see this done expediently and forget this night occurred.

"Introductions shall come with the pledge of loyalty. She already knows me. There is a matter I must speak with Merrick about, immediately." He narrowed his gaze, pinning Mikhail with a hard stare. "A matter I presume you are aware of already."

One corner of Mikhail's mouth lifted with the hint of a smile. "You have met our guests."

"Aye."

"Very well then. We shall do things your way." His smile returned to span his features, and Mikhail looked to Noelle. "Dr. Keane, is it?"

"Yes." Short and concise, Noelle answered without hesitation.

Mikhail's steely silver eyes sparked. He reached over the desk, clasped Noelle's hand and brought the back of it to his lips. "We are indebted to the work you have performed, Noelle. Many centuries have passed with the Holy Son's legitimacy in question. 'Tis long past time for the truths to be unveiled."

Farran nearly groaned aloud. Of all the things to say to Noelle, Mikhail chose the worst. Farran could think of naught that would spur her faster into giving freedom to her tongue. And what would inevitably tumble off those soft lips, he did not wish to hear.

To his surprise, Noelle merely chuckled. Her long hair washed over her shoulders as she shook her head. "I'm sorry, but really, I've done nothing. It was a job, among many others." Her laughter died immediately and every inch of her five-foot frame tightened. Behind her wire-rimmed glasses, her gaze sharpened into pinpoints of harsh light. "A job I must return to. I'd like to speak to Gabriel, and I know someone here knows how to reach him."

Farran's stomach turned over. The urge to drag Noelle into the hall and shake sense into her possessed him. One simple request. He had asked one small favor. Yet she did not hesitate to shame him mere moments after she uttered her promise. Why this pained him, he could not say. 'Twas no more than any other woman would do. He had come to expect such. But that spark of hope had lit. The damnable cinder that only served to remind him how vulnerable he could become if he did not keep his wits about him.

Mikhail released her hand with a weary sigh. He gave an absent shake of his head and shuffled through a stack of papers atop his desk. "I fear that is impossible, Noelle. Gabriel travels to find the rest of your kind. His work cannot be interrupted. He shall return in due time."

Seeking to put an end to the disastrous conversation, Farran took a step forward. "The oath, Mikhail. We would speak it now."

Noelle clamped her teeth down tight and scowled at the back of Farran's head. The oath. The damned oath—this had gone on long enough. She had work to do. An entire stack of boxes from a site in the Middle East awaited her. For two days, she'd allowed herself to be dragged across the countryside on this ridiculous journey. It was time to give up the game. Allow her to return the Sudarium and get back to normal life.

"Sir Farran, you will bide your time until I am ready."

At Mikhail's sharp reprimand, Farran's spine stiffened and his shoulders snapped to attention. His simmering gaze focused on the wall behind Mikhail, not on the man's face. A face, Noelle reluctantly admitted, that rivaled some of the oils she'd seen in the Smithsonian. Mikhail, whoever he was, was so flawlessly perfect he almost hurt her eyes.

Rich chocolaty hair carried just the faint hint of red. Angled features, that on another man would look harsh and severe, blended smooth against a complexion that had surely never seen a day of acne. Tall and every bit as strong as the other men in the room, Mikhail cut a striking figure of power. One who clearly demanded the men's respect.

Particularly Farran's if his rigid posture was any indication.

"Noelle."

Her thoughts snapped back in place as Mikhail addressed her once again. "Yes?"

"Farran has told you what you are, has he not?" He moved around the desk, across the room, and stood beneath a hanging kite shield that bore the legendary Order's seal. With a touch of reverence, he pressed long fingertips to the pitted metal. "He has told you of the Templar plight?"

"Yes, but—"

"I am certain you have many questions. 'Twas the same for Anne when she arrived."

Noelle glanced at the petite redhead who sat in a chair beside Merrick. Had she too been brought here against her will? She didn't look at all uncomfortable or unhappy. For that matter, she looked completely content. And the way her eyes communicated with her husband left Noelle strangely envious. Affection like that only happened in the movies.

"Dr. Keane?"

Noelle blinked. As she looked back to Mikhail, she felt the weight of Farran's stare scorch into her. "I'm sorry. What?"

Humor glinted behind Mikhail's steely silver eyes. He covered a smile with a fist and a forced cough. "I asked you if you are prepared to bind yourself to Farran."

Bind herself? Hell no. But whatever it took to gain her freedom at this point, she'd try. If he wanted a few simple words from her, then so be it. She had a backup plan if that approach backfired. The Sudarium waited, and one way or another, she'd get out of this mess.

She shrugged. "Sure. Why not?"

The warm light in Mikhail's expression dimmed. "I am not certain you understand the seriousness of your status. You must be dedicated to your purpose. When you leave this room, your life shall be changed forever. Men will depend on you. Men will die for you, should such need arise. This is not a matter deserving of a flippant attitude."

Farran's fingers dug into her wrist, warning her to mind her tongue. Silently telling her if she didn't, she'd have to deal with him. Did she really want to risk his anger? She'd caught glimpses of it, but from the grim set to his features, she'd already pushed her boundaries too far. Still, it chafed to have her hand forced. To find herself without alternatives and the only present option to do what these people expected.

She took a deep breath and forced her expression into what she hoped was sincerity. "I am prepared to take this oath, or whatever it is, if it will let me go—"

"Noelle," Farran bit out between clenched teeth. Low

and threatening, the husky growl sent a shiver racing down her spine.

She swallowed, cleared her voice, and nodded. "I'm prepared."

For several long seconds, Mikhail stared at her as if he could see through to her soul. More correctly, as if he looked *through* her and could sense the dishonesty behind her words. The eerie feeling that he knew exactly how she felt settled into her stomach and churned it in a slow roll. She shifted her weight, tore her eyes away from his.

"Very well," he murmured. With a lift of his hand and a wag of his fingers, he beckoned to the three knights to her right. "Swear yourselves unto her."

Merrick untangled his hand from Anne's and drew his sword. As he moved in front of Noelle, the embellished blade glinted in the dim light. As the men had done when she first arrived, he dropped to one knee, set his elbow on his thigh, and bent his head. He laid his sword on the ground in front of the toe of his boot. His rich voice rumbled in the silence. "Merrick du Loire, commander of the Templar."

Wide-eyed, Noelle looked to Farran. Was she supposed to speak again? Damn it, someone could have at least prepared her for this insanity.

In a voice so low she had to strain to hear him, Farran said, "Return his sword, damsel."

Noelle bent forward to retrieve the blade. She wrapped her fingers around the ornate pommel, noting the familiar weight in her hand. How often had she dated blades dug up from the ground? This one certainly resembled the ancient craftsmanship. Nicely balanced, leather-wrapped pommel, and it even bore the telltale nicks along the blade that marked it as handcrafted. Sect, cult, renegade SCA members—whatever Farran's little group was, they took authenticity seriously.

She gently rested the flat of the blade on her fingertips and offered it to Merrick. Onyx eyes locked with hers, full of warmth and welcome. No wonder Anne looked at him as if he could move mountains. Those eyes held feeling. Genuine emotion. Under other circumstances, Noelle would have liked to get to know him better. He at least didn't suffer Farran's eternal grumpiness.

Then again, Farran didn't share the scar along the side of Merrick's jaw either. Nor did that comforting scent of woodsy citrus linger in Merrick's wake.

She steered her wayward thoughts back into line and summoned a smile as Merrick stood. He resumed his place at Anne's side, and Lucan stepped before her. "Lucan of Seacourt."

He too dropped to one knee, offering his sword in the same way. Noelle didn't wait for Farran's coaching. Anxious to have the whole ordeal over with as soon as possible, she gripped Lucan's plain broadsword and passed it to him. He quickly tucked the blade into his scabbard, then captured her hand before she could retract it. Lifting it to his mouth, he placed a kiss on the back of her knuckles. "Milady, welcome home. Should you want for anything, you only have to ask."

His gallantry floored Noelle. Men weren't supposed to treat women that way. Not anymore. And if they were . . . Well, what little she knew about the male population suggested many could learn from Lucan. Uncertain how to respond, or if she even should, she pulled her fingers free and tucked them behind her back. He rose with a cordial smile, then offered her a brief bow before assuming his former position against the far wall.

The third man approached slowly, as if it pained him to make the effort. Though he smiled, the gesture didn't reach his eyes, and the light behind those hazel depths carried a haunted effect. Sandy blond hair tumbled over his wide shoulders as he bent over his knee. When he set his sword on the stone, a soft grunt accompanied the action. Pain indeed. Enough that Noelle's heart twisted just a little.

"Lord Caradoc of Asterleigh."

Even his voice carried a heavy degree of effort. A sympathetic smile broke free, and Noelle hurried to relieve him of the uncomfortable position. She curled her hands around the guardless pommel and offered his sword. As he accepted, she dropped her hand to his shoulder and gave it an encouraging squeeze. Whatever he'd done, he had no business playacting tonight. He should be relaxing. Curled up in some comfortable chair where whatever ached could rest.

Caradoc stood and joined the others. At her side, she felt Farran tense. She let her gaze skim sideways in search of the reason. But his blank expression held no clue—beyond the fact his scowl had disappeared.

Mikhail's head snapped up. A quizzical frown tugged at arched eyebrows as he peered at Merrick. "Where is Declan?"

"I do not know," Merrick answered.

Something passed between the two men. Something Noelle couldn't identify. But whatever it was had Farran sucking in a sharp breath and Anne sitting on the edge of her chair. Tension crackled through the room. The two remaining men exchanged meaningful glances, and jovial features morphed into masks of harsh angles.

Trouble in the ranks? Or had one of their bunch of

merry men decided this Robin Hood charade wasn't worth his time? Maybe some of them had sense after all.

"Very well." Mikhail strode across the room to swing the door wide. "You are dismissed. The rest is reserved for Farran and Noelle alone."

In single file, the four traipsed out of the room. The door closed heavily in their wake, and Mikhail moved to stand in front of Farran and Noelle. He studied Farran with a curious frown. "'Tis your duty to pledge loyalty to her, Sir Farran."

"Nay."

Shock washed across Mikhail's face. He opened his mouth, then snapped it shut. With a frustrated hiss, he shoved a hand through his hair, then folded his arms across his broad chest. "Nay? Sir knight, must I remind you why we are here? On your knee." He gestured at Noelle. "Pledge yourself to her, as duty demands."

Farran puffed his chest out, every ounce the picture of rebellion. He met Mikhail's hard stare with equal determination. "Nay. My *duty* is to the Order. I will take my oath as is expected. My loyalty she may not have."

Noelle bristled. In one heavy heartbeat, the annoyance she felt over being kidnapped gave way to anger. *He* had insisted she belonged to him. Yet he, of all people, would not follow through on his expected role? Game or no game, farce or reality, Noelle's pride refused to back down. She tossed him a defiant glare and jerked out of his hold.

But before she could free the obscenities that lurked on her tongue, Mikhail lifted his hand to silence her. His pale features colored a faint shade of crimson. "You insult her. You insult the Almighty."

Farran set his chin and looked beyond Mikhail, to the wall once more. "I care not. I will do what is asked of me otherwise. I will lend my strengthened sword. I will work at her side. But I shall not swear loyalty to her. My vows are to my brethren."

The soothing tone of Mikhail's voice cracked as he exclaimed, " 'Tis unacceptable!"

"Mayhap." Farran punctuated his response with a curt nod. "Which do you desire more, Mikhail? The reinforcement of our Order or a petty vow that, should you force my hand, I shall not uphold?"

Long seconds passed as the two men stared each other down. Noelle pursed her lips so tight they began to tingle. How dare he. Wasn't it bad enough he made his dislike of her known in private? Did he really have to go and shame her in front of someone else? She might not be anywhere near as beautiful as Anne, or likely the other women he associated with, but she wasn't chopped liver either. She had good qualities. A brain for starters. And once upon a time, a guy had said her ass wasn't half bad.

Damn him. He could add insensitive jerk to his evergrowing list of faults. Asshole too, if she cared to be blunt.

She willed her emotions under control and forbade the rush of tears to stop before they trickled down her cheeks. She didn't care what he thought of her. It didn't matter. He was nuts, and she was going home. One way or the other.

"I do not care for this, Farran." Anger tucked away again, Mikhail resumed his soothing tone. "And yet you force my hand as well." He turned on his heel and strode behind his desk. A heavy drawer complained as he jerked it open. Shoving a hand inside, he pulled out a stack of leather-bound journals and tossed them onto his chair. On the second delve into the drawer's contents, he produced a thick, tattered tome. He thumped it down on his desk, sending a cloud of dust into the air.

Mikhail thumbed through the vellum pages until the book was three-quarters open. In jerky movements that revealed his masked anger, he turned it around and shoved it toward Noelle. A slender fingertip punched an inset block of Latin text. "These are your words, Noelle. Let us be done with this farce."

Nothing she'd heard since she left her laboratory sounded better. Getting this over with meant home. Home meant freedom from this unfeeling man who seemed to thrive on insulting her. If she were witty enough to think of a comeback, his words wouldn't cut so badly. As it was, however, she bled every time he opened his mouth.

"You know yours?" Mikhail asked Farran.

"Aye." He turned to her, the light in his rich eyes hard and punishing. "Remove your armband, Noelle."

She rolled her eyes. "Oh for Pete's sake. You know I can't."

He grabbed her wrist, slipped a hand beneath the oversized sleeve. Warmth seeped up her arms as his fingers worked over her skin, edging closer to the torc lodged around her bicep. Her stomach turned into a mass of wild butterflies desperate for freedom. So intimate, yet so benign, the simple caress steered her senses off course. She closed her eyes to brace against the onslaught of sensation and held her breath.

When his hand slipped free, she expelled her air on a hiss. Man, oh man, why did she have to like it so much when he touched her?

The scrape of steel against steel drew her back to the present. Opening her eyes, she found Farran with his sword drawn. He dropped the torc down the plain pommel and held it in place with his fist. *"Meus vires, meus mucro, meus immortalis animus, fio vestry."*

Years of working with ancient artifacts translated the Latin automatically. *My strength, my sword, my immortal soul, becomes yours.* Nice vows, if he'd actually meant them. They sounded like something suited for a wedding. Especially given their Latin origin. The English translation wouldn't carry the same effect. It lacked the depth of feeling only the ancient language could provide.

A strange shiver flitted down her spine, and Noelle struggled to ignore the pang of regret that followed in its wake. If he'd meant the vow, *if* he weren't nuts, if such a thing existed as an immortal spirit, she might forgive his crabby nature.

Mikhail thrust the book beneath her nose and pointed at the matching line he wanted her to recite. *My life, my love, my eternal light, becomes yours.*

At once, everything clanged together within her head. His insults, her wounded pride, her stomped-on feelings—they all rushed together until Noelle couldn't see through the flurry of tears that gathered in her eyes. Damn him for waking up all those dead feelings. Damn him for breaking open wounds she'd thought long healed.

She swallowed hard and lifted her chin, determined to prove to him she wasn't some meager mouse. He'd insisted on her cooperation. Her freedom depended on this oath. Yet nothing would convince her to utter something so filled with meaning. Not when the words were empty lies. When this whole ordeal stemmed from some ludicrous claim. It was beyond time for Farran to learn he couldn't have everything his way.

In strong, confident English, she uttered her vow.

CHAPTER 13

As the bronze serpents remained unmoving against his sword, Farran swiveled toward Noelle. Anger rushed through him, fast and furious. Glad he did not still hold her wrist, he curled his fingers into a tight ball and narrowed his gaze. The magic lay in the Latin, not the mere recitation of their meaning. She made a mockery of the very prophecy that carried the Templar through time. "You will say them in the language they are written."

Lush lips lifted with satisfaction. She took another step backward and shook her head. "No. Or as you would say, *nay*."

He resisted the fierce urge to grab her by the arms and shake her until she cooperated. Once upon a time, he would have slain one who dared show so much disrespect. Had on several occasions during his brief reign as lord of Clare. Yet her very sex prevented him from turning the blade he held to her throat. He had not killed Brighid, despite her greater offenses, and would not stoop to taking the lives of women now.

However, he did not shy away from punishing women who did not know their place. He tempered his outrage with a deep breath. "You will, damsel, or you shall find yourself regretting your defiance."

Her short laugh only served to fuel his fury. Accompanied by Mikhail's quiet chuckle, her amusement cut his pride into ribbons. Heat spread through his veins, and he snatched at her hand.

She pulled away faster. Her chest heaved with unspent anger. Pinpricks of color stained her cheeks. She marched forward, closing the distance between them and stabbed her finger into his chest. "I won't say them in Latin. I won't say them again, period. I've done what you wanted, and now I want to go home."

Farran sheathed his sword before his fury got the better of him. He grabbed her by the arm and jerked her so close her breasts brushed against his chest. "You will not leave until you utter the vow."

Her eyes glittered like amber gems behind her narrowed gaze. "I *will* leave. Mark my words, Farran, you cannot hold me prisoner forever. And when I do, you'll wish you'd never met me."

Mikhail cleared his voice, reminding Farran they were not alone. He straightened at the sound and relaxed his hold on Noelle's arm, yet he did not turn her loose. Ordering his anger to subside, he turned to Mikhail.

"Perhaps you would both benefit from some time apart." Mikhail lifted his eyebrows, a silent instruction Farran should not argue. "I believe you made mention of unwelcome guests. Perhaps you should attend to other matters and allow Noelle a reprieve from your tongue. I am certain she shall find her chambers to her liking."

Noelle protested, "I'm not stay—"

"Aye, you are," Farran gritted out. "You may have found a champion, but, Dr. Keane, you will stay until you assume your duty."

He ushered her to the door, none too gently. Yanking it open, he thrust her into the hall ahead of him.

"Let go of me." She pried at his fingers as he marched her down the stone corridor. "I'm not staying here. I'm going home, damn it. If I have to walk to town to catch a ride, I will."

Clamping down on his tongue, he refused to give in to his temper. God's teeth, this woman was far more infuriating than Anne. At least with Merrick's wife, he could expect her to retaliate physically. In stark contrast to Anne's forthright manner, Noelle struck out when least expected. She wove a web of words that offered encouragement, then used that silvery tongue to twist things in her favor.

Just like Brighid.

At the stairs, she sank her weight into her heels, refusing to budge. Undaunted, Farran gave her another push and sent her stumbling onto the first stone tread. Outclassed by his size, she stumbled up the steps ahead of him, muttering beneath her breath. He could not make out the words, but guessed he would not wish to hear them anyway.

At the top of the stairs, she twisted sharply to the right. "Let me go," she hissed through her teeth. "You're making a scene."

Farran set his jaw and ignored her demands. 'Twas not a man within the temple walls who had not experienced a headstrong woman. All would have done the same, were they to face the humiliation she had caused. Many would not be as gentle. Many more would not have waited until they were out of earshot to make their displeasure known.

He hurried her up the stairs that led to the second story and the seraphs' chambers. The door across the hall from Merrick's stood open. Light spilled into the hall. He led her inside, thrust her away from him, and kicked the door shut with his heel. "You gave me your word."

"My word?" she cried. Oblivious to her lavish surroundings, she stalked back in front of him. "My *word*? You insult me at every opportunity. You want me to believe this means so much to you, and yet you can't bring yourself to follow your own delusional customs? Don't you *dare* start in on me about my *word,* when yours is just as meaningless."

A foreign pang of guilt stabbed through his thick skin as she flung the truthful accusation. He had spoken falsely. His vow held emptiness, and were it not for duty to the Order, he never would have spoken a single syllable. Yet he could not bring himself to admit the wrong. Duty stood above all. The strength that would come from their union demanded he take the necessary measures. A fact he must make her understand.

He pushed a hand through his hair and willed his temper into submission. Studying her for several long moments, he focused on the easy in and out of his breathing. When he felt he had reduced his fury to a low simmer, he spoke low and clear. "Your role is to this Order, as is mine. What we think of one another is unimportant. There are greater things at stake."

On a frustrated groan, she sank her head into her hands and dug her fingers into her scalp. "This is insane. *You* are insane. I just want to go home."

"Then say the words, damsel, and you shall gain your freedom."

Dragging her fingers down her face, she shook her head, then adjusted her glasses. "No. I'm not about to do one thing more for you. You're all nuts, and I refuse to play your ridiculous game."

Farran reached down to his sword and pulled the torc off its pommel. He tossed it onto the overstuffed plaid couch beside her thigh. "When you come to realize you have no choice, I shall be waiting."

Noelle reached for the torc and hurled it at his head. Her aim failed by several inches. The torc thumped into the wooden door, bounced off, and landed on the hardwood floor. He watched it roll on its edge before it toppled sideways and came to a stop near the toe of his boot. 'Twas no matter—the holy relic would find its way to her arm soon enough. 'Twould not leave her as long as it sensed her true intentions lay in leaving it behind.

With a disappointed shake of his head, he turned for the door. Mikhail spoke wisely. A battle of words and wills would accomplish naught. She needed time. And he had demons to address.

He left her in silence and rapped on Merrick's door. Anne opened it quickly, her smile bright. "Farran, I'm so happy for you."

Giving her a perturbed look, he let himself inside. "Aye, you would be."

Anne drew back, her blue eyes wide. "What's that supposed to mean?"

"She who does not hesitate to bully everyone into her demands would find Noelle's reluctance amusing." Though his voice held the sharpness of annoyance, his heart lacked conviction. In truth, much as he despised admitting it, Anne grew on him with each meeting.

Merrick stepped through the French doors that separated their sleeping chambers from the front room. "She gives you trouble, Farran?"

"She plagues me overmuch." He massaged his temples between thumb and forefinger.

Merrick's mouth contorted with a smirk. His gaze flicked to Anne, then back to Farran. "'Tis the way of seraphs."

Farran shook off the humiliating encounter with a heavy sigh. "I wish to speak of it no more. I need your sword."

All traces of humor vanished from Merrick's expression. He dropped a hip onto the arm of their sofa. "What is your need, brother?"

Gesturing at the window and the trees outside, Farran answered, "There are demons lining the lane. We must dispose of them before Azazel learns of Noelle's arrival. She remains vulnerable until she swears her word."

Merrick stood and went to the rack of armor behind the door. As he pulled his chain hauberk free, Anne gnawed on her lower lip. It took only seconds before her attempt at silence failed, and her worry tumbled free. "Is that wise, Merrick? Your leg's only begun to heal."

When Merrick bent to place a gentle kiss to Anne's cheek, Farran looked away. Of late, he found he could not stomach the affection they openly shared. It rent wounds over scars long healed and brought back disturbing memories of a time when he too had loved deeply.

"I shall be fine, little demon. 'Tis a good way to test my strength."

Anne's sharp tone scolded. "And a good way to find yourself back in bed."

"A fate I would not mind overmuch," Merrick answered on a chuckle. "Come, Farran. Let us descend in to the barracks. We shall gather Lucan and Caradoc. Declan, if we can find him. The fight will do you good as well."

Aye, indeed. If he were lucky, he would not survive to see the light of morning.

The faint sound of a cat's meow brought Noelle's trajectory toward the exit to an abrupt halt. Her hand stretched toward the waiting doorknob, she slowly looked toward the closed pair of sliding panel doors on the opposite wall. "Scat Cat?"

Mrrf. Mrrf.

The inability to produce a full *meow* could come from only her cat. All thoughts of fleeing the temple fled, and Noelle marched over to the closed doors. She eased one cherry-stained panel into the wall, far enough that he could slip through. Like a wisp of smoke, he sauntered into the front room, then wound himself around and between her feet.

"Scat Cat," she whispered. The feline had always made coming home after a long day of work a delight. Yet never before had she felt so incredibly glad to see her fat, lazy, and often opinionated pet. She bent down, picked him up, and buried her nose in his thick fur.

His overly enthusiastic motor returned her affection.

With a heavy exhale that stirred his silky coat, she lifted her face. "What are we going to do, fella?"

He caught the finger she rubbed under his chin with both forepaws. Sharp claws urged her hand toward his mouth where he could contentedly lick her fingers.

A glint of silver from the corner of her eye brought her attention back to the glass-topped coffee table positioned in the center of the room. Her eyes widened. Situated in the middle of a carved inlay sat a distinctive ceramic bowl. A Beaker Gabriel had presented to her in the middle of summer. She'd aged the artifact as Middle Bronze Age. Other particles identified its origin as British, specifically part of the early settlement near Thanet. The Beaker Period.

What in the world was that thing doing here? Gabriel had said he was consigning it to a museum.

Scat Cat tucked in her arms, she moved closer. The same cracked edges, the same unique pattern of symbols along the jagged rim. The same damn piece.

Frowning, she exchanged her cat for the aged artifact and held it beneath the light. No doubt about it, no matter how she tried to search for a difference that would mark the object as a replica, she held the artifact that had been the highlight of her career. The piece that had established her lab as the premier experts with small quantities and accelerator mass spectrometry.

Unease shifted around in her belly as she looked to the glass-front bookcase. Her heart slowed to a heavy *thump-thump* as more objects she'd seen in her lab looked back from their places beneath a soft filtered light. A Grecian pot depicting Dionysus, a Mongolian helmet from the Yuan dynasty, a four-inch solid gold Set figurine from early Egypt—one by one, she recognized the familiar treasures.

She turned around, slowly taking in the rest of the room. Amid a scattering of wall hangings that shared the same age and value of the things on the shelves, comfortable furnishings lavished the room. The sofa was simple in color, a soft tan hue. Ebony accent pillows filled the corners and matched the two plush end chairs. Hardwood lay beneath her feet, adorned with a thick white rug. Comforts that matched her decorating style and mirrored her living room in D.C.

But how? Clearly Gabriel had a hand in decorating this room, but she'd never once invited him to her apartment. How in the world could he possibly know what she'd like? Seth maybe? Had to be. Yet that too spurred more questions—was Seth part of this? Had their run-in on the road been part of some plan Gabriel designed? Surely not. Seth wouldn't set her up like that. He'd know she would fire him in a heartbeat if he did, and his position as her assistant meant too much to his career. He wouldn't take that kind of risk. Not if he ever intended to work in their field again.

With Scat Cat at her heels, she wandered through the pocket doors into her evidential bedroom. Similar to her room at home, this one followed the same pattern of simplicity. A four-poster bed in cherry matched the dresser and large vanity. Though the furnishings bore carvings, the patterns were straight lines, neat designs that didn't detract or stand out ostentatiously. An overstuffed mattress was covered with a heavy down comforter, as was the bed she'd slept in the last ten years. The only difference between the two rooms—the color patterns. Where her apartment's bedroom sported muted blue and off-white, this room was a rich teal and deep burgundy. Not feminine. Not masculine. Elegant all the same.

Curiosity consumed her. She traipsed to the adjoining bathroom and flipped on the light, then drew back with a soft gasp. A large tub, easily able to accommodate three of her, took up the entire far corner. Veins of muted gold weaving through the marble matched the polished brass fixtures. And the same dark cherry wood stood out against an eggshell backdrop. As if someone had plucked a picture straight out of her imagination.

A shiver rolled down her spine. Someone must have overheard her talking at some point. Nothing else could explain how the very bathroom she'd seen in the one house she'd considered buying—and the sole reason she'd considered the house—now stretched out before her.

Feeling suddenly as if a pair of unseen eyes watched, she picked up her pet. His purr served to soothe the way her nerves stood on end. The feel of his soft coat beneath her roaming fingers eased the *trip-trip* of her heart.

She backed out of the bathroom and swallowed hard. "We gotta get out of here, Scat Cat," she murmured. "Before we can't."

No way would she spend another minute in this eerie place. And Gabriel San Lucee would never again set foot in her laboratory.

Determined to make her escape while Farran was occupied, she hurried to the door. Halfway across the room, she froze against the hollow echo of a knock.

CHAPTER 14

✝

Noelle took a deep breath and lifted her chin. If Farran had returned already, she didn't dare give any sign she intended to escape a second time. She had no doubt he'd make good on his promise to turn her into a prisoner. If he bound her, or locked her away somewhere down in that maze of tunnels, she'd never get the chance again. No, she'd be better served by playing his game. Going along with things until he gave her a few minutes alone again. All she had to do tonight was lock herself in that enormous bedroom and cooperate a little while longer.

Steeling herself against inevitable confrontation, she trained her expression into what she hoped was complacency and approached the door. She half expected that when she opened it a fraction, he would barrel through. When he didn't, she widened it enough to stick her head outside.

Anne stood on the threshold, a hesitant smile on her porcelain face. "Noelle, I'm sorry to disturb you. But while the men are away, I'd like to talk to you."

Noelle cocked an eyebrow. While the men were away? Could that mean Anne only pretended at the same game? As the memory of how Anne had exchanged affectionate looks with Merrick rose, Noelle's brow furrowed. Surely that couldn't be faked. Then again, maybe it could be. Maybe pretending just came naturally to some women. She could attest to that—couldn't she?

Noelle stepped back, allowing Anne entrance. "I'm not sure there's much to say, but come in."

"Thank you." Anne's smile widened as she stepped into the room.

"Have a seat, I guess."

Holding Scat Cat close to her chest, Noelle followed Anne to the sofa. To her shame, the redhead carried herself with grace Noelle could only dream of. Although they shared the same short stature, Noelle felt somehow smaller. More insignificant. Almost as if Anne's very presence commanded a level of respect Noelle couldn't quite define.

A feeling that only added to the particles of ice that clung to her veins. She didn't know this woman. She wasn't a head of state or some notable figurehead in the scientific community. There was no reason Noelle should treat Anne any differently than any other stranger.

She pushed her discomfort aside and took a seat on the opposite end of the couch. "How can I help you?"

Auburn eyebrows pulled tight and creases cut into Anne's smooth forehead. She considered Noelle for several silent seconds before she tried her smile again. It fell short, quivered at the corners of her mouth. "You don't look pleased to be here."

Understatement of the year. Noelle bit back a burst of laughter, opting for a shake of her head. "I have work waiting on me. Archaeologists I promised answers. The Egyptian Supreme Council of Antiquities is waiting on results. The curator of—" Noelle stopped, before her thoughts ran away with her tongue. She licked her lips and folded her hands in her lap. "No. I'm not happy to be here at all."

She waited for Anne's disapproving frown. Anticipated a lecture. When Anne's smile returned, brighter than before, Noelle drew back in surprise.

Anne let out a soft, musical laugh. "I wasn't very fond of it either."

"No?" A spark of hope lit. If Anne sympathized, maybe she could find an ally who would talk some sense into Farran.

"Not at all. But I didn't come here knowing the things Farran's told you." She paused to regard Noelle with a measured stare. "Farran *did* tell you, right?"

"You mean that nonsense about Templar knights and seraphs and predestined fates?"

The frown Noelle had been expecting registered behind Anne's bright blue eyes. It lasted only seconds, however, before she quickly covered it with a blank expression. Her voice assumed a faraway quality as she stared at the cabinet of antiquities. "I didn't understand why Gabriel chose me first until this moment."

"What?" Noelle cringed at the harshness in her question, and gave herself a sharp mental kick. Snapping at Anne wouldn't win her any friends. "I'm sorry. What do you mean?"

"I used to teach college. The prophecy names me the teacher, and you the blind. I understand now." Anne looked back at her with a wistful smile. "You don't know anything, do you?"

It took every bit of Noelle's concentration to keep her

tongue in line and not return the insult. She pushed her
cat out of her lap and clenched her hands together. "I
don't know what you're talking about, that's for sure."

"You really don't believe in a higher power, do you?"

At that, Noelle's laugh slipped free. She cut it off short
and cleared her voice. "You mean some mystical being
who controls our lives like we're puppets on strings? Or
do you mean the higher power who randomly chooses
who will live and who will die? Or, are you referring to
the social dependence on the need to believe in order to
give meaning to life?"

Anne chuckled. "I guess that pretty much answers
everything." She stood and dusted her hands on her
ankle-length skirt. Clasping them behind her back, she
wandered to the glass-encased artifacts. "You'll learn.
It's inevitable. Please trust me, Noelle. It's uncomfortable
now, and nothing makes sense. But Farran will teach you
if you let him. You'll realize this isn't such a terrible
place." She looked over her shoulder to add, "In fact, it's
really pretty wonderful."

"Right. As wonderful as a trip down a rabbit hole.
You've even murdered time." The sarcastic jibe slipped
free before Noelle could stop it. Eyes wide, she covered
her mouth with her hand. *Please, please, please don't let
her get that.*

Laughter rippled through the room, hearty and genuine.
Anne's blue eyes danced with merriment as she turned
around. "I suppose it would feel a bit like that. I'd never
quite thought of it that way. Farran must love your wit."

In the wake of Anne's amusement, Noelle's appre-
hensions filtered away, and she began to relax. This was
a woman who understood her wit *and* her intellect. Not
to mention she didn't take offense at her tendency for

bluntness. Outside this crazy scheme, they might have been close friends.

The opportunity to express the full weight of her frustrations was too great to let slip by. She grabbed at it like a life raft and let out a snort. "Farran could give the Queen of Hearts a run for her money."

Anne's shoulders slumped, and her expression twisted with sorrow. She returned to the couch and sat down on the edge of the cushions. "Don't be hard on him, Noelle. He's a good man. Aside from Merrick, I know no one more loyal. He'll take care of you, if you're patient with him. His secrets are his to share, but I know his past. What he must overcome . . ." She trailed away on a sad shake of her head. "In time you'll understand that as well."

The uncomfortable twist in Noelle's gut returned with a vengeance. Her stomach knotted down so tight she couldn't breathe. A spark of irritation ignited at the discomfort, and she shifted in her seat to keep her annoyance at bay. She didn't care what Farran had gone through. She refused to sympathize with him. Whatever had happened in his past didn't concern her, and she wasn't about to let the insinuation he suffered emotional scars weasel under her skin.

"Let me see your hand." Anne reached between them, her fingers outstretched. "I see things by touch. Maybe I can tell you something that will make this easier."

Noelle tucked her hand between her thighs. "I don't think that's necessary. Anne, you seem like a smart woman. I don't really know how you let them convince you into this cult, but I don't plan on being a part of it. I'm not staying."

"You don't have a choice." Anne set her hand on Noelle's knee. She closed her eyes and tipped her head to the side as if she listened for voices. Her brows puckered, relaxed, then furrowed deeply. Then she snapped her eyes open and withdrew, her features suddenly pale. With a toss of her long red hair, she leaned back against the throw pillow.

"No wonder you have so much to learn. You're a new soul."

Exasperation gripped Noelle and she snapped, "A what?"

"There are old souls who have been on this earth before, and new souls. I've only met one other completely new soul. When I did, I didn't know what I was seeing, and I asked my mentor. I see wisps when I look for your past." Her mouth pinched in thought, and she fell silent. After several expansive seconds, she explained, "It's hard to describe. You've seen pictures of space and the stringy particles of matter up there?"

Resisting the urge to roll her eyes, Noelle nodded.

"It's like that. Wispy. Only full of colors. Like a river of the energies of life." She waved a dismissive hand in the air. "Never mind. What's important—you're a new soul. Completely untainted and utterly innocent." Her eyes locked with Noelle's and intensified with meaning. "You were created for this purpose, Noelle. And you better accept it in a hurry."

"Uh-huh. I suppose lightning will strike me down if I don't?" So much for believing Anne might be sane. She'd just shot that theory all to hell. She was as crazy as the rest of them and perfectly suited for their little game of charades.

All traces of humor and sympathy vanished from Anne's expression. She hurried to rise, and opened her mouth as if she intended to say more. Evidently thinking better of it, she snapped her mouth shut just as quickly. Three purposeful strides took her back to the door. There, she hesitated again. Her head bowed, her shoulders bent forward. Her heavy exhale was audible in the silence that spanned between them.

With the gravity a surgeon would give to a patient's waiting family, she twisted to meet Noelle's gaze. "No. But you *will* die."

As the door quietly closed, Noelle flopped back against the sofa's arm. This was too much. Where these people came up with these ridiculous things, she couldn't explain. Still, she had to admit their game was tight. They took their role seriously, played the part to a T, and came up with things more fantastic than what she'd heard before. Anne's little drama had even succeeded in sending another shiver down her spine.

Priceless.

A chuckle worked its way free from her tightened throat. She gave in to the lunacy and began to laugh. Big, unchained bursts of amusement that stirred tears behind her eyes. She tossed her right arm over her eyes to swipe away the straying drops. Beneath her sweatshirt sleeve, something hard rubbed against the bridge of her nose. Something snugged securely around her bicep.

Her amusement strangled in the back of her throat. In slow motion, she sat up and looked to the place near the door where the torc had bounced to a stop.

Empty floor met her gaze.

Farran's body strained against two days of little sleep. Arm raised, he blocked the demon's baseball bat and shuddered against the heavy blow. His shoulders ached with the weight of his sword. His thighs burned from the effort of holding himself upright against the heavy blows. Yet he pushed the agony from his mind and eyed Azazel's foul minion, anticipating the next attack.

Behind him, Caradoc grunted against an onslaught of nytym claws. His back brushed Farran's, their close quarters a defensive tactic to improve their outnumbered strength. Farran used the momentum of Caradoc's stumble and lunged forward. In a powerful strike, he arced his sword across his body, aiming for the demon's unprotected arm. The blade sliced through flesh like a knife put to butter. A bone-chilling howl cut through the air, blending with another to Farran's left, and the demon stumbled off the road's shoulder into the tree line.

Farran pursued, unwilling to give the creature a moment's respite. One more blow, a well-timed drive, and the beast would return to the hellish pit it spawned from.

The demon surged forward, its once-human features now twisted with the evil of its spirit. Yellow fangs gleamed in the moonlight. Darkness shrouded its face, illuminating goatlike, yellow-green eyes. Baseball bat still clenched in bony fingers, it rushed headlong with a ghastly bellow.

Exactly what Farran awaited. He had played the demon, using his fatigue to his advantage. Now the illusion of being the weaker would give him the final upper hand. He bided his time, kept his pace deliberately slow. All part of his planned deception.

With a scream that could chill the very fires of Azazel's realm, the demon swung wildly. Farran sidestepped to avoid the blow. Gathering the last of his faltering strength, he thrust across his waist and sank his blade into the demon's exposed side. He jerked his broadsword up, deepening the wound. Shadows poured forth, ran in rivulets down the demon's leg.

Shock washed across the creature's widened eyes. As Farran sucked in a heavy breath, he gave his sword one last twist and wrenched it free. With a haunting moan, his opponent folded in on itself and vanished.

Farran braced himself for the darkness that would come next. Nine hundred years of combat, and he had yet to become accustomed to the invasion on his soul. He closed his eyes, dropped his elbows to his knees. In his mind's eye, he saw the shadows roll down his blade, soak into his hand. Darkness flooded into his veins, raced to his heart where it burst through his body. He gasped against the searing heat. 'Twould seem as if the pain intensified the closer he came to joining Azazel's ranks. Mayhap it did. Mayhap 'twas an effect of anticipating the agony. He could not know for certain.

As his heart faltered against the evil, struggling to maintain the rhythm of life, Farran dropped to his knees. Hard, wet earth jarred his bones and soaked through his jeans. Gradually the feeling of clawed hands turning him inside out faded, leaving pinpoints of light to flicker behind his eyelids. He breathed long and deep and lifted his chin to open his eyes.

Through blurry vision, he made out a figure as dark as the sky above. Ebony armor clad a powerful frame. Scratches on a heavy shield cut through the onyx color to glint silver in the moonlight. Eyes he had no doubt known once before peered down at him with hate. A dark knight, a fallen Templar. A transformed brother Farran had no hope of overcoming alone, given his exhaustion.

"Petty fool," the knight hissed. "The forest is mine. Your life belongs to me."

Farran clenched his hand around his sword. He would not surrender his life without a fight. If he must die, he would inflict what damage he could so his brothers could send the spirit home to the Almighty. He straightened his shoulders and flattened a foot to rise.

The gust of air caught him first. It rustled his hair, stirred the stench of death. He drew back in reflex. From the corner of his eye, he saw the shield. Before he could do so much as clench his teeth, it slammed into the side of his head.

A ringing erupted in Farran's ears. His vision failed him completely, turning shadows into pitch black. The sword in his hand tumbled free.

CHAPTER 15

✝

"Farran!"

Merrick's bellow lured Farran from the swimming of his thoughts. He fought for consciousness, struggled to silence the buzzing in his head. He squeezed his eyes shut and groped on the ground in front of him for his fallen weapon.

"Get back!" Closer now, Merrick's order came from his right. On trembling arms, Farran crawled backward what he hoped was four or five feet. Merrick could handle the knight. With his oath in place, his sword would emerge the victor. Whatever blows Merrick might take, immortality would heal.

He opened his eyes to find three of Merrick and the knight. His sword forgotten, Farran scrubbed at his face and bit back a stream of curses. Damnation! There had been no warning of a dark knight, just nytyms and demons, beasts easily overtaken by their small band. Had any of them anticipated that Azazel would send a knight to the very fringes of the temple, they would have roused the entire Order and combed the sparse woods.

Nay though, they had not, and the oversight nearly cost far more than Farran's life. Noelle's purpose would be for naught with his death—a blow the Order could not withstand. He was proof enough of their weakened state.

The three images of Merrick merged into one, and Farran watched as his commander parried off the fiend's attack. Steel clanged against steel, ringing a death knell. The healing Anne's light brought to Merrick could not be more evident. His sword arm moved with lightning quickness. His body arced with the practiced grace of one born unto battle. A frisson of envy sliced through Farran. If Noelle had but uttered the oath, he too would know the might he had once possessed. He too could step beside Merrick and fight off the glancing blows.

He would not be a useless heap upon the sodden ground.

Merrick lunged forward, entering the dark knight's open stance. With the deft thrust, his blade pierced through links of ebony mail and slid deep into the knight's gut. Though embedded in flesh, the broadsword gave off an odd, bluish-white glow that seeped through the rent skin. In the faint light, blood poured forth, thick and dark.

The knight doubled over on a vile hiss, and Merrick pulled his broadsword free. Taking it in both hands, he arced it over his head. In the moonlight, the ornate hilt that marked Merrick's sword as equal to Mikhail's glinted bright gold. He brought it down in a furious slice that sent the knight's head toppling from his shoulders. It tumbled to the ground, rolled chin over brow, and came to a stop before Farran's knee. Ghostly eyes stared up, unblinking.

Farran nudged it aside, unable to look upon the face of

the brother he had once known. Too many he had lost. Brave men who sacrificed everything to uphold the Almighty's name, only to die for evil's purpose. A shudder rolled down his spine, and he grimaced. Dimly, he heard the plaintive sigh of expiration, the last sound an avenged spirit would make before it ascended to the heavens.

Merrick's boot entered his field of vision. Farran looked up to meet his commander's grim expression.

"'Tis done." Merrick nodded at the men behind Farran. "There is naught left of Azazel here. Those we could not slay fled. How do you fare?"

"I live."

Merrick extended his hand to aid Farran to his feet. As he struggled to rise, he observed the way his commander kept his weight off his left leg. A glance down revealed Merrick did not escape the attack unscathed. His injured thigh bled through Merrick's white surcoat, staining it with crimson. Farran lifted a brow. "You tore open your wound."

Merrick glanced down as if he had not realized the injury. He gave a curt nod before releasing Farran. "Anne will mend it."

"If she does not injure you more." The hint of a smirk tugged at the corner of Farran's mouth.

A smile played on Merrick's mouth before quickly disappearing behind serious black eyes. "Come. We must report to Mikhail. I am certain he did not anticipate the presence of a fallen knight." He shouldered past Farran, heading for the road once more.

As Farran fell into step behind him, the severed head disintegrated into ash, marking it as one of the eldest fallen knights. Only those who had turned long ago disintegrated when death took their bodies. Giving his former brother the respect his death deserved, Farran stepped over the small gray mound and offered a silent prayer that the spirit's journey would be swift.

Lucan and Caradoc joined him in the march to the temple's front porch, both equally as silent. He knew the question that lurked in their minds, for it drummed inside his as well. *Why was no seraph sent to save their brother's life?*

One other haunted Farran—why had he been spared, when he would have willingly exchanged places?

Beyond the wide front doors, the temple lay in silence, as it had since Anne's coming. For a short time after her pairing, life returned to normal and men gathered in the communal room until the wee hours of morn. Yet now, with Noelle's arrival, they retreated to their chambers early to tend the wounds of despair alone.

At the top of the stairwell leading to the barracks below, Caradoc clamped a heavy hand on Farran's shoulder and brought him to a halt. "Your seraph rests upstairs, and yet your sword remains unchanged."

The reminder of Noelle's behavior brought Farran's teeth together so hard he grimaced. His body tensed. Warily, he lifted his gaze to Caradoc's.

Apology shone behind Caradoc's hazel eyes. "Nay, brother, I meant no insult. Was I not the one who journeyed with you from Clare so long ago?"

Farran blew out a heavy breath and let his shoulders slump. Of all the people who would understand, 'twas Caradoc. "Aye," he answered quietly.

"Your place is with her, Farran, not in the barracks amongst the men."

Involuntarily, Farran's gaze tracked up the ascending stairs. He chewed on his tongue, debating whether to tell Caradoc the difficulty his suggestion posed. Yet before he could find the words to explain Noelle's reluctance, Caradoc forged ahead.

"Do you think that Azazel's knight did not report to him the moment you drove down the lane? The fallen are the strongest of Azazel's creatures. In a whisper he can relay what we could over the phone." The grip on his shoulder intensified, urging Farran to turn around. "Mark my words, Farran. Azazel knows of Merrick's transformation—his sword announces it as clear as a trumpet. The dark lord knows he cannot harm Anne." Caradoc paused, his words taking on greater weight. "And he knows the woman you brought home is unclaimed."

A heavy ball of lead rolled inside Farran's gut. He swallowed against the truth—as long as Noelle refused the oath, her life was in jeopardy. She might detest him, he might find her unacceptable. But their personal concerns made no difference. The Order needed her. They needed the strength she would bring to his sword.

"You must convince her. You are a pair."

"'Tis not as easy as you suggest. She is—"

Caradoc lifted a hand, cutting off Farran's protest. "Whatever divides you, you must overcome. Do not retreat to your chambers, old friend. Go to her. Allow her to tend your wounds. There is no better time for you to learn to work together."

The memory of Noelle's gentle kiss as she set her mouth to his scar rose in Farran's mind. Tend him. Would she? A traitorous flicker of hope stirred deep inside his soul. Her fingers would be soft. Her touch tender. He had been but a boy the last time a woman showed him such care.

He squelched the stirring feeling before it could take life. 'Twas not emotion he desired from Noelle. Whether she tended him, mattered not. 'Twas too likely that, like

Brighid, the sight of blood would make her ill. "I shall go to her after I see Uriel. I am in no frame of mind to deal with a woman's weak stomach."

Caradoc's fingers refused to release him. He bore down harder, biting into Farran's sore shoulder muscles. "If she faints 'tis better she do so here than when she may be needed on the field. Make her accustomed to it now." The warning ran clear in his firm tone—he would issue an order as second in command, if Farran refused.

With his choice made for him, Farran yielded to the pressure on his shoulder and turned. He looked to the dilapidated window on the landing between the floors and drew in a fortifying breath. Reason lived in Caradoc's urgings. To put off duty only increased the odds another night like tonight would occur. As much as he longed for the comforting solitude of his sparse chambers, duty obligated him to take the stairs.

Noelle refused to look at the torc. Looking at it would mean thinking about how it ended up wrapped around her bicep, and she'd thought herself in circles trying to figure it out. She knew she damn sure hadn't put it there. Anything else meant . . .

With a shake of her head, she grabbed a throw pillow and hugged it tightly. She wasn't going there. The only explanation possible was that she'd picked it up, absently stuffed it back on her arm, and had been too distracted with anger to remember.

The ever-tightening knot in her stomach clamped down another notch. She huddled into her pillow to fight back the bitter taste of rising bile and concentrated on her breathing. For the first time since she'd met Farran, icy particles of fear pricked at her conscious. As much as she wanted to believe the tripe she'd created about forgetting to wear the torc, the brutal reality loomed before her—she hadn't.

Scat Cat nudged his way under her elbow, forcing her to give him room. When she released her death grip on the pillow, the feline crawled into her lap. Eyes narrow slits of gold, motor running, he massaged his paws against her thigh. She absently dropped a hand to the scruff of his neck and slid her fingers through his thick gray fur.

A knock at the door startled her. Her chin snapped up, her gaze locked on the barrier. Yet before she could do anything more than give Scat Cat a reluctant push, the door swung open. Farran entered, his gaze canvassing the room and finally settling on her. The tight lines around his mouth eased, and he dipped his head in a casual nod. "You are not asleep?"

Her nerves chafed at his bold intrusion. But the sight of him rendered her unable to speak. She stared, wide-eyed, at the strange man who had seemed so outwardly normal only a few hours earlier. Where he'd worn jeans and a casual long-sleeved shirt, he now dressed in a costume straight out of the Middle Ages. A long white surcoat, embellished with a bold crimson cross, draped down to his calves. Beneath it, he wore a hauberk of linked chain, complete with a coif to cover his sandy hair. Well-worn vambraces on his forearms matched the supple leather of his boots. The sword he'd brandished in Mikhail's office hung from a belt pulled so tight, it accented the trimness of his waist.

Only, where the actors she'd seen at the Renaissance festivals looked stilted and uncomfortable in their costumes, Farran wore his with the practiced comfort that belonged in the movies.

As if he wore the stuff daily.

Noelle blinked. She found her cobweb-covered tongue and managed to squeak, "What are you doing here?"

He pulled at the fingers on his gloves. One by one, they gave, and he slapped them lightly against his thigh before setting them on the small table near her door. "We are paired. Here is where I shall stay."

"Oh."

The short retort was all she could find, and she sagged back against the couch cushions. She ought to be surprised, ought to be furious. But the dilemma with the torc had sapped her energy so completely she didn't care. She'd spent the last two days with Farran. It was becoming almost natural to have him in her personal space. Besides, while she'd never admit it aloud, she'd rather not spend another minute alone and let her mind run away with possibilities.

"I shall sleep where you sit. The bed shall remain yours." Farran's hands dropped to his waist to give the buckle a tug. His belt fell away from his hips, and he leaned his sheathed sword against the wall. "I require a bath. Then I require rest."

His fingers stilled over the vambrace strings. For several silent seconds he gave her a thoughtful stare. He opened his mouth, then shut it. His brows tugged together. Then he let out a nearly inaudible sigh. "If you wish to watch your television, I could rest in the other room. I would remove myself when you are ready to retire."

The bone was small, nearly tooth size. Yet Noelle realized the thrown offering in an instant. His quiet tone, the warm light in his eyes, the sheer work it took to summon the words—Farran was trying to be friendly.

"No. That's okay. I can go in the bedroom. We can talk in the morning, right?"

Ale-brown eyes widened a fraction. "You wish to talk? Do you require something of me?" He slid the vambraces off and tossed them on top of his gloves.

A fool would blow past this intriguing side of Farran and push him back to his gloomy demeanor with complaints. The surprising politeness, the willingness to listen to her was too much of a treasure to spoil the few minutes of peace his newfound demeanor offered. She shook her head, dismissing the nagging need to plead to him to take her home. "It's nothing that can't wait until morning."

"Tell me what you need, damsel. As I said, we are paired. We must learn to speak to one another freely."

"No, it can wait." One more night wouldn't change anything. If she really wanted to be honest with herself, he looked tired. Who could blame him—he'd driven almost two days straight. While she longed for freedom and her apartment, she wouldn't pick a fight with him tonight. His efforts deserved at least that much consideration. She tried for a smile and added in a quieter voice, "I'm tired too."

"Very well." He took a step toward the paneled doors. "I shall wash." Halfway through the doorway, he stopped to glance over his shoulder. The perplexed look returned to his features, and the same war of wills played on his eyebrows. "If you would aid me in the removal of my mail, 'twill go much faster."

Oh, so that was it—he wanted her help. She, whom he couldn't stand. Whose touch repulsed him. No wonder he had such a hard time asking.

Her pride rose up, taunting her to toss the request back in his face. After all the demands he'd made, the insults he'd given her, she shouldn't lift a finger to help. If he'd been Seth, she'd have laughed in his face.

Only he wasn't Seth. He was handsome, grumpy, insane

Farran. A man who probably didn't have the first clue about his mood swings and behavior.

Her gaze tracked across his broad shoulders, followed the high planes of his cheeks. Scratches littered his face, tiny marks she hadn't noticed until he stepped beneath the light that poured from the bedroom.

"What have you been doing?" She asked as she rose to her feet. "Isn't it a little late for fencing?" Then again, when she'd been on the team in high school, there had been several who practiced at every stolen opportunity. Maybe he was no different.

A soft snort accompanied the bemused shake of his head. "You would not believe me."

She smirked. "You're probably right. Tell me anyway."

He leaned a shoulder on the door frame, and his gaze settled on hers, intense and probing. "There were demons in the woods. Sent for you, I am certain."

Demons? She'd expected something related to the Templar purpose and being the best he could be, regardless of the hour. But demons? The notion stirred her amusement once again. If he could put half these things down on paper, the man would make a fortune as an author. His imagination topped the charts.

She swallowed down the rising laugh and checked her expression. But what brought her to a stop wasn't the challenge in his eyes that dared her to argue. Nor was it the harsh line that his mouth had once again assumed. What rooted her in place and dropped her jaw was the jagged vein of crimson that flowed from under the crushed links of his coif and trickled down his temple. "Farran, you're bleeding!"

CHAPTER 16

⸎

Farran tensed. Eyes closed, he waited for the shrill scream, the shout for Anne to help. If he looked, the brief shock that had passed across Noelle's pretty face would be replaced with the hardness of anger. Silent repulsion would glint behind her doelike eyes. Too many times, he had seen the same in Brighid's sky-blues. He had been too blind with love to recognize it then, yet he now understood he had disgusted her even on his greatest successes.

'Twas foolishness to allow Caradoc to convince him . . .

The light press of Noelle's fingertips on his forehead brought his thoughts to a screeching halt. He drew back in surprise. Opening his eyes, he found her on tiptoe, concern etched into her delicate brow.

"Hold still," she scolded softly. Setting her hand upon his shoulder, she steadied herself and reached for his coif again. "This doesn't look good."

" 'Twill heal," he murmured.

As she pushed at the mail, it caught in his hair and

scraped against the rent flesh beneath. He winced, reflexively avoiding her touch. Her eyes darted to his, her slight frown chastisement enough. Holding his breath, he did his best to obey and yield to her gentle probing.

With the care a woman would give to a babe, she eased his coif away until it draped around his neck. "I think you need stitches. What did you do to yourself?"

Farran could scarcely draw a breath. Disbelief stole his words, shock cemented his tongue. Deep inside, something soft and wholly unfamiliar stirred. She did not tremble at the sight of blood. Did not draw away as if she could not stand the thought of touching him. Nay, in fact she stood so close the faint scent of jasmine that clung to her tickled his nose. He did not know what to do with this. What to do with . . . her.

Before his senses could flee, he reached up and caught her wrist. He pulled it away, terminating the mystifying contact. As he held her hand level with his chest, her gaze pulled to her bloodied fingertips, and she nibbled on her lower lip.

"You need stitches, Farran. I'll drive if you give me the keys."

"Nay, damsel. 'Twill heal come morn. 'Twould have already healed, were it not for the taint that infects my soul. Tonight the wounds need to be cleansed. If you would but bandage my head, you shall see."

He read her doubt in the set of her mouth. But for a reason he could not fathom, she did not protest. She stepped away and gestured at the door. "Go lay down. I'll get a washcloth. If you bleed to death, or you have a horrible scar, you can't blame me. You try, and I'll give you a bump to match on the other side."

Farran bowed his head to hide a budding smile. She

could not begin to heft the weight of a kite shield. Yet, if she insisted, he would allow her to try. The battle to bring the shield to her shoulders would be well worth the risk of injury.

At the edge of the bed, he stopped. Humor under control once more, he called out, stopping her near the bathroom. "Noelle?"

"Yeah?"

"I need your aid in removing my hauberk." The request felt strange to his tongue. Had she been Lucan, or any of his brethren, he would not have hesitated to ask. But the removal of armor was a task left only to a knight's most trusted—a dedicated page, squire, or in some instances, a wife. To ask this of Noelle was like entrusting his sword to a stranger's care.

She hesitated only a moment before she pivoted on a heel and slowly approached. "Tell me what to do."

"Pull off my surcoat. I lack the strength to maneuver it over my head."

Noelle studied him for a heartbeat. Then she climbed up on the bed to stand behind him. Her hands dropped to his waist. She tugged the heavy fabric up over his shoulders and eased it over his head. To his surprise, she managed to avoid all contact with his injury. The garment hit the floor at his feet.

"Now what?"

He bent at the waist, intending to remove his hauberk himself. But the pounding against his skull as the blood flowed to his head rendered him helpless. He grimaced against the pain. Through clenched teeth, he issued the rough instruction, "Guide it over my shoulders."

When she did as he desired, he took the heavy chain from her and laid it over the nearby chair. She vanished into the bathroom, giving him the opportunity to remove his sweaty shirt. It joined the soiled surcoat on the floor, and as water ran from the faucet, Farran stretched out on her bed.

Downy softness engulfed him, a stark contrast to the firm bed in his chambers that had served his needs for centuries. Savoring the mattress's embrace, he closed his eyes and relaxed. A bed like this spoke of luxury. 'Twas no wonder Merrick slept so soundly, if he too finished his day on feathers.

"Okay. I found peroxide in the cabinet. And a stack of gauze and tape." Noelle's voice came from beside the bed.

Farran forced his eyes open. He could not sleep here, no matter the temptation. 'Twas her bed, not his. This blissful respite he could not claim.

She nudged his hip with her knee, and he scooted over to give her room to sit.

"Oh. You're wounded here too." Her fingertips glided over his shoulder.

Looking down his nose, he inspected a short puncture he had not realized he bore. A jagged hole, about the width of a quarter, sank into the flesh above his left pectoral. The perfect size for a demon's claws when it lost the ability to hold its magical human form. He would have to inspect his mail come morning. Quite likely, the rend in the links was large enough to create a point of vulnerability.

He let out an annoyed grunt and pursed his lips. The hours required to repair his armor would eat a good portion of his morning.

"Well. Sit tight. This might hurt."

Her quiet murmur was the only forewarning he had before a warm washcloth grazed the lump on his head. He sucked in a sharp breath. Noelle's expression took on heartrending softness that stirred that unfamiliar feeling inside once more. He averted his gaze, unable to stomach the sensation.

"I'm sorry. Just a bit more."

She rubbed at the cut, dunked her cloth into a pitcher of water. Warm droplets rolled into his hair, then seeped down the nape of his neck. He closed his eyes to the tickle. 'Twas not bothersome. Nay, 'twas such a comforting glimpse of heaven he did not feel the touch of the cloth to his chest.

The slow rise and fall of Farran's chest told Noelle he'd fallen asleep. She dropped her hands in her lap and sat back to study her handicraft. Contrary to his conviction, he'd need to see a doctor in the morning—if for no other reason than to get a good dose of antibiotics. Until then, her bandages would suffice.

She traced a fingertip over a curling edge of tape and let her eyes drift across the broad expanse of his chest. A strange giddiness tumbled around inside her at the sight of hard muscles and taut bronzed skin. She'd never been so up close and personal to such blatant masculinity. The closest she'd ever come to a naked chest—let alone one as magnificent as Farran's—was her father's. Even her almost lover kept his T-shirt on during that brief disaster.

Her gaze tracked down to the shocking scar on Farran's abdomen, and Noelle surrendered to the part of her that was all woman. She deliberately forgot about why she wanted to leave, dismissed Farran's mental instability, and allowed compassion to fill her veins. For tonight, he was nothing more than a man. A man who had suffered too much for his thirty-some-odd years. A man who stirred something so profound within her, her fingers trembled as she reached out to trace the whitened flesh.

His skin jumped beneath her light caress.

She drew away with a wistful sigh and looked back to his face. Long lashes dusted his high cheekbones. The softness in his features told tales of a time when he hadn't always been angry. Faint crow's-feet at the corners of his eyes even hinted at laughter. Had the war done all this to him? Changed him so much? She'd heard stories about returning veterans, but nothing quite like this.

A shame it had affected him so greatly. But then, if it hadn't, she wouldn't be here admiring a stranger whom she ought to hate.

With a faint smile, Noelle brushed his long locks away from his face and bent over to press a kiss to his forehead. "Sleep well, Farran," she whispered.

She stood and collected her nursemaid's supplies. As she tucked them away in the bathroom, logic turned to torment. No matter what sympathy she felt for Farran, nothing had changed. She still needed to return the Sudarium to Spain and get home. This little holiday might have its perks now and then, but she had bills to pay. And her job wouldn't wait for Farran to come to his senses.

While they may have established a fragile truce this evening, tomorrow she had no choice but to shatter it. She had to make him understand she couldn't play along with his little game. Maybe he could live off veterans' pay and disability, but she couldn't. Wouldn't. The whole compound was nuts.

Or were they?

Her mind drifted back to the torc and the unexplainable way it came to be around her arm. Squeezing her eyes shut tight, she blocked the thoughts before they could root in. Nevertheless, the chill that had invaded her blood returned. She rubbed her arms to ward it off and braved a glance at Farran's sleeping form.

What if he isn't crazy?

No. Impossible. There was a logical explanation for everything. She'd been too angry to remember putting the armband back on. That's all. Nothing more.

Decided, she stalked back to the front room and the comfort of the couch. Scat Cat blinked up at her, then offered a wide yawn. With the remote in one hand, Noelle stretched out on the cushions, careful to tuck her knees around her cat, and flipped the television on.

As luck would have things, she found herself staring at the History Channel. Ancient ruins filled the screen, creating the picture of old world Israel and the al-Aqsa Mosque. The narrator's voice flooded the speakers:

Yet it seems the noble Templar may have been pardoned after all. Whatever they discovered beneath this timeless structure certainly contributed to their demise. But despite the Inquisition's torturous—and often successful—attempt to elicit confessions, discovery of the Chinon Parchment absolves them of heresy. If so, why did they feel the need to run, to dig underground, and vanish into time? Could it be they meet in secret now, and the Freemasons of today guard the truth?

She swatted the button on the remote so fast the controller fell to the floor. No more legends. No more unanswered questions. In particular, that one. It struck too close to home.

But the chill returned, as did the prickling of fear.

Maybe Farran wasn't crazy. Maybe Anne and the rest of them weren't really influenced by a god who didn't exist, but maybe they were on to something. Maybe they *were* the guardians of tradition and brotherhood that society had condemned.

Even so, that didn't explain Farran's wild story about her or why he'd brought her here. Nor did it explain the mystery of Gabriel's cursed piece of jewelry.

Possessed by the need to hold on to the tangible she reached down and scooped her cat into her arms. But the feel of his fur against her face only stoked her apprehension further. Scat Cat shouldn't be here. He should be at home, mewling at the door because she hadn't returned to feed him. Clearly this had been planned—her abduction. They'd brought her cat. The drawers in the bathroom held her personal effects. And while she hadn't inspected the dresser or closet, she knew without a doubt she'd find her clothes inside.

What kind of people kidnapped a person and brought everything important along with them? They treated her with kindness. They hadn't locked her away—Farran hadn't even locked the door. In no way did she feel threatened, beyond the fact she'd lost control of her decisions.

Anne had been brought here against her will too. Yet she seemed happy. Had they brainwashed her? Convinced her somehow all this was normal?

Noelle shivered as her thoughts slammed together in a mass of confusion. Each one took her down a dark path that only made her question all the things she couldn't explain further. And each one led right back to the inexplicable torc.

Desperate to find some fragment of understanding, she wrapped her fingers around the serpentine band of gold and tugged with all her might. As before, it refused to move. Helplessness engulfed her. Tears brimmed, trickled down her cheeks. She wiped them away, refusing to cry. She'd find a way out of here, a way back to the world of logic she understood. A world where jewelry laid in a box and waited for someone to pick it up. A world where men ignored her. A world where the most threatening thing she had to consider was what brand of cat food to buy for Scat Cat.

She had to leave, and there was only one way to accomplish that. Tomorrow she'd tell Farran about the Sudarium. The relic's hiding place was her ticket out of here. He'd be furious, but what he thought of her didn't matter. By his own word, he didn't want her. He ought to be happy he wouldn't have to interact with her further. Then again, all those things they hadn't done to her yet might come to fruition once he found out.

Nevertheless, she had no choice. She'd stand her ground until Farran conceded and allowed her to return the Sudarium to Father Phanuel. Then, when she managed to get overseas, she'd ask the priest for help.

CHAPTER 17

Farran walked in silence at Caradoc's side, the sun hot on his back. Ahead, the mighty wooden door to Clare's great hall stood open. Had word of his return reached this far? He could not control the nervous trembling in his legs or the way his heart skipped several beats at the thought of Brighid waiting within. How he ached to hold her. To run his fingers through her golden hair.

"You worry," Caradoc observed.

Farran nodded. "Aye. Two years is a long time."

Caradoc clapped a hand on Farran's shoulder with a short laugh. "Two years is time enough for a wife to forget her anger. Relax, brother. She has forgotten her imagined slight on her blood and shall welcome you with open arms."

Imagined, the slight was not. To Brighid, born of Saxon kings, the aid Farran gave to the Normans made him a traitor—even if William's war ended years ago. He held no hope she had forgiven the duty he owed to his best friend. His salvation lay in the possibility his service in the Holy Land would overcome the wrongs she vowed he committed to her kin.

He forced himself to smile. "Aye. 'Tis a warm bed I shall have tonight. And a willing wench." Glancing sideways, he gave Caradoc a teasing wink. "'Tis more than I can say for you."

Caradoc's usual good humor rumbled on a throaty laugh. "If Gabriel had not seen fit to allow those already married to retain their vows, you would not banter so freely." His expression sobered as they stepped onto the wooden planks that hung suspended over a rampart of wooden spikes. "What do you expect Brighid to say when you tell her what has happened?"

Farran chuckled for the first time since they had dismounted at the gates. "She shall be glad she no longer has to worry when duty takes me to the battlefield. She does not like it when my sword is called to arms."

"Nay, I cannot imagine she would. A mother does not wish to have her son fatherless."

Farran's heart stuttered at the mention of his son. Alefric would be six now, halfway to a man. He had lost count of how many times he had replayed the memory of their last summer together. The boy's laugh lived in Farran's heart, a sound that gave him courage even through the darkest secrets the archangels revealed.

"Come," he instructed Caradoc at the doorway. "Tonight we shall feast and celebrate."

The sound of feminine laughter drifted through the wide opening, giving Farran pause. He cocked his head and listened, unable to recall the sound. In seven years of marriage, he had never heard such gaiety. From the day he met Brighid, she had been as serious and stern as a matron. 'Twas one of the things he appreciated about his wife—he did not concern himself with the possibility she would flaunt and flirt herself into another's arms.

Anxiousness clamped a fierce hand around his gut. He swallowed against the ghostly finger that ran down his spine. "Brighid?" His call broke in the back of his throat, turning it into a hoarse rasp, as opposed to the strong bellow he had hoped for.

Caradoc encouraged him with a warm smile. "'Tis your home. Go in."

Farran strode forward, entering the shadowy darkness of the towering stone walls. Torchlight flickered around him, and the light laughter intensified. It drifted from the adjoining hearth room, where he and Brighid had spent countless evenings before a cozy fire. Farran followed the sound, his pulse aquiver with the way she would run into his longing arms.

As he pushed aside a heavy tapestry, he came to an abrupt stop. His wife, the woman he had taken these foul oaths of immortality for, sat upon a man's lap. She wriggled as he tickled her, squealed as his teeth nipped the side of her throat. Like a child, she beamed down at a face Farran knew only as *enemy,* and planted a kiss on Hrothgar's bearded cheek.

"Brighid!"

Two heads snapped his way. Hrothgar dropped a hand to his waist and curled his fingers around the hilt of his sword. Reflexively, Farran did the same. But his gaze remained fastened on his wife, frozen in place by the pain that lanced through his heart. "What is the meaning of this?" he croaked through a tightened throat. "You are my wife."

She possessed the grace to slide out of Hrothgar's lap. As she stood, Farran's bleeding heart splayed in half. He near choked at the sight of the swollen belly that protruded beneath her lavish gown. A child. She had sworn to him she desired no more than their son. He had heeded her request, content with his small family. And here she stood, laughing with the man whom he had gone to war against, proudly displaying the proof of her betrayal.

"Farran," she answered coolly. "You have returned."

Rage surged through Farran. He clenched his sword tighter, his muscles twitching with the need to wrest it free and slice off Hrothgar's head. Only the fall of Caradoc's warning hand stayed Farran's arm.

"A year late, I might add." She lifted her chin in disdain.

Farran glowered at Hrothgar. "Get out. I will not have your foul presence taint my home further."

Hrothgar's bushy upper lip curled into a sneer. With a gentle push to urge Brighid aside, he rose to his feet and drew his sword. "You are dead, de Clare. You stand in my hall. *You* will take your leave, or I shall remove you piece by piece."

Dead? Hrothgar's hall? This was Clare. Awarded to him by his uncle, Walter de Clare. 'Twas not Hrothgar's, 'twas not even Saxon land. Farran searched Brighid's placid expression for answers. But in her cool stare, he read all the things he could not stomach hearing. "You did this?" he asked in disbelief. "You told them I was dead?"

She shrugged. "What else was I to believe when you did not return?"

He ground his teeth together and bit back the bile that rose. Inhaling against the fierce desire to take her beautiful neck between his hands and squeeze the life out of her, he fought off the violent twisting of his heart. "You were to believe I would return, or someone would send word to you. As is custom. As you well know each time I leave for battle."

"Ah." The corners of her mouth turned with a faint smile. "I see my error. The noble Farran who runs with Normans expects his wife to remain loyal when she cannot stand to look upon him. Be glad you are dead, or Clare thinks you are. For I would have taken my knife to your throat, had you stayed."

He staggered backward, her blow more deadly than any blade of metal. Caradoc gripped Farran's elbow, halting his lunge at the deceitful pair. His bellow of rage strangled as Caradoc pulled him back. With a swift jerk, Caradoc spun Farran around to meet his warning gaze. So low Farran had to strain to hear him, he instructed, "You cannot. They cannot learn of our secrets when your wounds heal before their eyes. Fetch your son."

Farran hesitated, the war between what Gabriel demanded and his need for vengeance proved overwhelming. Brighid . . . He had loved her. Would have surrendered his life for hers. In return, she killed him more fully than if she had wielded a weapon. As heartbreak engulfed him, he bowed his head in acquiescence. Caradoc was right. The vile bitch could not be trusted, and though he despised her, he could not bring himself to take her life. If she witnessed how the Templar oaths changed him, he would have no choice.

"Where is Alefric? He will leave with me."

"He stays," Hrothgar countered.

"Nay, love," Brighid answered with a trace of the decency Farran had believed her to possess. "Alefric is his son. Let Farran take him . . . if Alefric will go." A rustle of her skirts said she sat back down. "He is in the yard behind the kitchens, Farran."

Unable to set his eyes upon her again, Farran strode from the room, through the hall, and out the door into the bright sunlight. He did not slow his step as he marched around the castle's wall, aware of the heads that turned to follow. Former servants made no move to acknowledge him, despite the fact he recognized several. Brighid's poison had spread to them; nothing could be more obvious.

Behind the thatched roof building where the scullery maids labored over hot fires, Farran found his son. Blond hair that matched his own swayed in the breeze as Alefric skipped a large rock into a small pile of pebbles.

"Alefric?"

The boy turned around, puzzlement written into his angelic face. "Aye?"

Farran's heart swelled with pride. He had grown taller. His skin spoke of good health. Strong, robust—Alefric would become a man to reckon with. Farran cleared the emotion from his throat and tried for a smile. "Do you remember me, son?"

Miniature eyebrows tugged together, and Alefric shook his head.

Farran dropped to one knee, his hand extended. "'Tis I. Your father."

A stubborn chin jutted forth. "My father died in the Holy Land. And if he lived, I would not wish to see him."

Another lance of pain stabbed through Farran. On a choked whisper he asked, "Why do you say such?"

Alefric's boyish features hardened into stone, and his blue eyes assumed a glint as sharp as glass. "My father is a traitor. He turned against my ancestors and disgraced my mother's name."

"Nay!" The bark broke free, against Farran's will. He stood up, clinging to the last of his control. "I disgraced no one. I did what was right."

For an instant, indecision passed across Alefric's face. Farran grasped at it and did something he never thought he would live to hear. He begged. "I live, Alefric. Do you not remember my face? The way we caught frogs in the creek the summer before I left? How I told you stories each night before you fell asleep? I am no traitor. You must believe me."

Slow, hesitant steps brought Alefric to stand before Farran. He tipped his head back, scoured Farran's face with inquisitive eyes. "You are Farran de Clare?" he asked quietly.

"Aye," Farran breathed.

As the fist around his lungs slowly eased, and he began to believe his son would embrace him, Alefric drew back. One tiny upper lip curled into a sneer before he spit on Farran's boots. "My father is dead."

Farran bolted upright in bed, the nightmare making him gasp for air. Sweat trickled on his brow, loosening the tape Noelle had used to secure his bandage. He ripped it off and tossed it aside. In the dim light of her bedside lamp, he glanced around the room, certain he would find Brighid laughing in a corner. When he found himself alone, he pressed a hand over his pounding heart and closed his eyes to the pain he could not escape.

Centuries had passed since Alefric's denouncement haunted his sleep. So many years he had begun to believe he had put the nightmare behind him. 'Twas Noelle's fault, this sudden stirring of memories he wished to escape.

The angelic touch of her hands, the compassion in her fawnlike eyes. She roused feelings he had not allowed himself since that dreadful summer afternoon in 1130. And with those stirrings, she brought his past to life.

Aye, indeed he had erred in staying here. He dared not spend another moment longer than he must.

He frowned as he realized she did not lie at his side. 'Twas long after midnight; she should be asleep. Had she used his exhaustion as a means to find escape?

Ignoring the dull throb behind his skull, he pushed to his feet and dragged himself through the door. If she had run, if she had played his weakness to her advantage . . .

The thought came to a skidding halt as he spied her asleep on the couch. Relief washed through him with such force he sagged against the door frame and expelled a heavy breath. She had not run. Had merely left him in solitude.

While he watched, she shivered.

Cool air kissed his bare chest, and he realized the chill in the room. Grumbling to himself, he crossed to her side. Touching her was the last thing he cared to do. Yet he could not leave her in discomfort. She had sacrificed her warmth, and he would not leave her in misery. Not when she had tended him with so much care.

Unwilling to wake her, he scooped her into his arms. His breath caught as she turned her face to his chest and nestled her cheek against his skin. Though he would not admit it, he liked the feel of her. The way she molded into him. The way one hand clutched at his shoulder as if she sought to bring him even closer.

Her cat padded along behind him as he carried Noelle to the oversized bed. With some difficulty, he managed to keep her from tumbling loose whilst he pulled down the thick mound of blankets. Yet when he sought to disentangle himself and lay her against the pillows, her fingers bit into his arm, refusing to let go. He leaned back to give her a perturbed scowl. Instead, he found half-open eyes looking up at him.

"Sleep, damsel. I have brought you to your bed."

"Stay," she murmured, once again snuggling in close. "I'm not scared when you're here."

Her confession bottomed out his stomach. For several heavy heartbeats, he froze, unable to make thoughts or words form. Stay with her. The invitation could not be more clear. Yet if he stayed, he could not be certain Alefric and Brighid would not return.

Through the haze of conflict shrouding his mind, one whispered word echoed louder than the rest. *Scared.* She was afraid. And that fear he alone could carry the blame for. He had brought her here. Had forced her to this place she did not understand. He could no more turn away from her request than he could deny their fated pairing. He owed her the security of her dreams, at least.

"Shh," he soothed. "Let go. I will stay." He slipped his arms from behind her and lifted a hand to stroke her silken hair. "Sleep, Lady Noelle. Sleep."

The fleeting realization he had called no one *Lady* since Brighid passed through his head as he eased himself into the bed beside her. When his head hit the pillow, she surprised him by rolling into his arms and setting a delicate palm over his drumming heart. Sensation shot through his body, tensing every muscle in an instant. He blinked against the pleasant contact and lay utterly still, afraid if he moved she would either roll away or snuggle even closer.

Which he desired most, he did not know.

After several never-ending minutes, the even cadence

of her breath brushing against his skin spoke of heavy sleep. Hesitantly, he set his hand on her hip. This was uncharted territory. He could not remember the last time he spent a night with a woman at his side. Even Leah, he left when the lust in his loins cooled.

Noelle, however, felt good. And the pleasant scent of jasmine that floated to his awareness beckoned him to press his nose to her hair and inhale deeply. He followed the urge, closing his eyes to the sweet comfort her warmth offered. Instinctively, he wound his arm around her waist and pulled her in tight.

CHAPTER 18

✝

Bright sunlight lulled Farran from the feel of soft curves melded against his body. He kept his eyes closed, unwilling to confront the light of day, longing to remain in the sweet haven of dreams. As he lay still, absorbing the full pleasure of a willing woman tucked within his arms, a quiet, feminine murmur triggered awareness.

'Twas not a mere dream. Noelle lay folded against his chest.

He cracked one eye open, hesitant to believe she would not fade away with the light. At the sight of her parted lips and lowered lashes, a deeply buried knot slowly unraveled. The sensation sparked pleasant heat within his blood, and he breathed in her sweet perfume. Against his thigh, he felt his cock thicken.

Taken aback by his body's profound reaction, he eased his chin free of her hair to better study her face. Lighter skin across the bridge of her nose and near her temple reminded him of the glasses he found so compelling. She had not worn them last eve, though he had not realized it until now.

He allowed his gaze to travel the length of her elegant neck, across a shoulder his palm could easily cover. The sensations stirring in his veins intensified at the discovery her fingers still pressed against his pectoral, and that tempting mouth nearly touched his bare flesh. He shifted a knee to ease the growing discomfort in his loins, only to have his thigh tumble against hers. With widened eyes, he shifted to inspect her positioning, and sucked in a sharp breath on finding her leg wedged between his.

Jesu. 'Twas no wonder his cock swelled. She fit against him as if they shared a night of intimate pleasure, not a mere eve with their clothes on.

He closed his eyes to an inward groan and lay unmoving. Sensibility urged him to disentangle their bodies. But the idea of removing himself triggered a far more primal response. His body tensed in violent protest. Something inside his chest that he could not name squashed in on itself. He could not move. He could scarcely draw a normal breath.

She stirred, drawing his eyes open once more. He looked down to find her fawn-colored gaze heavily laden with sleep. Yet as he held her quiet stare, those fathomless eyes drew him in so deep he could not hope to surface. The heat in his veins rose to intolerable limits, and the overwhelming desire to revisit the kiss they had shared before possessed him. Though it defied all logic, he must have one more taste of her. Must discover if the velvety slide of her tongue offered as much promise as he recalled, or if 'twas just a fragment of fantasy.

Rising to his elbow, he lowered his body into hers and eased her onto her back. She offered no protest, despite the way his knee slid between her thighs. To his astonishment, she did not encourage by shifting her body to give him room. Unlike the other women he brought to his bed, Noelle ignored the blatant press of his hips and offered only the faintest hint of a smile.

Even on his wedding night, Brighid welcomed the invasion of his body by lifting her head in search of his mouth. But then, he had learned not long after, he had not wed a maiden.

Farran ordered the wayward thoughts aside. Brighid had plagued him enough last eve. He would not allow her to intrude on this unexpected delight.

He dipped his head to Noelle's and brushed his mouth against hers, seeking entry. She parted her lips ever so slightly, her response as light as a feather's caress. What manner of kiss was this? Did she seek to play the innocent, or did she wish for him to stop?

Intrigued, Farran traced the seam of her mouth with the tip of his tongue. Beneath him, she shivered. The response rolled through him, vibrated down his spine, and stirred his swollen shaft. Fierce desire leapt to life, and he slipped one hand into the silken lengths of her hair. Curling his fingers against her scalp, he angled her head where he desired it and nudged her lips apart.

No more play. 'Twas time to make his intent unmistakable. If she wished to refuse him, she must speak now. For he intended to take full pleasure in the gift of waking beside her. He had spent too long away from Leah, and his body would not stand another moment of this ache.

Noelle met the urgent foray of his tongue with hesitant strokes. Unlike the kiss he recalled, she did not answer with hunger. The fleeting brush, the hesitant retreat, stoked a memory of the serving girl he had cornered behind the stables when he was but a squire of fourteen. She had tittered with laughter, blushed profusely, all evidence of her . . .

The meaning hit him with the force of a fist. *Jesu!* Noelle was innocent.

Stunned, he froze, his lips clinging to hers. *He* had kissed her in the adytum. He had been so affected by the tenderness his scar elicited, he had not given the stolen moment consideration. Yet now, as he replayed the brief encounter, he realized 'twas he who dominated. Even then, Noelle's response lacked the familiarity of one well practiced.

With a low groan, he succumbed to sensation he had never imagined possible. Untouched. Naive.

His.

It took every bit of self-control he possessed not to ravage her mouth and lose himself in her sultry flavor. With measured breaths, he encouraged her, told her without words what he desired. Proving herself a quick study, she responded eagerly. Velvety strokes sent his senses careening into one another. Moist heat that carried the lingering flavor of mint sent his heart thudding into his ribs.

Innocent. His seraph had never known a man.

Over and over, the discovery echoed in his mind, until he could not kiss her deep enough. Could not mesh himself close enough. He sank his body into hers, a slave to the tide of feeling that roiled inside. A light mewl that escaped the depths of her throat provoked his own hungry groan, and he gave in to the need to feel her flesh beneath his hands.

He slid his free hand down her arm, roamed his way up her ribs. His thumb stroked the fleshy side of her breast, and Noelle sucked in a gasp through her nose. He lifted his head to give her a moment to breathe. But holding her gaze, he covered her breast with his palm. Her eyes lit with liquid warmth. Her lashes fluttered against her high cheekbones. As he rolled a taut nipple beneath his thumb, he lowered his head and touched his lips to hers.

A crisp, demanding knock at the door stilled both his hand and his mouth. Curses, more vile than he would gift Azazel himself, screamed inside Farran's mind as Lucan called out, "Farran, the hour approaches noon. Mikhail orders your presence."

As Farran rolled to his back with a hiss, Noelle's mind reeled. Every fiber of her body pulsed with sensation. Every nerve ending arced as if live current ran in her veins. Her breath came in short, quick bursts that added to the rising heat in her cheeks.

He had kissed her. Not the aggressive pressure that came with his brief foray in the house in D.C., but something entirely different. An encounter Noelle couldn't describe with words. The only thought that rose was that he'd mastered her. And, damn it all, she didn't want it to end.

"I must go." Farran sat up and swung his legs over the edge of the bed. "Mikhail would not demand my presence lest something important has occurred."

The Sudarium. Noelle knew it in an instant. Mikhail had discovered her bag was empty. She bolted upright and fidgeted with the blankets as Farran gathered his belongings. "Farran, I need to talk to you."

"'Twill wait. We should have risen earlier."

"But—"

He glanced over his shoulder with a shake of his head. "Nay, damsel. There is not time."

If it was the Sudarium, she didn't intend to wait. She

had to get out of here before someone tried to tie her up and stuff her down in that stone maze because she'd duped them all. Legitimate relic or not, they believed in it. She needed to get Farran on the path of returning it—and her—before he sided with his friends.

"Let me go with you then." At least that way, she could plead her case before someone sentenced her.

"Nay, you were not summoned." He stuffed his feet into his boots and adjusted his jeans.

On a wince, she groaned silently. This wouldn't end well for her—she could feel it in her bones. Kiss or no kiss, by the time Farran returned, whatever had softened inside him would be as hard as coal. The truce they'd established last night would disappear. And she'd lose complete control of her fate.

A finality she couldn't allow to happen. "Farran, wait. Listen to me. You just . . . we just . . . I can't . . ." She floundered, then settled on, "We have to talk."

In the doorway, he paused to give her a backward glance. It was then she noticed he'd removed her bandages. Unbelievably, the ripped skin beneath pulled into a neat pink line. What the . . .

For a moment, a smile caught the corner of Farran's mouth, before it faded into passive nonchalance. "You have my apologies, Noelle. I swore you had no cause to concern yourself with my advances, and I broke my word. Rest assured, 'twas only a product of waking to find a woman in my bed. The kiss would have happened were it you or any other maid."

His words cut through her like knives. Sliced to the very core of her being, she recoiled. Lifting a hand to her mouth, she covered a gasp. Nothing. The kiss had meant nothing. While it had given her soul wings, to him it was little more than instinct. Testosterone overload.

Tears welled as he gave her his back and strode to the door. His steps held no hesitation, no indication his words were anything but truth. The proud lift of his shoulders, the way he didn't lift his eyes to so much as glance at her as he put on his sword belt, confirmed the harsh reality.

She knew men were capable of intimate acts without the involvement of emotions. Science proved that time and again. They lacked the branching networks in their brains to link everything together. But how a man could kiss with so much feeling and remain indifferent, she couldn't comprehend.

When the door closed with a firm *thump,* her tears broke free. Hating herself for caring, for *allowing* him to wound her so easily, she grabbed the pillow and clutched it tight. She knew where she stood. Knew he found her unacceptable. And damn it all, he was crazy—she shouldn't be this affected.

Still, she wept, as she had so many times before. Just once, she'd like to be desirable, to wield the power so many other women possessed. Even if her target needed psychiatric help, she'd like to hold the upper hand and the ability to bring a man to his knees because he found her irresistible. Dr. Martin, the forensic anthropologist who worked next door to Noelle's lab, could wag a finger and men fell at her feet.

Scat Cat leapt to comfort her by cleaning his teeth on Noelle's jeans-covered knee. On a watery sniffle, she lifted her head and dragged her fingers through his fur. "Scat, I want to go home," she whispered.

As if he agreed, he lifted golden eyes to give her a *mrrph.*

A shudder drifted through her as she met his unblinking gaze. What Scat Cat and she wanted didn't matter. In a few hours, maybe less, she'd find herself prisoner, and she had no doubts that Farran would make good on his promise to tie her up.

Possessed by the thought and her imagination's vivid illustrations of some dark dungeon amid the corridors below, she pushed Scat Cat aside and leapt off the bed to race to the dresser.

She had to leave. Before she couldn't.

As she yanked open a drawer and grabbed for a pair of clean jeans, pressure on her left bicep sent pain arcing down her arm. With a strangled cry, she clutched at the torc, attempting to pry it loose. Yet the more she pushed, the more fingers she tried to stuff between the band of bronze and her skin, the more the pressure intensified. Like hot coals pressed to her skin, heat inflamed her arm and scalded through her veins.

Unable to bear the torment, she dropped to her knees and doubled over with an agonized groan. Tears seeped from the corners of her eyes. She fought for the ability to breathe. Distantly, the memory of Farran's words rose.

The torc recognizes you. 'Twill use whatever means necessary to ensure you assume your place.

At the bottom of the stairs, where the cool air could temper his heated blood, Farran set a hand on the thick stone and let the myriad of sensations flow through him. He had wounded Noelle, aye. A blind man could have read the hurt reflected in her eyes. He had not meant to. Had pulled the only words he could find to mask the way his insides quivered. She had wanted to discuss their circumstance, and he did not possess the answers.

He lifted a hand to inspect the wound near his temple. It had healed . . . overmuch. With his soul so tainted, it should have seen the passing of a good three days before it began to scar. But this, like the flesh upon his chest he had glimpsed whilst he dressed, was undeniable. Could she have contributed to the healing?

He shook his head. She threatened all he understood. Ignited hopes experience told him were a fool's pursuit. Moments ago, he had yearned for nothing more than to lose himself within her embrace. He could have so easily forgotten his purpose lay in obtaining her oath. So easily discarded all but the physical pleasure.

And that fact alone terrified him more than any shade, nytym, or demon Azazel spawned. Noelle could make him vulnerable. Could turn him weak. With this accursed immortality, he dared not chance she might tear open the scars on his soul and make him bleed again. One betrayal he had survived. Another, he would wish for death—a fate duty to the Order forbade him.

Nay, the only course he could choose was the one he first assumed. He must obtain her oath, then take his leave. Before she could push him into senselessness.

He steeled himself against the twist of anguish that accompanied his resolution and strode down the darkened hall. It mattered not how much he craved her kiss, he would serve his purpose better without the worry she created. And once she said the oath, he need not worry about her safety—immortality would claim her as well.

With the light of angels in her soul, not even a Templar blade could take her life.

He pushed open Mikhail's door to find Merrick, Declan, Lucan, and Caradoc assembled inside. Added to his familiar band of brothers, he found Anne perched in a nearby chair, worrying her fingers in her lap. A frown tugged at his brow on seeing her, and he lifted an inquisitive gaze to Mikhail. "You summoned me?"

"Aye, we have waited all morn for you to decide to wake," Merrick teased. "'Tis high time you climbed out of bed."

Mikhail gave Merrick a scowl meant to scold, but humor crinkled the corners of his eyes, spoiling the effect. He openly displayed his smile. "Have you succeeded in obtaining her oath?"

"I am making progress." Farran choked back a snort. If indeed insulting her counted as progress, he had no doubt when he returned she would offer her vow willingly. Quite likely, he would find himself spending the rest of the afternoon trying to persuade her.

Mikhail looked unconvinced. "I will take that as a nay."

Uncomfortable, Farran shifted his weight and searched for a chair. Spying none, he assumed a position against the wall. Ankles crossed, arms folded over his chest, he waited for the reason of their assembly.

Anne slid out of her chair to stand before the men. With a hesitant glance over her shoulder, she sought Mikhail's permission. He granted it with a short nod. For several long heartbeats, she stared at her hands. Then, lifting her head, she fixed her sky-blue gaze on Farran.

Apprehension raised the hairs at the nape of his neck. Meaning filled her stare, a silent message full of warning. He jerked off the wall as her voice filled the small chamber.

"I've seen Noelle's death."

CHAPTER 19

Silence engulfed the room as the men waited for Anne to continue. Farran's pulse thumped dull and heavy, trumpeting the anxiety that rushed through his veins. He glanced at his brothers' faces, searching for some sign of disbelief, another who might give him reason to believe the seer spoke falsely. His heart drummed heavily when he found only shock on all but Merrick's. In their commander's expression, Farran read concerned acceptance.

In one heavy blow, Farran understood the gravity of his circumstances. He could not abandon Noelle when her life depended on his protection. No matter how he longed to separate himself from the confusing feelings she stirred, he could not leave her defenseless. She was his seraph. His responsibility. Until she took her oath, he could not entrust her fate to anyone else. Most especially now that the evil presences that had gathered beyond the temple's gates.

Elation blended with despair and turned his insides into nonsensical mush. He could not stay with her, yet he could not leave. To garner her oath faster, he must stay. To protect himself, he must leave. Damnation! Gabriel could not present him with a more intolerable situation. He had asked for naught of this.

"I saw only a brief flash." Anne's voice quavered. Her eyes darted between them all, refusing to settle on Farran. She breathed deeply, and her words came out in a rush. "She'll die at the hands of a dark knight. She's not afraid of this death, which leads me to believe she knows him."

For the smallest fraction of time, her gaze paused on Farran. He stiffened in defense, but before he could determine whether accusation glinted in her eyes, she looked away. The gesture, however, was not lost on Lucan.

Bolting forward in his wooden chair, he thrust an accusing finger at Farran. "You will kill her."

Fury launched through Farran with a catapult's ferocity. He lunged at Lucan, his hand on the hilt of his sword. Naught would make him harm a woman. He would take his own life before the darkness in his soul could drive him to such actions. "You speak your own death sentence."

Lucan met his advance by leaping to his feet. "Nay, I do not. You will fail to obtain her oath, and you will kill the seraph!"

Caradoc stayed Farran's arm before he could draw his blade. One angry jerk halted Farran in his tracks. With his free hand, Caradoc twisted Farran's arms behind his back and restrained him. Wanting naught else but to strangle Lucan for the insult on his honor, Farran twisted in outrage. His glare held Lucan's in open contempt.

As Lucan took another step toward Farran and opened his mouth to hurl another vile accusation, Merrick grabbed him by the collar. He hauled Lucan backward, separating the two men.

"Enough!" Mikhail's voice bit through the crackling tension. "You serve naught by fighting amongst yourselves."

Farran glowered at Mikhail. "His tongue begs punishment."

"Does it?" Mikhail's voice rose with authority. "Who amongst us knows the precise moment the change will come over them? Even I cannot say. It could be a knight, a demon, an insignificant shade. You cannot guarantee you will not kill her." His eyes pulled to Lucan, and he added in a softer, more meaningful tone, "Nor can Lucan be certain she will die at your hands."

Farran struggled for freedom, lurching forward against Caradoc's imprisoning hold. But his brother's arms held fast, refusing to grant him an inch of release.

"Declan," Mikhail addressed the silent Scot. "You keep your thoughts unto yourself. What say you to this?"

Declan pushed a hand through his auburn hair and rubbed a knuckle under his chin. "Given we canna ken her fate for certain, seems to me the guard you ordered upon her discovery should be enforced."

"Aye," Caradoc agreed from behind Farran. "We have neglected it with Farran at her side. 'Twould only be smart to return to it."

The idea of posting a guard outside his chambers struck Farran like a hammer to his knuckles. He would not have his brothers, not even Caradoc, overhearing what occurred between him and Noelle. He jerked against Caradoc's hold and barked out, "Nay!"

His reaction surprised even him. Shocked at the first thought that raced through his mind, he fell into silence. Why should it matter? He certainly did not intend to revisit another instance of this morning. All the guards would hear would be an occasional argument, mayhap his snores from the couch.

"Sir knight, calm yourself," Mikhail instructed. "None here seek to offend you. 'Tis only the seraph's safety we consider. Use your head."

Use his head. Aye, he could do with a good dose of logic. If only he could find it through the ridiculousness that haunted him after the taste of Noelle's sweet mouth. Saints' blood, he felt like a madman, best served by being locked in a forgotten dungeon.

He pulled in a deep breath and ordered his thoughts to behave. Noelle's safety was all that mattered. Had she been Lucan's, or any other man's, he would have uttered the same as Caradoc.

"Och! The lass should be told of her fate," Declan continued. "She canna resist an oath if she kens about her death."

A chorus of agreeing murmurs and nodding heads followed Declan's suggestion. Farran twisted a shoulder and freed himself from Caradoc's grasp. He shook his head in violent protest. Careful to keep his tone even, he argued, "You may have your guards, but you may not tell Noelle."

"All the more reason to believe—"

Before Lucan could finish the thought, Mikhail lifted a hand to order silence. He turned to Farran with lifted brows. "Nay? You do not think she would benefit from understanding the risk?"

Farran let out a heavy sigh and studied his boots. "She is already afraid. If you push her further, she shall run. Outside these walls, none can keep her safe."

"Then what do you propose, Farran?" Anne asked quietly.

He lifted his head to look squarely at Merrick. "We

shall teach her to fight, as you are teaching Anne. She is my responsibility. I will stay with her. The rest of you"—he glanced at each knight in turn—"shall look to her safety when I am not at her side."

On a decisive dip of his chin, Mikhail confirmed, "'Tis agreed then. Who will take the first watch?"

"I shall." Lucan stepped out of Merrick's hold.

Farran could not contain a derisive snort.

"That bothers you, Farran?" Lucan challenged. "Do you not trust me to protect the Order's treasure?"

The message was silent, but it gleamed behind Lucan's narrowed eyes and the tight set of his jaw. *I do not trust you with the seraph's safety.* Farran's arm twitched with the longing to slam his fist into Lucan's nose.

Before he could fully curl his fingers, Caradoc ushered him out the door. He urged Farran down the hall and into his chambers where he firmly shut them in. "Calm yourself, Farran. Lucan cannot help his words. You know the darkness makes him suspicious. As it fuels your anger."

An irritated hiss seeped through Farran's clenched teeth. Begrudgingly, he acknowledged the truth and sank back against the heavy wooden door. He buried his face in his hands, then dragged his fingers down his face as the fight left him. "His seraph should be found soon, or I shall have to strangle him."

The halfhearted threat elicited a chuckle from Caradoc. "What's this? Humor I hear? I have not heard you jest in so long, I know not what to say." Amusement fled his features like a veil drawn over his face. His gaze hardened. "If you seek to strangle someone, look to Declan."

Declan? What had the Scot done besides suggest the impossible? Farran queried Caradoc with furrowed brows.

Caradoc moved to his barren table with a slow shake of

his head and braced his hands on the scarred wood. "He is odd of late. Whilst you slept, he fidgeted in his chair as if he hides something from us. I know the injury I gave him has not healed enough to let him fight, so 'tis not his soul that concerns me. However, I worry all the same."

Farran shrugged. 'Twas not uncommon for a knight to seek the solitude of his thoughts when the darkness encroached. Sometimes 'twas easier to face the changing of one's soul when no one could observe. "He does not care for the fated pairings. You know this."

"Nay, 'tis something else. When Mikhail mentioned the return of the Sudarium, Declan volunteered to take it overseas. Too eagerly for a man who has spent the last several weeks in virtual seclusion."

"Could it not be he wishes a change of scenery? An escape from seeing the seraphs that do not belong to him? You know he took Anne's pairing hard."

"Mayhap. But when Mikhail mentioned Tane had begged to prove himself, even Merrick did not protest as much as Declan."

"Tane?" At the mention of the traitor, Farran bristled. "He stole a seraph. He should not be allowed within these walls."

"I agree." Caradoc straightened and clasped his hands at the small of his back. "But Mikhail does not. He has assigned the Sudarium's return to Lucan and Tane. Whilst he will not overrule Merrick's desire to have Tane banished, he insists Tane's sword is necessary."

Farran's mind snatched on to the one important factor. Dismissing all thoughts of Tane, he asked, "Lucan is leaving?"

A grin crossed Caradoc's face. "Aye. In four days."

"Thank the saints."

As the last of the tension fled Farran's body, he dropped into the solitary chair at Caradoc's table and tossed an ankle over a knee. "Tell me, old friend, how do you convince one who does not believe in the Almighty to take an oath that binds her into service?"

Caradoc's grin broadened and he chuckled beneath his breath. "Your work has become easier."

"Aye?" Relief flooded through him. The faster Noelle came to believe, the less time he would have to spend with her. At this point, the temple in Europe looked heavenly compared to spending another minute in the close confines of her room.

"Mikhail has granted Noelle access to the relics. The archangels have created a laboratory for her, at Gabriel's directive. He is convinced she will be unable to deny the proof that lies beneath her hands."

Relics. A laboratory. Farran could think of naught else that would please his scientific seraph more. He moved to his feet. "She shall enjoy it. When may I take her to the inner sanctum?"

"Whenever you wish."

"I shall do so now." Mayhap, in so doing, he could make amends for his earlier actions. He was not sorry he had spoken the words, but indeed, he despised the fact he wounded such an innocent soul. He moved to his feet, offered Caradoc a thankful nod, and swiftly exited.

Declan hurried down the stairs that led to the innermost heart of the temple. With a glance over his shoulder to ensure no one followed, he took the right-hand corridor. At the third closed door, he rapped three times, as he had been instructed.

The door swung open soundlessly.

He stepped inside, and a black robed figure shut him in.
Declan glanced around the room, noting four others also
bore the same ceremonial attire.

"You have reconsidered?" The voice that had approached Declan several weeks before came from behind
him.

He turned around, tried to peer through the heavy
folds that cloaked the knight's face and left only a scarred
nose and a ghostly mouth in sight. "Aye. I ken the truth of
what you speak."

The man seemingly in charge lowered his chin, allowing the hooded garment to completely shield whatever reaction he might have had. "You will give us your pledge?"

"Aye. For what meager time I am granted in this form,
I swear myself to the Kerzu's purpose of restoring the
Order's true design and eliminating those who threaten
us from within."

In unison, all five men lowered their hoods to reveal
faces he knew well. Against the wall, Eadgar, Aelred,
Godric, and Hrodgar stood unmoving. Men he had served
with when the last grand master, a pawn of the ignoble
Church, led them all to a slaughter at Saladin's hands.
Beneath a sun intent on burning them all to cinders, they
had fought unfaltering until wounds too grievous for a
mortal to survive forced them to fall down in false death.

Leofric, an aged man who had fought at the mighty
William's side and knew not the meaning of the word
dishonor, moved in front of the four men. His quiet demeanor, his stoic features demanded respect Declan
could not deny. He bowed his head in deference.

"What brought you to this conclusion, Declan?"

"They wish for the traitor's return."

"Tane?" Leofric drew back in surprise. He quickly

masked the shock with a thoughtful tug of his brows and chewed the inside of his cheek. Hands clasped behind his back, he paced the floor in front of the other four. "'Tis concerning news indeed."

He stopped suddenly, his gaze piercing Declan in place. "You understand you have been chosen because your soul is so close to changing?"

"Aye."

"And you further understand that we search for those who have fallen from our true purpose. That your work involves relaying what you discover to us. That, even if those you are closest to defy the oaths we swore centuries ago, you will hand them over to our means of justice?"

Declan swallowed thickly. Already Merrick had betrayed several of the vows. His very refusal to allow Tane's execution after Anne's abduction went against the Code. Traitors were to be removed from service by an archangel's blade. Further, the decision all four made to allow Noelle access to the relics before she swore her oath broke several more. To turn in those he was closest to bordered on a different type of treason. Yet he must do something to stop the ruination of the Templar purpose. He would not take a seraph, no matter the circumstance. Which meant his death was imminent. He could not leave this earth knowing he had allowed the Order to fail.

As if Leofric understood his torment, he smiled. "Worry yourself not with Merrick. He has sworn himself to Anne. His path is no longer our concern. Use only what knowledge you bring to this meeting to guide your actions when you leave."

Relieved from the burden of having to confess what he already knew, Declan breathed easier. From this day forth, this very hour, he would do what he could to guide his brethren on the right path. Or he would simply stay away. "My thanks, good Leofric."

Leofric gave a dismissive wave of his hand and his smile broadened. "There are knights amongst us who are not truly knights. 'Tis those we must locate. Now let us speak in more detail. We shall share what we know. Please, sit down." He swept his hand to a neat row of five chairs.

Declan and the other four shuffled forward and dropped into their seats. Perched on the edge of his, Declan waited, his life full of new purpose.

CHAPTER 20

✝

Noelle sat on her bed, her knees pulled up to her chest, her chin resting on them. She stared at the torc that poked beneath her short-sleeved shirt. Miniscule bands of red lay beneath the gleaming metal, evidence of the encounter that brought her to her knees. She tried not to think about it. Tried to convince herself the pain she'd experienced was a matter of her arm swelling while she slept.

In her heart, in the most scientific portions of her brain, she knew swollen tissue had nothing to do with the encounter.

Somewhere around the time she'd decided to give up the idea of fleeing and instead simply changed her clothes, the pressure reduced to little more than a firm press. That too defied logic. Inanimate objects didn't possess the ability to think or to adapt behaviors based on surrounding circumstance.

The damn thing behaved as if it lived.

A thought that made her want to laugh aloud. If someone had said it, she would have. The very concept was as fantastic as believing in the Tooth Fairy or sitting up all night and waiting for Santa Claus to shimmy down a chimney.

And yet, the torc, the pain she'd experienced, was as real as any lost tooth or present under a tree.

She turned to rest her opposite cheek on her knees and gazed out into the empty front room where Scat Cat lounged in the open doorway. Silence filled the small apartment, oppressive and foreboding. Any minute now, Farran would return, and she'd have to face inevitable punishment. Her stomach had balled up so tight over her imagined possibilities that even the pangs of hunger no longer registered.

If he didn't hurry up, she'd go crazy waiting.

Or she'd go crazy trying to figure out how a metal alloy suddenly acquired the high reactivity of a halogen.

A faint thump outside her door made her jump. Sitting bolt upright, hands fisted into the quilt beneath her, she stared at the door. He was here. Her freedom had come to an end.

Through a grimacing squint, she watched the door slowly open. As predicted, Farran entered. He took his time closing the door and removing his belt. Then, he turned around and his gaze blistered into her.

Damn, oh damn. If she had to be stuck with something magical, why couldn't it be a bottomless hole she could disappear down?

She closed her eyes, bracing for confrontation.

His footsteps padded closer. A floorboard creaked near the side of the bed he'd slept on. The mattress gave with his weight.

"Noelle?" His deep baritone washed over her, stirring

to life the traitorous butterflies in her stomach. "Does something pain you?"

Did something . . . What? Unconvinced she'd heard him correctly, she cracked one eye open, but didn't dare turn her head to look. "Huh?"

"You look pained." His hand fell to her shoulder, warm and weighty. Slight pressure from his fingers guided her to pivot in his direction.

Reluctantly, Noelle lifted her head and braved the fury behind his warm eyes. But when her gaze locked with his, concern probed gently. He wasn't angry. Which could only mean . . . he didn't know.

Relief unwound her tense muscles like a chain of dominoes. From the base of her neck to the tips of her toes, her body relaxed. On a controlled exhale, she answered, "N-no. I'm fine."

Golden eyebrows pulled together. "You are certain?"

She sat up more fully and found a tentative smile. "Yeah. I'm good. Could we have that talk now?" Anything to get the anticipation over with. At least if she spilled everything now, she could plead her case and stood a better chance of making him understand.

Disapproval quickly replaced his momentary concern. With his usual abruptness, Farran withdrew his hand and stood up. "Nay. I have been instructed to bring you to the inner sanctum."

Any relief she'd felt vanished. In one heartbeat, her chest collapsed, her stomach heaved upside down, and her limbs turned to jelly. *Inner sanctum* sounded foreboding. Like some tiny room where they stuck people they intended to forget. Maybe he *did* know. If not him, then someone else.

"Farran, I want to go home."

He inclined his head toward the band around her arm. "Say your oath, damsel, and I shall deliver you to your apartment."

Like hell. Though her pride still rankled at the prospect he couldn't fulfill his own set of obligations, nothing could make her say that Latin phrase after today. With her luck, it really *would* mean something, and given the unexplainable properties of the band around her arm, she didn't intend to find out what that was. She certainly didn't intend to explain why either. He'd take it as some sign she'd accepted his nutty story. If she let him believe that, who knew what else she might be obligated to after the fact, even if he swore differently.

Worse, she had a sneaking suspicion that torcs that defied the very nature of their chemical composition might not be the only objects to challenge everything she believed in.

Noelle settled for accepting his offered hand. She slid her fingers into his larger palm, and he tugged her off the bed. Yet as she extended a leg to stand, her foot caught in the tangled bedding. With a surprised squeak, she stumbled forward.

He caught her, but not before her nose flattened against his chest. The biting sting made her eyes water. Strong arms steadied her as she leaned back to rub the offended cartilage. "Damn," she mumbled.

When she blinked away her tears, she found him looking down at her. His eyes danced with amusement. "You have forgotten your glasses again."

Lips pursed, she extracted her foot and shook off his hands. "My vision's fine."

"I see that." He checked what resembled the beginnings of a smirk with a light cough.

"Oh hush," Noelle muttered. She plucked her glasses off the nightstand and slid them onto her throbbing nose.

To her surprise, Farran reached out and tucked a lock of her hair behind her ear. His fingers smoothed the strands as he dropped his wrist to her shoulder. Warmth filled his voice. "Would you like some ice? We can stop by the kitchen."

She didn't want his compassion. All it did was make her skin tingly. He'd made it clear he found her unacceptable—he shouldn't act like he cared. She twisted away.

Undaunted, Farran caught her hand. He took two steps toward the door, and Noelle dug her heels in. No way was she going to meet anyone with him. "Farran, really. I'd rather stay here. I'm too hungry to do anything else."

"Then you shall eat." He gave her arm a tug.

She grabbed at his fingers, intending to pry them loose. At the same time her nails grazed his knuckles, she felt the slide of cold metal around her bicep as the serpents shifted. The faint pressure increased, squeezing into her skin. Not enough to pinch, not even enough to make her wince. Obvious all the same.

For one heavy exhale, she froze in place. Her thoughts turned frenetically. Argue and suffer that sort of torture again, or follow and face a room of angry men. Possibly imprisonment. If she fell to her knees in agony, she'd have to explain to Farran. Explaining meant admitting the torc held power.

In a blink, she rushed to meet Farran's long stride. She couldn't admit that. Until she discovered what chemical caused the torc to react with her skin, she wouldn't give

Farran an ounce of room to feed her more fantastical stories. Not until she could fully explain them.

Each step she took closer to the door eased the pressure around her arm. By the time she stepped into the hall, all that remained was the faint sensation she might feel if she'd worn a necklace or a ring.

A shudder tumbled down her spine. Biting on her lower lip, she silenced a whimper. This wasn't right. Wasn't *natural*.

The sharpness of Lucan's gaze, combined with the stiffening of Farran's spine, drew her thoughts off the torc. *That* wasn't right either. From her brief observance earlier, those two were supposed to be friends. But Lucan looked as if he'd be perfectly willing to stuff a fist in Farran's jaw.

She slid her gaze sideways. Farran didn't look any too hesitant to do the same, for that matter.

What in the world?

Wordlessly, Farran led her past a stoic Lucan and held her elbow as he guided her onto the stairs. She shot him a quizzical glance, but the short shake of his head denied her curiosity. At the brief landing, he murmured, "'Tis not of your concern, damsel."

Of course—leave it to Farran to change the rules. Last night, he'd claimed they were a pair. Evidently, that only meant when he felt like sharing. She grumbled beneath her breath and trudged down the remaining stairs.

The rich scent of meat engulfed her as they stepped onto the main level. In response, her neglected stomach rumbled. She pressed a palm to her belly to ease the gnawing ache and did her best to ignore the delicious aroma.

Beside her, Farran's low chuckle rumbled. "Why did you not speak of your hunger earlier?"

Dumbfounded, she gave him a look that asked him if he'd lost his mind. "Um. You weren't here?"

"Nay," he conceded. "I was not. My apologies. Let us see to your meal."

Before she could think of urging him to get this meeting over with first, he ushered her through long rows of empty tables to a pair of swinging silver doors that stood at stark contrast with the simple furnishings of a dining hall.

"The men will not sup for another hour. We shall have to negotiate a plate from the cook."

"Negotiate? You have to negotiate food around here?"

Farran opened his mouth, but a deep bark from behind an overhead warmer cut him off. "Out! Out of my kitchen! How many times do I have to tell you the new menus will not be revealed until the meal is served?"

A portly, salt-and-pepper-haired man rounded the cooktop. He brandished a long knife. "I cannot have you coming in—" He stopped to openly gape at Noelle. Spluttering, his ruddy features reddened to deep crimson. The man recovered enough to exclaim, "Milady!"

Noelle grinned, despite herself.

"Milady, accept my apologies." The man dropped to his knee, long dark robes pooling around him on the floor. "I did not expect to find you here. I am Simon. Master of the kitchen." As he bent over his knee the way the men had in Mikhail's office, Noelle understood why this man did not wear a sword at his side like the rest of them. Where the arm that would have held it should have been, the sleeve of his robe was neatly pinned at his shoulder to hide an obvious amputation.

"Hi," she answered. "I'm sorry we barged in, but I'm awfully hungry."

"Of course." He stood with a flourish and swept an arm toward a long countertop of silver platters and earthenware bowls. "Whatever you desire is yours." His eyes rested briefly on Farran. "My apologies, Sir Farran."

In his typical churlish manner, Farran accepted the apology with a nod. He steered Noelle toward the counter and handed her a heavy plate. "Fill it, and we shall take it with us."

Her eyes widened a fraction. Take it with them? Maybe this wouldn't turn out half bad after all. They couldn't mean to lock her up and abuse her if they intended to let her eat. Unless this was her last . . .

She refused to complete the thought. Diving in to an array of greenery, she helped herself to a heaping salad. Moving down the long bar, she added a bit of shredded carrot, some crumbled egg, bean sprouts, and cucumbers. The finishing touch came with a generous dose of Italian dressing.

When she finished, Farran looked on with laughing eyes.

"What?"

"It appears Lady Anne did not err with her insistence there should be salad."

She glanced at her plate, then back at him. "Is there something wrong with salad?"

Farran fitted his hand in the small of her back and guided her through the swinging doors. "Naught at all. Only that it has not been a part of our menus for many years."

"I don't want to know." Reinforcing the statement, she plucked out a cucumber and popped it into her mouth. It hit her stomach like a rock, and she greedily stuffed another in.

"Aye, I assumed as much."

Too absorbed in the simple pleasure of eating, she vaguely realized the shift in her surroundings as they descended the central stairs. The cool air stirred her anxiousness, but she forced it down with a heavy swallow. If not for the patience Farran exhibited, and the relaxed nature of his usually harsh features, her fears would have mounted higher. Strange how a few days cooped up with a stranger could teach her so much about reading expressions. Two days ago, his lack of a smile would have made her swear he was angry. Now, the ever-so-slight upturn at the corner of his eyes spoke to good humor. Maybe not amusement, but something pretty close.

The look soothed her nerves and told her he couldn't possibly be leading her to a horrific fate. If anything, the restless brush of his hand against the waist of her jeans hinted he was anxious to reach their destination. He was always so still, always so in control of his actions. The motion of his thumb and the tap of his fingers revealed an additional layer of the man.

At the end of a long corridor, mounted torches cast an eerie orange light over a darkened opening in the wall. Two stairs peeked from the shadows, but the rest blended into the dark, creating the illusion they dropped into nothingness. Only when Farran took her by the hand and helped her down into the inky depths did she find it was merely a trick of lights. She could see, as well as she might under a full moon.

Noelle climbed down the narrow stone treads, delving deeper into a cavern of hand-carved glyphs and sigils. Icons of Christianity blended with images of the Templar. A Star of David, a horse with two riders, fleur de lis, and strange Gothic heads she'd never seen in any documented history—one by one they merged into a mosaic of art that could have adorned any medieval European structure.

They reached the long end, and Noelle froze in place at the image carved into the rock above her head. Twin serpents wound around each other, twining into three loops that matched the coils locked around her arm. Only, in this depiction, the snakes' heads lifted to stare up at a meticulous depiction of an angel with widespread wings.

"Come." Oblivious to her transfixion, Farran gave her a gentle tug.

She shook off the chill that weaseled into her blood with a short exhale and entered an enormous cavern that rendered her unable to breathe. Gold gilt columns extended several dozen feet above her head and spanned out across a carved and painted ceiling that rivaled the craftsmanship of London's Temple Church. Where stained-glass windows would have adorned the apex of the high arches, someone had even painted replicas in bright colors.

He'd said he was a mason—had he and his friends created this? Surely, they didn't possess this kind of talent. How could they have? Down deep in the earth this far, it would have taken years, maybe even decades, to work this kind of art.

And if they had, why on earth had they kept it secret?

CHAPTER 21

The awe that widened Noelle's eyes took Farran back to the first time he had stepped beneath divinely inspired work of the Order's masons centuries ago. He too had looked on in wonder, caught his breath at the carvings of masters. Marveled at the interwoven veins of gold.

Over time, the beauty became ordinary. Aye, he still experienced the same holy presence beneath the canopy, but seldom did he stop to appreciate what the Templar elders crafted long ago. Now, as he looked on, he saw the embellishments through Noelle's eyes. Felt the pride rush through his veins. He was part of this. It lived inside him, breathed as he did.

As it lived inside her. A fact she must soon accept.

Though he hated to drag her from beneath the splendor, he slipped his fingers through hers and pulled her closer. She would learn the truth no faster by gazing at the handiwork. What would change her mind lay beyond the distant pair of doors.

Echoing boots pulled her out of her daze before he

could utter a word. He looked as she did, observing Declan's approach. The Scot walked with Leofric, their
heads bowed in private conversation. 'Twas not the sight,
however, that gave Farran pause. 'Twas the room they
exited. Reserved for the singular purpose of offering last
respects to those Mikhail freed when their souls became
too dark to save, the room was forbidden to casual use.
The pair should not have been within.

Suspicion narrowed his gaze, and he watched as Declan accepted something from Leofric. Gold glinted in
the dim light as Declan held the object before his face. A
medallion, Farran realized, hung suspended from a rope
of leather. Though what the gold depicted, he could not
say.

A smile broke across Declan's face. He eased the trinket over his head, then tucked it beneath his shirt. Leaning a shoulder against a wide pillar, he folded his arms
across his chest and listened to whatever Leofric said.

Farran urged Noelle toward the relic room. Leofric
had long ago isolated himself from the rest of the Order,
swearing he could not tolerate the leniencies the archangels granted to the men. Of all the people Farran did not
trust, Leofric topped his list. He would not allow the man
to catch a glimpse of Noelle until she spoke her vows.

As he pushed the heavy door open and ushered her
through, her soft gasp cut through the air. He stopped,
half expecting to find a foe waiting in the shadows. But
fear did not turn her eyes to saucers or part her lovely lips.
Nay, she gaped at the wall of shelves, laden full with objects from the Templar past.

"Farran," she breathed. Rushing forward, she barely
tossed her plate onto a table before she caught a jewel-
encrusted goblet in her hands. "What is this place? This

is . . ." She trailed off as she turned the goblet bottom up. A manicured nail traced the molded metal, tapped against a large sapphire. "My word, this is museum quality," she murmured.

Turning wondrous eyes on him, she asked, "What's it doing here?"

He could not answer. 'Twas all he could do to remember to inhale. Beneath the low-hanging lamps Gabriel had arranged, Noelle's delicate features radiated the first true glimpse of happiness he had witnessed. Her bright smile held the sparkle of the jewels in her hands. Her eyes danced with the intensity of open flames. And in the radiant light, her hair held the glint of an angel's halo.

Jesu, she was beautiful.

His heart kicked against his ribs. Spellbound, he watched as she reverently restored the goblet to its place on the shelves and picked up an iron-handled dagger. Her fingertip tested the blade's sharpness, then slid down the shaft of metal to follow the path of the curved guard. As she tilted the tip toward the ground and sighted down the short length, his gaze dropped to her backside. Faded blue jeans hugged a heart-shaped bottom, fit snug around slender thighs.

To his amazement, he felt his cock shift against his thigh. Stunned by his body's profound reaction to her simple clothing, he clenched a hand at his side and ground his teeth together. 'Twas the relic room—she did no more than he had hoped she might. She gave him no reason to react physically when all she did was pick up trinkets.

Yet his blood warmed as he brought his gaze up the long lengths of her silken hair. It had felt so perfect against his palms. More splendid than any tresses he had ever touched.

"Where did you find these things?" Noelle spun around, incredulous.

Remembering himself, and his purpose for bringing her here, Farran cleared his throat. He nodded at a darkened corner where an array of modern metal waited. "I presume you find this to your liking as well?"

She let out a little squeal of delight and hurried to the assembled flasks, vials, holding tanks, and computer equipment. "A lab! Oh!" Her hands clasped tightly beneath her chin, she turned pleading eyes on him. "May I?"

"Aye. Gabriel asked that you might."

"Gabriel and his trinkets," she murmured with a light laugh. "Now I understand."

He was not so sure he did. The power of the room and the objects within it pressed down on him hard. Lightheadedness teased him with thoughts of what it might be like to let go and embrace his fated future. A sense of calm acceptance, of utter peace, swelled his chest. He closed his eyes, torn between the deep-rooted need to flee and the unacceptable rise of hope.

One thing he knew for certain—if he did not escape, in another moment he would forget his earlier vow to leave her untouched and take full advantage of those smiling lips. He backed away, edging closer to the door. It must be the room. Outside, all this feeling would cease.

"I take my leave, damsel. Enjoy your treasures."

He refused to give her opportunity to object and rushed into the spacious room beyond. Yet even with the door shut firmly between them, he felt her presence as keenly as if she stood at his side. Everything inside him called out for her, begged him to crush her close and mend the wounds that gaped and bled. He lifted a hand to the bump on his head. She had helped to heal his wound. Mayhap she could . . .

Nay. She could not. The passing of ten centuries had not sewn closed those jagged caverns. No woman could accomplish what time itself could not. What had transpired a moment ago was nothing more than pent-up lust produced from waking beside a woman. If he could trust Noelle's safety to another, he would rid himself of this unwanted desire in one short hour with Leah.

Sucking in a deep breath, he steeled himself against the storm that roiled within his mind and strode for the stairs. Declan. He must find Declan. Discover what that scene with Leofric was about. The Scot would serve as a much-needed distraction.

He took the stairs at a brisk pace and rounded a corner. The walls spanned out alongside him, identical to every other narrow hallway. Habit led him to the unremarkable door Declan claimed, and he gave the ancient timbers a heavy rap. "'Tis I, Farran."

Silence answered.

Farran tried again, using more force with his arm. The steady drum of his fist echoed down the hall. At the far end, another door opened and a dark head peeked out. A grunt accompanied the curious inspection, and the door closed once more, leaving Farran to confront Declan's silence alone.

He hesitated, cocking his head and listening for movement beyond. When he heard naught, his frown deepened. He had but seen the Scot moments ago. By all rights, he should have caught up with Declan on the stairs. Where had he wandered off to?

Turning away, Farran returned to the stairs and took

them to second floor. His gaze strayed to Noelle's chambers, but determined not to allow the tugging memory to take hold, he trained his focus on Merrick's room. There, he knocked with a light rap of his knuckles.

Anne pulled the door open in an instant, her smile just as quick. "Farran. Come in."

Damnation, her friendliness ground at his nerves. If she did not cease, he would truly come to like her. "Is Merrick about?"

He did not need to ask, for as he stepped inside, he found Merrick lounging on the couch. Much like Noelle's fat cat—belly up and eyes heavy with sleep. Farran marched to his commander's side, pulled the pillow from beneath his head, and thumped it against his belly. "You grow fat and lazy."

Chuckling, Merrick sat up. "I find matrimony suits me."

"Aye, as it suits a woman. Soon you shall be wearing skirts." Farran dropped into the empty cushion.

"Imagine that—Farran's grumpy," Anne teased from behind him. "I think I'll go lock myself in the bedroom where I don't have to hear you."

"Nay," Farran conceded on a grumble. "I shall not stay long. I look for Declan—have you seen him?"

'Twas Merrick's turn to frown. As Anne perched on the arm of the couch beside him, he let out a heavy sigh. "Has he disappeared again?"

"I saw him speaking with Leofric. I was not aware the two had become close."

Merrick lifted his head, his dark eyes sharp. "Nor was I. What did they speak of?"

"I do not know." Leaning back in his seat, Farran tossed an ankle over one knee. "Caradoc is concerned about him. 'Tis you and I who Declan chose to follow, and yet he says naught to us." He lifted his gaze to Anne. "Do you see his fate?"

She shook her head. "No. He's distanced himself from me since Uriel released him."

"'Tis my fault." Merrick stood and moved to the window. He gazed out at the late afternoon light, his back to Farran and Anne. "He believed Anne was his. 'Twill take some getting used to, I suspect. Caradoc is right to concern himself with Declan—I fear Declan will not come to me again. 'Tis best he report to Caradoc now."

Tapping his fingers on the upholstery, Farran considered Merrick's explanation. 'Twas indeed possible. Anne had changed many things within the temple, the least of which the menus. Many had yet to adjust to the discovery of the seraphs. Many more resented theirs had not been found.

But simple jealousy had never been Declan's fault. 'Twould not explain his sudden distance. For centuries, the six had fought side by side. Brothers beyond the immortal ties that bound. He would have, as Merrick suggested, turned to Caradoc for guidance. Instead, he kept them all at arm's distance and consorted with men he had never given a second thought.

"What does Mikhail say of it?"

Merrick turned around and shoved his hands into his pockets. "Mikhail says naught."

Farran grumbled beneath his breath. 'Twould figure Mikhail kept his thoughts silent. The archangels delighted in their mysterious ways.

"Come now," Anne chided. "Mikhail might legitimately know nothing. He's said more than once only Gabriel knows the Almighty's plans."

A spark of annoyance brought Farran upright. "Aye

and 'tis beyond time for Gabriel to share his knowledge. How are we to overcome Azazel if we are but pawns to the Almighty's game? We know not when Azazel will strike. Even his most trusted he leads around by the nose. We know not where the seraphs are. Yet we are told on their coming, the tides shall turn."

Anne's gaze slid to Merrick's, uncertainty playing on her porcelain features. He held her gaze as if weighing his options, then answered with a nod so brief, 'twould have been unnoticeable, had Farran not been staring.

The hair at the nape of Farran's neck lifted, his senses on sudden alert. "What secrets do you share?" He focused on Anne, his eyes accusing as they narrowed. "What have you seen?"

"I haven't *seen* anything," she answered, her voice merely a rustle of wind. Sitting taller, she continued in a stronger voice. "Which is the problem. I cannot find my sister. She won't answer the phone."

Farran blinked, dumbfounded. They spoke of seraphs and the Order's purpose, of the fate of all mankind, and Anne worried about a few unanswered phone calls? God's teeth, 'twas no wonder he had avoided tangling with women. They stewed over the most confounding things.

He dropped his foot to the floor and let out a disparaging snort. "If she is as headstrong as you are, I should worry not. She is probably—"

"She is a seraph."

Merrick's low interruption cut Farran's retort short. For a moment, he doubted what he had heard. No one knew the seraphs' identities. Even the prophecies stated the blood of siblings proved naught. One could be divine, the other uninspired. Yet Merrick's confident posture, the reassuring hand he set on Anne's shoulder, left no room for argument. Farran rolled the questions around on his tongue before settling on the one most likely to explain them all. "What do you mean?"

"They are not just siblings, Farran. They are twins."

"But the prophecies—"

Merrick lowered his voice as if confiding a great secret. "And on the day Anne received the serpents, Gabriel sent identical ones to Sophie."

Sophie. The seraph's name was Sophie. Farran's jaw dropped, and he fell back into the couch, speechless. A third seraph. One already known.

"I haven't been able to reach her for several weeks," Anne explained in a rush of emotion. "She lives in Malibu, but her cell phone's been disconnected and the apartment manager said she disappeared several weeks ago. Not moved out. *Disappeared.* And she said the apartment looked like someone had broken in."

Her emphasis was enough to restore Farran's ability to speak. Seraphs did not just disappear. They came to the temple or Azazel found them. "Gabriel says naught?"

"He changes the subject every time I ask." Her voice cracked on the last word, and she brushed a knuckle beneath her eye, smearing a stray tear. "I'm afraid something happened to her and he's afraid to tell me." She breathed deeply, struggling for control over her emotions. When she tempered them, she looked between Farran and Merrick. "I'd like to find her."

Merrick pulled Anne back against his chest, offering silent comfort. "I told her I would go."

What Merrick did not say, Farran heard all the same. The request lingered in his gaze, *Come with me, brother.*

Farran stood, torn between the oaths of brotherhood and the oaths of service. To go would defy Mikhail's order to stay near the temple. To refuse would shatter the promise to always stay at his commander's side. Worse, another troublesome thought rose—Noelle. Whilst the opportunity gave him ample freedom from her, a damnable part of his soul wanted to explore the giddy woman he had left in the belly of the temple.

He pushed a hand through his hair and went to the door, avoiding Merrick's heavy stare. He cloaked his indecision with the truth. "I swore to protect Noelle."

"I understand," Merrick replied.

Somehow, Farran doubted that he did. Merrick could not possibly comprehend the torment Noelle caused him. He turned the handle to leave, but Anne's sudden pleasantry stopped him short.

"Speaking of which, I told Merrick I'd see if she fits into my padded armor. Is she down in the relic room?"

"Aye." Farran almost shouted with relief. Unwittingly, Anne had given him a few more hours to absolve himself of the conflicted emotions. Hours he could spend exhausting himself with Leah. Once he had, he would return a sane man.

"Then I'll go get her." She hesitated as she slid off the couch. "Unless you had plans together?"

"Nay." A self-satisfied smirk tugged at Farran's mouth. "Though I am about to have plans with Leah."

Ignoring the sudden gray pallor to Anne's features, Farran entered the hall. His step felt lighter as he descended the stairs, the constriction in his chest not quite as tight. Relief lay around the corner. Freedom from the constant taunt of ill-fed desire. He had fed Noelle, he had introduced her to her private sanctuary, and now he would see to his own needs. God bless, Anne.

"Farran." From the landing, Anne's authoritative call echoed down.

He turned to find her bounding down the stairs. She caught his elbow, her blue eyes wide. "I beg you, don't do it. Don't do that to *her*. She's too innocent."

Annoyed, Farran shook his arm free. "Her innocence is precisely why I take my leave."

She reached for his arm, then thought better of it and dropped her hand to her side. "Don't. You'll taint her."

"Taint her?" he asked, incredulous. "What I do shall not affect her, I assure you. Do you think I intend to return and announce my whereabouts? Lest you inform her, she shall not know." He took the rest of the stairs in double time, anxious to be free of the condemnation that lurked in Anne's pleading gaze. Naught could convince him out of the drive across town. Two hours, no more, and he would find the man he had known only a few short days ago. The wild beast that strained for freedom he would chain no more.

"She will know."

Though her words were as soft as a whisper in the wind, Anne's proclamation followed him out the front door.

CHAPTER 22

✝

Beneath the bright intensity of the overhead industrial light, Noelle turned a curved slat of wood over in her hands. Time had worn splinters smooth where the thick coating of amber-colored pitch peeled away. She squinted at the exposed fibers and flicked off a bit more pitch with one nail. The faint, but distinct aroma of cedar drifted to her nose.

At her side, machinery that bore no manufacturer's labor whirred at twice the speed of her lab equipment. Another something she couldn't make sense of, but one she was grateful for, as its rapid output allowed her to skip the precious hours required to wait on carbon-dating test results. For this odd gift, she owed Gabriel a thank-you.

As she turned the wood in her hands once more, her mind worked at the discrepancies, snatching at bits and pieces, putting them together like a jigsaw puzzle that lacked the photo to illustrate the picture. Nothing delighted her more than anomalies, and this foot-long piece of wood contained dozens.

She glanced at the printed readout beside her and scanned the long column of figures. Her eyes jumped past the last line, the line she usually rushed to read. Once was enough to eternally etch the approximated date range into her mind. She didn't often encounter objects from the early Bronze Age, and what she did predominantly linked to the Egyptians. Moreover, the irony that this piece, dated from 2400 to 2000 B.C., paired too neatly with Farran's claims made her stomach uneasy.

Let alone all the other conflicting data.

Peering through the microscope, she squinted at the tiny piece she'd extracted from the object. Miniscule fibers separated with the evidence of water saturation. Evidence that supported her theory its curved nature and the heavier pitch along the horizontal edges saw water. Classic craftsmanship early fishermen would have used. Strangely, though, the final data included no trace of salt.

Not an oceanic boat.

Yet the trace minerals showed a high volume of sand. Grains she'd seen before, in the region surrounding Egypt, and further east near Syria. Slight differences separated the soil from the area's counterparts of Iraq, Iran, and Turkey—a lesson she'd learned through humiliation when as an intern she erroneously pronounced a recovered piece of pottery originated in what was now Baghdad. Her superior hadn't hesitated to prove her negligence by throwing the archaeological documents into her lap, documenting it as a piece discovered in an Egyptian pharaoh's tomb. For the next several months, he refused to allow her to work alone.

She chewed on her lower lip, absorbed in thought. There were plenty of freshwater rivers in the area, but again her data lacked the specific brackish qualities. For all intents and purposes, what soaked into this slat was as pure as a gallon of distilled water.

What could possibly have originated in the area and floated on a body of water large enough to saturate the splinters, yet contain no salt? She'd already proved the thing still floated, terminating the possibility someone had retrieved it from the bottom of a lake.

Even then, lakes large enough to support a boat in the region it indicated would have held a degree of salt.

On a sigh, she set the slat down and reached for the other object eluding her. She ignored the ancient word etched crudely into the surface. What it said meant nothing. Anyone could have carved *Jesus* for any number of reasons. Not to mention the name wasn't terribly uncommon.

The properties of this small plaque, however, paired too neatly with the slat. Almost as if they had been made by the same hands. Only, the plaque's age corresponded to the date on the Sudarium.

Another factor she didn't care to consider.

What intrigued her more was the same cedar/cypress blend of wood and the same disconcerting organic matter that paired the origin. If she worked with it long enough, she'd find the link that tied them together.

A knock at the door made her jump. She cringed as the plaque clattered to the floor. Bending to pick it up, she called out, "Come in."

"Hey." Anne's melodic voice accompanied the opening of the door. She moved to stand behind Noelle and peeked over her shoulder. "Hard at work?"

Noelle placed the plaque beside the slat and absently gave Anne a nod. "What do you know about these things? Are there records that document where they were found? Where they originated?" She tapped the shiny metal machine. "Do you know where Gabriel came up with this equipment? I'm not familiar with the model and my lab needs this. It works at double the speed."

At Anne's light laugh, Noelle looked up. Drawn from her immersion into the scientific realm, she struggled to find a smile and straightened her glasses. "Sorry. I didn't mean to be rude. I'm just preoccupied."

"I would be too." Anne grinned as she swept her hand toward the rows of shelves. "You should feel lucky. I wasn't allowed down here until I took my oath. You must be pretty special."

Noelle detected a degree of censure in Anne's words and shifted against the uncomfortable weight. "I, ah . . ."

With an elbow in Noelle's side, Anne laughed again. "Relax, I'm teasing. I don't know where Gabriel found the equipment, but what did you find?"

"I'm not sure yet."

"Well, put it aside. I'm here to free you from your prison."

Noelle lifted an eyebrow. "Free me?"

"Yep. Mikhail's ordered you to learn how to defend yourself."

Uneasiness tightened the base of Noelle's spine. Defend herself? If she needed defense lessons, someone threatened her. Though this place was more than a little odd, she hadn't felt unsafe. Who would with giant-size men and swords all over the place? "Um. To what?"

"C'mon." Anne slid a hand beneath Noelle's armpit and tugged her to her feet. "I'll show you. Swords are kinda fun. But I need to see if my armor fits you. Did Farran give you the tour?"

Unable to find her tongue through her confusion, Noelle echoed, "The tour?"

"I'll take that as a no." Anne grinned again as she opened the door. "Obviously you've seen everything down here—it's the nicest part of the temple. You'll want to stay away from the men's chambers. At least until you're oathed. But upstairs, on the main level, you can go pretty much wherever you please."

With little choice but to follow, Noelle struggled to match Anne's quicker stride. Still caught up in the oddities of the relics, her mind twisted in such a mess she could only dumbly repeat Anne. "The men's chambers?"

"Upstairs. The stone corridors."

"Oh." Inwardly, she cringed. A fool could have made the connection, given all the doors. "Right. I wasn't thinking."

"It's a little hard to do that when you first get here."

Anne made it impossible for Noelle to berate herself. Under the redhead's continual smile and her easy laughter, Noelle's embarrassment faded. She fell into a comfortable pace, and mounted the stairs at Anne's side. Her curiosity got the better of her, and slipping Anne a sideways glance, she asked, "Why did you stay?"

"The relics. I wanted to know what they found." With a conspiratorial wink, she added, "And Merrick was good in bed."

Her bluntness sent a rush of heat to Noelle's cheeks. She dipped her head, hiding her blush with her hair, and grabbed for an appropriate response.

Anne saved her once again with a reassuring squeeze of Noelle's forearm. "I'm sorry. I've made you uncomfortable."

"N-no," Noelle stammered. "It's okay. I'm just not used to such honesty."

"The truth is, I wanted to stay." Anne rounded the landing and pointed at the stairs that led to the main level. "It took me awhile to realize I wanted to stay forever, but I was never opposed to a short visit. I had to fall in love before I knew I couldn't leave."

"And you don't miss home?"

"This is home. I hope you'll come to think of it that way too. It'd be nice to have another woman around."

Doubtful. She might have an amazing lab to play in and a room full of artifacts that could occupy her for months, but it didn't change the fact home was in Washington, D.C. Unlike Anne, Noelle didn't have a guy trying to convince her to stay either.

She stumbled as she took a step. What the hell was she thinking? Even if she did have a man sweet-talking her, she wouldn't consider staying in this place. She wasn't that desperate.

Anne grabbed Noelle's elbow, steadying her. "You okay?"

Noelle summoned a grin, along with a shrug. "Just clumsy."

"Well, we'll work on that. We can't have you stabbing yourself in the thigh."

Another grin stirred Noelle's humor, and she found herself laughing. "That would be my luck." Although, to her credit, when she'd taken fencing in high school, she hadn't been half bad, even though she hated every minute of it.

"If that happens, Farran will never forgive me. Here, come this way. This is the entertainment room. Over there"—Anne pointed at the arches Farran had led her through earlier—"is the dining hall. Meals are served at six, twelve, and six. Right now, they're pretty simple, but I'm working with Simon on some new chefs and new menus. Give me another month, and meals will be edible."

Noelle glanced around at the conglomeration of over-sized sofas, recliner chairs, and rough-hewn wooden tables. The wide-screen television at the far end sat dark, as unused as the furniture. Strange they'd have such niceties and rarely use them. Seth was always carrying on about football and beer and having the guys over.

Her expression must have revealed her confusion, for Anne explained, "The men haven't ever really embraced modern conveniences. They shoot some pool, but they'd rather train in the yard when they aren't out watching the gates."

"The gates?"

"Yes." Anne opened her mouth to say more, then covered her words with a smile. "I'll let Farran explain the gates."

Noelle shrugged. Probably better not to hear more talk of the supernatural and unexplainable coincidences. Beyond the fact her mind had experienced more than enough for one day, the idea of spoiling an amicable conversation left a stale taste in her mouth. As long as she could pretend Anne was normal, she could like her.

"Let's go see if my armor fits you, and I'll show you the other things on the way to the indoor commons." Without waiting for Noelle's response, she hurried her up the stairs to their neighboring rooms. "Merrick's already waiting on us," she said as she motioned Noelle through the door.

Absent or not, Merrick's presence hit Noelle like a physical force. His cologne lingered in the air. A shirt lay draped across the back of a chair. In the corner, a tall stand supported chain mail that matched Farran's, complete with an identical white surcoat. Noelle's gaze pulled to the couch where an afghan lay in disarray. Beside it, tucked against the foot of the couch, two pairs of socks nestled together—one fuzzy and feminine, the other large and masculine.

Each way she turned, something that marked this room as much his as Anne's caught her eye. A belt on the bed, the open wardrobe that exposed both his clothes amid Anne's skirts. In the bathroom, their razors sat side by side—Anne's pink and lavender, Merrick's chrome and black.

The merging of belongings struck a chord of longing in Noelle's heart. What would it feel like to share everything with a man? To have someone be as much a part of life, as all the things that identified someone? They slept in the same bed, a treat Noelle had enjoyed for a scarce few minutes before Farran spoiled it all. How would it feel to spend every morning waking to kisses like the one he'd shared with her?

"Over here."

Anne's voice pulled Noelle from the wanderings of her mind, and she followed the sound to a small closet in the corner of the bedroom. Inside, Anne tugged on a heavy padded vest. She thrust it at Noelle with a grin. "Try this."

One look at the garment, and Noelle knew it wouldn't fit. Anne's bust exceeded hers by at least a full size. No way would that thing begin to do anything else but hang like a bulky sack. Nevertheless, she held her arms out and allowed Anne to slip it on her. Her fingers quickly worked the laces along the sides, snugging the strands of leather tight. When they would close no further, she stepped back with a frown.

"Well, it's a little big. But it'll work until Raphael can have one made in your size."

It would work? Noelle glanced down at the weighty covering with doubt. If she had to execute any move of skill, the darn thing would fall down to her elbows. A wry smirk tugged at her mouth. She shouldn't care. It'd just be another example of how terribly she lacked grace.

"Now what?"

"Now we go to the yard. We'll work with wooden swords today. But Merrick won't wait to pair you with metal. A couple days at most, and you'll have your own short sword."

Joy. She'd been overjoyed to quit fencing and be free of all the aches and pains. But this had to be better than sitting in her chambers alone all night. If relearning swords gave her company until she could tell Farran about the Sudarium and go home, she'd put up with it.

Anne elbowed open the door. "Merrick won't take it easy on you just because you're new either. Expect to go to bed sore."

"I'm really not too sure about this, Anne," Noelle protested at the top of the stairs.

Anne hesitated and looked over her shoulder. Her blue eyes hardened. Her voice lost its lighthearted lilt. "You are a seraph, Noelle, whether you want to believe it or not. Azazel, the Lord of Darkness, will do all he can to kill you. Farran has sworn to protect you, and you were chosen to save him. To do so, you must protect yourself."

An unexplainable shudder wafted down Noelle's spine and needled particles of ice through her veins. Anne's tone, the absolute conviction in her expression, left little room to accuse her of being crazy. Yet she couldn't possibly be right. The Lord of Darkness? Even what little Noelle recalled of Sunday school said Satan was the master of evil. For that matter, she couldn't even remember hearing the name Azazel.

"Hurry, there's a movie on I want to see tonight. It starts in an hour." Anne's joviality returned along with her bright smile. She rushed down the stairwell, forcing Noelle to take the stairs in double time.

As they reached the main floor, the front door swung open and a dark-haired man stepped inside. He glanced around, his eyes darting wildly until they came to rest on Anne. For a moment, he looked as if he might smile. But the pull at the corners of his mouth disappeared as quickly as they stirred. "Is Merrick present?"

Anne answered with a slow, tenacious nod. "He is. But it wouldn't be wise to approach him, Tane. Can I help?"

Tane twisted his hands together, then shoved them into his pockets. He shifted his weight, looked at his boots. "I wanted to discuss the money."

"Oh that." Anne chuckled softly. "Don't worry about it, Tane. I'll talk to Merrick and get it for you. I promise. But you should go. Before someone sees you here."

Hope lit vivid green eyes, and the smile he'd tried to contain broke free. "You will contact me?"

Moving closer, Anne gave his arm a squeeze. "Of course. What you're doing's noble. Merrick knows that. He just doesn't want to see you."

"Very well then, milady. I shall await your call." With only the briefest curiosity, he looked to Noelle before vanishing out the door.

Noelle turned to Anne, eyebrows lifted.

"That was Tane." She chewed on her lower lip, her expression tight with concern. After several seconds of silence, she explained, "The men here all suffer from tragedy. The longer they live, the more difficult it becomes to separate from those issues. It's why Farran's always angry. Why Lucan is suspicious . . ." She trailed off, her stare fastened on the closed door. "And why Tane kidnapped me."

"Kidnapped you?" Disbelief lifted Noelle's voice several decibels. "He *kidnapped* you, and you're helping him? My word, Anne, just what kind of crap did they feed you here to make you think that's okay?"

"You'll understand in time." With a wag of her fingers, she beckoned Noelle down the hall. "Tane is trying to open a shelter for homeless teens. The Order has money like you wouldn't believe. He can't help himself, and working with those kids gives him purpose. I've seen how they respect him. He can make a difference."

"But . . ." Unable to find the words, Noelle trailed off with a tight frown.

"Farran's good to you, isn't he?"

The abrupt subject change caught Noelle off guard. At once, the memory of his kiss, of the weight of his body pressing into hers, slammed into her. She shivered with the impact, recalling just how good Farran could be when he wasn't carrying on about demons and angels. "Sometimes," she conceded in a whisper.

"Like Tane, like most everyone here, Farran's a good man. He's a little rougher around the edges than the rest of them. But give him time. Let him prove himself to you. Like Tane, he can make a difference in your life. The real man will show through if you give him opportunity."

Give him opportunity? Did that mean she could do something that might make him find her more desirable? She flinched at the idea. Even if she wanted him to find her irresistible, she didn't have the slightest clue how to accomplish that. When it came to men, they were as foreign as that piece of wood in the basement.

The twisting of her heart made the obvious unavoidable. Reluctantly, she surrendered to the illogical realization she *did* want to make a difference to Farran. She couldn't keep him, couldn't abide by his beliefs, and yet every time he stood within two feet of her, her heart did a little tap dance against her ribs. And the kiss, that incredible kiss . . . She'd give her eyeteeth for this morning to have meant something.

From the corner of her eye, she studied Anne as they walked down the hall. She knew Farran. She knew *men*. Maybe Anne could give her some advice.

A blush crept in fast and furious, negating the thought. No, aside from Farran, Anne was the last person Noelle wanted to look stupid in front of. She'd only feel more insecure if she confided her naivety. Better that she say nothing at all. In a few days, it wouldn't matter. She wouldn't be here to care. Farran, along with Anne, would be strangers she'd leave in a dark corner of her memory.

They passed the commons, stalked down a wide carpeted hall, and entered a padded room the size of a gymnasium. Merrick sat in a folding chair in the middle, two wooden swords lying across his lap. He stood, his eyes only for Anne as they approached, and again Noelle felt the foreign pang of yearning. To be looked at like that, like no one else was present . . . She surrendered to a wistful, inward sigh.

"Are you ready, Noelle?"

Before she could answer, Merrick arced an arm across his body, and the flat length of the makeshift weapon thumped into her stomach. She doubled over, gasping for breath.

"Use that to remember. Never allow your opponent to anticipate your actions," Merrick instructed in a low, even tone.

CHAPTER 23

Farran rose and dusted his hands on his jeans. The crisp winter breeze stirred his hair. In the chill, he caught the scent of snow. Christmas would come again. Each year it passed, another day of celebration and merriment he did not share. This year would be no different.

He turned his face to the full moon, seeking answers in its silver glow. For centuries, he had sated his physical needs in exchange for a handful of coins, unashamed. Not even the Order's code of chastity, nor the punishment for breaking it, gave him pause. He was a man. He would suffer the temporary loss of sword and robes to keep himself sane. And oft he had.

Yet Anne had run him through like a pike.

She will know.

So deeply did the claim puncture, the prospect of a stolen hour of escape with Leah soured.

'Twas what brought him to the gardens to sit in the dark. He should not care whether he wounded Noelle. It should matter not if the truth of his preferences moistened her fawnlike eyes.

Still, for a reason that eluded him, he did not wish to cause her pain. He knew only that he wished to keep intact the happiness she had shown him.

Make it blossom.

A realization that shook him to the core, for it rang too similar to the innocent hope he had harbored, a long-ago summer, with a maid named Brighid.

He blew out a breath, watched it cloud before him. The breeze stirred again, and he embraced the cold. Icy fingers slid beneath his clothes, across his skin, and into his veins where the biting sting tempered his overwarm blood.

Lowering his gaze, he scanned the perimeter's iron gate. Beyond, the rustle of dried leaves set his senses on alert. Azazel could send his foolish shades. He could order all the horrific nytyms to attack. He could even instruct his shape-shifting demons to aid his foul knights. Farran would meet them all with a smile to match their wickedness. But Azazel would not harm Noelle. Not as long as breath remained in Farran's body. He would walk with Azazel's minions in hell before a claw could touch her pretty face.

The simmering of anger stirred in his veins, and he looked away. Tonight they would fight again. But not now. Not yet.

A shadowy flicker behind a distant window made him squint. Silhouettes faced off, swords in hand. In a dance he knew by heart, they circled slow. A hand thrust forth. A body jerked back. Long hair slashed sideways, and the evader returned the strike.

Curiosity prickled his skin. Did Noelle practice? He

shuffled a heel against hard-packed earth, fighting the pull of discovery. Before his eyes, the figures came together in a clash of blades, and one stumbled back. Fell.

Like sparks set to dried rushes, his temper flared. He ground his teeth together and stormed across the lawn. The rear door gave easily beneath the slap of his palm, and he stalked down the hall to the indoor training room. If 'twas her, he had words to say. She was too inexperienced to parry thus.

As the doors swung open, Farran halted in place. Where he had expected to find his seraph still in a crumpled heap, she stood toe-to-toe with Anne. Pulled back in a ponytail that brushed her waist, her long hair swayed with the graceful rhythm of her body. Perspiration dampened straying strands that clung to her face, and her cheeks were flushed. Rosy, to match her parted lips.

To his amazement, exhaustion did not slur her actions nor cling to her expression. If his eyes did not mistake him, behind her glasses, excitement gleamed.

Farran stood unmoving, counting off the elementary paces in his head. Parry, back, parry, thrust, parry . . . Feint? Where had she learned to feint?

Anne stumbled against her own force, Noelle's surprise maneuver catching her off guard. She rose, her back meeting the edge of Noelle's blade. Beaten, Anne set her hands on her knees and panted.

"Again," Merrick barked. "'Tis twice she has caught you in that trick, Anne. Use your head."

Twice. 'Twas not a lucky step. Pride swelled through Farran. With the sudden infusion, his heart thumped hard. A heavy beat he would have never imagined possible, yet one he could not hope to deny. With the next weighty drum, his awareness of Noelle intensified. The way her body arced and twisted, the way her hair swung wild. With relentless persistence, she pursued Anne, each clack of her wooden blade drowning him deeper in all she was. Simple scientist, innocent maid, aggressive warrior, gentle healer—he knew not which he preferred, but he craved them all.

She possessed so many different layers. And God help him, he wanted to peel every fascinating one away until she stood before him, utterly bare.

"She is good. 'Tis as if her arm is blessed by the Almighty," Merrick commented at Farran's side. "Tomorrow, I shall give her a real blade."

Unable to tear his eyes off the vision of angelic beauty before him, Farran could only murmur, "Aye." Indeed, she took to the sword naturally. A fact that contradicted the clumsiness he found so inexplicably enchanting.

Noelle was all too aware of Farran's unexpected presence, and her nerves kicked in. She struggled to keep her focus on Anne and the effortless way she wielded her wooden sword.

She'd been doing good, damn it. Good enough she didn't feel quite as insecure around Anne. What Merrick had instructed after his surprise attack had somehow connected with her former lessons, and like before, her scientific mind clicked them in place. Swordsmanship was like physics. The calculations only a derivation of theories. Once she'd grasped the hang of the heavier weight in her hand, everything else came naturally.

Even her clumsy feet recalled the long-ago dance.

But now, with Farran watching, the cadence in her mind

stuttered . . . along with her arm. She hesitated a split second too long, giving Anne the advantage. Anne swept in to drive her sword down on Noelle's wrist.

A startled cry escaped at the biting smack, and Noelle's hand faltered. Her fingers released. The blade clattered to the floor.

"Enough," Farran barked. His harsh tone softened as he added, "For tonight. Noelle grows weary."

A low growl threatened to possess her. Weary? How the hell would he know? She had another few rounds left in her yet.

In defiance, she picked up her sword and faced Anne in an open stance. Anne's slight head shake, however, terminated their spar. "Go with him," she urged quietly.

Noelle turned around to find Farran marching toward her, his features tight. He stopped a foot away and grabbed at her smarting wrist. Strong fingers probed with the gentleness she'd come to cherish. He chewed at his lower lip, turned her arm over to inspect the opposite side.

When he lifted his head, and his eyes met hers, Noelle's breath caught. Annoyance didn't create the grimness of his mouth or the deep furrow between his golden eyebrows. No, concern gleamed within those ale-brown pools. Bright enough it burned.

"Can you turn it?"

The question jarred her. She blinked to ward off the power of his unsettling stare. "What?"

Farran bounced her fingers in his. "Your wrist."

"Oh!" As heat rushed to her cheeks, she hastened to tug her hand free. "Yeah. It's just a bruise. I'll be fine."

He looked unconvinced. "'Twill swell. 'Tis best if we ice it."

As if she were some fragile doll apt to break under too

much force, he moved around her carefully. Never once did his fingers stray from her skin. His hand slid to her elbow, around her ribs, then settled into place at the small of her back. As he took her free hand in his, his gaze held hers, conveying messages she couldn't begin to interpret. Whatever they were, they possessed him, and the light within his mesmerizing eyes took on a darker hue. She shivered against the sudden wash of warmth that seeped into her where they touched. Butterflies seized her stomach. Tingles broke out in their fluttering wake, and Noelle's pulse skipped several beats.

Dumbstruck, she allowed him to lead her into the hall. He didn't hurry. Had abandoned his usual purposeful stride. In a manner that defied all she knew about Farran . . . he strolled. As if he would be content to have their walk last all night.

"Where are we going?" she asked to break the thick silence.

"To your rooms." His rich baritone took on a rough, hoarse edge. He cleared his throat and avoided her curious gaze. "Have you practiced swords before?"

"I was on the high school fencing team my sophomore and junior year. Why?"

"You are gifted in the art." Before he fell quiet, he brushed his hand across the small of her back.

She joined him in silence as he escorted her to the kitchen for a bowl of ice, uncertain how to react, or even what to think of this side of him he rarely let her see.

Up the stairs he led her, then through her entry and into the shadowy confines of her bedroom. There, he turned her loose and clicked on the bedside lamp. He lingered over the nightstand, his chest expanding as he pulled in a deep breath. Noelle caught the closing of his eyes before he straightened and looked at her once more. His features were normal again—an impassive wall of tight lines and stiff muscles. Whatever troubled his thoughts, he'd wrestled into place.

Immediately self-conscious, Noelle rushed to excuse him from a chore he obviously didn't relish. "Really, I'm fine, Farran. I can take care of this myself."

"I know you can," he snapped. The same harsh rasp clung to his words. It scraped across her, a strangely pleasant chafe of sand and gravel that tightened her throat.

"Sit." He motioned to the bed.

When she did, Farran retreated into the bathroom. Cabinets banged, drawers rattled. The rush of water replaced the rush of her blood in her ears. What had happened to him? Why was he treating her like a . . . She frowned. Like a princess?

Before the answers could take shape, Farran reappeared and knelt at her feet. He picked up her arm to examine it under the light. "It already swells."

"Really, it's fine." Noelle tugged on her wrist, the heat of his fingers unbearable.

Farran held fast and shot her a scolding lift of his eyebrows.

Resisting the urge to squirm, Noelle resigned herself to Farran's ministrations. He wrapped the ice in a water-soaked washcloth, then situated it around her wrist. His hands worked quickly, his touch light, yet laden with tenderness. Using long strands of bandage tape, he secured the loose ends and fastened the wrap in place. Precise. Meticulous—the compress fit snug around her defined bones, yet loose enough it didn't create further pain.

Finished, he rocked back on his heels and caught her free hand in his. A smile touched the corners of his eyes.

"Remove it in fifteen minutes. If you wish to bathe then, the hot water will aid further." Standing, he gave her good arm an easy tug. "Up. I shall help you with your laces."

She rose, bewildered by his unexpected tenderness. When he dropped her arm, then nudged it to the side, she raised her arms and twisted to give him access to her vest's tight leather laces.

Farran stepped closer, so near the heat of his body ebbed into hers. The faint scent of woodsy-orange mingled with the aroma of the outdoors, teasing her senses into high alert. How divine it would be to lay her head against his chest, close her eyes, and breathe him in. Every fiber of her being rose in search of the contact, the comfort of his protective embrace. She needed only to take a half step more, and that pillow would touch her cheek.

Instead, she stared at his shoulder, determined to keep her mind off his close proximity. She didn't dare be so bold. He'd laugh, and then she'd die of shame.

"Damnation," he muttered.

Noelle glanced down to find him fumbling with Anne's knots. She lifted her arm a tad higher, and Farran muttered something incomprehensible, the sound little more than a hiss. As he plucked at it once more, those hands, those strong fingers that always seemed to know exactly what to do, shook.

Her eyes widened a fraction.

With an agitated yank, the ties gave, and he eased them apart until the padded protection hung loose off her shoulders. Avoiding eye contact, he slipped the vest off to set it on the edge of the bed. As he moved, his body brushed against hers, sending a shockwave of pleasure coursing down her spine.

She closed her eyes to the sensation and willed her

heart to cease its frantic beat. *Kiss me.* The silent plea rang so loud she thought he'd surely hear it. Wanting nothing more than to cure this illogical reaction, she sought distance by stepping to the side.

Farran's hand caught her hip, refusing her escape. Firm pressure held her in place as he nudged her arm aside and ran a solitary finger along the length of her ribs. "How are your bruises?"

"F-fine," she stammered.

The unintentional brush of his thumb against the side of her breast turned her knees into a wobbly heap. She bit down on her lower lip to silence a whimper and refused to look up into his probing gaze. If she did, she'd crumple. Her resolve would crack into a million pieces, and she'd throw herself into his arms, whether he wanted her there or not.

But the weight of his stare teased. Though he said nothing, he made no move to distance himself. Beneath the absent caress of his thumb, her nipple tightened into a hard bud. In the silence, she became aware of the shortness in his breath, the heavy rise and fall of his chest. Her body disobeyed her will, and Noelle leaned into the gentle weight of his hand. Her gaze strayed to his.

Farran's eyes held hers. For several heavy heartbeats, she hung suspended, waiting for him to step away, praying he'd pull her in tight.

He did neither. Letting loose of his hold on her hip, he lifted a hand to push a lock of her hair behind her ear. He cupped the side of her face in his palm, and in perfect timing with the hand on her ribs, he stroked her cheek.

Words came unbidden, ignorant to her fear of rejection. "Farran, kiss me," she whispered.

CHAPTER 24

✝

Noelle's whispered request snapped Farran out of his stupor. He snatched his hands away and raked them through his hair. "Nay, I do not want you."

Instantly, he regretted the lie. Her eyes glistened with hurt, her flinch as forceful as if she had kicked him. He would have rather suffered the blow of her foot, for indeed he deserved it. Yet he knew naught else that might cease the feeling that surfaced every time he stood near this woman. If he said the lies long enough, mayhap he would come to believe them. Mayhap she would grow to hate him enough that he would cease to care.

God's teeth, he knew not what to do anymore. Never had such simple contact stirred him so profoundly. His body thrummed with the need for more. His heart felt so large he could scarce claim a normal breath. And the desire that flooded through him when her body naturally responded to the touch of his thumb had lifted his cock to attention.

He did the only thing he could think of to cease the

torment—he turned away. Noelle was a greater danger than any trebuchet, for she would lay siege on his heart until his faltering defenses crumbled completely. If he surrendered, if he let her through the barricade he had so carefully constructed, she would claim, plunder, and destroy.

Nay, whether it tainted her or not, the only choice he had to end this torment was to exhaust himself completely with one who demanded naught. One who knew the stakes, and held no desire for anything beyond the tariff of a handful of coin. He would go to Leah, as he had intended earlier. Spend this fruitless desire until he purged Noelle from his system.

"What is it about me?"

Her broken murmur lanced through him. At the door, he stiffened, but he dared not look back at that anguished angel's face. One glimpse would haunt him to the ends of the world. Better to keep moving, to walk away and pretend he cared not.

Farran closed the door behind him and stared down the stairwell with a ragged sigh.

"Problems, brother?" Declan asked from the shadows of the hall.

The question was all Farran's tormented thoughts required to clash together in a violent storm. Saints' blood, he could not do this to Noelle. He could not do this to himself. He ached for her in so many ways he could not describe them all. She belonged to him, damnation. *She* was who he wanted, not some whore whose touch lacked any trace of tenderness.

He spun on his heel and shoved Noelle's door open. The sight of her sitting on the bed, her knees pulled to her chest and slowly rocking back and forth, unwound something so deep inside him, he felt her pain as if 'twas his own. He rushed through the doorway that separated them, stepped over her cat, and dropped to his knees on the mattress in front of her. Gathering her face in his hands, he tipped her gaze up until her tear-filled eyes locked with his. "'Tis not you, Noelle."

She tried to turn her head, but he held her steady, refused to allow her to look away. He searched her face, willing her to understand all the things she could not possibly comprehend. Words formed, but before he could master them, they eluded his grasp. What could he say to her? He did not wish her shame. Could not tolerate the idea of giving her the ammunition she would need to destroy him. If he told her about Brighid, he would have no defenses left. He could not expose himself like that. 'Twould be like riding to battle without his mail.

At a complete loss, Farran followed instinct and brought his mouth to hers. The tang of salt blended with the softness of her lips and provoked a gut-deep sigh. Heaven. Her kiss was the closest he would come to a glimpse of that promised salvation. And her hesitant response unlocked the vise around his throat. "I lied," he exhaled. "'Tis you I want. This."

Caught by the mesmerizing satin of her mouth, he wound his arms around her and claimed her in a hungry kiss. Every last bit of conflict poured out through the tangle of their tongues. The greedy way she welcomed him spiraled him down a path he knew he had no chance of retreating from, and Farran surrendered to the longing in his soul. To the hope he dared not feel, but could not help.

His hands slid up her narrow back to twine through her hair, and he tipped her head to possess her more fully.

The sweetness of her perfume made him light-headed. Her warmth soaked into his blood. As desire sparked down his spine to tighten his body into hewn stone, a low groan rumbled in the back of his throat, and his shaft swelled to painful limits.

His. Noelle belonged to him. Innocent, angelic Noelle. *Mine.*

With fierceness to match the horns of attack, the thought raged through his mind. The Almighty sent her here for his pleasure, and by all that was holy, naught would make him turn away tonight.

He trailed his lips down the fragile skin at the side of her neck to nibble at her throat. She arched into his body, her breasts stabbing through the thin cotton of his shirt and into his chest. Farran released her hair, and supporting her back with one hand, he slid the other between their bodies to cup one full mound in his palm. At his gentle squeeze, she gasped.

The sound seeped through the haze of desire that clouded his thoughts and brought sense to the surface. He could not rush her. Could not think only of his own needs and ignore her innocence. Nay, he must bide his time. Teach her the pleasures of the flesh and not behave like some uncivilized barbarian.

He steadied himself on a deep breath and rocked back to sit on the mattress. Pulling her along with him, he drew her into his lap and guided her legs around his waist. When she settled against the confined hardness of his cock, his body jerked. But he beat into submission the urge to lift his hips into hers and found the will to sit still. To give her the freedom of becoming comfortable with his body. As he plied the ice pack off and set it on the floor, he held her gaze, tried for a smile. It faltered, but broke through to lift the corners of his mouth.

She dropped her eyes, a blush staining her delicate cheeks. "Farran I've never . . ."

"I know." To his own ears, his voice sounded hoarse.

Surprise widened her eyes. "You do?"

"Aye." Strangely touched, Farran tucked a lock of her hair behind her ear and plucked her glasses from the bridge of her nose. He set them aside, then leaned forward to kiss her forehead. "Touch me as you wish, Noelle."

Farran dropped his hands to her waist and gathered up the hem of her shirt. "Like this," he whispered as he eased it over her head.

Cool air hit Noelle's skin, prickling it with goose bumps that intensified the nervous quivering of her belly. Half of her mind demanded to know what she was doing. Why she was allowing this to happen. The other half, the portion that suspected Farran wasn't as crazy as she wanted him to be, urged her to stop thinking. To just feel the amazing warmth of Farran's palms as they cupped her breasts, lifted, and brought them closer together.

When he dipped his head and pressed a kiss to the deep V he'd created, she closed her eyes. *Just feel . . .*

The tip of his tongue seared along the lace edge of her bra. His stubbly whiskers scraped against skin that had never known more friction than a heavy sweater. Nothing near as pleasant as the chafe of a chin, the brush of a cheek. His fingers teased, the roll of his thumbs over her taut nipples enticing enough she arched her back, wanting more.

Her womb tightened with anticipation, and Noelle

clutched at his strong shoulders. Between her legs, where their bodies joined, his arousal was evident. Hard and seeking, it brushed against her sensitive nub each time he moved to trail his lips further, plunge his tongue deeper. Every absent caress sent sensation rushing up her spine. Breathing became difficult. Sitting still near impossible.

Following instinct, she pressed her hips into his. A thrill shot all the way down to her toes, and she rocked forward, chasing the unexpected bliss.

Farran feathered his lips across hers. Winding her arms around her neck, she sought the contact of his skin against hers.

"Not yet," he whispered against the corner of her mouth. A shift of his hips distanced his lower body from hers.

Disappointment escaped with her quiet whimper. But the plaintive sound morphed into a gasp as Farran nimbly released the closure to her bra and those big, strong hands covered her bared breasts. His hair tickled across her shoulder as he rained kisses down her throat. A nudge of his head asked her to give him room, and she loosened her grasp enough to lean away. His body followed, a gentle yet insistent press that urged her onto her back. She yielded, too bewildered by the newness of feeling to think of resistance.

When those moist lips closed around her distended nipple, Noelle's body nearly jerked off the bed. "Farran . . ." Filled with blissful shock, her throaty cry cracked through the still air. Her eyes flew open, and she looked down her body to find Farran's eyes closed. The sight of her flesh in his hands, slipping against his mouth, sent heat gushing through her veins. It pooled in her belly, spread lower to fan between her legs. She clamped her thighs together to curb the growing ache.

His chuckle whispered against her overheated skin. He lifted his lashes. Smiling eyes met hers for the briefest moment before a nip of his teeth sent her tumbling back into the bed.

Wow. Oh, wow. The night of college graduation when she'd let Alec Yates bare her down to bra and panties before he insulted her and passed out in a vodka-induced haze hadn't been anywhere near this thrilling. In the years that followed, she'd had fantasies, but her imagination hadn't created something like this. Something so incredibly perfect, and yet intolerable all at once. She speared her fingers into Farran's hair, wanting more, and at the same time wanting the torment to end.

Farran complied by lifting his head. Hovering over her, he looked down, his eyes a rich amber. Though they sparkled bright, his momentary humor had vanished. His gaze dipped between their bodies to canvas her exposed skin, and self-consciousness flooded Noelle. She didn't have a model's body. Was too thin in all the wrong places. Bony hips, flat boobs—nothing at all remarkable as Alec had so endearingly pointed out. She looked away, unable to witness the disappointment that would flutter through Farran's face.

"Look at me," he instructed.

Reluctantly, she obeyed.

Farran's gaze burned into her. He sank his hips into hers, letting her feel the full extent of his arousal. "Do you think my body would crave you as it does if you did not please me? There is naught to be ashamed of, Noelle." He dusted light kisses over her nose, her cheeks, her eyelids. Against her mouth he murmured, "You are more beautiful than any woman I have ever known."

The ferocity of his kiss left no room for doubt. Under it,

something deep and unnameable unraveled, and the last of her insecurities fled completely. Beneath the inquisitive caress of fingers that explored her body as if he sought to read Braille, she believed. And as he drew the kiss to a close, then bent to capture her opposite breast with his mouth, he told her his sincerity without words. Each velvety stroke of his tongue, graze of his teeth, and gentle suckle took her to a place where all the insults had never happened, and she gave in to her body's natural inhibitions.

Bunching his shirt in her fingers, she tugged it up, asking him to let her touch as he did. He complied by sitting up. A roll of his shoulders helped her pull the Henley off, giving her the most amazing view of smooth bronzed skin and corded muscles. She glided her fingertips down his chest, fascinated by the way his skin jumped beneath her nails. He closed his eyes, his breath as unsteady as hers, and that amazing mouth curved with a faint smile.

Her heart fluttered at the sight, and the pressure between her thighs increased. As if he understood her torment, his hand drifted to her hip, slid behind to lift her into him. The squeeze of his fingers against her inner thigh made her world tilt. The feel of his erection, nestled so close to the most intimate part of her body, provoked her into a low moan. She closed her eyes, unable to tolerate the dizziness holding his gaze created.

His mouth returned to her breast, but he didn't suckle as she'd anticipated. Instead, Farran flicked the tip of his tongue around her nipple, then trailed a searing path down the valley of her breasts and lower. Lower still, until his teeth raked across her belly. While he scattered light kisses over her goose-pimpled skin, his fingers toyed with the button on her jeans. When it popped open, he flattened his palm against her abdomen and worked the zipper free.

Knowing she was about to cross a line she shouldn't, Noelle shimmied with his tug and helped him ease her jeans down her thighs. He took his time removing them, showering every exposed inch of skin with the feathery caress of his mouth. Calloused palms scraped pleasantly down her calf, strong hands held her ankle as he lifted her leg to pull the garment free.

What happened next shook her to the core. Warm, moist heat washed over her aching flesh as Farran nuzzled at her panties. His breath teased. The tickle of his fingers against the sensitive skin at the juncture of her thigh made her squirm. He kissed her there, a lingering brush of lips that brought her body off the bed and her hands to his hair. Her womb quivered in response, and instinct demanded she part her legs.

When she did, his fingers dipped beneath the satin to pull the loose elastic aside. His mouth fluttered through her feminine curls, the heavy rasp of his breath full of erotic promise. At the touch of his tongue, Noelle sucked in a sharp breath and curled her nails against his scalp.

Slow, provocative strokes brought her hips into a dance that matched his languorous rhythm. Feeling swelled to impossible heights, driving her to an unimaginable plateau. She knew the only way to make the fever that consumed her go away, and yet she couldn't define exactly what she needed. All she understood was Farran's mouth held magic, and if he stopped, she'd shatter to pieces.

As he suckled at her sensitive nub, he slid a thick finger inside her opening. At the pleasant invasion, Noelle cried out. She clamped her thighs together, and clung to the fistfuls of his hair. He eased his hand away, lifted his head. Entering her once more, he rasped, "Give your body freedom, Noelle."

She didn't know what he meant, but the push of his finger, the way she felt him deep inside, made her tremble. When his thumb pressed against her sensitive center of nerves, a tidal wave of heat flowed through her body. Another thrust, another rub, and all the engulfing feeling crashed together. Release took her, dropped her off that high plateau without so much as a parachute. She plummeted into an abyss of sensation and cried out with ecstasy.

"Aye, angel. Aye," Farran whispered. "Like so."

The motion of his hand slowed in time with her body. As the last of her climax pulsed through her, he withdrew completely and scattered light kisses across her navel. Sense slowly returned, along with her embarrassment. Here she lay, completely exposed in the bright light, and had just screamed. Damn, what had she done? How had she managed to forget herself like that? Heat infused her cheeks. She turned her head to the side, unable to look at Farran.

The rustle of his clothes told her he undressed. His body covered hers, his erection hard against her swollen flesh. On a thick swallow, she grasped for the bliss she'd felt moments earlier. His mouth found hers, soft and tender. But all Noelle wanted to do was cry.

CHAPTER 25

E very bit of fierce, aching need ground to a standstill as Noelle's mouth refused to respond. Farran pulled his thoughts away from the intoxicating satin of her skin and the throbbing of his body. Something had changed. Drastically. And he had been so blinded by her pleasure, he had failed to observe when. Or why.

He let his lips linger, hoping beyond all measure her distance was only temporary. That she would come alive once more and take him to the sweet release he yearned for. Though she smoothed a hand across his lower back, naught else offered encouragement. Her lips touched tentatively, as if she wished she were far from here. Far from him.

Allowing his weight to sink into her, he framed her face between his hands. "What troubles you?" he whispered.

Light reflected off the welling moisture in her eyes, and Farran cringed inwardly. She could not despise him, could she? Moments ago, she had let go, gave in to feeling in a way he had never experienced with a woman. Brighid had but laid there. The others . . . he had not bothered to even pay attention to their false words and encouraging hands.

Noelle let out a shuddering breath. "I don't know."

He exhaled heavily and touched his forehead to hers, surrendering to the reality the pleasure he craved would be denied. 'Twould take little to coax her back into his arms, to return her to the ecstasy he knew she had felt. Yet he refused to indulge in selfish pleasure. He wanted a willing partner, not one who responded because her body had little choice.

Rolling onto his back, he tossed an arm on the pillow above his head and welcomed the cool air against his overheated flesh. His cock throbbed in protest, his body screamed. But Farran ignored the ache and attempted to train his thoughts away from how close he had come. He should be relieved she stopped him, for continuing down this path would only bind him where he could not stay. And yet, the longer he lay in the stillness, her thigh so near they almost touched, the more impossible it became to deny he would cut off his sword arm to lose himself in her.

Noelle rolled onto her side and flatted a hand over his drumming heart. "I'm sorry."

He wanted to speak. To tell her he understood, that she need not feel guilt over her refusal. His throat, however, refused the order. So overwhelmed by the enormity of sensation that flowed in his veins, he could do little more than swallow. God's blood, if she would but give him the slightest hint of welcome, he would roll her onto her back in a heartbeat and bury himself to the hilt inside her slick warmth.

Her hand spanned across his chest, drifted lower to his belly. As tempting as a siren, and as innocent as a babe, her touch burned. Beneath the power of her fingers, his cock bobbed against his abdomen. He caught her by the wrist, ceasing the wayward path of her fingers. "Do not touch me, Noelle." Hearing the harshness of his bark, he softened his command with a whispered, "Not yet."

She jerked her arm away, as if he had scalded her. But Farran refused to let her retreat into the place in her mind where she believed he found her lacking. He held fast to her wrist and compromised by settling her palm back upon his chest. When she stopped fighting, he threaded his fingers through hers, and covered the back of her much smaller hand.

They lay together in silence, their breathing matched. Yet naught would cool the fire that burned in Farran's blood. He could not tolerate another moment of this damning nearness. Sitting abruptly, he rolled off the bed and stalked toward the bath. If he could retreat into the bowels of the temple, and know she would not take offense, he would. As such, he had little choice but the meager flow of water.

He cranked the faucets on, adjusted the temperature to lukewarm. Stepping beneath the spray, he purged his frustration with a hiss. What had that little slip of a virgin done to him? 'Twas unlike him to be unable to shut off desire. Yet one innocent scientist wheedled so far under his skin he had lost control of himself. Even now, well removed from her presence, her perfume lingered in his nose. Her silken skin swathed his calloused hands. And the deeply etched scar upon his belly tingled from her naive caress.

He should have expected she would turn away from him. That she would find her pleasure and care little for his needs. Her name was woman, was it not?

As the thought crept into his mind, he groaned against

the falseness of it. Noelle was no temptress. She may have brought him to this state of intolerable arousal, but she did not coerce him to her bed.

A vision of the way she arched beneath him rose to argue what he knew was fact. On another haggard hiss, he took himself into his hand, intent on relieving his ache the only way he could. Yet as he wrapped his fingers around his swollen length and pumped, disappointment hollowed out his gut. Biting back an oath, he snatched his hand away. 'Twould serve no point. 'Twas not release he craved, but something else.

Something he refused to name.

Noelle pulled on her T-shirt and crossed her arms over her chest. Cross-legged, she sat on the bed, staring at the bathroom and the sounds within, certain she'd just become the biggest fool to ever walk the earth. Her first orgasm with a man—she was supposed to be elated. The numbness in her limbs, the weighty feel of satisfaction, should have left her giddy. Instead, she'd behaved like an idiot and spoiled everything.

Damn it, why couldn't she get her act together? She'd waited a lifetime for what Farran offered. He'd even confessed he found her attractive. Hell, he'd even smiled. That alone should have given her confidence enough to shed her insecurities.

On an inward mutter, she pushed a hand through her hair. If only she could undo the damage and convince him back into bed. She'd tried, but he'd clammed up as tight as she had. Now he'd retreated completely, and judging from the stiffness of his shoulders, she'd made him angry once again.

She flopped back into the pillows, curled on her side,

and willed him to walk out of the bathroom wearing that faint smile. As she waited, she took stock of the new sensations coursing through her veins. Already her muscles in her legs twitched with weakness. She must have strained something—no surprise really, given the abandon she'd shown. Her lips stung with the chafe of being kissed too thoroughly, but despite the uncomfortable tingle, she couldn't say they hurt. If anything, the reminder stirred her pride. Farran—gorgeous, out-of-her-league, sexy Farran— had kissed her. This time he made no attempt to hide the fact he'd wanted to.

No single part of her body had forgotten what they'd shared. Her breasts felt heavier, her head lighter, and a strange warmth enveloped her despite the cool air that seeped through old windows and chilled the room. The more she replayed the memory of their loving, the more she came to terms with her behavior. And what had seemed so embarrassing became intriguing.

Did all women forget how to think? Did all men show the tenderness Farran gave her? Better yet, did men share this same feeling of utter exhaustion blended with an underlying thrum of excitement?

The precious smile Farran had given her flashed in her mind with the clarity of a candid snapshot. He'd come close to a grin before, almost found a smirk once or twice, but he'd never shown the slightest hint of happiness. Not as he had when she traced the firm planes of muscle along his chest.

The tingles started again, stirred by the thought she was responsible for that rare treat. Her IQ might be near genius, but she didn't need extreme intelligence to understand how special that little glimpse of emotion was. She'd made him happy. Somehow, someway, she'd provoked what he otherwise refused to show. If she hadn't turned into an ice cube, he might be here now, lying beside her, giving her more. They'd spend the night together, wake in each other's arms. And tomorrow morning, there'd be none of his harsh words to shatter her perfect fantasy.

If only she could take her fumble back.

A shadow fell across the threshold to the bathroom. Noelle scrunched down into the bedding. Her heart tripped into her throat, and she waited, anticipating the worst. Preparing for more of Farran's biting words and angry scowls.

He walked through the archway as naked as the day he'd been born. Long hair dripped over his shoulders, clung to the thick cording of his neck. Little rivulets of water trickled down one firm bicep, dampened the ridges of his chest. Perfect masculine splendor.

She felt the predatory weight of his gaze, but Noelle couldn't tear her stare away from his body. She took him in, every fantastic inch of bronzed skin and tight, toned muscle. Her eyes dipped lower to trace the stark white scar across his abdomen. Again, her heart rolled over, twisted by the thought someone could be sadistic enough to cause him such pain. She blinked long and slow, banishing the vision of torture that always came with the sight of his injury.

When she looked again, she sucked in a sharp breath. Still swollen with arousal, his cock jutted forth from a nest of dark hair. Under her perusal, the smooth tip bobbed against his abdomen. Shocked to the core, she hastily averted her eyes. But curiosity got the better of her, and as Farran moved toward his pile of clothes, she let her gaze slip sideways. Thickly veined, it stood proud and erect, sure evidence she hadn't imagined the feel of that insistent length against her core moments before he'd rolled off her.

Her innocence came rushing back to her, along with the questions. Before she could catch her tongue and stop the silly words, she asked, "What's it feel like for you?"

Bent over, about to snatch up his shirt, Farran came to a halt. His fingers didn't so much as twitch as he asked, "What?"

A blush crept in, heating her face and neck. Had she asked that? Damn. Well, she'd stuck her foot in her mouth far enough—might as well discover the answer. "Orgasm. What's it feel like?"

Slowly he stood and turned around. For a moment, she thought he hadn't heard. He simply stared, blinking as if he tried to make sense of the question. He opened his mouth to speak, then closed it. The light in his eyes sharpened, and he watched her like a lion stalking the gazelle it intended to feast upon. His throat worked as he swallowed, and at his thigh, one hand clenched into a tight fist. "Were you to bring me there, there would be no words."

He'd heard her all right. At his raspy answer, the heat returned to Noelle's womb. It clenched tight, wound into an uncomfortable knot.

"Damsel, you stare."

His observation deepened her blush. She fumbled for her tongue, searched for an excuse, and settled on, "I'm sorry."

"Nay," he murmured. "Do not be. I regret only 'tis not your hands that inspect so thoroughly."

Noelle's pulse skipped. Invitation lay before her, an opportunity to reverse the sourness her insecurities had created. But could she? Could she really cast aside her modesty and give in to what she wanted most—to do exactly as he suggested? She summoned all the courage she could find and whispered, "You wouldn't mind?"

Farran's exhale rushed out on a prolonged whish of air. "God's teeth, nay, Noelle. I hunger for your touch."

Slowly she sat up and lifted her eyes to meet his searing gaze.

Farran did not know whether he had sentenced himself to hell, or whether he had opened the gates to heaven. But as Noelle crossed the room, her head bowed with modesty, she peeked up at him with a shy, hesitant smile, and he lost the ability to move. He stood motionless, expectant and uncertain.

When inquisitive fingertips caressed his chest, he closed his eyes to the perfect pleasure. Her hands were so gentle. Healing in so many ways. The light scrape of her nails tightened his flesh, the tickle of her journey across his ribs stirred a chuckle.

"Oh, sorry," she exclaimed, her voice a hushed wash of air against his chest.

With a shake of his head, he dismissed her apology. Not opening his eyes, he caught her free hand and pressed it firmly to his body to encourage her further. "Never again apologize, lest you have truly wronged me."

The flutter of her lips on his shoulder had him gritting his teeth. His body tightened at the softness of her palm as she smoothed a hand down the length of his abominable scar. When the cotton of her long shirt brushed against his thigh, and she stepped so close the scent of jasmine engulfed him, his throat closed tight. Jesu, she would tempt even the purest of saints. 'Twas all the strength he possessed to keep his hands still and not crush her close and ravage her until time stood still and Azazel, the demons, their crossed purposes, all faded away.

Her hands skimmed lower, across the stiffened muscles of his thighs. One lone fingertip traveled the length of his swollen cock, from base to tip. His breath came out on a hiss. He moved his hips away, not trusting himself. To his absolute frustration, she ignored the subtle warning and closed those searing fingers around the length of him.

"Noelle, 'tis not wise—" He choked on his words as she gave him a tentative squeeze.

"Tell me what to do, Farran?"

Quiet, curious, her voice pummeled into his awareness like cannonade. He groaned aloud, knowing he should not look, yet unable to stop his eyes from opening and his gaze from locking on the sight of her delicate fingers possessively wrapped around him. Nature took over. He undulated against her hand, aching for the promise of her brazen exploration.

Knowing he damned himself if she should stop, he closed his hand over hers and guided her into a slow up and down motion. When she shook off his hand and brought her other into play, Farran's knees threatened to give out. His body surged into her hands, and he stumbled backward, grateful the wall was there to hold him up. He reached for her breasts, cupped them, and squeezed.

But the pleasant friction of her palms overwhelmed him. He moved with her, unable to cease the press of his hips even if he had wanted to. Sensation surged through his veins. He trembled with the effort of holding himself back. His chest contracted, denying him air.

"Noelle." His protest was feeble, a mere whisper he could scarcely hear.

At the touch of her tongue, Farran's world ground to a halt. He sucked in a jagged gasp, braced against the dizzying rush of heat that threatened to consume him. As she pumped, she teased his throbbing flesh, swirled that tantalizing tongue over his sensitive tip. The close of her lips as she took him into her mouth pushed him over the edge. On a hoarse bark, he grabbed her shoulders and dragged her upright as ecstasy ricocheted through him. He crushed her to his chest, spilling himself against the palm she refused to remove with a fierceness he had never before experienced.

Her hand slowed in time with his body. She let go slowly and wiped her palm on the hem of her shirt. Farran held her close. Head buried in her silky hair, he struggled to catch his breath and floated down from the otherworldly heights she had taken him to. He pressed a soft kiss to the side of her throat. The strong vibration of her pulse against his lips revealed something else he had not anticipated—shared arousal.

Lifting his head, he met the bright sparkle of her eyes. A smile made the corner of his mouth twitch. What surprised him more was the swelling of his heart. It felt too tight, too large for the small space behind his ribs. He brushed a strand of hair away from her cheek and traced the pad of his thumb along her delicate jaw. "Let me make love to you, Noelle. As a man should. As we were fated."

He waited for her refusal. Hated the sound of the words long before she spoke them.

Instead, she pressed a kiss into the meaty flesh of his hand and whispered, "Please."

CHAPTER 26

✝

Farran knew he would soon visit a paradise many men would give limbs to glimpse. Slowly, reverently, he scooped Noelle into his arms to carry her to the bed. She nestled close, her long hair tickling the length of his arm. The gentle press of her palm against his chest turned his heartbeat into the low, resonating beat of a death knell. Only when this short trek came to a halt, he would not find himself strung from high ramparts and left as carrion fodder. Nay, only the crumbling walls that kept Noelle at a distance would perish.

How he would fare against their destruction, he did not care to consider. All that mattered was that she had said yes. Had welcomed him into her bed, her fears a thing of the past.

He took a step forward when something caught his ankle. Glancing over her shoulder, he found his shirt tangled around his foot. He gave it a shake to dislodge the cloth, only to find it wrapped tighter. Failing to consider how Noelle's slight weight might throw him off balance, he stepped on the shirt with his other foot and tried to pull himself free.

Noelle's giggle made the chore more difficult. He scolded her with a false frown. Chagrined, she bit down on her lower lip, but the humor lingered in her bright eyes.

With a derisive grunt, he shook his foot again. When it pulled loose, he could not quell a satisfied smirk. As a bit of the man he had once been broke free, he winked at Noelle. "I will not be deterred from honoring the damsel's request."

He regretted those words with his next step. Where he thought he had freed himself, he soon discovered his error. Trapped by the weight of his other foot, the material snagged midstride, pulling tight to halt the forward motion of his leg. He stumbled.

All sense of grace and poise shattered as Farran fell forward. 'Twas all he could do to hold Noelle tight and prevent her from tumbling out of his arms. The floor rose to meet him, and in a vain effort to cling to some of his dignity, he twisted to keep from crushing Noelle beneath the impact of his body.

His shoulder crashed into the carpeting, jarring the wind from his lungs. Pain shot through his arm. With a grimace, he released Noelle and rolled to his back. Humiliated, he stared at the ceiling. Christ's toes, he could look no more foolish if he tried.

Spread across his chest, Noelle lifted her head. Laughter brimmed behind her eyes, though she tried to temper a smile. "And I thought my feet got in the way."

He pursed his lips and scowled. But when he opened his mouth to tell her how much he disproved of her amusement, a foreign sound rumbled in the back of his throat.

A sound he had not heard in the passing of hundreds of years. His laughter.

Rich and hearty, it burst free to vibrate his chest. Shake his shoulders. With the noise, the soul-deep tightness he bore each day unwound. The pain of betrayal shook loose. The weight he had carried through centuries rolled away to give him freedom he had believed he would never know again.

Noelle stared spellbound. The smile that lit Farran's features dazzled brighter than any star. His eyes gleamed, radiant with the first glimpse of utter happiness she'd seen in this man. Those dormant crow's-feet took on new life and deepened. And the sound . . . The husky velvet of his laughter swathed her like rich fabric.

She luxuriated in the strength of his arms as they wound around her waist and he fastened her in place. The giggles she'd tried so hard to silence slipped free. She laughed with him, at him, at the irony of it all. In between great gulps of air, she teased, "You should give me pointers on how to fall with so much class."

On a playful growl, Farran rolled her over and pinned her beneath his powerful body. He nipped at her nose before he grinned. He swiped at the tiny teardrop that crept from the corner of his eye. The effort it took to control his amusement showed in the warring lines of his mouth. They tensed, twitched, then smoothed as he laughed more softly. "It requires much practice."

She smirked. "I'm sure it does."

"Aye. If you were truly practiced, you would have never caught yourself on the stool at the adytum. You would have crashed to the ground."

At the reference to her embarrassing moment in the kitchen, she gave his shoulder a push. But his wince spoiled the playful punch. He tried to hide his reaction with another chuckle, but the effort fell short. He couldn't hide his hurt.

Noelle traced her fingertips over his warm skin. "I think you need the ice now."

"Nay. 'Tis a mere bruise."

The magic that bringing him to orgasm conjured disappeared, replaced by a far more enjoyable comfort. Laying in his arms, feeling the comfortable weight of his body against hers, sharing laughter with this handsome enigma satisfied in a way Noelle couldn't remember ever experiencing. She liked it here. Liked this side of Farran. Too much, if she wanted to be honest with herself. He had changed tonight somehow.

And truth be told, he had changed her. Beyond introducing her to sex, he'd changed her perceptions, made it impossible to believe he was anything less than sane. The man in her arms knew the full spectrum of human emotion, and while she'd wager every penny she owned he'd never want her to witness his sensitive side, he'd exposed her to too much. Tonight he held nothing back, made no pretense about what he wanted, how he felt. That kind of raw honesty, even if his actions revealed more than his words, couldn't exist if everything else was a web of lies.

She lifted a hand to trace the faint scar near his temple. Mystified by the wound that had healed so quickly, she whispered, "Tell me the story again?"

His gaze clouded with confusion. "Which story?"

A portion of her mind seized against the idea of inviting him to retell the fantastic impossibilities he'd spouted in the adytum. She didn't want to hear them. All they would do was wreak havoc with what she thought she understood. Yet she knew if she intended to make sense of this at all, she had to hear them once more.

Holding his gaze, she forced the words through her tightening throat. "About what you are."

For a moment, Farran went rigid. His shoulders stiffened, the light faded from his eyes. He searched her face for the certainty that she knew what she requested. She encouraged him with a short nod, and the tension in his body dissipated with his quiet sigh. "Aye. Let us move to the bed. 'Tis a more comfortable place to talk."

Easing himself to his feet, he reached down for her hand. She accepted the aid and allowed him to pull her upright. He kept his fingers twined with hers as he led her the short distance to the bed, then pulled her in beside him. Stretched out on his back, he guided her head to his shoulder. A bounce of the mattress announced Scat Cat's intrusion.

Noelle snuggled in close. Beneath her cheek, his heart drummed a steady beat. She splayed her fingers across his chest, slipped one ankle between his legs, and smiled despite herself. Ignoring the tiny voice that insisted she stay silent, she instructed, "Okay. Go on."

Farran skimmed his hand down Noelle's back, beyond the cotton hem, to rest on the firm cheek of her bottom. Her nearness stirred his body's natural response, and his cock flinched against his thigh. Although something feral and untamed rumbled quietly in his blood, a greater gratification soothed the agitation. That she had brought him to laughter satisfied more than any physical need. The inner peace she created was enough to still his roaming hand and savor the way she burrowed into his arms.

He rubbed his cheek against the crown of her head and tightened his embrace. "I am an immortal member of the Knights Templar. I spoke my oaths of service to Merrick in 1129. From that day forth, I have existed for one purpose—to protect mankind from Azazel's evil."

As he had anticipated, she stiffened. "That's impossible, Farran. Merrick just waved a magic wand?"

His brow tightened, but the lightness of his spirit prevented the customary burn of annoyance. He scolded by giving her bottom a light slap. "'Tis you who wished to hear. Now allow me to speak."

"Sorry."

"Ten years earlier, Merrick rode with Hugues de Payens to the Temple Mount. There, where they were forbidden to explore, they discovered ancient scrolls. You would know one as the Copper Scroll."

She tipped her head, dislodging his chin and met his gaze with wide eyes. "The Copper Scroll? Who doesn't know about it? It lists Jerusalem's lost treasure."

Farran caught her slip, her failure to qualify her words with legend or myth about those who might believe. He said nothing, choosing not to call her lack of hesitation to her attention. That she listened showed progress. Mayhap the afternoon in the relic room brought her closer to the truth of the Almighty. Mayhap the pliant nature of her body reflected a supple mind. He forged on. "Nay. Whilst scholars believe such, they do so because Azazel planted the thought within their minds. The scroll identifies the gates to hell. Azazel disguised it to tempt man into his clutches."

"Farran—"

"Hush." He softened his harsh command with a light

chuckle. "Because we were forbidden to touch that scroll, the archangels cursed us with immortality and the duty to guard those very gates, to slay Azazel's vile creations. Spread through the world, our purpose exists as it has from the start, to protect and guard the holy purpose."

"And you don't die."

He paused, unwilling to lie and yet unable to find words to explain how the darkness from the creatures he slayed crept into his soul. He did not want her to fear him. If she should believe the truth—that soon he would become as evil as what he hunted—the fears she had confessed would deepen.

At the same time, if she understood her oaths would give him back his light, she might be more inclined to take them. Assuming she cared if he lived or died.

Nay, he could not leap to such conclusions. Though tonight transformed them into lovers, it spoke naught of what she felt for him. Pleasures of the flesh had little to do with stirrings of the heart.

On a deep breath, he compromised with a half-truth. "I weaken over time. I can be killed by a Templar blade. Raphael infused our swords with divine light, and the weaker I become, the more I am at risk." The explanation omitted the fact his taint made him vulnerable, that the blade was designed to eradicate darkness, but 'twould suffice. When he knew fear did not haunt her, he would supply the rest.

When she said naught, he waited. In the silence, her fingertips drew a lazy pattern on his chest. Her hair tickled his face. And though the shirt she wore prevented him from experiencing the full warmth of her skin, his body flushed where they touched. Saints' blood, he could become accustomed to this. No woman had ever fit so neatly into his arms, nor had one evoked such a fierce desire to cast all else aside.

A hollow screech beyond the window stiffened her spine. As the sound drew out into a yawning howl with the brittleness of breaking glass, her fingers dug into his shoulder. She jerked her head up and struggled to rise. "What was that?"

Farran tucked her back into place. He looked over the top of her head at the window as he answered, "A nytym."

"A what?"

"A creature of Azazel's. Smarter than shades, they possess some ability to change shape. Unlike more intelligent demons, they cannot speak."

'Twould only complicate matters to tell her the creature should not be so close. Distantly, he recognized the sound of a slamming door, the rush of boots through the entryway below. Beyond the thin pane of glass, mail clinked and swords clattered. He reached behind him to extinguish the light, then gathered Noelle in both arms and maneuvered her onto her side. "Sleep, damsel. They cannot hurt you." Brushing his lips across her shoulder he murmured, "You are safe with me."

The knock he expected resonated through the outer chamber. In answer, her cat meowed. He slipped his arm around Noelle's waist and tucked her back against his chest.

"I should get that," Noelle commented on a yawn.

"Nay," he whispered. "They shall fight without me tonight." Inhaling the sweet jasmine scent of her hair, Farran did something he had never once given consideration. He ignored the call to duty.

* * *

Noelle stared out the window and listened to the noises outside. The clink of steel, a faint bellow, another chilling scream. Down deep in her core, the chill the first grotesque howl created spread. It filtered into her veins, seeped through to prick her skin with goose bumps. Shivering, she huddled closer to the sheltering wall of warmth behind her. Farran's arm lay across her like a protective shield, heavy yet comforting. She ran her palm down the hard perfection of his forearm and slipped her fingers through his, over the back of his hand.

He answered with a light squeeze, but the rhythmic rise and fall of his chest betrayed his exhaustion.

Demons. Immortality. Alternate theology. How could any of what he'd said be true? Yet she couldn't think of any reason so many people would go to such fantastic lengths to maintain a fiction. While she'd like to believe they were all nuts, two hundred or more people couldn't be that committed to make-believe. The cults she'd heard stories about—even at the height of their popularity, they didn't twist *everything*. They focused on specific points, exaggerated portions of truth. Actively solicited members through condemning the accepted beliefs and offering utopian paradise. Children, and the need to train the young, played a prominent role.

Farran didn't criticize. He didn't offer her an escape from persecution. Hell, he hadn't really mentioned the vow he wanted her to speak the last day or so. And no animal she knew of made the horrific noises outside, even if the people in this building were missing a screw or two.

Anne spoke of a prophecy. One where she was a teacher and Noelle was blind. Could it be possible that everything science could prove was only evidence of something more divine? All the theories, all the postulations, all the

math . . . Until today, everything had a place, a pigeonhole
to fit into. Artifacts had precise properties. Chemical
compounds, carbon footprints, and exact atomic mass.
Men didn't find her desirable. Her father had been the only
one to ever call her beautiful, and sex was something
she'd written off to movies.

Now she confronted objects she could touch and hold,
and yet by all scientific reason, they didn't exist. She lay
in Farran's arms, the heat of his half-mast erection nestled against her bare bottom evidence he desired her even
in sleep. He hadn't only told her she was beautiful, he'd
made her feel that way. And she knew, without being
told, he'd give up his last breath to protect her.

But protect her from what? Whom?

She closed her eyes on a heavy sigh and took a deep
breath of the woodsy-orange that ebbed off his body. Another haunting moan beyond her window had her edging
backward into his body as far as she could go. She trembled as the sound died off on a high-pitched whine, and
another memory of Anne's words resonated in her mind.

You will die.

CHAPTER 27

As sunrise turned the heavens into lavender, Lucan sheathed his sword. He bent down to collect the onyx blade at his feet. Beside it, the broken remains of his brother, William, lay in a headless, bloody heap. Three dark knights had come. Three they had conquered, but with great loss. Five Templar gave their lives. One returned to Azazel's lair with the retreating demons. The others perished at the end of holy blades, before the darkness turned them on their brethren. Including William, who met the angels' songs at the end of Lucan's sword.

He stepped back from the lifeless body as strong hands hefted it off the ground. His gaze lifted to the curtained window beyond the iron gates where Farran slept. If any were to know the extent of darkness that descended on Farran, 'twould be the man himself. Mayhap his soul suffered enough he dared not lift his sword. If indeed such were true, however, Noelle faced greater risk.

Each day they spent together placed her in greater peril.

She grew to trust him, and as long as Farran resisted the oaths, he came closer to fulfilling Anne's prophecy.

"Lucan, join us inside. James shall see to William and informing Mikhail. Your watch is soon to start." Caradoc hollered from the open gates, his arm raised to beckon Lucan inside.

Aye, his watch. Though he delayed assuming his position, he had not forgotten. 'Twould be another shift of minding a closed door. Another opportunity lost to warn Noelle of the danger she faced.

He took one last look at the ground where William had lain and kicked fresh dirt over the blood-soaked soil. Though few seldom traveled this road, the evidence of death would only raise suspicion. As he crossed the road to join Caradoc, his conscience nagged. His suspicions were naught else but Azazel's power. What he accused Farran of bordered on treason. Farran was a hard man, scarred and weathered as they all were, but his loyalty had never faltered. He would not risk the Order's future.

Good reason existed for why he failed to join his brothers on the field.

Reason mayhap Lucan could learn if he stayed at Noelle's side, instead of guarding her door. If she chose to leave, he could draw her into conversation. Discover what Farran may have told her, and in passing conversation guide her to be wary.

Inside the temple's gates, he shed his surcoat and mail. His gaze followed the procession of men and decapitated brothers through the front doors. Mikhail would bless them. After, the broken shells that once held gentle souls would join those who fell before them in the crypt beneath the temple's cold stone floor.

With his armor slung over one arm, Lucan fell into step

behind the solemn march of brethren now turned pall-bearers. Anne waited in the entry, her arms laden with towels meant to clean the mess. Her gaze rested briefly on Merrick, and she offered him a faint, supportive smile. They would grieve together later.

Lucan departed from the group to ascend the stairwell leading to Noelle's rooms. In the shadows, he set his mail on the ground and leaned against the wall. His stare fixed on the barred door ahead of him, his thoughts deviated from their usual course. He exchanged his suspicion for a fleeting stab of envy. Many centuries had passed, but well he could remember the comfort of a woman's arms.

Mayhap he would live to know that peace again.

Farran awakened to the low call of a dove, every bit aware of the woman sleeping next to him. The swollen nature of his cock, along with the accompanying ache in his loins, made her impossible to ignore. He lay embraced by her, the firm cheeks of her delicate bottom framing his hard length. Her feminine warmth called like a siren's song, and against his will, his hips lifted into her, seeking that sweet haven. The slow undulation brought her body closer. Moisture dampened his straining flesh.

God's blood, he would spill himself if she moved again. That, or he would bury himself so deep inside her she would not have time to decide whether she desired the invasion or not. He drew away, teeth clenched tight.

This newness of feeling confounded him. In years past, waking to find a woman in his bed brought no hesitation. She was present. Therefore, willing. Yet this was not his bed. 'Twas not his room. And the woman slumbering beside him had yet to welcome him between her legs.

He eased from the bed. Last night he had found comfort. A strange peace his matrimonial bed denied. He had rutted with Brighid enough to produce a child, and yet all the passion they had shared lacked in comparison to one night spent sleeping beside Noelle. It unnerved him. How could he experience such intimacy, when he had done little else but talk?

Farran stood naked at the foot of the bed, watching as Noelle slept. The goose bumps on her skin where he had blanketed her told him of the room's chill. Yet he felt none of it. His body thrummed with heat, a fire he could not quench.

Part of him insisted he return to the bed, rouse her with his mouth, and entice her until she could not think to deny him. That insolent part of his mind refused to acknowledge the suffering she could bring. It screamed at him to let go, abandon his fears, and trust in the divine promise that she was his salvation.

The other part of his soul raged that he had already allowed her in too far. Demanded he retreat behind barriers of stone before she could land a felling blow. She had already coerced him into neglecting his duty. He had sent his brothers off to battle, too unwilling to leave her warmth.

Mayhap his first idea, to remove himself from her, had been the best. If he did not have to look upon her each day, he could not become soft. For as certainly as the sun peeked from beyond the gray sky, he traversed a dangerous path.

He shook his head. The thought of leaving her produced an equal agony. He knew not when she had become his weakness, when lust had overridden common sense, but he must stop this nonsense. He must make her understand that though he treasured what had happened between them, he wanted naught more from her than her seraph's oath.

'Twould hurt them both. But he must protect himself before she made him bleed.

He quickly donned his clothes and strode from the room. Tonight he would press her. By morn, he would be gone.

Outside her rooms, he greeted Lucan with a glower. Silently he dared his brother to speak and give him reason to engage his fists. But Lucan merely averted his gaze, denying Farran a means of soothing his internal ache. Farran stomped down the stairs, hand on the pommel of his sword. He would seek the training yard. Find a partner who did not mind a beating.

Caradoc stopped his angry march to the indoor arena with a crisp shout. "Farran!"

Slowly he turned, his annoyance creeping out through narrowed eyes. "Aye?"

"We missed your sword."

The subtle reprimand cracked through Farran with the power of a lash. He grimaced inwardly, turned on a heel, and strode for the arena. Caradoc followed, his heavy step a matched cadence to the footfalls of Farran's boots.

Farran punched through the doors with enough force to rattle them on their hinges. When they slammed shut behind him, he drew his sword and whirled on his brother. "Come at me. I crave the fight."

Caradoc frowned, but made no move to grab for his sword. Instead, he set his hand on the tip of Farran's blade and pushed it toward the ground. "I shall give you your outlet. But first you will hear my words."

Farran shook his sword free with a snap of his wrist. "I have talked enough to last me a lifetime, brother." Lifting

his blade, he widened his stance and stood at the ready.
"Come at me, before I leave you no choice."

On a slow shake of his head, Caradoc drew his blade.
He mirrored Farran's position, feet braced wide, shoulders
loose, arm at the ready. Caradoc moved around him in a
slow circle. Methodically, Farran stepped in the opposite
direction, matching his pace, looking for weakness.

Caradoc caught him by surprise. In an act uncharacter-
istic of the seasoned swordsman, he rushed at Farran.
Farran met the wide arc of Caradoc's blade. Steel clanged
together, echoing through the wide arena. The impact
rolled down Farran's arm and jarred his bones. Yet he
welcomed the harsh burn, the tingle in his fingers.

Lifting his sword high, he returned Caradoc's strike.
The battle had begun, though Farran fought not the man
opposing him. He combated himself. All the rage and
frustration he could not channel into any useful means
poured through the arc of his arm, the twist of his body.

Step-by-step he pushed Caradoc toward the wall. Blow
by blow Caradoc countered, driving Farran back to the
spot where they began. Equal partners, matched in skill
and experience, they sparred as if their lives depended on
victory. Years of fighting at Caradoc's side gave Farran
advantage, but weakness came with the fact his opponent
shared the same knowledge.

Parry met thrust, slice met the flat defensive blade. The
angry song of clashing steel ricocheted off the walls. The
sound of his own heavy pants filled Farran's ears. Sweat
broke over his body, and the heavy weight of his weapon
settled into his shoulder.

With lightning speed, Caradoc thrust his blade at Farran's chest in a potentially devastating blow. Farran
grunted as his broadsword took the impact. He managed

little more than defensive parries as Caradoc drove again and again, quickly outmaneuvering Farran.

Caradoc struck down on Farran's blade, lifted his sword, and struck again. Then in a surprisingly agile maneuver, he attacked from the opposite side. Farran blocked the strike, but a stumble left him wide open. Caradoc moved in. Victor raised his sword, brought it down hard, and knocked Farran's weapon to the floor.

Color filled Caradoc's cheeks as he drew in a sharp breath and snapped, "She is not Brighid!"

Stunned, Farran came to a standstill. His empty hand closed in a fist, and he lowered it to his side. As the truth passed between them, Farran clenched his jaw. He bent to retrieve his sword, but Caradoc kicked it aside.

"Do you forget I was there? Do you think I do not know what poisons you against her?" Caradoc sheathed his sword, but challenged with a piercing gaze. "'Tis your fear Azazel takes advantage of. Your heartbreak he twists to his favor. You let him win each time you turn away from her."

All the raw, unchecked emotion Farran had closeted away burst forth, and he dropped his head into his hands with an anguished moan. He curled his fingers against his scalp, hating himself for the weakness he could not hide.

The press of a pommel against his stomach brought his head up. He glanced down to find his sword extended in offering. Silently he accepted and sheathed the weapon. When he looked to Caradoc once more, his brother's expression no longer held accusation. Instead, Farran found compassion.

Caradoc gestured at the floor, then assumed a seat. "She is your *seraph*, Farran."

"I know," he said, exhaling as he dropped to sit across

from Caradoc. He looked above the sandy brown head at the stark white wall beyond. "It shames me, brother. I failed in duty because I did not wish to leave her side."

"You feel—there is no shame in that. 'Tis when you try to cease what the Almighty intends, it eats at you like a canker. Brighid was a whore whose father sought to get her out of his hair. Noelle is naught like that vile bitch. No devilry lurks behind the eyes that follow you. And indeed, they do follow you. They look for you when you are not present. Ask Anne, for she told me the same."

Did they? He had been so consumed with the terror of his past, Farran could not answer. Instead, he hung his head. "I do not know how to believe in goodness, Caradoc."

"Then do not. Trust in the Almighty's plan. He brought you here. Carried you through the loss of your son. Allow yourself to feel. Anne tells me Noelle is pure. She is your gift. Your salvation. 'Tis time you embraced your fate before you drive us all mad with your morose moods."

Frowning, Farran shifted against the uncomfortable twist in his gut. He did not know how to respond. No words existed. His chest felt tight, his throat dry. What Caradoc suggested terrified him more than a proposal to stand toe to toe with a dark knight. In a battle with a fallen brother, he knew what to expect—his soul would fail. He would die. But when it came to Noelle, he could predict naught.

A streak of rebellion snatched at opportunity, and Farran sought to cloak his discomfort by turning the discussion in his favor. "You are one to talk. You ran from Isabelle. Her mortality you could not face. The pain of losing her plagues you now."

Caradoc's earnest expression flickered with sorrow be-

fore his eyes took on a harsh light. "Indeed, you are right.
But you do not find me living in the past, do you, brother?"

He stood with effort, grimacing at the ache in his bones.
He clapped a hand on Farran's shoulder, his gaze fixed on
the distant doors. "I leave you to your thoughts. But, my
friend, I urge you. Do not make the same mistakes as I."

With purposeful steps and a firm shut of the door, Caradoc left. Yet the weight of his words lingered long after
the sound of his boots disappeared down the hall. Farran
reeled from their impact. His head spun. His hands trembled.

CHAPTER 28

Noelle chewed on a fingernail as she paced in front of the chrome laboratory equipment. It hummed and ticked in ominous harmony with the whirring of her mind. She still couldn't explain how it managed to work at such an incredible rate of speed, but after sampling a shard of a cracked wooden bowl that she'd dated earlier this year for Gabriel and discovering the same results, she couldn't doubt the equipment's accuracy. Now, in minutes, the readout for the strange wood would drift into the printer's tray. She knew what it would say—the same things it had said the first three times she'd run the test. The same data it spit out yesterday.

She cast an anxious glance at the curved wooden slat. Sadly, she didn't care. The rote activity of repeated testing kept her busy. Helped to soothe the agitation Farran left behind.

She told herself the reason she couldn't keep him off her mind was because he'd introduced her to what it meant to be a woman. That this ridiculous giddy feeling had nothing to do with caring about the man and every-thing to do with the by-product of a release of oxytocin. Like mothers who experienced the rush on the birth of their child, orgasm saturated her with hormones and led her false.

All scientific fact. Yet every bit of it a bald-faced lie.

Waking to an empty bed had left her more cold and empty than the night he'd brought her out of the snow. Why had he left? Where had he gone?

Why did she care?

A soprano beep signaled the counter had finished, and Noelle wandered to the printer. She picked up the print-out, but didn't bother to scan the columns. Tossing the paper aside, she pressed her palms to her temples and grimaced. She could read it a hundred times and never make sense of all the conflicting data. The only concise fact—the cedar/poplar plank was an anomaly to all she understood.

She went to the shelves for something less compli-cated, less threatening. Scanning the tall stacks of arti-facts, she spied a handful of broken pottery bits that bore a striking resemblance to the Celt marks on the Beaker bowl in her room. As she gingerly picked up the shards, they left behind a powdery residue. So fragile had the particles become, they nearly disintegrated in her palm.

Careful not to jostle them unnecessarily, Noelle re-turned all but one to their resting place on the shelf. Air-tight canisters—that's what Gabriel needed here. If he intended to preserve some of these things much longer, he'd have to make the investment.

She took the solitary piece to her worktable. With the press of a stylus, she split the half-dollar piece in two. Both portions crumbled, making the work ahead easier.

She prepped one sample for beta counting of the carbon-14 decay. The other she set aside to chemically analyze while the gas counter measured the first.

Absorbed in the process, her mind strayed from Farran for the first time all day. She added the chemicals to clean the carbonates, then set the vial aside. While she waited, she divided the remaining sample into five small subsets, each to fit a different test.

Enraptured by her love for her work and the insatiable curiosity of her mind, Noelle lost track of time. Before she had time to stop and consider why Farran had left her to wake alone, she stood before the gigantic maze of metal tubing awaiting the final result, while her stomach rumbled, reminding her she hadn't eaten all day.

Excitement set her pulse into a staccato beat, and she gnawed on her fingernail once more. Chemical data revealed the pottery shared a similar composition to the one in her room. Right down to the faint copper residue. The hand-carved patterns were so eerily alike she couldn't help but hope. If the two were related . . . Her heart jumped into her throat at the prospect. Not one, but two Beaker artifacts would cross her path.

The printer went off and she dove for the printout. As she scanned the graphical representation, she let out a bit of the breath she'd been holding: *archaeological age: 1900–1800* B.C.

She whipped around on a gasp as the door opened. But when Farran stepped inside, her breathlessness gave way to an excited squeal. She rushed across the room, flung her arms around his neck, and threw herself into his startled embrace. "Farran, you'll never believe what I've found!"

* * *

Farran staggered backward under the force of Noelle's elation. He caught himself before he stumbled, yet nothing would curb the enormity of feeling that swept through his veins on hearing her joy. Could it be she had missed him?

The possibility swelled his heart to intolerable limits. Instinctively he sought to block the sensation and stiffened. If he allowed himself to believe . . .

Allow yourself to feel.

Caradoc's suggestion bellowed like a horn, and Farran swallowed hard. He released the vise of logic. Cast it aside to embrace the heady pleasure of Noelle's soft body molding against his. He wound his arms around her waist and held her close as he nuzzled the side of her neck. "What have you found that has kept you from joining me for supper?"

She wriggled free, to his dismay. With a smile bright enough to rival the moon's silver light, she waved a piece of paper in her hand. "It's a Beaker!"

He peered at her with a perplexed frown. But as he opened his mouth to speak, she caught him by the hand and dragged him to the tall shelves on the far side of the room. There she nearly bounced in place as she pointed at a handful of broken shards of clay.

"Beaker pottery. A Neolithic society—the first to bury their dead in graves. They introduced Britain to metal. But there's no archaeological evidence to prove they used the tools themselves. Their pottery is distinctive, loaded with sigils and intricate designs."

Though her words came out in a mad rush that only served to further scatter his disorganized thoughts, her smile warmed him from the inside out. Behind her glasses, her eyes blazed with excitement. And the constant motion of her hands stirred an equal thrill in him. As he studied her, slowly processing her explanation, he found himself fascinated by what drove her to such joy. Save for the men who craved the thrill of battle, he had never met someone so enchanted with her work.

He glanced around, noting for the first time the intricate labyrinth of metal tubing and canisters that connected to a cylindrical chamber. Aye, though he had witnessed the equipment before, he now saw it through her eyes. Compelled by the deep-rooted need to understand what stirred her passion, he gestured at the device. "Tell me of this? How you discover the age of these artifacts?"

She blinked. For a moment, he feared she would refuse. He knew not why it mattered, but the possibility left him holding his breath. He wanted to know. Needed to understand.

At the nodding of her head, his anxiety dissipated. She gave him a shy smile, then tugged on his arm to draw him closer to her tools. "Everything has a carbon footprint. It comes from an unstable isotope, carbon 14, which is formed by the earth's atmosphere when cosmic neutrons hit nitrogen 14."

She spit the foreign terms out so quickly, Farran's eyes widened. Saints' blood, he had not realized she was versed in multiple languages.

Her soft chuckle sent heat to his cheeks. Nay, he was wrong. The light in her eyes laughed at him. He shifted, suddenly uncomfortable with his age.

"I'm sorry." Rising to tiptoe, she placed a kiss on his cheek. "All you need to know is everything living has carbon 14. When an object dies, carbon 14 is frozen, more or less, within it. To find it, we take samples, combust them, then pass them through chemicals. The process gives off a gas, which this machine analyzes and counts the particles." She tapped the cylinder. "This is a gas proportional counter. It can give a rudimentary age, but my lab uses the accelerator mass spectrometry method, which destroys less of the sample artifact and determines age by passing liquid carbon through light refractors."

He listened as she walked him through the process. Now and then, when she sensed his lack of understanding, she backtracked to clarify the scientific terms that flowed so smoothly from her tongue. The confident scientist who emerged in the place of the shy, modest woman he had put to bed the night before captivated him. She hesitated not. Carried herself with grace as she maneuvered him around the room. And her zeal for her work was naught less than catching. Before he realized what had happened, he found himself asking questions, encouraging her to tell him more. Anything that would keep her face aglow with excitement and those mesmerizing eyes shining bright.

And by the saints, she excited him. With every hard beat of his heart, heat flowed through his veins. The slight touch of her hand when she set it absently on his arm drove him to distraction. Her voice caressed, until he could not take another moment of its silken feel. As she led him past the end of the table, he dragged her to a stop. Gathering her in his arms, he crushed her against his chest. Her mouth dropped open in surprise, and Farran used the moment to his full advantage.

He backed her into the wall and pressed his body along the length of hers. He braced his hands on the hard stone at her shoulders, dipped his head, and captured her mouth. She offered no resistance as he nudged her lips apart and indulged in her sweet flavor. The kiss was hot, full of all the relentless yearning that coursed through him like a tidal wave. Where their bodies met, heat ebbed and flowed between them. And the subtle undulation of her hips swelled his cock to painful limits.

He dropped his hands to her waist to still the restless pursuit of her body. If she did not cease, he would take her here. Against the wall. Oblivious to the unlocked door and unconcerned with the fact anyone might stumble upon them. But his hands acted on their own accord. His fingers dug into her hips, drawing her close even as he pressed her flat to the stone. His body knew what it wanted, and he was helpless against it.

She sensed his need and slipped her hand between their bodies. Great horns of alarm went off as her fingers fumbled with the button to his jeans. He should stop. Back away. Take her upstairs where he could spread her on the bed. God help him, though, he could not bring himself to move. The velvety stroke of her tongue, the short breaths she sucked in through her nose, spiraled him beyond all measure of self-control.

When her fingers slipped beneath the denim and encircled his throbbing shaft, he cursed himself for teaching her so precisely. His hips bucked forward at her firm squeeze. The slow pump of her hand stirred a soul-deep groan. His body quaked as she manipulated him into hewn stone, and on a raspy gasp, he tore his mouth from hers too dazed to do naught else but breathe.

"Jesu, Noelle . . ." His body convulsed, and he sank his forehead to her shoulder. Ecstasy poured through him, bright and burning. With one last heedless thrust, he felt the warmth of his seed trickle down his abdomen. God's teeth, 'twas not what he wanted. She must think him weak.

The constriction in his chest eased enough to allow him a normal breath, and still panting, he lifted his gaze to hers. Heat blazed in her fawnlike eyes, along with something else. Something Farran could not believe.

Happiness. The same elation he had witnessed when she launched herself into his arms glowed fierce.

"You want me."

She said it not with accusation, as if she sought to hold his lapse over his head. Nor did she gloat as if she had set out to prove his weakness. Nay, her simple observation held a note of wonder. She had doubted? After the eve they spent together?

"Aye, Noelle." He grazed his teeth along the delicate skin at the side of her throat. "But not like this." Reluctantly he took a step back.

"Don't move," she ordered quietly before she ducked beneath his arm. From the nearby table she retrieved a scrap of cloth on which she dried her hand. Returning to him, she cleaned his belly, then planted a chaste kiss on his lips.

A knock at the door interrupted the blissful innocence of her mouth, and Farran hastened to fasten his jeans. "Aye?" he barked, displeased at the interruption.

Anne's merry voice called out, "I've come to collect Noelle for swords."

Farran looked to the door, then back at Noelle. He could not stomach the idea of sharing her company with others. He had let go as Caradoc advised, and now he wished to bask in the glory of true feeling. He would not stand to have that freedom interrupted by the necessity of cloaking all he felt for this woman from the eyes of men.

"Nay, Anne," he answered roughly. "I shall see to Noelle's lessons tonight."

Noelle's light laugh cascaded through the room. "Why do I have a feeling your lessons have nothing to do with swords?"

He shook his head. "We shall practice in the arena. Your safety comes first."

Though her smile did not falter, he detected a touch of disappointment within her bright eyes. That she yearned for the same things he did sent a fresh rush of heat through his veins. Yet he would not be swayed from duty so easily this time. She must learn to defend herself.

He reached for her hand. She twined her fingers through his. Drawing her close he bent his head and drew his teeth along the delicate shell of her ear. He suckled at her earlobe, then released it to murmur against the hollow beneath, "The lessons you speak of, I will grant after. If you shall allow me."

He felt her shudder. Heard the catch of her breath. Beneath his lips, her throat worked to swallow. On an airy exhale she whispered, "I will."

CHAPTER 29

Noelle stumbled backward against the ferocity of Farran's advance. Though he used less than half his strength, as his sword came down hard against the middle of her blade, pain sizzled up her arm. She let out a yelp and dropped her smaller weapon. It clattered to the tiled floor at his feet.

Wide-eyed she met his wicked grin. "That's unfair. I tripped, and you know it."

"Nay. Such is battle. You look for your opponent's weakness and manipulate it to your advantage. You could have easily nicked me under the arm as you recovered." He took a step back and his eyes assumed a harsher light. "And you should have."

Frustrated beyond all measure, she resisted the overwhelming urge to scream. "But you aren't wearing any armor. I'd have hurt you."

His long fair locks brushed against his shoulder as he shook his head. "I would have healed. You, however, would have learned a valuable lesson."

He had a point. Though the healing was debatable, she'd realized her error the moment victory leapt to his eyes. From that point on, he'd been relentless in his attack, offering no quarter to the arc of his arm and searing slice of his blade.

She muttered beneath her breath, too ashamed of her error to admit it aloud, and bent for her sword.

Farran set a booted toe on the pommel. "Nay, no more." With catlike grace, he bent over and retrieved the weapon. Rising, he tucked it into his belt beside his now-sheathed broadsword. "You are good, Noelle. 'Twill not be long before you can stand against me as my equal, but you have much to learn. And you are weary. When we began tonight, you would not have made such a careless mistake."

He clasped both her hands in his much larger ones and brought them to his lips. Light stubble on his chin scraped pleasantly as he pressed a kiss to her knuckles. His gaze shifted, darkening in hue, and filling with the same hot light she'd witnessed every time he kissed her. "Besides, we have other sport to practice."

A flush crept over her chest, up her neck, and into her cheeks. She averted her gaze in a desperate attempt to hide the way the same heat spread through her belly, down lower to stir the ache between her legs. He caught her chin in his calloused palm and lifted her face. His eyes searched hers like a falcon watching prey before it swept in for the kill. To her shame, her body betrayed her and her nipples pebbled.

Farran's gaze dipped down to her breasts, and a satisfied smile pulled at the corners of his mouth. He slid the hand beneath her chin down her throat, over her collarbone, and traced one tight peak with a solitary fingertip. She closed her eyes as every last nerve ending above her waist rose to attention. Her womb clamped down so hard her lungs felt tight. She craved the feel of his palm. Yearned to have him close those fingers around her taut flesh and massage.

Instead, Farran turned his back to her. With her hand tucked securely in his, he led her from the room, down the hall, and up the stairs. Each step led her closer to the inevitable moment she'd brazenly agreed to. Now, as it loomed closer, her damnable modesty rose up to cry foul. She didn't do these things. Couldn't. She shouldn't go to bed with a man who made it clear he didn't intend to stick around.

But the idea of denying him brought even greater discomfort. She wanted this. Wanted him. Everything he had to give. And that fierce longing kept her moving forward through her door, into the bedroom beyond.

He didn't stop at the bed as she'd expected. On the contrary, he led her into the bathroom where he turned on the tub. Stark terror turned the blood in her veins to ice. He couldn't mean for them to bathe together, could he? It was easy to tend his arousal, to bring him to pleasure. But let him witness her undressed? Last night she'd found freedom only once she had her clothes partially back on. She'd never survive the mortification of peeling them off right in front of him in the bathroom. At least in the bedroom, they could turn off the lights. She wouldn't have to look at herself to know how inadequate she was. But this . . . This involved bright lights and a complete lack of covers to hide beneath.

"W-what are you doing?" she stammered as she looked for a quick means of escape.

He reached a hand behind him, grabbed the collar of his long-sleeved shirt, and doffed it in one quick motion.

At the sight of all that smooth bronzed skin, her pulse leapt into her throat. But the sight also intensified the terrified quiver of her belly.

"We will share your bath."

Oh crap. *No!* She backed toward the archway that divided the room from the bed. Not in a hundred lifetimes. And most especially not on the very first night she made love to a man. He might have seen her naked last night for a few brief moments, but this was altogether different. She could excuse last night to hedonistic impulse. This spoke of planning. Deliberateness.

"Do not run. 'Twill be enjoyable."

Right. Kind of like having her fingernails plucked out at the root. Maybe he'd get a kick out of it, but standing before him when he could take full count of all her imperfections was the last place she wanted to be.

Denying her opportunity to retreat, Farran caught the hem of her shirt in his hands. He tugged it over her head before she could protest, then reached around her back to unclasp her bra. Slow, unhesitating fingers drew the loose straps over her shoulders, down her arms, off her hands.

She stood before him exposed. Alec's long-ago words bellowed in her head. *God, Noelle, you could pass for a guy, you're so flat.* To alleviate the embarrassment that accompanied the unwanted memory, she crossed her arms over her chest. "Really, Farran, this isn't a good idea."

Oblivious to her discomfort, he settled his hands on her waist. One firm tug erased the distance between them and brought her into his arms. With one hand, he caressed the length of her back. The other freed the button at her waist and eased the zipper on her jeans apart. Thick fingers slid beneath the denim to push the garment over her hips.

As he shucked his own, cool air kissed her skin. She shivered as goose bumps broke out in the wake of the chill. But the frigid sensation brought another awareness front and center. He hadn't just removed her jeans. He'd taken her panties with them.

Feeling much like a mouse trapped by a hungry cat, Noelle crossed an ankle over the other and attempted to huddle into herself. She couldn't bear the thought of looking at him, of seeing the disappointment in his eyes.

The hand returned to her chin and tipped her head up where she couldn't hope to avoid his frown. "What troubles you, angel?"

No way could she tell him. She'd sound like a stupid fool, and the same thing that happened last night would occur again. She'd run him off. Spoil everything. She couldn't stand that possibility. Not when all she wanted was to do this differently. Preferably in a manner that gave her room to hide. Like in the bedroom, without the lights.

"N-nothing."

His brows dove downward as his frown deepened. He cocked his head to the side and studied her. Slowly one eyebrow crept into a curious arch. The creases in his forehead smoothed. And as understanding filtered into his unblinking gaze, Farran gave her a tender smile.

He trailed his fingertips around the curve of her breasts and gently lifted them into his palms. His rough whisper soothed some of her discomfort. "Look, damsel. How perfectly you fit into my hands. Nay, do not close your eyes. Look, Noelle."

Hesitantly, she did as he asked. Her skin stood out against his, a surprisingly pleasant contrast of creamy white and sun-kissed tan. He stroked with his thumbs, massaged with his fingers. His caress held deliberateness, but the feeling was nothing less than heavenly. Her nipples puckered tight, and the soft flesh rose to attention, hungry for more.

In answer, Farran rolled the hard buds beneath the pad of his thumb. Shock arced down her spine, tingling in its wake, and Noelle let out a sharp gasp. Arching her back, she invited him to indulge.

He did, but not in the way she had anticipated. With a half step backward, he dipped his head and swirled his tongue around one aching point. Through heavy-lidded eyes, he looked up to her, the light in them full of wicked promise. As long lashes fluttered shut, he drew her nipple into his hot mouth and suckled.

The sight of her flesh sliding against those sensual lips turned her inside out. The aching between her legs that had vanished at the prospect of a bath returned tenfold, and she squirmed to find relief from the growing pressure in her womb. When he scraped his cheek across her skin and exchanged one turgid nipple for the other, she felt herself grow shamefully wet. Breathing became a chore more difficult than thinking. Thought was a thing of the past. He took her back to the place where linking words together became impossible and sensation dominated.

As he dominated her.

He lifted his head, nuzzled the deep valley of her cleavage. His chest heaved as hers did, the fall of his harsh breath matching the wild intensity of his gaze. "Watch," he murmured. "'Tis naught to be ashamed of. You fit me as no other could." As he spoke, his hand drifted down her belly. Lower. Fingers slid through intimate curls, and his warm palm cupped her feminine flesh. He pressed a thick finger to her moistened folds and rubbed the sensitive nub there. "Like so. Does it feel naught else but right?"

Oh sweet merciful God in heaven. *Yes*. Yes it did. But she couldn't get her throat to work and answer. She choked out a whimper as her body moved against his touch. Dimly, she realized she'd just acknowledged the creator he wanted her to believe in, but with the next fantastic press of his hand, the oddity spiraled out of her mind. She grabbed at his shoulders to steady her weak knees and lifted her hips into his palm.

Farran's mouth tracked a hot moist path across her throat, skimmed over her cheek, and rested briefly on hers before he murmured, "You are not watching." His eyes held hers, tawny depths scorching like fire. Then he slid his gaze away, raking a scalding path down the length of her body as he looked to where he touched her.

Against her will, her eyes followed his. She watched in fascination as he slowly slid a finger through the length of her quivering sex and withdrew his hand. Moisture glistened on his fingertip, dampness that embarrassed her yet brought to life sinfully vivid visions of erotic play. She glanced in the mirror wanting to see them both, wanting to somehow verify this perfection he spoke of.

He refused to let her. Capturing her chin between thumb and forefinger, he turned her head toward him, brought her gaze back down between their bodies. "Do you see how you affect me? My hunger for you is insatiable. If you were flawed, I would not ache for you."

His arousal was impossible to ignore. His shaft stood at full attention, thick and anxious. As if he felt the heat of her stare, his erection bobbed. A bead of moisture gathered on the smooth head. In a strange, surreal way, she knew when he took her, Farran would treat her with the same gentleness he gave her now. He would take away her pain, as he erased her fears each time he took her in his arms.

Farran settled his hands on her hips. Holding her in place, he angled his body into alignment with hers. "We will fit together just as perfectly." The gravelly tone of his voice agitated the restless hum in her blood. Time moved at a sloth's pace as Noelle stood trapped in the enveloping heat of Farran's body, unable to look away. Hard and hot, his shaft nudged at the juncture of her thighs. Slipped between her sensitive skin to slide along the slick folds of her sex. His body moved in. Molded their hips together.

And as his arms wound around her waist to hold her so close not even the air separated them, he nestled between her legs.

"Farran," she whispered as she moved against the tantalizing feel. She rubbed against his length, mystified by the pleasant friction. Last night his mouth had worked wonders. But this exceeded that ecstasy. This felt right. As if all her life she'd waited for him. For this moment. The insistent nudge against her opening came with deeper feeling. More profound sensation. As if making love to Farran somehow gave her honor.

His moist breath kissed her shoulder, and he cupped her bottom in his hands. "Aye."

The simple affirmation dissolved what remained of her hesitation. She allowed her hands to wander, to memorize the curve of his spine, the solid mass of muscle that comprised his back. As she curled her fingers into his tight buttocks, she turned her head to the mirror once more.

The sight set her aflame. His body mirrored the undulation of hers. Her curves fit into all his flat planes like interlocking jigsaw pieces. She looked so slight, and he so powerful, and yet their reflection retained grace. None of the awkwardness she'd imagined. He held possessively, but with the reverence one might give a cherished treasure.

And for the first time in her life, Noelle felt beautiful.

She turned away from the mirror and scattered kisses over his shoulder. Farran gradually let go, hesitating to take his hands off her as he stepped toward the full tub. One hand wound around her wrist, he brought her to the edge and turned off the faucet. "Come, let me bathe you."

This time, she didn't hesitate. With the confidence of a queen, Noelle stepped into the tub. Before he could pick up the waiting washcloth, she pulled it off the hook.

Farran cursed every saint he knew in English then in French, then did it again as Noelle rained water on his body. The press of her hand, the boldness he had desired, but didn't know what to do with, drove him to lunacy. If she had been any other woman, he would have hauled her onto his lap and impaled her to ease the ache in his loins. But she was not. No matter what courage her hands and mouth held, beneath it all, she was still as innocent as a lamb. He could not allow himself to forget that fact and allow his desire free reign.

He sat stock still as she lathered his chest. The *plunk* of the rag into the water, the pelt of water as she squeezed it out, the slide of her bare leg next to his, all left him shuddering.

He would not survive much more of this. Their hot play had done too much damage to his already weak control.

Inhaling a sharp breath, he caught her wrist and wrested the cloth from her fingers. He could tell by the heavy flutter of her lashes she felt the same ache he suffered. But he could not understand why she did not seek to find relief. Why she did not ease herself into his lap, down upon his straining shaft, and take them both to paradise. The water would ease her discomfort. 'Twas what he had hoped. That this bath would bring them together at the pace she preferred.

Clearly, he had assumed wrong.

He dipped the rag beneath the surface then pressed it to her breast. Her nipples pebbled beneath rivulets of water. Her skin glistened soft pink from the arousal he had stirred. He could not recall a greater pleasure, and pride infused him with a swell of warmth. She responded to him like no other. Even at this relatively innocent caress, she arched her back, closed her eyes.

He leaned forward to lap at a drop of water that clung to the soft swell of her breast. "Noelle, I ache to ease my desire inside of you."

The tremble that vibrated through her and into him flared his senses. If 'twere possible, his cock stiffened even more. He raked his teeth across her shoulder, then nipped the tender flesh at the base of her throat. Her hoarse moan rendered him senseless. Sliding a hand up her silken thigh, he found the sensitive flesh at the juncture of her legs and manipulated her tender bud. She leaned back a fraction, giving him enough room to delve deeper.

Finding her mouth, he kissed her with all the pent-up hunger he had stored away and eased one finger into the warm recesses of her feminine sheath. Her slick folds tightened, the heat of her enough to scald. The water sloshed against the basin as she moved against the slow steady thrust of his hand. Each time she brought her body forward, he pressed his palm against her most sensitive spot until she shuddered and her teeth pricked his lower lip.

Shocked, Farran drew away on a hiss. But where he had expected to find a trace of annoyance, some outward sign that this was not what she wanted, he found her eyes closed, her expression soft with rapture. God's toes, she had not even realized she bit him.

His chuckle came out in a rough bark, and he chose the safer haven of her delicate neck to sate his need to taste her. Fervently she lifted into him. He entered her once more, and the moist warmth that sheathed him gripped tight. "More . . ." With the quiet cry, her body convulsed.

'Twas all Farran needed to dismiss any hesitation he might have had about her wishes. He stood and scooped her into his arms. Heedless of the water that pooled behind them on the floor, he lifted her out of the tub and carried her to the bed. There he laid her down with care and eased his body onto hers.

Her lashes lifted, her smile sated and sublime. She looped her arms around his neck, encouraging his mouth to hers, and spread her legs to accommodate the width of his hips. Long past the ability to temper his body's demands, Farran eased the head of his throbbing cock into her tight silken flesh that further verified her innocence. Noelle went rigid in his arms.

He halted, his spine as stiff as steel, as he tore his mouth off hers. She stared, her eyes as large as saucers, and pushed at his shoulder in an attempt to dislodge him. It took several deep gulps of air to curb the instinctive need to thrust in deep and find strength enough to speak. "Relax, angel. 'Twill hurt only for a few moments."

In truth, he did not know. He had never had an innocent before. But he counted on the wise words once spoken to him and his father's timeless guidance to prove him right. God's teeth, she was so wet and tight. 'Twas hell on earth to lay here motionless, waiting for her body to accommodate him.

Noelle, however, took matters into her own hands. She squeezed her eyes shut tight, dug her nails into his shoulders, and thrust her hips hard. He slid through her tight sheath to find himself seated at the mouth of her womb. Air spilled from his lungs in a rapid rush, sensation pummeled through his body. *Jesu.*

Robbed of thought, of the very ability to function under his own power, he yielded to instinct. Finding her mouth once more, he tangled his tongue with hers and drew her into the timeless dance of lovers. The heat their bodies created infused him with such ecstasy a familiar tide of feeling surfaced. But this was somehow different. Somehow richer. As release pounded at him, a more unsettling sensation broke free. One that lacked words, or definition.

Noelle's body demanded all he could give, and he gave it freely. Knowing he was lost, knowing he could not return from this bliss she carried him to, he thrust and slid, plunged and retreated, each stroke a promise of loyalty he dared not speak. They glided together as one, their bodies slick with sweat and the remnants of their bath. Their breaths mingled, their lips never parted for more than the time it took to recapture their kiss.

The tide inside him crested, built to intolerable heights. As it crashed over him, he drowned in perfect pleasure. Noelle's cry joined his hoarse shout. Her legs wrapped around his waist, holding him tight, forbidding him to move as if he could so choose. Her flesh milked his seed until he had naught left to spill.

The rhythm of their bodies slowed, along with the velocity of their breathing. Utterly spent, Farran collapsed into her heavenly embrace. He had done the unthinkable. He had let her through every barrier he knew. And to his horror, he had come to care for this little scrap of a woman.

He closed his eyes on a contented sigh. He did not regret doing so. No woman who bared her soul so freely could be capable of betrayal.

CHAPTER 30

†

M*agic.*
It was the only word Noelle could find to describe what she'd just experienced. Not illusion, for the man in her arms was no trick of lights and mirrors. The pleasure he'd given her wasn't the product of a sleight of hand. He'd exposed her to the purest form of divine intervention she could imagine.

She furrowed her brow, catching her second reference in one evening to a greater power. God, to be exact. No, maybe not God. She wasn't ready to go that far. Until she could transport everything she'd discovered back to her lab in D.C. and the mass spectrometry equipment she trusted implicitly, the possibility for answers still remained. Though the margin of error grew smaller, she wouldn't surrender to the concept of an all-powerful creator until she'd eradicated all alternatives.

But Farran's body was magic all the same.

She snuggled deeper into his arms, luxuriating in the feeling of having him deeply embedded inside her. In a million years, she'd never dreamed a man could fit so right. As he dusted his mouth against the side of her neck, she let out a sigh that matched his sated exhale and dragged her fingers through his long hair.

"That went a little better than I thought it would."

He chuckled. "Ah, Noelle, how you amuse me. Your innocence is naught less than enchanting." Easing himself out of her body, he rolled to his side and lifted on one elbow. Head propped in his hand, he splayed his fingers over her belly. "Should it concern you, I am incapable of producing a child."

"Oh." Though nothing could explain the brief disappointment she experienced with his words, she felt it all the same. She told herself it didn't matter. That children with Farran had never been a part of her imaginings, and she didn't care if he could father kids or not. But still, the knowledge this incredible man couldn't ever experience the joys of fatherhood left her with a strange sadness.

She pushed the uncalled-for reaction aside and found a smile. "I guess I should have thought about that."

"Nay, you have little to be concerned with. I cannot give you sickness either. The only taint I shall ever carry is the darkness of Azazel."

The hair at the back of her neck stood on end at his subtle reference to his claims of immortality. Her gaze jumped to the faint scar on his shoulder, nearly invisible two days later. The mark on his forehead was the same—nothing but a narrow line she had to squint to see. He'd needed stitches. No medical advances could heal that quickly.

Her mind fought against the obvious. She didn't want to believe he was some ancient knight who'd live forever. Couldn't. That she even considered the possibility made her feel like she belonged in the loony bin. And yet, how could she argue when his wounds healed at extraordinary rates and every last damn word he uttered came with earnest conviction?

Not to mention the torc wrapped around her arm.

She fingered the thin metal band, drawing Farran's gaze onto the glinting bronze. He reached out, encircled the trinket, and slid it down over her elbow and wrist. Holding it to the light, he studied the rich play of colors in the patina. "My duty is to protect you. I cannot fulfill that responsibility so long as you refuse your oath. Will you take it, now that you know how it shall be between us?"

Noelle blinked. Her heart seized as she came to the startling realization all the tenderness he'd shown her could be nothing but farce. She sat up suddenly and peered at him. "You think I'll make some vow that will keep me here because we had good sex?"

His forehead furrowed in a deep frown. "Why would you not? 'Tis your duty."

White-hot anger blistered through her. The cad! The arrogant, deceitful jerk. She snatched at the sheet and tugged it over her nakedness. *Fool!* She should have known better than to trust his pretty words. All he'd wanted was to coerce her into agreeing to that promise. Just like every other guy she'd mistakenly believed in, Farran disappointed the moment her defenses dropped.

Fury turned her hands to tight fists she clenched into the sheet. "How could I be so stupid? I *believed* you, Farran."

It was his turn to bolt upright. His scowl cut sharp. "Believed what, damsel? That I would forget my responsibility to you? I seek only to keep you safe."

She shook her head. "No. You only care about what

you want. The fact you'd seduce me to obtain it sickens me. Get out. I might be naive, but I'm not stupid."

He spluttered, his expression a mask of disbelief. "What manner of absurdity . . ." He snapped his mouth shut, opened it, then closed it once again. Blinking several times, he stared as if he couldn't believe she'd seen through his thin disguise. "Noelle . . ." He reached for her.

She moved faster. Jerking the sheet free, she scrambled from the bed. "Get out, Farran. I don't want to hear any more of your pretty words. They've done enough damage. You could have had me so easily. But the fact you went to this extent . . ." She trailed away as her voice cracked. "Just get out," she finished on a choked whisper.

Farran tried once more. Lunging across the bed, he attempted to catch hold of Noelle's hand and drag her back into the pillows where he could talk sense into her. Damnation, what had gotten into her head? Was it so difficult to believe he meant his words—that he wanted to ensure no harm could come to her? Had he not proven himself worthy of her trust?

As she recoiled as if his touch would scald, annoyance cracked through his diminished patience. Fine. If she wished for him to leave, he would. He would not beg. 'Twas not part of his nature. Once mayhap. Never again. When she could use the logic she so prided herself on, he would explain.

He threw himself from the bed and stormed to the bathroom to collect his clothes. But when he returned to the bedroom fully dressed and found her huddled on the edge of her bed, his annoyance turned on him instead. Saints' blood, he could not blame her for misconstruing his words. He had been vague, and she had yet to comprehend the deeper meaning to the oath her position demanded.

"Noelle, I would not play you false." He approached the side of the bed he had lain on and curled his fingers into his palm, resisting the urge to reach for her a third time. "I worry for your safety. With the oath, you shall gain my immortality. 'Tis the only way I know to keep you from Azazel."

Her disbelieving snort lanced pain through his tightening heart. "And I suppose you're ready to suck up your pride and fulfill your part of the bargain?"

He hesitated on the word *aye*. No matter how he tried, 'twould not dislodge from the back of his seizing throat. His pulse quickened at the prospect, but the deeper-rooted fear of betrayal wound an impassible barrier between his mind and his tongue. He cared for her, aye. But he was not ready to take the final vow. To give his loyalty to her and be bound for eternity to place her above all others.

She looked over her shoulder awaiting his response. The tears gathered in her eyes tore him into pieces. He swallowed hard, knowing he must make this right, yet unable to grant her request.

"Like I thought." Sadly, she shook her head and turned away. "Nothing's changed. I'm still just a pawn in your stupid game. Take me home, damn it."

Farran opened his mouth to protest, then slowly closed it. He dropped the torc on the bed. What use was it to argue when he could not grant her what she needed? He had pushed, aware he should not. Spoiled the most incredible night he had ever experienced. The enormous cavern between them left him hollow and wanting. If he could but somehow bridge it . . .

He turned for the door, hating himself. Hating Brighid for the monster she had turned him into.

Noelle refused to cry. As the door thumped shut, she pulled in a deep breath and forbade the tears to fall. Soft purring from the foot of the bed drew her out of her dismal thoughts, and she instinctively reached for her cat. Scooping him into her arms, she buried her nose in his fur and exhaled with a shudder.

When she closed her eyes, all the images she longed to forget tormented. Farran holding her, Farran's mouth at her breasts, Farran's body possessing hers in a way that made her light-headed. She shut the images out with a groan and looked out the window. If she had to sit here all night and replay what had turned into disaster, she'd go crazy. She needed to move. Change scenery. Go home.

If she were in D.C., she could jump into her car and spend the restless energy at the gym. Run on the treadmill until her legs burned so badly that by the time she got home she'd pass out.

But she wasn't in Washington. She was stuck in this beautiful room, her only companions the voices in her head and her faithful cat.

Still, she didn't have to sit here. Maybe someone would be in the commons and she could forget with a good movie. Or maybe she could weasel in on a game of pool—not that she had ever played. At the very least, she could raid the kitchen.

Unwilling to look at the clothes Farran had peeled off her, she quickly donned a comfortable pair of sweats and a navy blue T-shirt. She stuffed her feet into her sneakers, gave her cat an affectionate pat, and trudged out the door.

Caradoc greeted her with a cordial smile, which only reminded her more of her current circumstance as quasi-prisoner. But the subtle trill of Anne's light laughter that floated through her closed door, stopped Noelle's trek toward the stairs. Conversation. Another woman to commiserate with. Maybe even get some answers to the things she didn't really want to know.

She pivoted, hesitating only a moment before she knocked.

Anne's laughter grew louder as she approached. The door cracked open, and her bright smile greeted. "Noelle. Come in." She swung the door wide.

Noelle shifted her weight. "If it's all the same, I'd rather not. Is there wine around here anywhere?"

From the concern that filled Anne's sky-blue eyes, Noelle guessed the redhead had noticed her teary eyes. Anne stepped into the hall, dragging the door closed behind her. "No wine—alcohol is forbidden within the temple. But we can find some tea."

They descended the stairs in silence. The same quiet engulfed them as Anne ushered Noelle into the kitchen and poured steaming water from a tall percolator. She passed Noelle a mug, dropped a teabag in, then gestured at a small table tucked into the corner.

Noelle sank into the metal chair. She stared at the cup she held, uncertain what to say now that she'd dragged Anne out of her room.

"You want to talk about it, or do you just want the company?"

On a heavy sigh, Noelle leaned back in her chair. "I'm not sure."

"I heard your door slam not too long before you knocked. I assume you and Farran had an argument?"

"You could say so." Noelle dunked her teabag for good measure. Convinced it had steeped long enough, she dropped the soppy pouch onto the table and watched as liquid pooled around it.

Anne reached a slender hand across the table to clasp Noelle's. "Things are only complicated if you ignore what's in your heart."

"Anne, there's so many things I don't understand." The words came out in a rush that gained momentum with their freedom. "Torcs aren't supposed to move without help. Pieces of wood can't be buried in sand yet saturated with water. Puncture wounds deep enough to fit my thumb in up to my second knuckle don't heal overnight."

Anne's hand squeezed more tightly, offering encouragement, yet she said nothing.

"I slept with Farran. It was incredible. I thought he was really, you know, *there* with me. Really feeling the same things I was. I don't know how he couldn't have. And then, I find out it was all an act. A great seduction just to get me to say those stupid words."

Withdrawing her hand, Anne gave Noelle a sympathetic smile. "I've never known Farran to be anything less than honest. Maybe you misunderstood?"

Noelle waved her hand in dismissal. "Oh he had pretty words. Plenty of them. He tried to cover his mistake by telling me he was worried about me. That he wanted to keep me safe. But when I challenged him to follow through on his part, he couldn't answer. Wouldn't. He left."

A frown touched the high arch of Anne's elegant eyebrows. In her thoughtful stare, Noelle observed secrets. Things Anne knew but wouldn't tell her. Sincerity mixed with that private knowledge, however, making it difficult for Noelle to believe Anne would tell her lies.

"Aside from the evil Farran battles, he has his own private demons to fight. I'll tell you two things, Noelle, and I pray you listen. If you don't, I fear the devastation you'll cause."

A chill wafted down Noelle's spine. The urge to run away before Anne could tell her things she didn't want to hear pressed hard. She squirmed in her chair, caught by an even greater, warring curiosity. "Go on," she muttered.

"Farran's not lying to you. The oath he wants will keep you safe. It will save his life too."

Exhausted by the same spiel, Noelle let out a heavy sigh. "He's said as much."

"Don't press him. When he's ready to let his past go, he'll tell you everything. You'll understand, and whatever you feel for him now will only deepen."

She took a moment to process the information. Not entirely certain she understood, she frowned at Anne. "You mean he's got some tragic past?"

"Yeah. Something like that." She took a sip of her tea and smiled over the rim of her mug. When she set it down, the smile vanished into sharp warning. She lowered her voice, leaned in closer. "Tell him the Sudarium is in Ohio. Before Mikhail does it for you. If you tell him *why* you hid it, he'll understand. But if you don't, Noelle, I don't know if you'll ever be able to make it right."

Noelle recoiled, sending her chair rocking precariously on its rear legs. She leaned forward before she toppled backward, and the chair crashed in place with a *thunk*. "How do you know?" she cried in a whisper. "I was the only one there. I've told no one."

"I told you I can see things. When I held your hand just now, I saw the board you loosened in the floor. *Tell him.* Before you can't."

Anne drained her mug and rose. "He's outside in the gardens, where he goes to think." Standing at the side of the table, she smiled down at Noelle. "While you're at it, you might also mention how you really feel about him. I think you'd be pleasantly surprised."

Speechless, Noelle stared at Anne's back as she retreated through the swinging silver door. How she really felt? How could Anne know? Noelle wasn't even sure she understood all that Farran made her feel. And how in the hell had her being upset over Farran's rejection ended up in a lecture on where she'd failed?

She turned her mug in lazy circles, grumbling to herself. If anything Anne had said was true, it was the Sudarium. Though she couldn't explain how Anne knew it rested beneath floorboards in Ohio, Noelle wasn't foolish enough to think if she didn't come clean with Farran, whatever chance she had at holding on to him would slip through her fingers. No man liked to be lied to. And that's exactly what she was doing every time she avoided the subject or hoped it would simply go away.

Her stomach in knots over what she must do, she stood and smoothed her palms on her sweatpants. Outside. If she could find the gardens, she'd get this over with. It had waited too long as it was. Besides, she'd rather tell him now when he'd hurt her as much as he could, than give him the opportunity to soothe the wounds and make her bleed later.

Maybe, just maybe, he'd take her home before he could get close enough that she didn't want to leave.

CHAPTER 31

✝

Farran palmed the pommel of his sword as he scanned the fence for the predators he could feel. Unholy eyes watched and waited. Vile beings scurried amongst the dried foliage. Branches snapped, leaves crunched. The whispered hiss of evil floated on the slight breeze. But only shadows met his watchful eye.

The darkness in Farran's soul stirred in recognition of its kind. It brimmed in his blood, tormented his thoughts. Urged him to step beyond the protected boundary, engage, and join their unholy ranks.

They would fight again tonight, and he with them. Soon, though, battle would become an impossibility. If his next kill did not wrest him into that black abyss, the act of fighting would rent pain far worse than any injury.

'Twas what Caradoc battled. With each sunrise, Caradoc's pain intensified. Each night he drew his sword, Farran prayed his brother would return. God only knew how long any of them might linger on this earth. If God was kind, Farran would hear Noelle's oath and be spared the chains of inescapable agony. Yet Farran had learned centuries ago, kindness was not part of the Almighty's composition. The very exchange with Noelle in the bedroom proved such. The Grand Creator asked for naught less than all a man could give. And for Farran, far more than he could manage.

Footsteps behind him brought him up short. He spun around, reflex tightening his sword arm. At the sight of Noelle, he swore beneath his breath. Arms crossed over her chest to ward off the cold, she picked her way through the remnants of snow. In the moonlight, a halo of silver illuminated her creamy skin and danced off her silken hair. Were it not for the breath that clouded around her, he would have sworn he looked upon a specter.

The creatures in the trees stirred. Hushed voices took on an anxious hum. Anger that she would risk her safety by venturing outdoors cracked through Farran's momentary awe. He clenched his teeth tight, his fingers even tighter, and scowled.

"Farran, I need to talk to you."

"Go inside!" he snapped. "You should not be out here."

Defying him, she continued to close the distance between them. "I'm not a prisoner. You said so yourself. I need to talk to you, and it won't wait."

As she arrived at his side, he swiped an arm out to push her away from the iron fence. She stumbled, but moved forward. At the pressure he continued to apply to her shoulder in hopes she would retreat the way she had come, however, she dug her heels in and pushed back on his hand. "Stop it!"

"Nay, get yourself inside, damsel. We will talk come morn."

She twisted free of his hold and flung his arm aside.

"No, we won't. I've done something I'm not proud of. You're going to listen to me while I have the courage to tell you!"

Something deep inside him splintered at her words. She regretted their joining. He had dared to hope, and had erred. Could the Almighty be more cruel? As the fist of darkness around his heart squeezed and its vile claws pierced, he turned away before she could see how her rejection affected him. "Go inside, Noelle," he repeated in a flat whisper. He inhaled deeply to strengthen his voice. "There is no need for you to clear your conscious. That you regret what we have done 'tis obvious."

Tiny hands clawed at his shoulder in a futile attempt to turn him around. Her touch burned like a hot poker. Unable to stomach her insistence to speak the words, he braced himself against the pull and took another step forward.

Noelle darted around him and pulled on his arm, forcing him to come about. Her voice rose several octaves as she cried, "What is the *matter* with you? Is it always about you? Always what you want? Damn it, Farran I'm not talking about—"

Her words strangled to a yelp as a shadowy fist shot through the gaps in the fence and wrapped around her throat. The demon jerked her backward, slamming her back into the metal posts. Terror leapt to her eyes.

Farran's heart lurched to a standstill. Though he drew his sword with a barbarian's frenzy, he could not move fast enough to stop the vile claws from sinking in. A trickle of blood rolled down Noelle's fragile neck.

She clawed for freedom, kicked a leg out behind her. Another hand snatched at her foot, binding her in place.

Enraged, Farran let out a bellow. Fear so great his

blood turned to ice and consumed him. He charged forward, driven by the instinctive need to stop her pain. Hacking his sword through the narrow opening, he brought it down on the unholy hand, neatly severing it.

Noelle lurched forward gasping. But the claws that held her ankle toppled her to the ground. Another hand snaked out, determined to catch her free foot and drag her through the gate. A second set of claws crept through, waiting to capture what other parts of her they might touch. She let out a hoarse scream. Digging her fingers into the cold hard earth, she tried to crawl to freedom.

"Nay! You cannot have her!"

Like a madman, Farran swung. His sword struck the ground, jarring his arm all the way to his shoulder. He shook off the stun and sliced again. They would not take her. Not Noelle. Not the woman he had bared his soul to.

The hand around her ankle broke off with a sickening squish of vile flesh. Before the other could grab Noelle's freed foot, Farran lobbed it off as well. Freed from her restraints, Noelle scrambled several feet away. From the corner of his eye, he caught her watchful gaze as he quickly disposed of the remaining set of claws and swiped his blade on the leg of his jeans. He stuffed the sword into his scabbard and rushed to her crumpled form.

Scooping her into his arms, he cradled her trembling body close. She turned her face into his chest with a soft cry. He dug his fingers into her hair and held tight, uncertain whom he sought to comfort more. Though the danger had passed, the ghastly scene replayed in his mind. He had almost lost her. If she had been out here alone . . .

He shuddered and tightened his hold. Brushing a kiss against the top of her head, he murmured, "Shh. You are safe. 'Tis over."

He knew not how long he held her, but the quaking of her body ebbed. As did his. When she rubbed her cheek against his shoulder and touched her fingertips to her neck, he eased her far enough away he could inspect the wounds. She tipped her head, allowing him the freedom.

Three jagged tears marred her delicate flesh, but the wounds were shallow. The puncture of claws had missed her vital veins. But already he could see the rise of deep purple where the viselike fingers strangled.

"Come. Let us take you inside."

He helped her to her feet, but her legs refused to hold. She wobbled into him, her fears having exhausted her strength. Farran lifted her into his arms. As if she were grateful for his aid, she laid her head on his shoulder and expelled a shuddering breath. With quick, purposeful strides, he carried her through the front entry where he gently deposited her at the foot of the stairs.

"Anne!"

The door upstairs thumped at his bellow. Footsteps pounded down the stairs, a matched pair of boots and sock-clad feet. "Oh God, what happened?" Anne's question blended with the scrape of Merrick's sword.

Farran lifted his gaze to Merrick's knowing stare. "Merrick, rouse the men. The demons attacked Noelle. We must clear the trees once and for all."

Noelle snatched at his arm. "Please don't leave me."

He gazed into her wide eyes, wanting naught else but to stay at her side and offer the comfort she needed. But 'twas his fault this had occurred. Mayhap if he had fought the night before, none of Azazel's creatures could return to his foul realm and solicit reinforcements. He reluctantly pried her fingers free and bent to press a chaste kiss to her forehead. "I must go. Anne shall see to your wounds."

He looked away before her pleading gaze could deter him and nodded at Anne. "If you must, take her to Uriel."

"Of course, Farran." She assumed the place he had abandoned at Noelle's side.

In the privacy of Anne's room, Noelle let the tears fall. Holding them back had become too much effort, and with Farran unable to witness her absolute failure of strength, she gave in. They rolled down her cheeks in silent rivulets that dropped into her lap.

Anne grabbed for a Kleenex and pressed it into Noelle's hand. "Hold on, almost done." She dabbed a bit of salve on a finger and smeared it down Noelle's throat. "There. You'll be fine."

While the ointment soothed the burn, it did nothing for the scald in Noelle's throat. She swallowed with difficulty and managed a short nod.

Anne's soft gaze pled with her. "Please don't be upset with Farran. This is what they do."

"I'm not." The effort of talking made her throat ache even more. And truth to tell, she didn't want to speak. What had happened moments ago shattered all her illusions. She couldn't pretend to understand anymore. To continue to swear the extraordinary events could all be explained by science.

Demons had attacked her. She'd seen the shadowy hand, the horrific claws. Felt the icy touch of death. Smelled the fetid breath.

Anne gave Noelle's knee an affectionate pat. "I'm going to go down to the kitchen and get you some tea."

Noelle nodded in thanks. When Anne left, she sank into the overstuffed couch and stared out the window at the unseen noises beyond. Her hand moved absently over the torc. If demons existed, everything else Farran claimed existed too. Immortality. Seraphs. Archangels. Anne could see through the veil.

Which also meant that silly cloth she'd hidden wasn't just a meaningless scrap of fabric. She'd hidden the Sudarium of Oviedo, and the things that wanted her, wanted it. She'd almost died over that shroud. How many more car wrecks would it take to drive that point home?

She groaned to herself. Blind—she'd been absolutely blind. But then, Anne had said she was. Some prophecy marked her as such.

The same prophecy that dictated she should pledge herself to Farran. The man who couldn't bring himself to offer the same loyalty to her.

Her brows furrowed as she considered another possibility. Anne had said taking that vow would save his life. How? Maybe she did descend from angels, as hard as it might be to believe, but how could saying a few words in Latin save an immortal's life? He could still take wounds. By his own words, the sword he used could kill him. So what difference would this oath make?

And then there was tonight. She'd have wagered her very soul Farran felt something for her. Maybe he had. Whatever it was, though, it wasn't enough to overcome the things he hid from her. The secrets Anne knew.

Another tear fell to her lap as reality settled in. She didn't mean enough. He might have opened up, but she was still just a tool. She'd given him everything she had to offer someone, and now he had her faith. He, however, was still as distant as the life she'd known in D.C.

Damn it all, it shouldn't bother her. Yet no matter how she tried to fight it, she couldn't avoid the fact she cared. About him. About this silly oath that was supposed to bind them for eternity. She didn't know exactly when she'd fallen in love with the grumpy, arrogant, jerk, but God help her, she had.

Voices comingled in the night. Dead. Demons. Templar—shouts clashed as severely as their natures. Above the din, the song of striking steel rang a clear, eerie note. Farran gripped the leather-wrapped pommel of his sword tighter. The darkness from his kill roiled in his veins, burned through his limbs. At his side, Tane, who had happened on the battle moments after it began, neatly hacked his way through a pair of confused shades. Heads lobbed off shoulders, rolled to the ground. Tane also staggered under the infusion of unholy taint, but he recovered with a sharp upper cut that sank his borrowed blade deep into a nytym's soft underbelly.

A flash of yellow-green drew Farran's attention on the trees. He kicked aside the pile of shadows near his feet and shouldered past Tane. The pinpricks of pain on his face did not deter him. If anything, they pressed him harder. He had attained that sacred place where survival dominated all thought. Where instinct honed by years of training narrowed his focus on his foe alone. Save for the fleeting picture of Noelle's stricken features that flashed in his memory and hardened his resolve.

Sword in hand, he elbowed aside a thatch of thorny foliage and stepped into the underbrush. It snapped back into place, lashing across his face. He expelled an annoyed hiss. Squinting into the dark, he searched for the hidden creature.

A rustle to his left spun him in the direction of the sound.

As he took another step into the starless copse, the

rush of wind behind him whipped his hair. In the next instant, pain split through his skull. Darkness infringed on his vision. He tottered forward, catching himself on a thick tree. His mistake shot into his awareness. In his blind chase, he had left his brethren behind. Walked right into what could be a deadly trap. Christ's toes! Only a squire would suffer such a foolish error in judgment.

Above, the trees quaked with the vile presence. The birds had long fled, and even the crickets fell to silence. Evil pressed down upon Farran like a heavy fist intent on smashing through his chest. Cold. Oppressive.

Nearby.

With a violent shake of his head, he cleared the blackness from his vision. He dragged in a deep fortifying breath and adjusted his grip on his sword. He heard the hollow cackle long before he saw the creature. Filled with the aching sorrow of a thousand lost souls, the chilling sound filtered through the overhanging branches to caress him with a promise of slow death.

He had only enough time to bring his sword in front of his chest, and the trees broke. A pair of snarling demons, too enraged to hold their human forms, hurtled toward him. With no way to retreat, Farran did the only thing he could. He flattened his back to the hulking oak and prepared to defend.

The first struck out like the lash of a whip. Claws raked down his chest, tearing links of mail apart. Then 'twas gone, and the second lunged forward. Farran blocked the blow to his left side, prepared to counter, but the creature retreated before he could do so much as twitch his arm.

'Twas a favorite game of demons. Pick off pieces until naught was left but bone. They worked in pairs to overwhelm their opponent. When they finished toying with their prey, they would share the spoils.

Farran studied their movement, attuned his mind to the rhythm of their coordinated strikes. Lunge, retreat, lunge, retreat—he counted off the paces. When the beast on his left rushed in, he swung his right arm in a wide arc across his body and cleaved the ghastly head in two. The demon's body fell to a shadowy heap, and its vile spirit quickly did its damage.

Agony wrenched through Farran's body. Through clenched teeth, he let out a strangled cry. But the expulsion did naught to lesson the blinding strike of lightning that set his blood on fire. His knees gave out, and he buckled to the ground.

A hideous battle cry deafened him as the remaining beast lumbered closer. Farran struggled to right himself, to see past the blearing of his vision. He squinted through the beads of sweat that rolled into his eyes, but the sting made focus impossible. In the time it took to swipe his forearm across his eyes, the demon struck home. Claws cut through Farran's clothing where his mail had been torn. He felt his flesh tear. Screamed at the scrape against his bone. Blood poured forth, oozing down his ribs into the waistband of his jeans.

Panting, he doubled over, trying to squeeze the rent flesh back together. He fought for the strength to rise. Between great rasping gasps, he eyed the evil predator. He would not give up the fight. If he were meant to die here, he would do so with his blade stuffed in the creature's gullet.

'Twas then he noticed his attacker's hand. Where claws should have curled in synchrony with the other mangled fist, naught but rent flesh dangled from the useless limb. A fresh new bout of rage erupted within Farran's soul, and as the demon lunged for him again, he threw his weight into his sword.

The blade sank deep into the creature's gut. Beady yellow-green eyes went wide with shock. On a grunt, Farran pulled his sword free to plunge it in once more. He jerked his arm up, widening the wound. A gargled noise burst from the demon's throat, and then it collapsed.

As the shadows pooled into the barren ground, Farran yielded to the darkness he was to become.

CHAPTER 32

✝

Merrick surveyed the men around him, counting his brothers. All were present, save for one. Lucan bled from a wound to his head. Caradoc favored a wrenched knee. Tane cradled a cracked wrist. Even Declan left the field holding his arm, his former injury not yet healed. But Farran was nowhere to be found.

Not wanting to call attention to the matter after last night's bickering, Merrick limped to Caradoc's side, his own wound aggravated in the fight. He set a hand on Caradoc's shoulder, gaining the younger man's attention. "Where is Farran?"

Caradoc's expression turned to ash. He straightened to his full six-foot height to look over the gathered heads. His gaze stopped on the same faces Merrick's had, then canvassed the remaining knights gathered near the gates. With a slow shake of his head, he conveyed he did not know.

Merrick nodded at Declan, indicating Caradoc should inquire. When he started for the Scot, Merrick turned for

Lucan. Distracting Lucan with the same unobtrusive gesture, he asked, "Have you seen Farran?"

Lucan's frown was as harsh as the man's they sought. "Nay. He is not present?"

A deep dark foreboding settled into the base of Merrick's spine. He had witnessed Farran in the midst of battle. To leave the field was not in the hardened warrior's nature. That he did not gather with the rest of them spoke ill. Of possibilities Merrick did not wish to consider.

"He passed me not long ago," Tane supplied as he stepped up to join the pair.

Merrick automatically tensed. To be certain, they had needed the banished knight's arm, but Tane had trespassed too severely for Merrick to welcome his presence. Whilst Anne might find forgiveness easy, 'twould take far longer than the passing of a month for Merrick to do the same.

He looked beyond Tane, unable to meet his stoic stare. "Where?"

"There." Tane indicated a place in the road where two tree limbs jutted out at an angle. "He went within."

"Damnation," Merrick muttered. As dread turned his gut into a fist of iron, he scowled at Lucan. "Gather the others."

The silence spanned heavily whilst Merrick avoided conversing with Tane and waited for Lucan to return. He shifted his weight, rocked on his heels.

Tane broke the quiet first. "Thank you."

Cringing inwardly, Merrick slid his oath-breaking brother a sideways glance. "Do I wish to know what for?"

"The money."

Ah. The explanation for why he had come. Anne must have sent for him. She had spent the last several days pleading Tane's defense in hopes Merrick would relent and bequeath the desired funds. He had, if for no other reason than to cease her wheedling. But he had not expected she would send for Tane on the very day he relented and gave her the draft.

He cleared his throat. "Aye. It seems you have a champion in my wife."

"Lady du Loire is the truest lady I have ever known."

To Merrick's relief, Lucan returned with Caradoc and Declan. He turned to his men, his expression grave. "We must find Farran." Or what was left of him. "Tane saw him go into the trees."

Five men marched to the broken branches in silence. They ducked under the thorny sprigs, brothers as they once had been before Azazel had used their weaknesses to create divides. For the first time in many years, no suspicion, pain, jealousy, or self-doubt could rend the bonds of unity. Farran dominated their thoughts. Brought them all together.

They spanned out a sword's distance apart, each responsible for the eight-foot diameter path he walked. Their boots crunched dried leaves. Their breaths curled out before them. And in the oppressive silence, they fell into the comfortable patterns they knew as intimately as they knew their names.

"Over here!" Caradoc hollered from Merrick's left.

Merrick cut through a thick clump of dead shrubs and rushed to the grove of flattened grass Caradoc stood upon. Behind him, the hurried tromp of boots announced the others followed.

The bitter taste of bile rose to the back of Merrick's throat as he looked upon the bloody scene. Crumpled at the base of a hundred-year-old oak, Farran lay unmoving in a scarlet heap. His sword rested just beyond his open hand. Beneath him, the ground pooled with crimson.

Merrick had witnessed death a thousand times before. So oft had he heard the guttural cry of life snuffed out, he had become immune to the sound. Yet now, as he looked upon one of the truest brothers he could claim, all the centuries of combat could not quell the churning of his gut. He choked back the sudden, violent need to vomit and forced himself to join Caradoc at Farran's side.

"He breathes, but barely," Caradoc murmured.

As Merrick reached down to test Farran's pulse, Caradoc's arm shot out to block his hand. "Nay. The darkness taunts him. Though he is broken, he still retains the need to fight."

And so it had come to this. When Farran's salvation lay in his very bed, he would meet a different kind of angel. One who came with the quick slash of Mikhail's sword. Merrick turned away, unable to stop the unexpected rush of moisture to his eyes.

Of all the people who would come to Farran's defense, Merrick had never imagined 'twould be Lucan. He bent down behind Farran and stuffed his hands beneath his arms. "We will take him to Uriel. Not to Mikhail."

"Aye," the collective male chorus agreed.

Together they lifted him, avoiding Farran's struggles. Where Farran found the ability to fight, Merrick could not imagine, but he too had come this close. Had turned on Caradoc in a blind rage. Mayhap hope remained.

But as he assumed a position near Farran's right shoulder and drew the man's weight onto him, Farran's broken whisper explained far more than curses brought by arch-angels.

"Do not . . . let her . . . see me."

'Twas Noelle, not darkness, that possessed Farran to fight. Encouraged by the discovery, Merrick hastened his step.

At the base of the stairs, Noelle gnawed on a fingernail. Beside her, Anne paced as she had since the rest of the men returned. Noelle knew without being told, someone was hurt. The grave expressions on the passing knights' faces said all she needed to hear. And when one man made the fatal mistake of holding her gaze too long, the sympathy reflected in his green eyes told her everything else. The someone was Farran.

Worry consumed her. Even the night her parents had died, she hadn't felt so hopeless, so on the verge of complete breakdown. The man had turned her inside out. Twisted her so tightly she didn't know which end was up or down. Less than one week, and she couldn't tolerate the thought she might lose him.

"They come! Fetch Uriel!" a voice ordered from the window in the billiards room.

A second later, the door burst open and the men clamored inside. Two at his feet, two at his head, one holding his hands on his belly, they carried Farran in a stretcher hold. At the sight of his blood and the scarlet trail he left behind, Noelle's empty stomach heaved. She rushed to him and clutched at his hand. "Farran." Her other hand dropped to his side, coating her palm with warm wetness.

Somehow, unbelievably, he managed a hoarse chuckle. His eyes opened to laugh at her, but the light that glinted within was dark, void of the warm tone of ale. "You have . . . what you . . . desired." A rasping cough possessed him, and the men struggled to maintain their hold.

Anne came up behind her, drawing Noelle away by her

elbow. Noelle stepped back to let them pass, yet she failed to move far enough away she couldn't hear Farran's heartless words.

"You . . . shall go home now."

Her hand flew to her mouth, silencing her gasp. Surely, he couldn't think she'd want him to suffer this, just to go back to D.C.? That she'd be glad if he died?

The pressure on her elbow increased, and Anne urged her toward the stairs. "There's nothing we can do, Noelle. Uriel will take care of him."

Noelle jerked free. All the frustration, all the pent-up confusion, and every last drop of annoyance she felt for Farran broke with Anne as its target. "Let go of me! I'm sick to death of everyone treating me like a child. I don't give a damn what you want me to do—I'm going with him!"

The first sign Anne could be anything but sweet shone in the harsh, angry lines of her face. She caught Noelle's wrist, clamped her fingers down so hard her nails bit into Noelle's skin. With a fierce jerk, she dragged Noelle toward the ascending stairs. "You may think you understand, but you've hardly scratched the surface. You're going upstairs before Farran kills you."

Noelle didn't have time to process the words. Anne yanked again, and Noelle tripped over the bottommost tread.

Eyes closed to block the brightness of light, Farran lay in the infirmary, taking stock of what he knew, what he thought he knew, and what he could no longer comprehend. He could not understand why no one had blocked Noelle from seeing him. Why they had given no consideration to her fears and allowed her to wait with the seasoned Anne in the entry hall. Her stricken features, her ashen complexion, was obvious even to him as he wavered on the edge of consciousness. 'Twould be a wonder if she could ever look on him again and not see a monster.

He knew he had hurt her with his words. The darkness he had consumed would not let him stop them from sliding off his tongue. He knew too that his brothers feared 'twas more than his tongue he could not control. And although evil boiled in his blood and threatened to snuff out his senses, he held it at bay, the last vestige of light inside his soul far stronger than he had ever imagined.

He would swear upon his sword when Noelle had touched him, her fingers restored warmth to the ice flowing in his veins. He could not decide, however, if 'twas a caress of divinity or his body's mere reaction to having her show such care. He would further swear he had heard her shout she would attend to him in the infirmary. And yet she made no appearance. Had she changed her mind, or were her words a mere product of his fantasy?

He sighed, the effort of which shot pain down to his toes. Grimacing, he tried to temper the burn, but it sizzled like the blade once pressed to his belly.

A comforting hand came to rest upon his shoulder. "'Twill heal, brother. But will you?"

Farran turned his head to find Declan studying him. A fresh new scar on the Scot's face tugged around the hard set to his mouth. Too healed to have come from this night of fighting, it puzzled Farran. Until tonight, Declan had made no appearance at his brothers' sides for several weeks. When had he earned the scar? What creatures did he fight?

Not wanting to consider the possibilities, Farran told himself 'twas not unusual for a Templar to follow duty even when Mikhail forbade them to attend the gates alone. He found the strength to answer, "I am fine."

A touch of Declan's good humor sparked behind his rugged face. "Och, Farran, 'tis a hole the size of a fist in your side! I donna think you are as fine as you claim."

"Uriel has stitched me shut." Farran's gaze flicked back to Declan's, and he furrowed his brow, hating to reveal the extent of his craving for Noelle. Yet the nagging voice that demanded to look upon her heavenly face would not stay quiet. "Send Noelle to me. She will speed my healing."

Declan took his hand away. With one step backward, he sealed the doubt in Farran's mind. "She doesna wish to see you, brother."

The words were not unfamiliar. More than one serving maid within Clare had said the same. Yet the brittle rejections hundreds of years ago did not carry the sting of daggers quite like Declan's low murmur. Before Declan could observe the shameful mist that gathered in Farran's eyes, Farran turned his head back to the wall.

Declan exited the infirmary under Leofric's expectant stare. He took a deep breath, squared his shoulders, and gave his new commander a crisp nod. "'Tis done."

Deep inside his shadowed soul, a splinter festered. He had wounded Farran. Used the man's fears against him to earn a place within Leofric's honorable faction. With Farran's insistence on staying with Noelle before their oaths were sealed, he had disobeyed the edicts. He brought impurity upon the Order. Yet the awareness Declan had twisted the eternal dagger embedded in Farran's heart did not carry the same reward Leofric had promised. He did not feel proud. He felt naught but shame.

Leofric rewarded Declan's actions with a tight smile. "It becomes easier."

Indeed, he hoped so. He lacked the time to waste. His spirit shied at slaying Azazel's creatures, and the lifting of his blade required far more than strength of arm. He was not long for this world. When he left, he wished to make a mark upon it.

The tap of feet upon the stone stairs sent Leofric into the shadows beyond the mounted torch. His waspish whisper scraped through the empty hall. "She comes. I shall stay to witness. When you finish with her, we shall discuss your next responsibility."

Declan took his position at the infirmary's door. He lifted his eyes to the stairwell as the soft treads grew nearer. In the next heavy drum of his heart, Noelle emerged. She looked left and right, ensuring no one witnessed her approach. And then her widened eyes settled on him.

She had not expected to find a guard.

Her composure returned with the adjustment of her glasses. She took a bold step forward. "I wish to see Farran."

The words he must utter tasted as vile as horse piss. He could not stand the thought of wounding this lovely creature. This woman who had done naught. She belonged to Farran. How the Almighty brought them together should not be tampered with.

And yet, Leofric's words surfaced to give him strength. *Their bond cannot be pure if they first indulge in sin.*

Declan drew in a deep breath and held her defiant gaze. "He doesna wish to see you."

CHAPTER 33

✠

Noelle pushed away from the window and the gray skies beyond. She gathered up her cat and cuddled him close. Her tears had stopped, but the ache in her heart lingered. Even after the passing of two days, and still no word from Farran, she couldn't convince herself not to care. Couldn't stop the worry or the pain of Declan's words.

For more than forty-eight hours, he'd lain behind those guarded doors, and she couldn't bring herself to try again. Anne swore he improved. That this distance was some result of misplaced male pride. But Anne hadn't heard his whispered barb. All Anne—and everyone else—could seem to think about was some foolish idea Farran would hurt her.

He'd never been less than gentle, even at his maddest moments. And that gentleness haunted her. The images that rose each time she looked at the bed where they'd last slept tormented more than Declan's statement. They had driven her to rest on the couch—sleep had been out of the question.

She loved a man who didn't want her for anything but physical pleasure. And some misbegotten oath. Why that surprised her, she couldn't really explain. All her life she'd faced rejection. It wouldn't be the first time she cared about someone for no good reason.

But it bothered her she couldn't absolutely convince herself that Farran saw her only as a plaything. Each time she tried, each time she let the suspicion creep in, a little voice cried out in disbelief. He couldn't possibly go to such lengths to comfort her if he felt nothing.

The oath plagued her even more. As incredible as the claim sounded, if it could save his life, she'd caused his injuries. If she'd taken it sooner, maybe he wouldn't be bloodied to a pulp. Then again, he'd said even with the oath a Templar blade could wound. Hadn't he? How could that be possible? And if it were also true, her silence hadn't done anything a simple fight wouldn't.

Regardless, she wouldn't pledge herself to someone for eternity if he wasn't willing to make the same sacrifice. He wanted her loyalty—demanded it. She had every right to expect the same. Only the very weakest of women would accept anything less—and while she had insecurities, she still had self-respect.

No, she'd pledge herself in spirit, but she would not utter a simple syllable of that coveted phrase until Farran dropped to his knee and yielded his sword. If he couldn't come to trust her, to believe in her, his fate was his. After all, she'd come this far. Changed her very foundation and the principles she understood. He could find it within himself to give up a little of his pride.

A rattle at the door brought her pacing to a halt. She looked up at the same time she lowered Scat Cat to the ground. When Farran stumbled through, her heart forgot how to beat. All the anger, all her hurt, vanished as time stood still and his tawny eyes held hers. Her legs itched to run, to fly across the distance separating them. Her arms longed to wind around his neck. He was alive. Walking. *Standing in her room.*

"I've come for my clothes." He nodded at the jeans heaped at the foot of the bed.

Just like that, he crushed her budding hope into pieces. "Oh." She turned her back to him, her eyes closed to the tumult of shattered feeling. On a hard swallow, she bit back a threatening sob and returned to her perch at the window. He could leave if he wanted to, but not without the fight he'd long deserved. He'd brought her here. Forced her to change. Forced her to love. He wasn't walking out under her silence.

"So you blame me."

He moved behind her, his presence so enormous it shadowed over her and turned her skin to gooseflesh. The quiet grunt that escaped him as he bent for his clothes twisted her heart. His scent, that heady aroma of woods and citrus, enveloped her. And deep inside a longing for the beauty they had shared not so very long ago stirred.

When his footsteps retreated without answer, she turned to scowl at his back. "Are you such a coward you can't accuse me as you want to? You can't look me in the eyes and tell me you're walking out because I put you in danger?"

The taunt had the desired effect. He whipped around so fast his hair pelted the side of his neck. His glower made her pulse skip. But his subsequent wince and the press of his hand to his ribs spoiled the seeds of fear. She lifted her chin in defiance, silently daring him to speak.

When his pain had eased, his gaze narrowed. Through clenched teeth, he answered, "No more a coward than the damsel who cannot stand the sight of her knight's blood."

"What?" Disbelief cracked her voice. She stomped across the room to stand in the doorway that separated them. "I'm not a coward, Farran. That I'm still here is proof to that!"

His eyes burned hot, full of all the fury that boiled in her veins. "Do not feed me lies. That you have no way to return to your beloved Washington is proof to that, damsel."

It took effort to keep his voice under control, to stop the bellow she knew rumbled in his chest. Yet she felt no need to show the same temperance. She gave her anger freedom and reveled in the surge of it. "No. Open your eyes, Farran. There's at least a dozen cars parked in that lot. I could have run when you slept." She flung her arm to the dresser, indicating a simple keychain near her hairbrush. "You left those behind. I could have left whenever I wanted. But I stayed. For you. Don't you *dare* accuse me of cowardice."

The overwhelming urge to draw Noelle into his arms and crush her so close she would feel the pounding of his heart made Farran's hands curl. Against his will, his gaze dropped to the keys she referenced. The force that punched him in the gut equaled the throb of his sewn flesh. Saints' blood, he wanted to believe her. But that she had not once asked about him, had not even seen fit to come to the infirmary, made Declan's claim bellow that much louder. He had almost convinced himself the Scot spoke false. But Noelle's continued absence said more than words.

As he watched the furious rise and fall of her breasts, he fought the protective instinct to slam the door between them and forget what she made him feel. He had blocked himself so many times that doing anything else felt foreign. However, the challenge in her fawnlike eyes provoked the warrior. The man who was not afraid to risk the condemnation of his kin and stand up for what he believed in. He had accepted the brand of traitor. He would never accept *coward*.

"Yet you saw fit to stay closeted in your room?"

"I did no such thing!"

He could not help but snort. "I slept much, but I assure you I would have known if you sat by my bed."

Noelle stalked up to him, her pretty face stained with crimson color. "First, Anne dragged me up here. Second, when I snuck out the first time while she took a bath, Declan ran me off." She punctuated each ticked-off item with a stab of her finger to his chest. "Third, I haven't been able to *leave* because everybody around here seems to think you're going to kill me."

At the last, he groaned aloud. 'Twas the same reason Caradoc now stood beyond the door awaiting his exit. He had tried, with little success, to explain he felt the darkness but wrestled it under control. Still his brothers surrounded him like hornets.

She jabbed him once again. "You want to explain that? Or do you want to run off and hide?"

Choosing neither, he slid his hands around her waist. Her body yielded the fight. Soft curves molded into him like down. Her warmth seeped beyond his skin to melt the chips of ice around his heart. He dug his fingers into her silken hair and held on as if her very nearness could carry him to a place far from here. A time before he had known the vileness of immortality.

"Jesu, Noelle, what have you done to me? I cannot think straight anymore." He buried his face into her shoulder and nuzzled the side of her neck. "Declan told me you did not wish to see me."

She clung to him, her body trembling with tears she did not shed but hoarsened her voice. "He told me the same." Fervently she twisted in search of his mouth. "I thought you hated me. That you blamed me for your injury."

"Nay," he whispered against her seeking lips. *I love you.* As he released the thought, he allowed her sweet flavor to consume him. Their tongues twined, hungry and full of unspoken need. Under the assuage of her mouth, he felt not the pain from his stitches. All he knew was bliss. An ecstasy he did not deserve, but one he would die without.

Aye, he loved her. He would fall upon his own blade to protect her. He would tell her now, in the only way he understood. But tonight, when the temple was at rest and he took her once again into his arms, he would tell her with his voice. He would kneel, set his sword at her feet, and they would never suffer the doubt of one another again.

He broke the kiss to look deep into her impassioned eyes. All the confirmation he needed reflected back at him. She bared herself completely—how he could have ever doubted her innocent spirit he could not fathom. She trusted. She loved.

Farran stroked her cheek with his thumb. "I have missed the feel of your body against mine."

Her shy smile touched him. "I have too."

"You will have to help me. My wounds . . ."

One hand drifted to the sensitive flesh covering his ribs. When gentle fingers spread over Uriel's meticulous stitches, the same warmth he had recalled ebbed through his body. "I will take care of you, Farran," she murmured as she bent to mend the wound with a soft kiss.

Noelle led Farran by the hand. Her heart soared with hope, pride, and above all else, love. He'd wanted to see her. Expected her to come. And though she didn't understand why his friend would tell her lies, she didn't care.

At the edge of the bed, she helped him to remove his clothing. Mindful of the great gash along the left side of his body, she eased his shirt free and dropped to her knees to tug down his jeans. His arousal sprung forth, begging for the caress of her hand. With the boldness he'd given her, she took him into her palm. As she rose, she scattered kisses over his stark white scars, across the wiry stitches. Her hand pumped steadily as she worked her way back to his mouth. When she landed there, he caught her in a savage kiss.

She indulged, but only for a moment. With effort, she tore her mouth away. Eager for the feel of his naked skin against her body, she released him to rid herself of her own clothes. She shucked them without care, then stepped out of the jumbled heap. As she stepped back into his sheltering embrace, Farran lowered himself to sit on the edge of the mattress. Hands fastened at her hips, he drew her between his legs. Thick thighs trapped her into place. The wide head of his erection nestled in her feminine down, full of heat and promise. He cupped her breasts slowly, reverently, and teased pebbled nipples with his roughened thumbs.

When he dipped his head and gently suckled, Noelle's

entire body flared hot with desire. She had found heaven, and he had brought her here. She curled her hands into his hair and pressed his head to her harder. The flick of his tongue, the subtle pull of his mouth, sent a frenzy for more humming through her blood. She arched her back, bent her knees to accept his swollen length a little more.

He slid against her inner folds with such ease she nearly blushed. What he could do to her defied logic. She was like sculpting clay in his hands, waiting to be shaped. Molded. Transformed.

"Oh, Farran," she exhaled.

His low groan vibrated through his lips to arc a shiver down her spine. One large hand slipped behind her bottom to tease through her damp curls. A thick finger slid along her nether lips to press against her opening, and Noelle's body moved of its own accord. Her knees buckled, drawing his fingertip inside. At the same time, his rock-hard arousal pressed against her sensitive nub and sensation blistered through her. She whimpered at the shock of pleasure.

In response, his shaft jumped against her flesh, and Farran drew in a sharp breath. He lifted his head, withdrew his hand, and cupped her chin to tip her mouth to his. His kiss held the lazy freedom of summer, full of the same suffocating heat. When she feared she'd never breathe again, he eased it to a close and his feral gaze locked with hers.

Awkwardly, he reclined across the bed, drawing her with him. His wince betrayed the effort moving required, and Noelle automatically looked to his injury. A tiny drop of blood trickled from a pulled stitch, then rolled off his side to disappear beneath him. She pressed her fingertip to the rend and exhaled with disappointment. "You're bleeding."

Undaunted, Farran guided her atop his lap. "I know." His wicked smile made her want to laugh and scold at the same time. He had no business indulging like this. And she should have known better than to encourage him, no matter how badly she wanted him.

"Farran," she protested with a light laugh.

He gripped her hips and lifted, easing her onto his hot, hard flesh. She sucked in a deep breath. He felt so good. So perfect. So . . .

With one firm push, he slid within her slick sheath, and Noelle let out a gasp. His grin deepened, tugging to life a dimple she hadn't noticed before. "Would you like me to stop, damsel?"

"No," she said as she rotated her hips to accommodate his size. The tip of him pressed against the mouth of her womb, turning her body into molten wax. Captured by the sheer ecstasy of feeling Farran deep inside, she twisted her hips.

Farran's body bucked beneath her. His grin vanished, and the light in his eyes darkened with feral hunger. A thrill bubbled, coaxing her to repeat the motion once again. When she did, his hands dug into her hips, bracing her down as he thrust up hard. Their hoarse cries blended with the same perfection of their bodies.

Nature taught Noelle what to do, how to move. She chased the sensation his body stirred and lifted in time with his slow, rhythmic thrusts. But as the heat they shared intensified, wild need demanded harder, faster. She braced her hands on his wide chest and let him take the lead.

He did not disappoint.

His body glided in and out of her like a piston. The brief glimpse of the erotic slide that she caught between her lowered lashes curled her nails into his tight pecs. She held on as Farran lifted her higher, and the swell of feeling built until it crashed upon her like a stormy tide upon a rocky reef. She cried out as wave after wave of pleasure slammed together.

Farran joined her in release. His hips drove into her a final time, and his body convulsed. He dug his fingertips into the soft flesh of her bottom, and she felt the wash of his hot seed against her womb. As his hips gradually slowed, he drew her down against his chest and wrapped the arms she loved so dearly around her slight form.

"Noelle," he murmured against her hair, "a man could wage war for you."

CHAPTER 34

As Farran's breath gradually returned to normal, he pulled his fingers through Noelle's long, thick hair. The slow motion of his hand helped to ease the pounding of his heart and restore his thoughts. Saints' blood, she had uttered but three sentences, and he had melted like wax. The powerful effect she had on him disturbed him. Aye, he enjoyed this carefree feeling she aroused, the security of knowing she would not play him false. But the way she bared him open made him vulnerable to whatever she may wish.

He had been fooled once by a maid's tongue, and although he did not believe Noelle capable of such trickery, 'twould take time to rest at ease.

She pushed up to her elbows and planted a chaste kiss on his mouth. "Why would Declan lie to us both?"

He frowned at the remembrance of his brother's deeds. In the warm languor of their lovemaking, he forgot to mind his words. "I do not know. But Declan's soul has long suffered the darkness. The change has pressed on him longer than the rest of us. I suspect he does not know the trouble he creates."

The instant those tawny eyes clouded with confusion, Farran recognized his error. He grimaced at the questions he knew would come.

"The what? What do you mean his soul's suffered darkness?"

"I do not want to tell you, Noelle." The last thing he wanted to do was give her reason to fear him, especially now, when he planned to say his oath tonight.

She would have none of his excuses. Rolling off his body, she sat up at his side. "I don't care if you want to or not. I want to know."

Groaning aloud, Farran tossed an elbow over his eyes. If ever a man was doomed, 'twas surely him. "Can this not wait?"

"No, it can't."

"Aye, then." He let out a heavy sigh and dropped his arm to the mattress. He stared at the ceiling, unable to bear witness to the condemnation he would cause. "The curse I told you of. 'Twas not just immortality Gabriel gave us. Nay, 'twould be too easy to live forever. He gave our souls a taint. A piece of Azazel's darkness that festers as we age."

Sensing he had not told her everything, Noelle pressed, "And?"

He glanced at her, then quickly looked away. The last of his explanation came out in a rush. "Each time I kill Azazel's creatures, it grows. In time, I shall become a knight under his service. An evil being." He rose to sit, grimacing with the effort.

She scrambled after him. Her fingers cut into his shoulder, and she pulled him around to meet her accusing glare.

"*This* is why everyone's been saying you'll kill me?"

"I am not going to kill you, Noelle. 'Tis a preposterous claim. But aye, 'tis what they believe."

She stubbornly folded her arms across her breasts. "If it's so preposterous, why does everyone think it?"

God's teeth, she would not relent until he told her all of it. He expelled a hard breath and frowned. After a moment's pause, he swiveled to catch her hands in his. The answer would not sit well. If she chose to run, he intended to stop her flight. He chose his words with care. "Anne believes she has seen your death. She claims 'twill come at the hands of a dark knight—the creature we are *all* capable of becoming. Because she says you are unafraid, they have assumed 'tis me."

She drew back, but shock did not fill her features as he had expected. Instead, anger glittered behind her eyes. His frown deepened with confusion. He had told her of her death—why did she seem unconcerned?

"So it is possible. You kept this from me. Why?" Sharp and brittle, her voice cracked through the room.

Difficult—her name was woman. He let out an exasperated sigh. "Is it not obvious? I did not wish to scare you."

Consternation settled into her mouth, pursing rosy lips tight. 'Twas such a misplaced expression for such delicate features he could not help but chuckle. He cupped her cheek and leaned in closer to kiss that puckered mouth. "You are not angry?"

With an indecipherable mutter, Noelle ducked out of his grasp and under his arm. She bent to his side, inspecting the stitches there. The tender probe of her fingertips made him shiver. But the sensation passed all too soon. She drew away and rolled her eyes. "You're already healed where your stitch popped loose."

He considered telling her his suspicions her hands had more to do with his healing than Uriel's talent with a needle. Before he could decide how to begin, she slid into his lap and laid her head on his shoulder. "No. I'm not mad. But don't keep things from me. Even Anne had the decency to tell me I'd die."

Farran bristled. Anne had no right to tell Noelle such. 'Twas not her place. The damage she could have caused . . . Even Declan's lies would not come close to such disaster.

At the remembrance of his brother's strange behaviors, Farran eased Noelle out of his lap. "I must speak with Mikhail about Declan. 'Twill not take long." He let his lips linger against hers, hating that he could not lie down beside her and nestle into her warmth. But this strange comfort of sleep would come soon enough. He could wait the twenty minutes necessary to fulfill duty. Besides, the little bit of distance his absence would create, would give him time to prepare for the offering of his eternal service.

Her eyes remained on him as he dressed, their brazen path as heated as her hands.

Noelle sank into the pillows as the outer door thumped shut. She had her explanations and had done her best to pretend the truth didn't bother her. Honestly, the meaning of her oath disturbed her greatly. With it, another voice joined in. Farran's as he tried to tell her what she was.

I shall gain the light that lives in your soul.

On the heels of his haunting echo rose Anne's reminder that the oath would save his life.

It didn't take a scientist to come up with the translation— those Latin words held the key to his salvation. In keeping silent, she doomed him to a fate she didn't entirely understand, but knew could only be horrific.

She had no right to barter with his life.

Then again, he'd said the fighting made the darkness grow. If she found a way to keep him from battle, she wouldn't be playing Russian roulette with his soul. From the way he had made love to her tonight, she sensed his feelings deepened. Could it take that terribly long to win his loyalty? His love?

She'd settle for his loyalty. Once she earned it, his love couldn't be far behind.

Decided, she curled into the pillows and gave in to a soft smile. Tomorrow she'd tell him about the Sudarium. When she explained why she'd hidden it, he'd have no reason to be furious. Especially not when he'd kept things from her as well.

Hushed voices beyond Mikhail's door stilled the hand Farran lifted to knock. Mayhap now was not the best time to cast more suspicion on Declan's character. If he waited for morning, he could ease the news of deliberate betrayal with the declaration he had won Noelle's oath.

Aye, he would start the morrow fresh. Spend the night with Noelle. Learn to live again.

He turned away to do just that, when the mention of his name brought him to a halt.

"You can't tell Farran, he'll be furious," Anne insisted.

Mikhail countered firmly, "'Tis his seraph. Her mistakes become his as well."

Farran cocked his head, his scowl intact. What wrong had Noelle committed whilst he slept?

"No, no, no!" Anne exclaimed. "I didn't tell you so you could drive another wedge between them. Can't you do whatever it is you do and magically make it reappear?"

The heavy scrape of chair legs against wood signaled

Mikhail left his desk. His voice grew closer. "I have already done so. 'Twill be here in a few hours."

Anne's voice rose an octave. "Then *what* is the big deal? Do your stuff, Mikhail. Fix it."

"I cannot." He paused before adding, "Will not. The *big deal,* as you say, is a quarter-sized hole in the fabric where a mouse feasted. What would you have me do, Anne, claim ignorance? 'Tis dishonest. Noelle will face her wrongs."

"Phanuel's an angel," Anne argued. "He'll under—"

No longer content to eavesdrop, Farran barged into the room. If Noelle had erred, he would know about it now. Whilst he had yet to speak the words, in spirit she had his loyalty. His duty was to defend her, even if she committed wrongs. And he could not bring himself to believe anything Noelle had done was more than a misunderstanding. "What wrong has Noelle committed?"

Anne's squeak drew his dark scowl. She backed up as if his glare threw fire, her face as white as a ghost's. "Farran."

"Aye, Farran. Now tell me what you speak of."

Wild eyes darted to Mikhail, who had resumed his chair. Farran followed the path of her gaze, and when she offered naught more, he challenged Mikhail. "Do you suffer from the loss of your tongue as well? Tell me what wrongs you accuse Noelle of!"

Mikhail folded his hands in his lap, his stare unblinking. "I see you have pledged yourself to her. Congratulations, sir knight, for making such a monumental step." He eased to his feet, crossed to the cabinet behind his desk. From the lower drawer he produced the satchel Noelle had sent with Lucan. He tossed it across the mahogany surface where it came to rest in front of Farran. "You are prepared then to defend her for hiding the Sudarium. She will need your sword should it not return with Gottfried tonight."

Farran stared at the leather bag in disbelief. He had seen her hand the very sack to Lucan. She had not touched it since. Mikhail's claims must be false. He shook his head against the closing of his throat. "You are mistaken. I have been with her since she gave the bag to Lucan. He brought it here. It has not left your office."

"Good, good." Mikhail nodded. "You shall need the meaning behind your words."

His goading tone needled beneath Farran's skin, striking fury. Farran curled his hands into fists to fight the urge to reach across the desk and grab Mikhail by the throat. Every muscle stiffened like a board.

"Striking me will solve naught, de Clare. Curb your temper before you come to regret it." Mikhail strode around his desk, grabbed the satchel from the top, and pushed it into Farran's hands. "You shall find it full of clothes. As did I when Anne came to me this morning. Noelle kept the relic in her purse. She hid it in her room at Bethany's adytum."

Each word Mikhail uttered pierced through Farran's heart and turned it into a sieve. As his chest constricted to agonizing limits, he looked to Anne, hoping beyond all measure she would claim Mikhail false.

She shattered him with the sad shake of her head. "It's true, Farran. The only reason I told Mikhail—"

"Damnation!" He slammed his fist down on the desk hard enough to make it shudder. Absolute devastation rose to choke him, and he spun for the door before it could suffocate his air.

"Stay where you are," Mikhail commanded. "There is more for you to hear."

By God, he could stomach no more. Noelle had betrayed him. Deceived them all. He had thought her pure, and behind her innocent smile, the same vile nature Brighid possessed lay in wait. Did no woman not know the meaning of deceit? Even Anne betrayed, for with her rightful honesty, she condemned Noelle.

One hand tight around the doorknob, Farran halted, yet he did not turn around.

"Noelle will face her misdeeds, Farran. Should the Sudarium arrive as planned tonight, tomorrow she shall take the damaged cloth to Phanuel. There she will confess what she has done to the Angel of Judgment. As your ward and mate, you will accompany her. The punishment Phanuel demands, you too shall share."

His spine stiffened to stone. Traverse the seas at her side, when he could not bear to look upon her? He would rather descend into Azazel's hell. "Nay, find someone else. We have exchanged no vows."

"She is your seraph. The duty is yours alone."

Farran jerked the door open and stormed into the hall. How dare she play him false. To think he had been minutes away from swearing himself to her. If he had, he would have no choice but to champion her to Phanuel. Her misdeeds would be seen as his, and once again, he would carry the mark of traitor. 'Twas bad enough she would bear the brand. That he must stand and bear witness to it. But *he* would not pay the price at her expense.

"Farran, wait!" Anne called from behind.

"Leave me be."

She caught up before he could round the corner and grabbed him by the elbow. "Wait. It's not what you think. Ask her to explain." Her voice held urgency. Her eyes begged. "Please, Farran. Don't shut her out."

He looked down to where her fingers dug into his arm.
"Take your hand off me before I give Merrick reason to
draw his sword."

Her gaze flickered, and her lips parted as if she meant
to speak. When she said naught, Farran shook his arm
free and left her standing in the hall.

He mounted the stairs two at a time. Each step that took
him nearer to her room distanced him from Noelle. She
had played him for a fool, and like the fool she thought he
was, he had fallen into her wily trap. She would explain
herself, but not before he made it clear she meant naught
to him. That he would take his leave the very moment
they returned from Spain.

He let himself inside her room and slammed the door
shut. The bang brought her upright on the couch. She
whipped around with a startled yelp.

In the next instant, Farran knew her act had been deliberate. Her body pulled away, distancing herself from
him like a cornered mouse. And those tawny eyes he had
come to adore filled with shame.

"I can explain." Despite the frantic stutter of her heart,
Noelle held Farran's furious stare. She told herself she
wasn't afraid of him, only of what might happen between
them. That he might walk away from her forever. Anne
had predicted devastation . . . Clearly, she'd been right.

But only someone who lacked the value of life would
mistake his deadly glower. If she'd been a man, she'd
have found herself facing down the point of his sword.
Maybe already run through.

"I care not to hear your words."

She rocketed to her feet, her fear replaced by sudden
anger. She'd given him the chance to explain. Had even

forgiven. While she wouldn't hold out for his acceptance, she refused to suffer his belligerence. "Well you're going to. You came back here for something—what was it, Farran? Your keys? Maybe your belt? It damn sure isn't me, is it?"

His jaw clenched so tight she was certain his teeth would crack. He took a threatening step toward her, then thought better of it and stopped. "Do not test me, damsel. You will not emerge the victor."

"I don't *want* to be the victor. This isn't about who wins, who loses. We are partners, not pawn and master."

The anger that rolled off him crashed into her like waves. Though he stood several feet away, the heat of his body burned. His nostrils flared, his eyes glinted like sharp daggers. In every way he was a dragon, and she the prey he sought to trap.

Trap her, he did. Three determined strides brought him in front of her. He grabbed her by the shoulders, his grip fierce enough to make her flinch. Dipping his head, he brought his gaze level with hers. "We are *not* partners. *We* are finished, Noelle."

She did her best to find her courage and ignore the biting sting of his words. With a shake of her shoulders, she twisted out of his grasp. "You of all people should understand. You kept your secrets. You didn't want me to be afraid." When he reached for her again, she evaded his grasp. "I *was* afraid, Farran. I thought you were crazy!"

"Aye, I was crazy to believe in you." Abruptly, he turned and disappeared into the bedroom. When he reemerged, he carried a pillow and the heavy comforter. He tossed them onto the couch, then sat down, once more in control of his emotions. As he snapped the blanket out, his voice rang eerily flat. "I returned to inform you we leave in the morning."

"We? I thought you said there was no *we*. And just where are you taking me?"

Farran smoothed out his pillow. Reclining, he tucked his hands behind his head. "Mikhail has ordered you to return the Sudarium. I am to escort you, to ensure follow-through. You will tell Phanuel what you have done, and you will assume the blame for the relic's damaged nature. You will, in all ways, subject yourself to his judgment." He glanced up through the tops of his eyes. "And damsel, you shall do so alone."

That he could dismiss her so easily wafted chills down her spine. She crossed her arms to warm herself, and stood watching him for several silent moments. He looked at ease. As if he didn't give a single damn he'd cut her loose from him.

Damn him.

Inflamed by his refusal to give her the same opportunity for explanation that she'd given him, she stalked to her room. The slam of her door satisfied her wounded pride, however, it did little for her breaking heart. Like a scrap of trash, he'd tossed her aside. One error. One insignificant act. Nothing like his failure to tell her he would turn into something evil. Or that by staying with him, she risked her life.

CHAPTER 35

✦

Farran stood in the shadow of Spain's majestic Sancta Ovetensis, his mood as black as the building thunderheads above. He had tossed and turned all night. Woke once to the sound of his own shouts when the nightmares returned. Not long after, he had awakened to find Noelle nestled in his arms. He had held her then, grateful for the peace she offered. Despising himself for the weakness she created.

Why she had comforted him when he had treated her with such disgrace, he could not fathom. But as he reflected on their argument, he realized she did not throw her errors in his face and place the blame on him. Unlike Brighid, she did not fault him for her failures.

And the more he compared the two, the more difficult ignoring Noelle became. He had feigned sleep on the plane, stared out the window in the taxi. She made no attempt to draw him into conversation, yet she made her presence known with the occasional brush of her hand, the touch of her eyes, her refusal to stand less than two feet away.

Now as twilight descended upon the concrete court-yard and they approached the cathedral's arching door-way, he could not understand why she did not turn from him in disgust. 'Twas what he wanted her to do. 'Twould make abandoning her to her mistakes much easier on his guilty concious.

Last eve, he had treated her worse than a dog. When he ached to hear her explanation and longed to believe the words she would speak, he blocked himself to every-thing, including all consideration.

He paid the price now, as she confidently thumped on the private entrance. She should be the one who hung her head. Yet nay, 'twas he, who felt shame.

The heavy door creaked open, dwarfing the minor priest who stuck his head outside. On seeing them, a hearty smile smoothed ruddy cheeks. "Good eve! Please, come in. Father Phanuel expects you. He is most anxious for your arrival." The thick Spanish accent that clung to his words gave his voice a melodic cadence.

As they entered, Noelle extended her hand. "I'm Dr. Noelle Keane. This is . . ." She glanced at Farran, her eyes full of unspoken question. Recovering from her brief hesitation, she put more effort into her smile and finished, "My companion, Farran."

Companion. He almost snorted. He was her *guard*. As he had been when he met her—no more, no less.

The priest beamed under the bright glow of Noelle's smile. "Ah, Dr. Keane! Spain is indebted to you. That you have finally proven what we've long suspected brings pride to Oviedo."

What would the priest say once he knew her carelessness caused the shroud damage? Before he could consider the thought fully, the man ushered them into a wide, echoing hall.

"I regret Father Phanuel is not here to greet you. He is with a patron in need of guidance. He asked me, please, to show you to the Cámara Santa where he will attend to you shortly." The man stopped before a barrier of iron bars. Upon producing a set of ancient keys, he inserted one and twisted an equally ancient lock. The gate squealed open. "You may enjoy Christ's treasures while you wait."

As he followed Noelle, Farran took in the bright lamps that beamed down on glass cases and jewel-encrusted gold crosses. But what caught his breath was not the manufactured light and ancient relics. 'Twas the overhead incandescence, one that came without a source and lacked the sharpness of man-made light. A holy aura that flooded the stone chamber and soaked into his soul. He basked beneath it, feeling small and insignificant. As if his place within the Almighty's plan was naught more than a passing speck of dust.

Noelle browsed with nonchalance, no single sign she was naught but comfortable within the sacred chamber. He bent to her ear. "Do you feel no shame, damsel?"

She looked up startled. "Why should I?"

His gaze dropped to the satchel that hung from her shoulder. "For the damage you brought to the sacred cloth."

Noelle smiled then, a bright confident parting of lush pink lips that baffled him. The gentle shake of her head sent her hair tumbling over her shoulders like spun silk. "No. I'm human. Made to make mistakes. The Almighty knows what's in my heart and will forgive." She shrugged her shoulders, and the sparkle in her eyes brightened.

"Mikhail said as much this morning. Phanuel's an angel—he'll understand."

Farran's air fled his lungs as if she'd punched him. Mikhail had forgiven her? Why had he said naught?

He did not have time to contemplate the meaning before Phanuel's voice boomed down the hall. "Dr. Keane. Farran de Clare. How happy I am to see you!"

Long dark hair fell in soft waves around a face that held so much beauty the archangel could rival Raphael. He moved with the grace of divinity. The same sublime light glinted in his watchful eyes. Though Farran had never set his gaze upon anything more than a watercolor depiction, Phanuel resembled naught of his imaginings. He was slight of stature compared to Mikhail, weak of arm compared to Uriel. And the Angel of Judgment gave off an air far less threatening than the mighty Gabriel.

"Come, allow me to show you the cathedral. It's not often I may have a bit of pleasure before business. The Lord's work is constant." He beckoned them into the wide hall with the hearty manner of a parent who welcomed a long absent child.

Farran shifted his weight. 'Twas disconcerting to be greeted by a stranger with such warmth. He gave Phanuel a respectful nod and assumed his place at Noelle's side. The need for normalcy, for what he understood no matter how objectionable, made him reach out for Noelle. He settled his hand in the small of her back and ignored the quizzical lift of her eyebrow. But he could not mistake the sway of her body, the subtle shift that brought her closer to his side. Her jasmine-scented warmth washed over him much the same as the light in the Cámara Santa. He suffered his body's natural response. His blood stirred with awarenes. His pulse skipped several beats. And against his thigh, his cock flinched.

God's blood, even when he longed to despise her, his body refused to listen. He gritted his teeth together and tried to focus on what Phaneul was saying.

"Bishop Alvarez began construction in 1308, but what you see now was completed in 1388."

Noelle reached out to trace a finger over an ornately carved stone column that supported the spanning arched ceiling. "If the early eleventh-century chapel was so honored, and the Church began housing relics before the bishop's improvements, why then are there no marks of the Almighty's master masons?" Her gaze settled on Farran in a pointed reference to the Knights Templar. "None of the artistry matches what I've seen."

"You are sharp." Phanuel let out a short laugh and directed his answer not to Noelle, but to Farran. "Those who held our secrets became a threat to the corrupted Church. As Farran can attest, the year before, the Inquisition, under the directive of Azazel's pawn, King Phillip IV, and the false papacy in Avignon, took great measures to eradicate our noble knights."

Snapshot images of his torture flashed within Farran's mind. Though more than seven hundred years had passed, he could still smell the burning of his flesh, hear the false priest's vile laughter. He dropped his hand to his belly and fingered the scar beneath his shirt. When he caught Noelle watching, he stuffed his hand into his pocket.

"Although the knights were secretly pardoned at Chinon the same year Alvaraz commissioned work, Alvaraz himself was a product of Avignon. He had the sigils destroyed and new ones crafted in their place. Look here."

Phanuel tapped a small relief not much larger than a door-knob. "You can still see two legs of the Templar cross. They are disguised amongst the detail and have been compromised, but they are still present." His grin broadened as he gave Noelle a wink. "Lazy masons."

The long heavy roll of thunder rattled a nearby stained-glass window. Phanuel looked toward the ceiling and frowned as if he concentrated on a distant thought. As the racket faded into silence, a heavy rain pelted down, and his jovial demeanor disappeared. He gave Noelle an apologetic look. "I'm afraid we must attend to other, more important, matters. You have the Sudarium."

Farran cursed beneath his breath. He had not intended to linger so long. Indeed, he had planned to return outside once Phanuel bade Noelle hello. Now he found himself unable to escape. Forced to stand at her side as she faced her misdeeds. He would share whatever judgment Phanuel decided.

Noelle shrugged the satchel off her shoulder and passed it to Phaneul. "It's inside, along with all the documents verifying its age." Her confidence faltered for the briefest of seconds, her anxiety reflected in the shaking of her hands.

As Phanuel released the lock and took out the fragile cloth, Noelle cleared her throat. Farran held his breath.

"You'll find a quarter-sized hole in the lower left quadrant. I apologize, Phanuel, for damaging the relic. I did not understand"—her earnest gaze shifted to Farran—"many things."

Phanuel clasped her by the hands, studying her. Farran's pulse slowed to a stop. Afraid to do more than breathe, he watched. Would the angel whisk her away?

Condemn her from this place? Or would he, as Noelle suggested Mikhail had done, grant her pardon?

The archangel did neither. They exchanged no words. Confounding Farran further, she gave Phanuel an understanding nod. In turn, he bent to grace her cheek with a fatherly kiss. After a slight squeeze to her shoulder, he withdrew. "I have some other business to attend to. Father Ricardo will escort you to your room. Let us meet again tonight and take our evening meal together."

Her smile returned, as radiant as it had been before. "I'd like that."

"Then it is agreed." At the lift of Phanuel's hand, the first priest materialized from the shadowy hall. "Meet me in the Cámara Santa a half hour from now. No more."

With that, Phanuel stalked away, his long dark robes lapping at his ankles, the Sudarium tucked beneath his arm. Farran found himself at the mercy of Ricardo—and an imminent room with Noelle.

Saints' blood.

As Farran ducked beneath the door frame and entered the sparse room, Noelle eased the door shut. She had one opportunity for a few undisturbed minutes alone with him, and she refused to waste it. Phanuel and Mikhail had both forgiven her, yet Farran could not. His reasons couldn't just revolve around the fact she'd kept secrets.

When he stretched out on the simple iron bed and shut his eyes, pretending she didn't exist as he had all day, she pounced. "When I hid the Sudarium, I thought you were crazy. I intended to leverage it for my freedom."

His body tensed. The hand at his thigh clenched into a fist. She ignored the signs of warning and stumbled ahead. Whether he wanted to hear it or not, she was going to explain.

"The night I was attacked, I came outside to tell you. I understood my mistake then, but everything happened so fast. Then you were in the infirmary. When you got out, I frankly forgot about the damn thing."

Driven by determiniation and the hope he could not ignore her touch, she sat on the edge of the bed and rested her hand on his arm. "If you hadn't left last night, I would have told you this morning. I wasn't trying to deceive you."

He jerked his arm away and crossed it over his chest. "Leave it be, Noelle."

The burn of anger started in her belly. It crept through her chest, out to her fingers, and up her throat. "Leave it be? You kidnapped me, badgered me, *humiliated* me, and then made love to me. Now you want me to just *leave it be*?"

He twisted onto his side, giving her his back. Incensed, she pried at his shoulder. But against her slight weight, rolling him over was like trying to move a boulder. At her wit's end, she let out a frustrated hiss. Wanting a reaction, any kind of a response at all, she punched his shoulder.

The strike succeeded. Farran bolted out of the bed. "Damsel, mind yourself!"

"Or what?" She gestured at the sword around his waist. "You'll run me through? Maybe you ought to. Murder would make more sense than your stubborn pride. Take me home—I've had enough of your abuse." Leaping to her feet, she held two fingers in front of her face. "Two archangels have forgiven me, Farran! Who are you punishing me for? Was she so cruel you can find no goodness in anyone at all?"

Like the lash of a whip, Noelle's words cracked through the air. They pierced through Farran to clamp a vise around his chest. His ribs screamed against the pressure, his gut hollowed out.

She stood before him, her chest heaving with fury. Her eyes blazed such scorching fire he was certain he would burn beneath their gaze. Righteous in her anger, defiant in her unyeilding stare, she dared him to confront the past.

Brighid's laughter and Alefric's rejection roared within his head. The pain surfaced once more, tangling his insides into briars. He grimaced at the agony, the heartbreak, the overwhelming loss.

In that instant, he knew Noelle had revealed what he could not bring himself to face. His anger was misplaced. Her error held no treachery, no malice meant to ruin him. She had done the only thing she could think of in an effort to survive. In her place, he might have done the same.

His anger came not from her, not from the hiding of a relic. It came from Brighid. From the need to punish his traitorous, unfaithful wife.

Instead, he punished an innocent. A woman who stood at his side when he least deserved a champion. A woman who knew naught but love. And now, he had lost her. Driven her back to the mindset where all she wanted was to return home.

He staggered under the weight of understanding. At once he felt the need to move, to take her in his arms and apologize for all he was, all he had done. Yet he could do no more than swallow.

Noelle took a bold step forward, her expression softer. "Tell me, Farran, was an oath all I ever meant to you?"

Through his tightened throat he rasped, "Nay." He

found the strength to move and reached for her hand. "No-elle, I do not mean—"

A deafening roar from the hall beyond squelched his apology. Stone splintered. Glass shattered. The ground shook, and she stumbled into his arms. He held her tight whilst horns of warning blared inside his head.

As the tremor ebbed, Farran pushed her away. "Stay here!"

Sword in hand, he bolted through the door to the sound of unholy laughter.

CHAPTER 36

✠

Stone dust fogged the hall. One glance at the toppled beams, and Farran knew no act of man had caused the blast. The columns that had tumbled were the very ones Phanuel had referenced. Beyond, above, where he could recognize the earlier indiscriminate sigils of his brethren, the stone remained untouched.

Sword ready, Farran pressed his back to the remnants of an interior wall and inched along the debris. Ahead, behind a mass of crumbled rock, a bright glow infused the rubble with golden light. As he drew nearer to the source, Phanuel's voice rang out.

"You have found a weakness, but you will not have the strength." The light intensified, blinding in its intensity. A tortured howl rang out, one Farran recognized as part demon and part man. A dark knight.

He rounded the column of crushed rock and crumbled mortar, and set his eyes upon the radiance. Priestly robes shed, Phanuel stood in full glory. He bore no sword, no staff. He wore no shield, nor armor. Cloaked in pristine white, he held his hands before his body. At his feet lay the Sudarium. With the beat of gossamer wings, a ball of light shot from his hands. It barreled toward Azazel's knight and sank into its skin. Another bellow filled the cavernous hall, and the fallen Templar crumpled in a life-less heap.

Phanuel's brilliance dimmed. Once again, the man took form. But the halo that crowned his dark head proved Far-ran's eyes did not see tricks. Phanuel moved to the shad-owy form and bent at his side. His words were hushed, murmurs Farran could not make out. But as Phanuel straightened to his full height and picked up the relic, his voice rang clearer. "Go home, where you have always be-longed." He made the sign of the cross over the man's punctured chest.

As if in answer, a sigh whispered through the air. From the pile of shadows, a faint, wispy beam of light rose heavenward.

Phanuel strode past Farran with the instruction, "Stay back. I will not have you sacrifice your soul for a handful of dark knights. Azazel has forgotten we are equals."

The warrior in Farran objected. His hand tightened around the pommel of his sword. He was trained to fight. Bound by duty. To turn away·went against every principle he knew.

"That is an order, Sir Farran." The air stirred with the fluttering of wings Phanuel had disguised. "I must return this cloth." He gave the Sudarium he clenched in his left hand a shake.

Farran felt the presence before it spoke. The hair at the nape of his neck lifted. Chills drifted down his spine. Deep inside, the darkness in his soul stirred to life.

"Phanuel, you are a fool!"

Fear pressed down upon Farran, his skin breaking out in a sweat. Slowly, he turned. What stood before him struck terror in his heart. The same imposing vision he had glimpsed moments ago loomed in the place where Phanuel had stood. Only this one bore no trace of brilliance. Ebony wings spanned full against the wall of stone. With their subtle undulation, the shadow seemed to grow in height. The face that Farran looked upon held equal beauty to the archangels he served, but in its fair creation, he saw malice.

"The coward shows his face at last," Phanuel exclaimed. "Be gone from here, Azazel! This is a holy place!"

Azazel. Farran's blood curdled. He had heard tales, knew the legends by heart. But all who had witnessed the dark lord paid the price with their life.

The mighty fallen chuckled, a sound not unkind to the ear, yet evil nonetheless. "And you stand in taint. Give unto me the cloth and the seraph, and I will spare you for the final battle."

At the reference to Noelle, Farran's stomach heaved. But before he could do more than exhale, he found himself trapped between the clash of light and darkness. Behind him, Phanuel's brilliance cast great shadows on the floor. Ahead, Azazel blocked out the divine light.

"Move!"

The voice bellowed inside Farran's head. Distantly he made the connection why he had not heard the words Phanuel exchanged with Noelle. A bolt of light shot forth, grazing his shoulder as it passed. The force shoved Farran to the ground and rolled him aside. He lay against the wall, stunned into motionlessness, and watched.

The angels came together with the fury of the Titans. Walls shook, stone crumbled. Phanuel gained easy advantage and sent Azazel to his knees. But with a mighty shove, the Lord of Darkness slammed divinity into the high ceiling. A jagged crack issued between the columns, large enough to let the rain drip in.

Farran dared not move. Between the chunks of falling rock and the terrific blows of battle, he could do little more than shield his face with his arm. His sword lay on the wreckage beneath the angels, dropped when he had fallen to the floor. Without it, he was naught. Though even had he held it, 'twould have been worthless. Ten men could not confront Azazel and expect to become victor.

Phanuel hurled Azazel into a cracked column. The impact provoked an agonized scream. Blood as black as night spilled to merge with the crimson stains that spattered the foundation. They both bled. They both weakened. They both made costly mistakes. Azazel rushed too quickly, giving Phanuel opportunity to throw another ball of light. It thumped into a chest of ebony. Phanuel saw victory too soon and moved in for the kill. His hands held high, he did not witness the shifting of Azazel's body.

Within striking distance, Phanuel summoned once more the light. Azazel's hand shot out. Claws fastened into gossamer wings. With one swift downward jerk of his arm, he tore off the bent and tattered limb. Phanuel's cry wailed into the night.

At once the victor, Azazel scrambled to his weakened feet. His body heaving with exhaustion, he clutched Phanuel by the throat. "The folly of salvation has always been the belief in honor. The cloth is mine." He plucked the fragile wrap from Phanuel's bloodied hands. "And so are you."

Grabbing Phanuel by the neck, Azazel lumbered toward the darkened hall. There his voice rang out with harsh authority. "I have the Sudarium. Find the seraph. Bring her to my hall. The others await you there."

In the next instant, the dark presence that bore down on Farran vanished. Eerie silence filled the ruins. His mind raced, his eyes widened with terror. *Noelle*. He must get her out of here.

With a sharp breath, he struggled to his feet and retrieved his sword. As he turned around, a familiar image filled the narrow exit. Broad of shoulder, significant in height, and adorned in garb Farran had worn too many times to count, a fallen brother raised an onyx blade.

Despair launched through Farran. To get to Noelle he would have to kill the knight. In so doing, he would take the being's place. Anne's prophecy pounded in his head. He would kill her after all. God's teeth, why had he not learned to listen to the seer's gift?

Mayhap there was hope yet, and he could avoid combat all together. He glanced around the chamber in search of another exit. When naught but blocks of stone rose beneath his seeking gaze, he swallowed hard. Nay, he would not kill her. He would bait the knight. Pretend he lacked the strength to battle, and in so doing gut his foe severely enough to stop his purpose, but with the precision required to prolong Farran's life by keeping the darkness at bay.

'Twas a risk. One that could easily backfire. But 'twas the only way he could buy the precious moments needed to beg for Noelle's oath.

As a deathly stillness descended on the cathedral, Noelle sat in the dark that had emerged in the absence of electricity. Her nerves strained with the restless need to move, to know the reason for the deafening noises and

terrible screams she'd heard only moments ago. She
chewed on her nail, her worry for Farran turning her
belly into a mass of quivering worms. He was out there
with whatever creature had made that racket. Hurt? Gasping for his last breath? Dead?

A chill enveloped her with the thought she'd already
lost him. She'd never survive that kind of emptiness. Not
even with a hundred angels to guide her through the pain.
He had become everything to her, even if he didn't feel
the same.

As she exchanged one fingernail for another, her
thoughts drifted to Phanuel's last words. *Be strong. For
you will need all your faith soon.* Was this it? Some sort
of test designed to challenge her strength? If it was, she
wanted no part of it. Sitting and doing nothing didn't
have a thing to do with strength.

She shoved off the bed to her feet. She wouldn't sit. If
Farran was out there injured, she'd move heaven and hell
to get him help. She wouldn't just wait around because
he'd told her to stay put, and let him die. With a shaking
hand, she cracked the door open.

The same unearthly stillness waited beyond. Distant
light marked the place where the ceiling had caved in.
Faint movement beyond the resulting pile of rubble drew
her attention. With slow footsteps, she followed the sound.
All around, the ornate columns she'd admired lay in
crumbled heaps. Where stained-glass windows had portrayed brilliant pictures of the divine word, now gaping
holes opened to the storm outside. Good God, what had
happened here? She tripped over a sliver of ancient timber.
Bending, she picked it up in case she needed a club.

She poked her head around the narrow crevice separating her from the noise. A flash of lightning brightened

what had once been the cloister. The very place they were to meet Phanuel. Movement caught her eye, but vanished as the lightning passed. Breath held, she waited for her eyes to adjust again.

With the next bright flash, metal glinted near a shadowed heap. She squinted, identifying a cracked blade. Though it was as black as the shadows surrounding it, where the tip had broken at an angle, the metal shone silver. Testament to its original holy design.

The fall of rock as it cascaded down a heap stopped her in her tracks. What she saw in the faint light stopped her heart. Sword crossed in front of his body, Farran backed into what remained of the high wall.

Lightning struck again, slicing through the wide opening where the tower had once stood, to arc across twisted metal and light the crumpled wooden supports several feet to Farran's left. In the dull firelight that quickly spread, she saw him more clearly. He and the dark knight who steadily advanced. Farran's arms bled freely from a multitude of slashes. His shoulders sagged with the heavy acceptance of defeat. And in his eyes, all the wondrous light she loved had burned to flat nothingness.

His name rose to the back of her throat. She tamped back the cry, knowing her words couldn't help him. Maybe her oath, but he was too far away for the serpents around her arm to do him good. Moving quickly, before either man could notice her presence, she exchanged her makeshift club for the broken blade.

Words might not help, but he'd taught her how to fight.

She tested the heavy weight of the broadsword between both hands, then gripped it firmly in her right. More accustomed to the short sword she'd used in her training, her shoulder protested. Noelle ignored the burn and set her feet apart. A moment of fear made her arm shake. But as she recalled Phanuel's words, she somehow found strength.

This was what he meant. He'd known this would happen. Had, in fact, played a direct role by instructing them to come here. For whatever reason, whatever the outcome, this was preordained.

She lifted her chin, glared at the dark knight's back, and shouted the words Farran had once bellowed. "You cannot have him!"

The dark knight spun around. In that moment, that stillness of time where his empty eyes held hers, Noelle knew she would not survive.

Azazel's servant lunged down the debris, rapidly closing the distance between them. She breathed deeply in acceptance.

"Noelle, nay! Get back!" Farran cried.

Ignoring Farran's demands, Noelle braced for the barrage of the knight's attack. His sword sung through the air. She lifted hers to meet the violent blow. Steel clashed, and Noelle stumbled backward with the force of impact. She quickly regained her footing and crouched, moving in the circle Merrick and her early fencing years had taught her.

Like Anne. He's nothing more than Anne, she instructed silently. Though she knew from practicing with Farran the knight's strength exceeded Anne's by five, the lie tricked her underlying fear. She drew him in close enough to land a glancing blow to his thigh.

Outraged, he charged.

From the corner of her eye, Noelle observed Farran do the same. He half ran, half slid down the pile of rubble.

She shut him out, unable to divide her concentration. Focusing on the cadence of their aggressive tango, she let her body move naturally, a vessel to the algorithms of her mind and her long-ago competitive duels. He sliced wide at her arm. She twisted her shoulder, fending off the strike. On a lucky backhanded maneuver that returned her blade to its natural position, she caught him in the side.

Blood was her reward. It trickled down the edge of her blade, though the injury was slight. The sight of it gave her pause. But at the flash of steel, her mind recovered from the shock. She dodged to her left, evading a well-timed thrust. She moved too quickly, though, and the unfamiliar weight in her arm threw her instead closer to the knight. So close she felt the hot rasp of his breath against her hair.

Panicked, Noelle braced her left hand on his shoulder and shoved with all her might. Searing heat leapt beneath her palm. The knight let out a bellow of rage. He drove in on a wild frenzy, his sword as fast as lightning and every bit as deadly. She arced and twisted, ducked and turned, faltering under the strength of his attack. Summoning stamina, she moved just often enough to prick his armor and remind him she was still worthy of a fight.

On the second pass around him, Noelle felt Farran's nearby presence. She redoubled her efforts, determined not to let his noble virtue rise and draw the knight on him. She would not let him die. Nor would she be the cause of that death.

As the knight stepped sideways and also noticed Farran, his arm hesitated. She spied her opening, glimpsed the unprotected area beneath the juncture of his arm and shoulder. The mercy she'd shown Farran when she observed the same, she wouldn't do again. With a cry to add strength to her blade, she summoned the last of her willpower and moved in for the kill.

The broken tip caught for an instant. In the next, bone scraped along the deadly edge of steel. Blood poured forth to slicken her fingers. The knight's eyes went wide with shock. She wrapped her other hand around the first and hauled backward on the blade, intending to strike once more.

To her horror, the broadsword refused to move.

The dark knight's eyes glinted with victory. With a raspy laugh, he shoved his blade into her stomach and quickly pulled it free.

Pain erupted through her veins. So great, her throat closed, strangling her scream. She stumbled backward, a hand pressed to the gash in her midsection. Sticky warmth seeped through her fingers. Before her, the knight dropped to the ground where he lay motionless. She lifted her eyes to Farran's ashen face. As her vision blurred with unshed tears, she crumpled to her knees.

"Nay!" Farran thundered as he raced to Noelle's side.

Every bit of emotion he had ever felt swamped him. Anger, hate, envy, and love, yes *love,* warred inside his heart. Not Noelle. Anyone but her. What hell did the Almighty seek to damn him to? Had he not already paid the price?

He dropped to his knees and cradled her in his arms. Her breath came faintly. Through his fingers, her blood ran hot. His gaze pulled to the gaping wound beneath his hand. When he saw the jagged flesh, his heart crumbled like the walls around him.

"Noelle, what have you done?" His throat caught on his whisper. He had just found her. He could not lose her now. What life he had remaining, he could not bear to face.

She struggled to find a smile. It graced her lips, touched her eyes, but did not linger. "Saved you," she answered with effort.

He held her closer, unmindful to the wet warmth that seeped into his clothing where their bodies met. She had saved him. For what reason he could not comprehend. Of all the people who deserved to die, 'twas he for the cruelty he had shown to her.

His heart broke all over again as she struggled for a breath. Pain flashed across her face with the flinching of her brows, and he watched as her captivating eyes drifted toward some unseen object.

Filled with the desperation of centuries of suffering, he snatched at the serpents around her arm. The torc tumbled into his palm with ease. Holding her awkwardly, he picked up his sword and dropped it down the blade. "Say the oath, Noelle. Save your life. I will take you to D.C., take you wherever you wish to go, but for God's sake, say the oath and live!"

Her lashes fluttered, her focus once again on him. When she did not answer soon enough to his liking, the dam around his fears burst. He yielded to the moisture that pooled in his eyes. Tears fell down his cheeks, washed across hers, and disappeared into her hair. "Say it," he begged in a whisper. "Can you not see I love you? If I could undo all the wrongs I have done to you, I would. I love you, Noelle." His voice cracked with emotion, and he gave her an insistent little shake. "Dear God in heaven, I will not live with myself if you should die. Please, say the words. Let my last memory be of your smile."

She did smile then, as displaced as it was. Her pale lips parted and she moistened them with the tip of her tongue. Against his fingertips, her pulse fluttered faint. *"Meus vita . . ."* A wheezing cough possessed her. She grimaced against the agony. Beneath his hand, she bled even more.

When she looked at him once again, sadness filled her eyes. "It is too late . . ." She swallowed with effort and gave him a shake of her head. "For you . . ."

His tears fell harder. Unashamed, he let them flow. He could not breathe. Could not think beyond the silent prayers he recited that she would find the strength.

She drew in one last rasping breath. On her heavy exhale, he heard the words. Faint and weak, she whispered, *"Meus vita, meus diligo, meus eternus lux lucis, fio vestry."*

My life, my love, my eternal light, becomes yours. The meaning rang in his head as she went limp in his arms.

Before he could release the sob that choked him, his sword flared with white light. A warmth unlike any he had ever experienced ebbed through his veins. Where he had known naught but anger, profound peace settled into his soul. He watched, spellbound, as the serpents came to life. Two golden heads converged, then drew apart. One slithered to the small golden cross etched into the point of balance on his blade. The other sank tiny teeth into the matching sigil at the pommel. One shared body undulated slowly, then moved no more. Bewildered, he traced a finger over the length of the warped quillons. The Almighty's barrier. No more would shadows creep into his palm and through his blood.

Noelle twitched in his arms. He looked down to find her expression soft, the deep etchings of pain now smoothed into her usual pretty features. At the side of her neck, the vein that had barely vibrated with her pulse now thrummed with the heavy beat of her heart. Beneath his hand, the wetness ceased to flow.

She lived!

His heart leapt to his throat and fresh tears rose to replace the salty trickle of sorrow. He cared not if she said the words to merely save her life. If her oath was not a product of the love he felt for her. She lived. 'Twas all that mattered. Fighting back the urge to shout for joy, he scooped her knees over his elbows and rose to his feet. She could heal at the European temple. When she had, when she woke and he was certain of this miracle, he would honor his word and grant her freedom.

CHAPTER 37

†

Noelle awakened in comfort. The small bed was similar to the one she'd witnessed in the cathedral, but unlike that iron-framed slab of rock, this one supported her with down. A mountain of covers weighed down on her naked body, cocooning her in warmth. But the comfort wasn't the one she wanted. She wanted Farran.

She struggled to sit, but the ache in her body made it impossible to rise beyond her elbows. At the door, she spied a brawny figure. Without her glasses, however, she couldn't identify the man.

"Milady, you are awake."

Noelle fell back into the wealth of softness with a grunt. On his best days, Farran wasn't capable of that sort of kindness. Not to mention, this man's voice lacked the soothing timbre of Farran's voice. "Where is Farran?" she asked, her throat surprisingly dry.

"I shall fetch him. He bade me wait until you woke, then bring you food and drink. I shall also fetch you a tray."

She lacked the strength to tell the man she couldn't eat a bite. Where the hell was Farran? He'd said he loved her. She'd fought the hands of death to stay with him. For days now, it seemed, she dreamed of him. Of waking to hear that cherished whisper and experiencing the joy when at last she could tell him the same.

The door eased closed, the stranger thankfully gone. She closed her eyes against the too-bright light and inventoried her aches and pains. Her stomach felt as if she'd been ripped in half. But when she pressed her hand to the place the dark knight's sword had pierced, she found smooth flesh. Not even the pucker of a scar now healed rose beneath her fingertips.

But the lingering protests of her sword arm told her she hadn't been here long enough to heal naturally. Strange she could be so mended, yet still feel as if she'd been hit by a truck.

She lifted her left hand, curious as to why it tingled. Tiny red blisters marred her palm, giving her a moment's pause. She held the sword with her right—how had she injured her left?

Her head hurt too much to think about the oddity. A yawn escaped. While she waited, she imagined the feel of Farran's arms. How it would sound to have his heart beat beneath her ear. The warmth of his body. The scent of his skin.

Farran jumped at the knock on his door. Dread arose, and at once he felt the urge to retch. There could only be one reason the sound issued from his door. And though he had prayed for it, he despised it as well.

"Aye," he barked.

The door opened, and Gareth poked his head inside. "She is awake."

"Aye," he repeated more softly. With a heavy sigh, he brought himself to his feet. When he found the younger knight still standing in the doorway, he scowled. "Take your leave, I know where she sleeps."

Gareth gave him a thoughtful look. A hint of a smirk played at his youthful mouth. "'Tis a sorry day when a maid so fair and lovely asks for a scowling grump."

Asked for him? His heart swelled to twice its normal size. As he pursued Gareth out the door, his step felt lighter than it had in centuries. She had asked for him. Mayhap they could . . . *Nay.* He had given her his word to return her. 'Twas her freedom that brought about her oath.

He made his way up the stairs to the sparsely occupied recovery hall. Though the two temples bore similar craftsmanship, the original here in Europe had many more benefits. One of which—the private healing chambers. But Uriel refused to give up his vast infirmary, and here Zerachiel healed. At Noelle's door, he lifted his hand to knock. On reconsidering, however, he let himself inside. They were oathed, her body he had seen before. Whether they parted or not, no secrets would ever come between them again.

She looked so tiny amidst the covers he could not help but smile. He went to the bed, anxious for the brightness of her smile.

Instead, he found her sleeping, her captivating eyes cloaked from his view. His shoulders fell as he sighed in dismay. 'Twas best, he supposed. For in truth, he did not wish to see her celebrate her freedom.

He eased himself to his knees and brushed a lock of hair away from her cheek. He gathered her left hand between his, brought her knuckles to his lips. "If ever you need anything, damsel, call to Gabriel. I will come." Turning her palm up, he scattered kisses over the blisters that marked her true gift. His whisper thickened. "No matter what shores divide us, what mountains rise between, I will stand at your side." With effort, he released her hand, stood, and pressed a kiss to her silken hair. Breathing deeply, he etched in the memory of her sweet jasmine perfume. "But if I must only keep you in my heart, I refuse to return your cat."

With that, he turned away and strode from the room. The agony began again. Each step toward Raphael's large office tightened the noose around his heart. He despised the thought of leaving her. But if he stayed, if he took her where she wished to go, he would not have the strength to walk away. He must do so now, before she could honor duty and convince herself she wanted to stay.

His knock rang hollow, in mirror of his soul. At Raphael's welcome, Farran entered the office that doubled Mikhail's in size.

"Farran. How is your seraph?"

"She woke, but sleeps again. I come to request a favor."

His blue eyes clouded with concern. "What is your wish?"

"When she wakes again, I shall be far from here. Take her where she wishes. Send word to Merrick I will accept the duty he requested on my immediate arrival in America. Tell him to bring the cat."

One thick golden eyebrow arched with suspicion. "I do not like the sound of this, sir knight."

With a respectful bow of his head, Farran backed toward the door. "I am not yours to command, Raphael. Please honor my wishes. I will subject myself to Mikhail."

* * *

Noelle woke again to twilight. On the bedside table, a soggy roast beef sandwich waited. Droplets of water dewed a glass whose ice had long since melted. She pushed to her elbows once more and found herself alone.

Damn it. She'd sleep at Farran's side tonight if she had to drag him to the bed. She couldn't take another moment of yearning for his nearness.

Every muscle screamed in agony as she eased out of the bed and pulled on a robe someone had thrown over the back of a plush chair. A wave of dizziness threatened to topple her over. She fought past the swimming of her head, gritted her teeth, and stumbled toward the door.

Thank God for small miracles—it opened without effort. She poked her head outside to scan the empty hall. Muttering beneath her breath, she padded barefoot toward the stairs. Halfway down, a knight dropped to bended knee and tossed his sword on the tread below her feet. She almost fell the rest of the way down.

She scolded the man with a blistering frown. "Oh for Pete's sake, can't this wait? Where's Farran?" With her toe, she pushed the blade in the man's direction. "You're crazy if you think I'm bending over to pick that up. I can hardly stand."

Apology widened the man's scarred features. He hastened to stand. "Lady de Clare, forgive me. I was not thinking. Might I aid your descent?"

Noelle had never been more grateful for a bit of chivalry in her life. Accepting his offered hand, she gave him an enthusiastic nod. "Please. I need to see Farran."

"He is in his room." The man flashed her a warm smile. "I am Alaric le Goix, commander of the European

Knights Templar. 'Tis an honor to have you within these temple walls."

So that's where Farran had taken her—the European temple. Feeling a bit more secure, she indulged in a smile. "Dr. Noelle Kea . . ." No, not Keane. She'd said her oath. Her smile brightened as she amended her introduction. "Noelle de Clare. And if we don't hurry, I think I might pass out."

For an instant, she thought Alaric might bend to carry her. But as if he thought better of the notion, he shook his head and offered more support to her arm. Slowly they descended to step into another winding hall. This one reminded her of the chambers beneath the temple in Missouri. Lighted by torches, unadorned door after unadorned door lined the narrow corridor.

Alaric guided her past so many she lost track of the twists and turns. Her legs burned. Her side flared hot. She did her best to keep up with him, convinced if they stopped to rest, she'd sink to the floor and never get up again. She could sit when she found Farran. If he wanted her to move, *he* could carry her wherever he wished to go.

At last they stopped at a door, and Alaric rapped sharply. At Farran's bark, he pushed the door in and let go of Noelle's arm. "I take my leave, milady."

Mystified by the strength she still possessed, Noelle let herself inside. Farran didn't turn around. Instead, he hovered over a black bag, his hands in constant motion. As he doubled a piece of fabric she recognized, and stuffed it in the satchel, Noelle's eyes went wide. Surely, he wasn't packing.

She peered at his broad shoulders. "What are you doing, Farran?"

Farran's hands stilled over his duffel bag. Slowly, he turned around. The shock of finding Noelle standing in his room almost bowled him over. She had come down here? How? Who had helped her find his room?

Saints' blood, he did not want to have this exchange. He let out a sigh, turned back to his task, and stuffed another shirt inside the bag. "I am joining Merrick in the hunt for Anne's sister."

A heavy moment of silence passed between them. He felt the weight of her stare, the piercing of her frown. At her sigh, he flinched.

"I guess I can travel. I'm not certain it's smart, and I know I'll pass out if I move another step, but if you want to leave so soon . . ."

Farran closed his eyes on a deep breath. He had waited too long. 'Twas as he suspected—she already felt the call of duty. Wishing beyond all measure their circumstances were different, he sadly shook his head and braved her troubled gaze. "Nay, Noelle," he murmured. "I gave you my oath to return you. I will honor it. I will not have you stay where your heart does not wish to be." He breathed again, ready now to admit his errors. "I made that mistake once. I shall not suffer through it again."

To his absolute surprise, she did not beam with elation. Indeed, she did naught but ease herself into the chair. Her expression turned thoughtful, and she lifted one hand to gnaw upon a fingernail. "That's why you've been such an ass? Because you married a woman who didn't love you? Let me guess—you were betrothed?"

The question stunned him speechless. He had expected her protest. Her admonishment they were bound to the Almighty's plan. He had in no way prepared for her to ask about his past.

As he considered where to begin, it occurred to him the memories no longer ached. Though Alefric's rejection would always prickle, even that did not twist his heart to pieces. He held Noelle's gaze, sank a hip onto the table. 'Twas best for her to understand where it all began.

"I was born in Tonbridge, the year 1102, and the nephew to Walter de Clare. He had no children. On his death twenty years later, I inherited holdings in Sussex, with the condition I take a woman he recommended as a bride. Her family was proud Saxon, as was she. I am of Norman blood."

Thought drew Noelle's brows together. She opened her mouth to speak, but he cut off her words with the lift of his hand. "Though the war was long over and William's might established, pride is oft a difficult thing to set aside. Resentment harbored within her heart—though she hid it well from me."

"She hid it? How can you hide something like that?"

He shook his head. "In part, 'twas because she did her duty without complaint. She never protested her position, and she did not hesitate to bear my son. In part 'twas also my blindness. I loved her from the moment I set eyes on her golden hair."

"Do you still?" she asked in a near inaudible voice.

Farran chuckled despite himself. "Nay. 'Tis you I love." He did not give her opportunity to dwell upon his confession. Before she could speak, he forged ahead. "Five years after we wed, my closest friend—also from a Norman family—pledged his sister to a Norman lord. My wife's cousin coveted the lass. On her journey to her wedding, he attacked her guards and took her as his own."

Noelle blinked. "He kidnapped her. Is this some sort of . . . trend?"

God bless her, she knew how to make him smile. He indulged in it, and became lost in her laughing eyes. Time hung suspended as he fought the need to take her in his arms and taste her honeyed lips. As he struggled with the ache that stirred when he did not.

"Go on," she encouraged softly.

He shook off longing with the closing of his eyes. "When my friend called for aid, I had no choice but to answer. Together our armies laid siege upon the Saxon's holdings. After the passing of a week, naught but charred cinders remained. His army lay in shambles, tattered remnants of the might they once had been. And the woman was delivered to her betrothed as she desired."

The memories rose again, taunting him with the dark chasm of hate he had once drowned in. He gathered strength from Noelle's quiet stare, the curiosity that gleamed bright. "I returned to Clare where my wife pronounced me traitor. Through a long winter I suffered her sharp tongue and the threats of her family."

With obvious effort, Noelle dragged her chair closer and twined her fingers through his. Farran reveled in the warmth of her palm, the press of her slight nails. He held tight, the gesture full of suffocating meaning. He knew not how long she remained unmoving and silent. But he spilled the story of his journey to the Holy Lands in an effort to reclaim his noble name. He told her of the nightmare that had haunted him so long—his return, Alefric's poisoned words, Brighid's lechery with the Saxon who had begun the war. He even told her of Alefric's death not six years later when Hrothgar allowed the boy to fight.

When Farran finished, he felt not the shame he had anticipated. Instead, a great weight lifted from his shoulders. He had shared the one secret he had told no one, save Caradoc, and the freedom he experienced he could not put into words.

Noelle pulled her hand from his. Using the edge of the table for support, she rose to her feet. At her audible whimper, Farran supported her elbow and eased her weight to his arm. "You should not be out of bed."

With a soft chuckle, Noelle shrugged free of his hand. She guided it to her waist, tugged the other free to do the same. "There's something I don't understand." With one uneasy step forward, she looped her arms around his neck.

She stood so close, his body prickled with awareness. 'Twould be so easy to catch her mouth and forget his determination to think of her needs, not his own selfish desires. "Aye?" he whispered.

"You said you loved me. As I recall, you begged me to take this oath and bind us for eternity. Why haven't you packed my bag as well?"

"I told you—"

Her mouth descended onto his, silencing his answer. For a moment, he could not believe the silken slide of her tongue was not a dream. But when she nudged his lips apart and demanded his participation, he awakened with a groan. He kissed her thoroughly, full of all the tumultuous emotion he had experienced in the last few days.

Noelle tore her mouth away, her breath hard. "Farran . . ." Their lips clung for a heartbeat. "You really are insane." Her lips caught his once more, forbidding him to fully process her insult.

As feeling swelled and desire thrummed through his veins, she tormented further by drawing completely away. Her eyes held his, ablaze with the passion that flowed between them. "You didn't offer me my freedom. You gave me your loyalty. With three words, you effectively turned me into your wife. If you think you're leaving me at this roughshod altar, you're every bit as crazy as I thought you were."

A smile lit the corners of her mouth, and she brushed the tip of her nose against his. "Crazy, handsome Farran . . ." She let out a soft laugh that reached in and turned his heart upside down. "I love you. Those aren't just words. There's not a part of me that doesn't mean them. Not a part of my heart that doesn't beat for you. I *love you,* Farran. And if you walk away now, as soon as I've recovered, I'll hunt you down and run you through."

The threat broke past his dizzy thoughts, spurring him into laughter. He gathered her close, her injuries forgotten, and crushed her in a tight embrace. Only when she yelped did he think of the pain she must suffer. He let her go quickly but chased down her mouth for another sweet kiss.

When he eased it to a lingering close to tell her he would never go, she sagged against his chest, her strength expired. "Take me to bed, Farran. I long to sleep within your embrace."

"Aye," he murmured as he scooped her into his arms. Come morning's light, he would tell her of her healing gift, of how he had witnessed the way she had dealt a critical wound to a fallen knight with her palm. For the moment, he had a wife to obey. And for the first time in his life, he did not mind the knowledge his loyalty lay with a woman. With a smile he could not hope to dampen, he carried her to the bed.